Parthian Stranger
6 Agency of Spies

Stewart N. Johnson

Order this book online at www.trafford.com
or email orders@trafford.com

Most Trafford titles are also available at major online book retailers.

Printed in the United States of America.

ISBN: 978-1-4907-4708-8 (sc)
ISBN: 978-1-4907-4710-1 (hc)
ISBN: 978-1-4907-4709-5 (e)

Library of Congress Control Number: 2014917199

Trafford rev. 11/21/2014

www.trafford.com

North America & international
toll-free: 1 888 232 4444 (USA & Canada)
fax: 812 355 4082

ACKNOWLEDGEMENT

I want to first start off with my investor, Breanna Gibson, thank you, without your efforts, this book would not be possible, but it's because of you I can see this in print, and many more to come. To my wife, to whom, is off and away, so making this book was the hardest to date, but the show must go on, I want to thank her for the cover which she drew, and to her continuing support from a far, she is truly missed.

And thanks to James the Book Guy, in Joplin Missouri for being the first to carry and distribute my books.

Other Published Works by the Author

Parthian Stranger 1 The Order
Parthian Stranger 2 Conspiracy
Parthian Stranger 3 Supreme Court
Parthian Stranger 4 Enzo Bonn
Parthian Stranger 5 Belarus

CONTENTS

CH 1

Meeting of the minds

High above the skies was a 757 jumbo jet, carrying passengers from Ramstein AFB Germany, outside the window, looked a woman who remark,"Look at the canoe shaped windows, they are of blue, yellow and red, in color."

As another said,"Don't you know, that is the UN building."

Inside, all the spies were led into the auditorium, as an advisor said "Through these doors, take a seat and we will begin."

The doors opened to see these curved like seating. It was like it was going to a live play. All filed in, some marveled at seating configuration, while others could care less. Jack found his way in and sat alone in the back. Someone up at the podium said, "Quickly take your seats, let's go, please,"as that Advisor left.

Jack saw on the stage, a door slide open, and two older men came out, one wrote on the chalk board while the other was at the podium, to say, "Welcome spies, from all over the world, my name is Professor Claude Benz, I'm from Germany, and my partner is Professor Gustave Goins he is from France, we will be speaking in English, for those who seek some translation, place on your headsets now, and this will be translated to your native tongue."

"Look up at the chalk board, we have the current world rankings for spies, but with this turn out and any one of this spots could be up for grabs. this where it currently stands, "Number one, is Vadim Adonis, of Russia, Number two, Alexei Putin, of Russia as well, of the famous Putin dynasty, Number three, Chu," is from Japan. Number four, is, Hendon Aziz, from Iran." "Number five is Thomas Jones, of the famed British, secret air service, or SAS for short." "Number six is Jonathon Razor, from France." "Next number seven, Alexander Yashin, from Russia." "Number eight, Chung, from China, Next up is Number nine, is Tad Jones, son of famed Thomas,from Britain." "And Number ten, is Louie Bellini, from Italy. For the rest of you, some we may have heard of you, but to be a member, you need to be pledged in, by someone of the known, some of you operate as a spy in your own countries, that the UN has no real control over such as the United States, Canada, and Russia, for that group, well their simply left to do as they please. Mark my words, you can look around the room, at the older agents and you ask yourself what are they doing different, than yourself, or are not really in the game at all, the current life span of a true working spy is two years, after that you're looking over your shoulder, for those wanting to take down the best, and even today in this room there is probably some sort of retribution from the Russians, so they think, over the debacle from the kidnapping of Victoria Ecklon, problem is what US and UN investigator found down below."

"Hush" said the other Professor.

The Professor Benz composed himself to say, "We will start out with a pre-qualifier, to insure that you can qualify to be a spy, tomorrow morning, there will be a fundamental race against the clock, those that qualify will be told so, and may come back here".

"Let's talk about tomorrow, we are trying to create real world situation, by having you go through a few test's put on by the SAS, and in coordination with the UN, several other detachments also will be there to assist, so for the time being, we are through till tomorrow, exit through those doors, and you will be shown where you will stay. Good bye and good luck."

Everyone got up and filed out, as Jack followed in order, as he saw some Russian's together, as they went through a tunnel, down ward, to an open door, to Quanson huts, for one tough SAS member said,"Between the four huts, is a bunk, take a bunk, anyone, there all the same, Jack went to the furthest one, in a hut by itself and waited, as time passed it filled up with 89 others. He was in the back, a signup sheet, was placed up, for all to hear, "Put your name down at the time you wish to do this?"

Jack got up and went to the board, as people were putting 1pm down, he chose 8 am, he figured to get it over with and went back to his bunk and rested.

Meanwhile another jumbo jet landed, and taxied, and pulled in next to prop plane, it dropped its ramp, and over one hundred and twenty women exited, along with the support teams and Jim saw Debby, the two embraced, and kissed, for her to say,"Looks like I'm here to help out". Then she told him what was going on. "The UN has decided to open this competition up to the women. So there are these, our top twenty, plus anyone else may try out for this, such as Jill, and Gia?"

"I'll let them know" said Jim, to add, "What about you, what are your plans?"

"I guess I don't know yet, we will play it by ear," said Debby, to add,"I wouldn't mind going back in?"

The strike team was called for assembly, for Jim to say, "Jill and Gia, I was just informed that the UN is opening up the competition to women, do you all want to participate?"

"I don't know, what did Jack say?" asked Jill.

"That's just it, you're here to train as spies, so I think he would say yes" said Jim.

"Then count me in", said Jill, as Gia said, "Why not, how hard can this be, as the two looked over at the other US women, some they knew, others not so much, for Jim to say," Drop your gear and weapons, and follow the girls in." Jim, motioned for them to go, as they dropped their gear and handed Brian their weapons. Jill and Gia followed the girls into the UN, as one by one, they took their turn, undressed, and redressed in the UN gear, for one senior UN lady to say, "This is nothing compared to these super spies, what is their credit limit?" she asked her advisor.

He said, 100, thousand, and a daily of five hundred on per diem card." She turned to see Jill, to say,"The red card is your expense card, and white is per diem, such as for the base store, and mess, now move along."

After all two hundred plus, went through processing, they were all led to their floor, where Jill saw, Michelle, and went into a room, took a seat next to her, as she saw several other girls from the plane.

An advisor, came in and introduced himself as Professor Gustave Goins, said, "Ladies take a seat, thank you, all of you have some sort of affiliations with the men, that are the spies, for those that are purely the wives, and don't want to participate, stand up and proceed through those doors, where you'll be waiting to hear if your men have qualified, for those of you who are spies, and work with a male counterpart, stay here". Michelle was torn, from doing this or to be available for Jack, as she saw her competition, and knew she could take anyone of them, even the Russian girls, so she went along with the program, to hear, "Fine, now, unlike your male counterparts, we will tell you what will be going on, first each of you will participate in a fitness test, five, pull ups, 100 sit-ups and 100 pushups, then a two mile run, and three mile bike ride, finally a swim, oh sorry, I read this wrong, it's all the opposite, does anyone think they can't handle this? After all this you will come back and the training will start."

A few got up and left, but Michelle just shrugged her shoulders and is ready to go. The meeting was over, and all were led out, to a floor, where it opened up to a huge squad bay, with at least enough bunks for them, as each took a bunk, as they peeled off the line, and heard, "There is a sign-up sheet, as Michelle, got up and saw the early one, at 9am, and took it.

Next morning was a base wakeup call of 0530, which gave you one hour to shit, shower and shave Same for the women, everyone was dressed in camouflage gear, as was assigned to them, after going through the early morning call line, then it was off to mess, at 0600- to 0630. Jack loaded up on whatever they served, scrambled eggs, bacon, sausage, hash browns, fruit, four milks, of them two chocolate. Jack ate rapidly, and was done in ten minutes, and deposited his platter, and went back to his Hut, as he heard, "One hut partied way into the night, did you hear?" Jack sat on his bunk, he took the time to make it tight, enough to drop a quarter on it, waiting till when they would be off.

Back in the hanger, Gregory and Jonny, the UN guys, met up with the Black Ops group, to say;"How would you guy's, care to help us out again?"

Casey looks him over, to say; "Sure" as Gregory was trying to see what was inside the plane, for Casey to say, "She isn't here?"

"Who, what, what do you mean?" asked Gregory.

"Jill and Gia both went in to try for the next big spy thing."

"Oh" said a rather disappointed Gregory, to add,"Have your team ready by 0900."

Casey shook his head, and told the rest of the remaining team.

Meanwhile back at the quanson huts it was 0700 came and went, to a call at 0730, for those to be ready. Jack got up, and went to the door, where a big guy blocked the entrance, to say; "So you're the famous Jack Cash, you don't look that intimidating, at least not here, anyway, where's all your gadgets?, Now that they are off of you, sometime during this event, I'm coming with several of my friends, to kill you" said Vadim, the Russian, and the World's number one spy.

Jack thought about striking him in the knee, and crippling him and in that instance Vadim allowed Jack to pass, to hear,"I'll be watching you" said the tall Russian with a smile.

Jack shrugged it off, and fell in with others, as they all took a truck ride, over to the lake, all got out, and onto the platform, all 75 of those that wanted to go first, the boat took off, it was more like a platform, with a steering box and an engine. The water on lake Geneva was fierce, as they got to the middle, as a guy with a bull horn spoke, "An on the count of three, you'll swim to shore, 3, 2, 1 Go", with that Jack dove into the water, as others simply jumped into the near freezing water and hung onto the platform, as Jack took the early led, swimming, in full camo gear, and boots. Meanwhile on the shore, a group meeting was held, "Now each of you line up, and whom ever comes out first, help them get changed into shorts, a shirt, which has the name of the spy, and make sure, each get a water pack, and a protein bar."

The line formed quickly, as an announcer, said,"In the lead, is Jack Cash, followed by a New Zealander, Steven Smith". And that was it, as guys were flopping around, as countless others simply quit, so from 75 instantly they were down to 50, and still others were flopping around. Jack was near the boat ramp, as his feet touched bottom, as he was out, and up as a girl named Christina, said "Right over here, is your bike, care to change?"

"Nah, I'm fine", said Jack, putting on the shirt with his name and the water pack and in hand a protein bar, and pedaled off onto the course, still in the water was countless others, as he did a long lap, came back, dropped off the bike, as his boots were dry, he picked up another protein bar, and went off running, meanwhile others were coming on shore, Jack took to the course, up a hill, and down, and then through a field, he noticed, something off to his left, as he made his way up, and instantly, someone came out and attacked him, Jack had the man in a rear naked choke hold, on the ground, as he used his feet to subdue him, and he was out, and threw him off, and got up and saw the other SAS commandos. Jack saluted them, as they saluted him back. He was at the halfway mark on the run, and then there was nothing, all the way to the end, was the finish line, where a board monitored his time of 32:15, as he saw Christina, to say, "Now the time has stopped, all you have to do is the sit-ups and then the pushups all you can do in five minutes, go, as someone held Jack's feet, he laid on his back, as Jack began and Christina counted, five minutes later, the count was 246, instantly he flipped over, as Christina placed her hand under his chest, as he went for it, and for the first hundred he was good, then tapered off quickly, to finish with 152, now tired, he saw the make shift high bar, for the cocky Christina, to say, "You need at least three pullups to qualify, Jack went to the bar, hoisted himself up, and Christina, began the count, 1,2,3 and more,and just like anything Jack does, he got into a rhythm, she counted out ten, twenty, thirty, forty and at five minutes, he ended and at fifty five. Jack let go, to hear, from Christina, "Your Qualified, Jack Cash, you can go into the UN and follow me to your room, and I'll be your advisor for the rest of your time here."

"Great" said Jack, as Jack followed Christina, and saw that there were still men out in the water flailing along.

Back in UN HQ, it was another story, as the two Professors were in sheer panic, as Claude says,"Now we have to push everyone back an hour."

"Who do we have next?"

"The women."

"Fine, let's get the rest of the men out of there, I sure thought we would have had more than two qualify," as it hit the one hour mark, and the rest were non-qualifiers, some was fished out of the lake as dive teams were called, as one had drowned, and one was missing, for Claude to say, "Lets reverse this whole process, and get all the men down here at 1pm." to add, "Once those men are cleared away, bring on the women, how many do we have?"

"Two hundred twenty six, prospects, plus give or take some volunteers?"

"Good lets reverse the course and see who emerges on top."

"You know a thought had occurred to me, what if the top ten spies don't give it their all, and were left with those that have the guarantee and those that really want this position, of three."

"Then let them go, let's use those that want to be here and get rid of the old guard."

"I second that, now let's see if Miss Hohlstein is on board with that?"

"She will, if its Jack Cash, and now that he is qualified, all others don't matter, you know I was reading a profile on him, as he knows 96 ways to subdue a man, his go to is to rip the cartilage from the knee, maybe the ranking are miss-screwed, take for instant Jonathon Razor, who has corruption ties, we really should consider who we put on that list, just to find agents that will obey, rather than on their own agenda."

"So this is what we will do, allow those that qualify in, and train, and we will reserve the right to cut as we see fit."

Back at the women's barracks, the women were told to all assemble, and told all would compete now, after the rest was ready, they were then led down to the playing field, to hear, "Pair up, as their was groups of two to equal 102, for a total of 204 participates, and now the nine o'clock start time, and with that the SAS and UN and Black Ops, Casey and Clark was all there, to watch five minutes go by, and the women were dropping like flies, then it was time to switch, and now it was down to 157, the other side did it for five minutes, same results, six rested on the ground, and quit, exhausted to leave 151of 204. Next up was the pushups, Michelle led the pack, with a clear, 196, in five minutes, her partner she egged on, to do 36, at five minutes, the blonde, dropped, another 12 quit, leaving 139, overall, next was the pull ups, and the high bar, it was the single biggest factor, in wiping out over half, leaving 70, at five minutes. Next up was the second half, led by Michelle was at forty two, easily the clear winner, her companion quit at two, and another 24 dropped out, leaving 46 to move on to the run, and on the start line, three distinct groups formed. Then an advisor called out,"Ready, on your mark, 3,2,1, Start", the gazelles took off, such as Michelle, Jill followed her, and paced her, as for another American, Cami Ross, took the early lead, those three had a three minute lead, going onto the bikes, and was completing it as the others broke to the bikes, they were turning in, as Michelle was the clear leader overall, and had a good time, as the last event was the swim, Michelle swam, to easily out distancing the others, as she hit the platform, with a time of 35:26, easily making her the top woman, as the others were finishing, in the following order; Jill Hoyt, US, Cami Ross, US, Lea Lucas, of Monaco, Simone, from US. Then another group led by Protima, from Brazil, Colonel Tam-Lu, from China, Chloe Ryan, from Ireland. Behind them was this group, led by, Raisa Sergel, from Russia, Dana Scott from US. Behind them just getting off the bikes, and diving into the water, was Callista Leander from Greece, Rebecca Adams, from Russia, Kendra Augustus, from Russia. Following them was another so called group, led by, Ellie Morgan, from England, Roxy Carr, from US, Peleruth Jaizem, from Poland, Maja Quincy, from Columbia, Nina Ivan, from Russia, Esmeralda Romero, from US-Spain, Z'sofia Baptiste, from Turkey, Nina Toop, from Russia, Nika Kenna, from Romania, Erica Adams, from US, Darlene Lewis, from US, Kellie Ryan, from US. Then it was all closing off, as the time was close to a hour, as the last group was left and accepted, as they got in the water, led by, Joana Celek, from US- Portugal, Freya Lyons, from US, Grace Fabian, from Wales-Britain, and Dayle Amos, from Mexico. All in all, twenty nine, as the last name was read off, all others were led off the course, to tell them it was over. The platform took all 29 back to shore, whereas they were escorted, back to the UN and up to their distinct floor, where they passed two rooms of size, the mess room, and into an open courtyard, to see all glass suites. Michelle was in the front, followed by those that finished, as the UN Advisor, Mark, said, "Follow me into Suite one," as Michelle was first in, as the door slid open, as others marveled at the rich décor, brand new smell, of a fresh clean room, from right to left, Mark said, "As you can can see, everything is brand new, a counter top, sink, a cooler, and cabinets, as we turn around, it is a tv room, complete with sofa's, and through that door, is a pool, and hot tub, as others went to explore that, for Mark to say,"Behind me is three bedrooms, currently we have ten suites available, with two still under construction." As the others went snooping, Mark said,"In each of the room, you need a card key, as it will be keyed to the room you are in, and you will be the only one who has access to that, now in this room, is Michelle Quan from the US and Callista Leander, from Greece." Now lets go to the next room?" as Mark tried to herd them out. The group all went to room number two, As Mark waved his pass, to say, "Jill Hoyt, her two roommates, are, Rebecca Adams and the other one is Dayle Amos".

Next room, over, was was number three, "Cami Ross, Kendra, from Russia, and Grace from Britain." Next room was number four, privileged "Lea Lucas, from Monaco, Ellie from Britain, and Freya, from the US". Room five had all US, "Simone, Roxy, and Joana." Room six was diverse in many ways, Protima, Peleruth, from Poland, and Kellie from the US". Next room was seven, "Colonel Tam-Lu, Maja, and Darlene Lewis", from the US. Room eight, had "Chloe, and Nina Ivan of Russia, and Erica Adams from the US". Room number nine has, "Raisa from Russia, Esmeralda from US and Nika from Romania." Last room, number ten, "The famed Dana Scott, US, Z'sofia from Turkey, and Nina Toop from Russia, as they all settled down, to see Mark leave their new surroundings, everything was lavish, three separate rooms, with each sharing a bathroom. A man from the UN came into number one suite, as both Michelle and Calista saw him, take out the extra bed and hauled it out.

Outside the UN and around the lake, clean up began over the women, as those that either quit, or didn't make the cut, simply were asked to leave, as the UN prepared for the rest of the men, Casey asked Clark?" have you seen any of our girls?"

"Nope it was way too fast, all I know is some girl from China won it, I think her name was Michelle."

"So what do you think we should do when the men comes out here?"

"Find Jack and help him out," said Clark.

Jim received word from the UN, by phone, Jim put it on speaker phone, said, "Michelle pre-qualified for the spy training for women, and that Jack also qualified, and needs another replacement inside, but before Jim could ask, Debby said, "I'll go in" without thinking Jim said, "I have a one, Deborah Snyder?"

"What is she to Jack Cash?" asked the UN advisor.

"She is his supply sergeant."

"Really, would she like to carry out those duties in here?"

Jim looked at her, as she said, "Why not, more on the inside the better we are off."

"Yes, she said she would do that" said Jim.

"Have her come into the staff room, on the south side, now, who else do you have, for Jack Cash?" said the UN advisor.

Carefully, Jim was running out of options, as this wasn't to plan, and little did he know, that some of the girls were coming out, so Jim said, "No one, not yet, call me back in six hours."

"You got one, Jim."

Miss Hohlstein, saw that she had a request from one of the UN advisors, so she called him to hear, "This is Mark, yes, we have a bit of trouble brewing, with a candidate, a Michelle Quan, is torn, on how to proceed, either fulfill her duties of protecting Jack Cash, or go it alone and become a spy, she is seriously considering quitting."

"We can't have her do that, send her to my office, I'll talk with her."

"Yes Ma'am."

Over the intercom system, in room number one, it said, "Michelle Quan, you presents is requested to visit Miss Meredith Hohlstein, of the World Council, can you be ready in ten minutes."

"Yes", said Michelle as she hit the intercom button. Then went and took an apple out of the refrigerator, noticed there wasn't even a assurity sticker, on it, it was similar to the fruit she saw in Jack's room, all fresh, thinking this is nice, and bites into it, pure deliousness, then saw the door open and the advisor, Mark with a clipboard, as she exited her suite, for the advisor to say, "How is your room mate?"

"She is alright, I'd rather it be Jack Cash," she said smugly, as they stepped into an elevator that went down one floor and straight across, where it came to a stop, as if they were on a train or had they switched cars, thought Michelle, realizing being a spy is crazy. As she exited, with her apple nearly finished, he said, "I'll take the remains?"

"No you won't that's the best part, as she took it in two bites the entire thing, seeds and all.

The UN advisor, escorted Michelle, to the room, knocked, to hear, "Please come in", the door opens, to see her, as Meredith meets them at the door, to say, "Come in Miss Quan, go run along, Mark till I need you again", as she closes the door, to say, "Have a seat, let's talk."

The tiny Michelle curled up in the chair, to hear,"So what's this I hear you want to quit?"

"I come here for one person only and that one person is Jack Cash."

"What if I were to get his approval, releasing you from this obligation."

"That's just it it's not an obligation, its duty, and especially what happen in Belarus."

"What happens if he is alright with you participating in this program, would you still quit?"

"No, I'm not a quitter, I did the fitness test out of a sense of duty and adventure."

"How did you like it?"

"It was fun and exciting", said Michelle.

"According to the records, your excellent rifle shot, and combined with your striking features you're a perfect spy candidate, what would you say, if we paired you both up, in the same room, would you stay then?"

"Perhaps" as she was wearing down her excitement for this promotion was too much too soon, everything she asked for she got, and she couldn't complain about that as she watched as Miss Hohlstein got up, to say, "I'll be right back," as she called Christina, the UN advisor, to hear her say, "Yes, Miss Hohlstein, I'm having lunch?"

"Where is Jack Cash?"

"Oh, I think he went to the spa."

"Really, you said the spa?"

"Yes that's what I said, why?"

"No worries." Said Meredith on the move to the spa, thinking, "Very seldom people goes in there, she thought, to add, "For some reason or another, she thought, but if Jack was enjoying, then fine with him. Jack was in the middle of a three hour rub down from three different spa attendants, only to be interrupted, to see an older woman barge in, to say, "Could you leave the room please", as the girl exited, she said, "Sorry for the intrusion, I want to tell you that Michelle Quan has qualified to become a UN spy."

Jack said sleephisly, "Good for her."

"So you approve of her appointment?"

"Yes, why not, I'd never stand in her way of progress especially if this is something she wants to do."

"Well in that case, I have several girls I could give you in replace of her?"

"Nah, it's not needed, I think I have found paradise here, so as far as I'm concerned, I'll stick it out till next week."

"Well about that, Jill Hoyt has also qualified, actually number two, in the current standings."

"Well good for them, especially her." That was the last Jack saw of her, as she bolted out of there, as Jack saw his sexy attendant, who put her hands all over him, but on a professional manner.

Meredith made it back to her office, to see Michelle, to say, "As of today you're an official UN pre-spy in training, congratulations?"

"Wait, what did Jack say?"

"He was happy for you and he wasn't going to stand in your way for success."

"No that's not what I mean, I'm here to serve and protect Jack Cash, and I'll only do this, if he stays on the women's floor with me, in suite one."

"What of your current roommate?"

"So ship her off, I don't care, but how bout this, I go stay with Jack, on the men's floor?"

"Enough, go get permission from your roommate, its Callista right?"

Michelle left the office of Meredith Hohlstein, realizing the games were just starting, she needed to be on her toes, as at the door, was her advisor, Mark, who led her into the elevator, and back to her room, whereas lunch was called, all the girls had their own mess, similar to the boys, Michelle caught up with Callista, to say, "Can I ask you of something?"

"Yeah, what is it?" as Callista turned her back to face the line, at the mess attendent, and to see Michelle was preoccupied.

Michelle got side tracked, and went down the line, and got as little as possible.

Debby entered from the south as an UN advisor, said, Please come, in, as per Miss Holhsteins approval, you will take over our internal supply operations, and look after Jack Cash whom is in Suite one, on the women's floor, all those pallets are for him, have some of the warehouse men, move them into his room, in addition, were converting a room in that suite to be a walk-in cooler, for all of his fish and produce, any questions?"

"Only one, do I have a service cart?"

"Yes, in there but you will have to make it up, I remember now, you have been here before, I think for your President."

"Yes, so show me the way."

One P.M. rolled around, as the SAS arrived, at the event, by the lake and all rest of the men who had to walk, whereas normally would have rode a bus, so they were not there yet, it was a mess all around, several spies were protesting their treatment, and would participate, but under duress so it was Vadim, searching for, and calling out, for, Jack Cash "Where are you?", only to find out a little later by SAS he went early, much to Vadim's dis-satisfaction, as he vowed some revenge and retribution. A lot of in fighting was happening, but it was those that played together stayed together, Russian, well with Russians, were actually by themselves as others kind of moved in, namely a one named Carlos the Killer Gomez, instantly fear was on their faces, as Alexei, put an arm around his old friend, to say, "Calm down fella's, Carlos and I go way back, although your thought of as a legend, never mind what Vadim said about revenge and retribution."

"I'm not, I guess you didn't know he is my brother-in-law?"

"Really, I or we weren't aware of that", as he waved off his other two companions, to add,"So are we cool?"

"Just as long as you stay away from Jack Cash, do I make myself perfectly clear" said Carlos, staring down his old friend, as two handlers came up to them, to say, "Do we have a problem here, move along, as they broke apart, the two handlers backed off, to give them room, as they were told, "Line up in a single file line, and now sound off," as the cadence started, "Even, odd, even odd, and kept up through the whole song till the end, when the UN advisor, said, "Odds stay where you're at, Even's move around to face so your paired off". Then it was called out, "One's will be on their backs, the other will hold the feet, and for every sit-up call a number, and so forth and so on, ready to begin, you have five minutes the record is 375, held by Varfolomey Bartholomew", as they all were ready, as it was called out to begin. They all easily qualified, doing more sit ups than needed. Most qualified, with several over a hundred, but not like Jack's performance, nor even close to the record. Next up was the pushups, everyone, assumed the position, as Simon Jonas, took the lead, to say, "Listen up could I have your attention", as he jumped up on a platform, to say, "All we need to do is 100 pushups, so on my count let's begin, "Assume, the position, ready, "He yelled, Down, 1, down, 2, down 3, until he did his first hundred, while the clocked moved, and went for another hundred, till finally he finished with 224. There was so many that dropped from that pace that the field was cut in half, and there were three distinct groups that formed, the old school, and the super new breed, and then the wanna bees, lastly it was pull ups, on the high bar, most did five and qualified, the wanna bees, dropped at one, and were eliminated, the elite group didn't choose its members, it was those that wanted to be there. Then it was off for the run, as time kept running for the entire event not restarting after the condition test. The elite group broke away from the wanna bees, even so much as tackling, a few good runners, as the elite pushed the old guard along, and kept them safe, in the middle of the formation, as it wasn't even close, they ran together, and finish together, with a slight lead over the wanna bees. Next was the bike, same thing occurred, the old guard in the middle, and Simon Jonas, was up front, pulling the pack to a record time, he was strong and powerful, and a true team player, with such a lead on the wanna bees, the elite swam with the old guard, and paced them towards the platform, as the times came in, immediately there was a problem, but it was a UN advisor, who took their time anyway, and disregarded the wall clock, that said one hour, fifteen minutes, so he looked at his watch, and chose to use the stopwatch feature. First on the platform was Simon Jonas from the North Korea. The advisor called out; "At 35-35, at 36 min, was Andreas Stauros, from Greece. At 37, was Chung, from China. Number 4, with 38 min, Stephen Moss. Next at 39 min, was Jonathon Razor. Next was at 40 min, it was Jamal Oman, from Saudi Arabia. At 41, minutes, it was Tad Jones. At number 9, with 42 min, was Sean Calvin, for Pakistan. At the principality, of the famed Monaco, it was Gordon Roderick. Next up was at the 44 mark, it was Chu, Japanese professional. At 45 minutes was Benjamin Logan, he represents Columbia. At 49, was Louie, Bellini, he had a chiseled body, next at 50, was Mustapha, of Israel. Next up was Kyle Devon, from Egypt at 52. At 54, it was Joel Robb, from Croatia." At 55 minutes is the new standard was the first of the big ones, Vadim was ready to take some chances, but not with Simon Jonas leading the group.

Next was his fellow compadre Alexander Yashin, at 58 min, and their older much wiser was Alexei, he was old school. Benjamin Hiltz at 1 hour. Another fluffer was Thomas Jones.

At 60 min, he was tired and it showed. Next up was Carlos, the killer, at 1 hour 5min, as the UN advisor, knew something just wasn't right, as the last two came, from the elite group as Simon was in the water, pacing the last two in, first it was, Andrain Jonason from Norway, at 1-10, and lastly who took ten more minutes, and lots of prodding from Simon as he paced him in, very slowly, to finish at 1-20, was Hendon Aziz, who had never swam in a lake, in near cold weather, but had a huge smile on his face, as the UN waved everyone else off, it was over. The field was set with these twenty, three. The rest were sent away, as the elite group steamed back on the platform boat to the UN this time, parked and was escorted, up a tunnel, and over to a waiting room, to rest, as the advisor said, "Wait here till we get all of your rooms assigned."

As the UN advisor made it to his boss, Claude, who looked at the list, to say, I want Jack Cash off, and pair up the rest, so the UN advisor, went back down, into the room, to say, "I have your assignments, as he saw the three Russians, standing together, to say, in suite 1, will be Simon Jonas & Mustapha, suite 2, will be Andreas Stauros & Kyle Devon, suite 3 Chung & Steven Smith.

Next up is suite 4, will be, Stephen Moss & Joel Robbe, in suite 5, will be Jonathon Razor & Vadim Adonis, and in suite 6 will be Jamal Oman and Alexander Yashin. Next up will be, suite 7, Tad Jones, and Alexei Putin, next up is suite 8 Sean Calvin, and Benjamin Hiltz. In suite 9 will be, Gordon Roderick, & Thomas Jones. In suite 10, will be Chu & Carlos Gomez, in suite 11, it will be Benjamin Logan & Andrain Jonason, and lastly it will be suite 12, Louie Bellini & Hendon Aziz, so let's go take a look at your suites as one said, "Wait what of this Steven Smith, who is that?"

"He will meet up in your suite."

"Then what of Jack Cash", asked Vadim?

The UN advisor looked up at Vadim, for the advisor to say, "He is on assignment, and his return is questionable."

Jack was relaxing in the mud pool, newly erected at his request, flown in, from Latvia, set up in a quickly and professional made up pool, complete with stone bench, and neck gard, he was now in heaven, as he opened his eyes to see a scantily covered girl, refreshing his head towel.

Back on the Men's floor, the men were led in, past the mess room, into a open space where six pallets sat, everyone just walked past them, as the UN advisor, said "I have a pass to give to you, it's the only way you'll be able to get into your specific room, the card has your name and the Suite you are in, as he passed them out to say, "Suite one, all enter please, on the right, is a living room, each has a 55 inch plasma T.V. on the right is the kitchen, if you or your lady need to cook, late night snacks etc."

Andrain raised his hand, "Yes, sir, what is it?"

"Is that what those pallets are doing in the courtyard?"

"No, they're for another guest, were still waiting to see if he comes, as I was saying, and also I want to add, everything is empty, except in room, 12, where it will be cleaned out soon enough, as I was saying, here on the left is a hallway, on the right is a room, on the left is a room, both have private baths, and on the very left, is a shallow pool to swim, or rest in a hot tub." That was all he had to say, as everyone bolted for their rooms.

Meanwhile down on the Women's floor, things were a bit different, Miss Meredith Hohlstein, was the headmistress for the girls as she was scrambling to find enough senior women to help as UN advisors, and keep men off the floor, except for her prize one, Jack Cash, where she is ready to give him anything he wants, as she has her assistant Christina, at his beckoning call, and escort.

When Miss Hohlstein is on the floor you knew about it, as she called a meeting over the intercom, as the girls, assembled in the courtyard, outside of the rooms, a common place of sorts, Christina was there too, as Miss Hohlstein, stepped off the elevator to see all the smiling faces, to say, "Welcome Ladies, to the UN first ever spy training course, don't get too comfortable, the back two suites should be done this weekend, tomorrow you all will go to the rifle range for an all-day event, you must both qualify on both rifle and pistol, in order to be a spy, you must shoot a top 90 percent, also I have one question, for all of you, with a show of hands, how many would let one male agent stay in suite one, hands please, so all those oppose, showed nine.

"Christina, write those names down," said Miss Hohlstein, as one said, "Wait, can we know who it will be?" she pleaded.

"Nika, it shouldn't matter to you who it was, that was a test, besides you can't have access without a key card, now can you?"

"I want to change my mind, and so did others.

"Sorry ladies, in the spy world, every decision is due or die." Meredith left as she had come, so Michelle asked Callista to sit, as Michelle said, "What that was about, was my boss would stay with me, in my bed, as I saw you didn't care."

"I still don't, whatever, if you get a guy what about me?"

"That's just it, it's not like what you're thinking."

"Then tell me what I'm thinking, and who is he anyway?"

"Jack Cash, ever heard of him?"

"Yeah, who hasn't, yes, I loved for him to be our roommate", she said in a glassy eyed sort of way. With a smile on her face, as she had a secret she couldn't hold any longer, as she blurted out, "The Guy, the guy is Jack Cash, he is the one who is staying here with us."

All the girls froze, some had smiles, some had frowns, as some, their worlds were about to end, namely Protima. A tall red headed girl approached Michelle to say, "Do you think I could be his wife?"

"Perhaps, wait in line, and when he gets here you can ask him, in the meantime, try to keep yourself scarce."

Michelle finished her meal in the courtyard, to hear, "Hey girlfriend, I want you to meet my man, his name is Alexander, the two shook hands, for him to say as he whispered in her ear, "When do you think we can talk, business Blythe", she looked at him weirdly, then said, "When ever."

"How about now", said the forceful Alexander.

"Sure", said Michelle, getting up and depositing her tray.

"Can you follow us up to my room?"

"Lead the way" said Michelle.

Michelle followed them, to the huge hallway, then to a glass door, where they all swiped their cards, except Alexander, as he fell in behind Raisa, up a flight of stairs, past the Men's mess room, to the same configuration the girls had, except for the frosted glass showed how private it was, as Michelle entered into the room number 7, it was the same layout, as the clear door closed to see Raisa leave the room, to see the other two Russian, converge on her, to say, "So are you in on our deal?"

She went along with it, to say, "Yeah sure, what do you have?"

"You know the deal Ingrid, explained to you in Belarus."

"Oh, she really wasn't able to explain to me fully what you wanted, except to find a way to kill him."

"Precisely, it's simple really, you agreed to poison Jack Cash, for a million dollars and then becoming a full-fledged spy for us, the Russians", said the smiling Vadim.

Michelle was clinching her fists to believe someone would betray Jack, for a million dollars, and defect to Russia, as she regained her composure, to say, "Alright, we have a new deal, I want cash, in American dollars, washed in yellow printer's ink?"

She waited their response as they were thinking about it to say, "Why?"

"Oh, for the fact if the dollars are real or not."

"We were just going to transfer the money."

"It doesn't work like that, Jack dies and I have one million dollars, I don't want to be around when all hell breaks loose."

"Fair enough, said Vadim, to add, "Then it will be done, in the meantime, here is the vial, just open it up, and pour it in the bath, the skin will absorb it and he will die." She takes it from Vadim, to see it says, "Flavoroids, use with special caution."

"That's devious of you, why don't you kill him yourself?"

"That's what we have you for, now I want this done before Monday morning" said Alexander, who was pacing, he was agitated.

"Just as long as I have that cash in hand, then it will be done."

Michelle turned and left the Russian room, thinking, "They are sure cowards, I wonder what he would of said had he known that Blythe got her head cut off for the betrayal of Jack, she thought who to tell first the Giant, Ivan or Jack, nah it will be Jack. The suite door opened for her, to see all was quiet, as some time had passed. Michelle walked through the men's' area, to see Raisa had waited for her to say, "So what did the boys want?"

"A foursome, wanna join in?" said Michelle smiling.

"Oowe, no way gross, you're considering doing this?" asked Raisa.

"Sure why not, he offered me a million dollars."

"He did, did he, wow."

They past the men's mess, to a secure door and each had to swipe her card for entry, and back into the women's area.

Meanwhile Jack was through at the spa, was led by Christina, to say, "You'll be staying, on the women's floor, until the Suite is ready for you, you have two roommates, the first is Michelle, which you are aware of and the second one is Callista Leander, from Greece, so here is your key card, this gives you unlimited access everywhere, keep it around your neck at all times, do you understand what I'm saying to you?, in addition, to the card, your hand print, or voice may activate the doors."

"Yes, I get it", as he places it over his head, and swipes his card, to see it leads to the women's room, he goes to the number one suite, and swipes his card, immediately to see five huge pallets, wrapped up in cellophane, to seeing no one, as he looks around the room, in the cooler, was fresh fruit, so he takes an apple, and over to the hallway, where there was two doors, he didn't even look at the name plate, swiped his card, the door unlocked, he pushed it open, only to see a very nude, women standing facing him doing yoga, to say, "Please close the door, if you wanna watch, stay, if you wanna participate, come closer and get out of those clothes, and lastly, close the door, its drafty."

Jack was tired, but she was a fiery red head, with a figure like Blythe, so he came in, dropped his robe, and undid his swim shorts, took a bite of the apple and stood before her in all his full glory, for Callista to say, "Now you're a hung man, what are you doing tomorrow?"

"Why are you asking that, when I'm right here tonight," asked Jack, looking at her incredible body, as she changed the pose, to an upward dog, from the standing tree, her body glistened from her radiance, it was go time, only to hear, "Come over here and assume the position", Jack did as he was told, as he was near to finish the apple, one last bite and it was all gone and instantly the excitement faded away, as the real work was taking place, as the hour went by, he was strained in his arms, as he collapsed to the floor, for her to stand above him to show him what she had, to say, "Care to take a shower with me?"

"Nah, I'll pass, but maybe later?" as Jack got up, slowly, she even helped him, up, as he staggered a bit, as he was drained, he was helped by Callista, to the opposite room, he swiped his card, it opened, he staggered in, as she had a clear film, and slid it over the lock, and allowed him to collapse onto the bed. She had his robe and shorts in hand, as she went around, and pulled the spread back, he said, “Thank you I must get some rest.”

“No problem, I’ll see you early tomorrow morning to pick back up where we left off, lover.” Callista left the room, the door swung shut, then she tried it, it had a little resistance then it opened, to think, “Good that will do the trick, tomorrow you and me Jack Cash.” A second goes by and Michelle returns, thinks she just saw Callista naked, but shrugs it off, as she was at their door, she swipes her card, and then pushes the door open to see Jack was sleeping, and seeing Callista to think, “So Jack you got to know the roommate already, interesting.”

Michelle checked out the vial, as she opened the drawer next to her side, and slipped the vial in, then closed it, she wanted to tell him badly of this plan, but thought being a good spy is to let it draw out, then let him know, as she stripped down, to step into the shower, she could see he was watching, as the clear glass showed him everything, as his eyes watched her, till, she was through, she dried off, then entered into her side, and placed her hand on his side, and slid in next to him, and both went fast to sleep.

CH 2

Sunday's assassination plot...

Michelle woke up, but knew it was too late, Jack was gone, she got up and made the bed, picked up his clothes, and got dressed, she saw it was 0615, and off to breakfast she went. She entered to see that it was full of all the hopefuls, as was several UN advisors, she and the others had breakfast, then exited to see Christina to say, "Please listen up, go get your Camo on, and come back here to pick up a pack, and then assemble, and we will be marching out, under-stand?"

"Heard" said the group as they disbursed.

Meanwhile Jack had an early meeting with Jim, who said,"It's all clear, another day, find a place to relax, our focus today is on the rifle range and Michelle qualifying."

"Will do", said Jack, through a secret slide panel, as Jack sat on a plastic bucket, in the storage room, he exited, in flip flops and in his white robe, and strolled out, and down the hall past the library, and right into an empty mess room, where a gorgeous lady was behind the counter, he stared at her, as he made his way up to the counter, to say, "I'll have a three egg white omelet with ham, beef, and pastrami, stuff that with goat cheese, and top with mozzarella." He paused then said, "Add some hash browns, crispy, but not burnt."

"Anything else Mister Cash?" said Dany.

"You know me?"

"Yes, matter of fact I work for you, this is my entire staff, so day or night, just ask, it shall be yours, my name is Dany, your official chef, when you get back I'll be in the food court.." she got the idea she was talking way too much to shut up, as he continued, to say, "Can I have two pieces of Pecan smoked bacon?"

"Yes, would you like a sausage?", she opened the container lid, to see that they were gone, to wait his response, for Jack to say, "No, I see, you have some fruit", he takes that, then, she cooked the omelet for him, and hash browns, to present the plate to him, he took it, to say, "Thanks Dany, I like your smile, it kind of brightens the room, he took four milks, two of chocolate, as he was finishing the line, he saw some condiments, and a jar of some chocolate spread, so he took the whole container, set it on his tray, for the check-out lady to say, "Your suppose to scoop it out with a spoon, not take the whole container."

Jack said, "So I can't get the whole container?"

"No, it's sold in our store" said the woman and Dany said, here I can scoop some out for you?"

"Nah, here you go, and hands it to Dany, knowing it was wrong, but allowed it to happen, as he went to the end, swiped his per diem card, and went to take a seat. He sat in the middle as he saw the girls assemble, and Michelle saw him, she came to him, to say,"So a pretty rough night huh?"

"You could sure say that, I'm sore all over?"

"What did the two of you do?"

"You saw her?"

"Yep buddy, so tell me what you guys did in the nude?"

"Simple yoga?" said Jack, honestly.

"What, Yoga, what about sex?"

"Nah, I first swiped her room with my card, and there she was naked, I was like let's do this, only to go through several poses and I was dead, so your right, she did help me to bed, then I saw you, so what's up with all the gear?"

"We're going to the range to qualify, any suggestions?"

"Yeah, keep an eye on Jill, I don't know if she had ever qualified before, and I will see you tonight, for some make up sex"

said Jack rather loudly. "Hush, boy, or I'll cut you off" said Michelle kiddingly.

"I have a back up plan", said Jack seriously.

"Who's that?" said Michelle turning to leave as Jack said, "Our roommate."

"Nice try she is here with us." She left as the roll call went off, and one pack was left, as one said, oh, she is in the bathroom, "Alright let's go", said Christina, as one picked up the pack..

Meanwhile up on a steep hill above the UN sat the energy department, that supplied the UN its Energy, what this person didn't know was it was a dummy reactor. This terriorist climbed, the hill to the very top, got to the fence, used a plasma torch to cut the chain link fence, as UN officials, were seeing this live, to say, "What is he doing?, let's get someone out there." Said the UN officials in panic.

Back at the mess, Jack had finished his wonderful meal, and waved off to Dany, went out, to the hallway, to the spa, swiped his card, and he was gone, and back into paradise, warm inviting, and handed the manager, his unlimited card, to say, "The works again, please."

"So all day?"

"Yep."

"Another 20,000 dollars." Said the Manager Margaret, but then said, "Looks like the server is off line, I'll try later."

"Sure, just hold on to the cards, bye" said Jack knowing where to go.

The Manager, just shook her head, and says, to herself, "He is our only customer."

Outside in the hanger bay, the UN advisor stopped by and collected up the Black Ops team, for field work early, that left Jim, and Mitzi on the plane, Mark and Mike doing fabrications work, along with Jesse and Brian, and Trixie and Tami were resting in Jack's cabin, Jared went with the Black Ops team, to take Jill's place. When all of a sudden the hanger door blew, it rocked the underground structure, as UN ground forces were sent into action. The terrorist finally made it to the top portion, killing any resistance he encountered, the guy who got into the power company, climbed the tower, and blew the top, and instantly, systems shut down, and all was quiet in the UN, except in isolated areas where there was no power needed as the spa was eco-friendly, everything had natural light, as in the solarium.

Outside away from the UN, the women, started off marching, as Meredith Hohlstein, took a van, and waited for the group, and some time later, Michelle and Jill came in first, she had them, take water, and sit, as more came in till all was accounted for, as several went into the bathroom, as roll call took place and all was supposed accounted for, then assigned a lane, and asked to go to that spot. Each laid down on a mat, adjust a rifle that they were given, and a box of magazines as the caller and judges sat 500 yards back. A caller called out, "Ready on the right, ready on the left, I want you to place the butt in your shoulder pocket, an instructor will help you with the sling, now we going to give you three rounds to set in your windage, now look at the target it's one hundred yards away, think of a football field, now when you're ready raise your trigger finger, and the instructor, will load your magazine, now that all of you are ready, ready on the left, ready on the right, on my mark, 3,2,1, fire."

Callista went back to the room as the other left, and decided to wait for Jack, as she went into her room, undressed completely, and put her clothes in the dirty clothes hamper, and left her room immaculate, went and tried the door, it opened, and she went into Jack's and Michelle's room, to see the bed was made, and the place all picked up, as she went snooping, first through Jack's drawers, then on to Michelle's, only to stop at her nightstand to see a vial, that read, Flavoroids, as she said, "What is this here for?" and instantly un capped it, first to smell, it was some sort of citrus, and then took some on the tongue to taste the wonderful flavors as it was a party in her mouth, and put the cap back on, and set it back in the drawer, then closed the door, and then just like that she had a warm sensation speeding through her body, and she laid down on the bed, in the middle, with her head on the pillow, and her arms to her side, as her body swelled to double its size, as she expired and died.

Just like that the Chinese Commando's ascended on the UN, with rifles, blazing, in that instant, Jim was handing out weapons, as the plane was getting shot at, the ramp was raised, as it was over, as they blew a hole through a process door, facing no resistance, as they went down to the third floor, the secure locks were frozen, on the second floor, so the super agents could not come out of their rooms and help. They came to the set of frosted doors to the women's floor, someone blew the access panels off the wall, and going in, they saw walls drop, on each one they set a charge and blew it, as time was running out, as they were speaking Chinese, Debby, came out from the supply to see all the electrical problems, to see, those with guns, trying to blow the final glass wall to the Suites, so she ran back to the secondary living station was, to start pulling Ivan out of his bed, only he put up a fight.

Finally, they used most of all there charges, on that huge clear wall, on the women's level, as it erupted and rocked the UN, and cracked other suites, glass, once inside, they came to Suite one and blew the door, which shattered both glass, into a million pieces, and one by one raced in there, one stumbled, and lost his weapon, as the other four made it to Jack's supposed room, number one, and tried the door it opened, and to see a sight as they were filming it. Instantly they got a whif of death as the body had swollen twice more, as the Chinese were filming the action of one Jack Cash, it made it hard to recognize if it were a man or a women, one person, they set the small explosive on the body, and watch it sink in, as they got back, and closed the door as it blew, pieces everywhere, as the four waited after the blast went off, when outside, their friend was flying through the air, bounce off the glass, and not moving, out of explosives and ammo, it was the old fashioned way, hand to hand combat, as around the corner was a Giant, who was on the war path, his fists the size of mallets, he stepped in, to see them, as each came him at once, one swipe a woman did cartwheels, and landed upside down, as Debby went to assist the Giant, and zip tie them up, one punch sunk the man's head and his life, a punch to the gut, also ended the other man's life. The last girl waited, as it was Debby's one punch, clocked her and her light's went out. As just then the UN support came in and it was over, as those involved were taken away, as Ivan, took a look inside the contaminated room, to close it tight to go over and wash his hands.

Some time had passed and Jim, Brian and Jesse, with Mark and Mike's help fixed the damage to the electrical power plant, inside the hanger and brought it back on line, as Jim was calling home, to see if Erica or Lisa had any news yet, as the President received a disturbing tape, of something blew up. Boldly the Chinese took the responsibility for the surprise attack, that left 22 UN agents dead, some wounded and two top spies, feared dead."

As the US government, saw the tape, that read, Poisoned and killed, Jack Cash super spy, as they saw a bomb get thrown on top of the body, and it sunk down, then the door opened to see, pieces everywhere, as US sent investigators, immediately there, and placed a call to Miss Meredith Hohlstein, who was overseeing the rifle and pistol qualifications, which she answered, "Hi, Mister President, what do I owe this call for?"

"You don't know?"

"Know what, what's going on here?"

"Earlier, this morning, five Chinese nationalist, took the UN, and Jack Cash is gone," said the President sternly.

Tears began to streamed down her face, as she wasn't able to talk, as she ended that call and called up her team, asking them for a confirmation, of Jack Cash's whereabouts.

The President had other ideas, as he set the fleet of ships into the south china sea, as a trident class, submarine, began to fire ACM, 1600 pound payloads, at targets all through China, as the Prime minister of China called the US, for the President to say, "Yes, Tan Ming, through a translator, as he said,"This crossing into our waters is a violation of the UN treaty."

"Maybe you should of thought that when you took out my top spy?"

"How so, it wasn't me or anyone from my country, I assure, you abort your missile strike or I will retaliate, as he was watching the missile head his way to the HQ in Shanghai.

In Russia, the word reached number two, the second in command was Ivan Bresniff, who admitted to his friend he took our beloved President, Vladimir, his wife Victoria, to his Chinese counterpart, to add, "The American's won't retaliate with losing a spy, but watched the carnage at the UN go off. To further add, "Don't worry, have another drink, maybe some more broads, come on."

The President of the US, came to his senses, and aborted the five missles he let go, and detonated in the sea, and ordered them out of the south china seas, Tan Ming assured those responsible would be turned over and all would be forgiven.

Back at the UN, the clean-up crews, dressed in Haz Mat suits, came in as did Meredith who saw how much damage, and of a barely alive Chinese man, and another Chinese woman, but the prize was the one the Giant left behind and was holding by the scruff of his neck.

US Delta teams were asked to extract Clarance out of Belarus and bring him to the UN, so said Miss Hohlstein as she had Floyd flying in as well.

In all that chaos, Jack found the mud pits to be his favorite place to be at to survive the Sunday.

The rifle range went rather well, as all that qualified, one of those, was Dayle Amos, and was a non-qualifier, but strange thing on number 13, it was supposed to be Callista Leander, her first shot was a miss, so below on the mark line, the judge, waved a red miss, then the next shot, same results, that resulted in a call to change, as everyone, moved one over, and after that everyone fired near perfect, on the range. Now it was onto pistol, this was one woman, one shot, at 50 and 100 foot marks, and first was Dayle Amos, she shot horribly wrong, and literially dropped her pistol on the ground, and walked off in a huff. "Next please, Michelle Quan, was perfect, next was Jill Hoyt, she too qualified, next up was the Rebecca Adams, who also qualified, and all three had become friends, because of Jack Cash. Next up was a relative new comer on the spy club, but learned how to shoot, Cami Ross, her hard exterior, was evident as she took almost range record, of 250, and finish 249. Now for the failures, Maja Quincy, from Colombia, took the heavy .45, and broke her wrist, Grace Fabian, from Wales, missed every shot, she was out, another London project, Ellie Morgan, she shot 50 percent, she was out, now the borderline, one, Nika Kenna of Romania, shot 84, although impressive, it was still low, and Raisa Sergel, shot a 87, and she was out and lastly Kellie Ryan, shot 89, but it was one shy, or one of her first miss, that did it. The SAS waited for Miss Hohlstein's arrival, to continue on, as Mess was called, and into the barn all went. Tam-lu shot well, and still with her pistol, as she got word of the attack, and pulled her weapon, on the SAS, to say,"Get me a Vehicle.", only to feel a dart at her neck, as the armorer, tranquilzed her, as they subdued her. She was taken away to the brig. The Russian girls, having seen their friend and house mother Raisa go down, were pretty upset.

So for the day, the results were a combined score from the rifle range and pistol, it was the following; Nina Toop, shot 246, Nina Ivan, 244, Kendra Augustus, 245, Lea Lucas, from Monaco, 246, tough girl Peleruth Jaizem, 244, Protima, 249, and Z'sofia, Baptiste, 248. Chloe Ryan, shot a 248. Now the following US, was Dana Scott 246, and Roxy Carr, 247, Simone, 246, Darlene Lewis, 248, Erica Adams, 244, Freya Lyons, 242, Esmeralda Romero, 241, and barely above 90 percent, Joana Celek, 240, as told to Miss Meredith Hohlstein, by Christina, over the phone, to hear, "Fine, allow them back in, for her to say, "Let's send the boys out after lunch."

"Yes, Ma'am, as Christina said, "Load up in the van, girls, Christina sat next to Michelle, to say, Miss Hohlstein has asked me, to inform you that your rank is now Captain, and you can appoint a lieutenant, a master sergeant, two staff sergeants, and the rest sergeants, understand?"

"Yes, Miss Christina," said Michelle as Christina was showing Michelle, as the group broke into two groups, and got into the awaiting vans, the new living arrangement, she said, "I believe were all set, a total of 23, with Calista missing, you as elected Captain. And here is the new format, in Suite 1, you as Captain.

The rest will be switched around, as needed.

The vans moved as Michelle conteplated, who to assign what, and where was her roommate, Calista?, she looked over the list, to think about Dana Scott, Lieutenant, Simone Bailey, Master Sergeant, Freya Lyons, one staff, and the other Nina Ivan, the other Staff sergeant.

The C-130 was flying high above the clouds, as Casey keeps instructing Brian what to do, with the heavy pack on his back, as Casey ties up his front pack, above his secondary.

"Over the intercom, Jim said "One minute to drop zone."

"Remember it's easy, you hit the target, and Clarance will help you with the chute, get the balloon in the air, and hitch him up, you have about twenty minutes, to land and hook him up and we will return, are you alright, I could jump with you if you want?"

"Would you?," said Brian, seemingly bit uneasy.

"Alright hold on?" said Casey, as he made it back to the flight cabin, to announce, "I'm going with him."

"You got thirty seconds to jump, you got your assault rifle ready?"

"Always" said Casey, who hitched up his single chute, then went to Brian, to unclip his pack, and snapped onto his front, he wanted the balloon, but it was too late for that, he clipped on his rifle across his chest, on long clips, he saw the green light, and went past Brian and jumped out, he was in a tuck position, to read his GPS, and saw he was late, unlike Brian who was way late, he soared through the clouds, and saw he was close to 2000 feet, then waited till 1000 feet to pull the cord, he hit the target, just under a bank, out of cover, came out a well camouflaged Clarance, who helped Casey pull in his chute, as Casey pulled out the harness, and helped him into it, and released the weather balloon as Clarance said, "Where's the helicopter?"

"There isn't one?"

"How do I get back?"

"Look up?"

Clarance saw another, to say, "Did you guys jump together?"

"Yep, you're going and he is staying" said Casey.

"Here let me help you" said Clarance, to help Casey line it up, to say, "Do you know what this is all about?"

"I don't ask, I just do as asked, and you're wanted at the UN."

"Is Jack coming now?"

"No, Brian will relieve you."

"What him?" pointing up at Brian, still coming down, to say "You're kidding right?"

"Nope, but listen, be kind, he is Jack's armorer."

"I got you" said a perplexed Clarance, to see Brian, near to the ground to say, "Go help him out."

Casey ran out to help Brian, who hit the ground and fell over, as Clarance, was steadying the line to say,"Are you going back with me?"

"Yes, why?"

That plane is bearing down on us, lets go, get him up", as Casey helped Brian, as Clarance yelled, "Lets go now".

Brian, stood there with just his pack and rifle in hand, as Clarance motioned for him to get back, back to his face, as Casey latched him into him, as his GPS was counting down for pickup, he saw the canister, to say "Brian, take that and hide it I'll see you in two weeeeee........"

The two were yanked up, at supersonic speed, as they leveled off, and in minutes later, the cable was drawn in and just like that they were on the underside of the plane, they unclipped and went inside the cargo plane, Clarance looked at him to say, "And you do this every day?"

"Yep,we do."

"That was a rush of my life." Said Clarance.

Back at the UN, the boys, they were notified by messenger, that after lunch to meet at lower lounge at 12:45, for a bus ride to the rifle range. Miss Meredith was running the cleanup and telling people what to do, as Ivan, was being looked after. The cleanup was ongoing, the whole women's level, is being de-contaminated, so men in blue suits came out, and began the sterilization process, first it was the people of the UN, who went through a decontamination shower and some went to the bathing station and the Haz mat teams took an area, and worked it back to the suite one. As all six pallets were taken out and disposed of and In Suite one, was the highest concentration of the chemical attack, where the walls were torn out, and the whole kitchen redone, floors, carpet, and only place left un done, was the pool, they were all in a hurry up mode, to make it right, now, for the time being. The UN had over hundred craftsman to finish up the rooms. Meanwhile the women came back feeling renewed, for Michelle it was nice seeing Raisa, even though she is innocent, and sweet, she too was notified that she was continuing on.

All the men were released out of their suites, and told over the intercom, "All is safe, and the threat is contained, so go get some chow." All did as they were told and went to mess together, as another line had been formed, when a UN advisor, with a clipboard, said "Chung, could you come with me, they took a trip on the train, to Miss Hohlsteins office, they waited, and then was asked to come in, Chung, gets up and goes in, to see Meredith standing, to hear her say, "Who is Marisol?, Chung?"

He shakes his head, to hold back his feelings, for Miss Hohlstein to say, "I'm going to give you two options, tell us who she is and I'll allow you to just go home, or, keep your mouth shut, and allow our translator to extract that information out of you either way, its voluntary or probably in your case in-voluntary."

Just like he sprung up, and tackled her, as they went down, she stuggled with the China man and said, "That's all you got, young, guy, as she was throwing rabbit punches as he was trying to subdue her, as she reached up to hit a button, under her desk, just then, a few UN helpers came in and extracted Chung off of the Chief Justice, as he was zipped tied up and subduded Chung, who was saying, "I want my ambassador" his words fell on deft ears. Chung was led to a holding cell, and set in there. Then moments later, a woman's scream, then silence, then she is swung into the next cage, as Chung sees her, beaten bruised, as, she was crying and saying, "Sorry, Chung I gave you up, it was my only chance to save myself, "said Col Tam-lu.

Chung watched as two UN guards took her away, then instantly jumped back to seeing Ivan, the executioner, to say, "Your girlfriend was easy, she sang the plan on your attack on the UN and for your target Jack Cash, you succeeded, I will have to tell you, I usually, don't do this line of work, I normal, just execute them, especially scrawny guys like yourself."

"Let me out and I will show you who the boss is now."

"Fine I don't care, but, like me I have to wait."

Chung came closer, to say, "Wait for what?"

"For who, and he is, I guess the world's most deadliest interrogator, he breaks people, even if they didn't even do it, so you see your safe in there till he arrives."

"Who is he I got to know?" said Chung.

"The names, Clarance."

The guy shot back into the bed, for the Giant to say, "Clarance, You made it?"

"Yeah, first time in a supersonic jet, yeah I heard about Jack, so who is in there?"

"One of the co-conspirator," said Ivan the Giant.

"That's alright, he will be easy?"

"What do you have in mind, can I help out?" asked Ivan.

"Maybe, but I'll ask him a few questions, to figure out what he likes."

"I'm right here, what do you want to know?" asked Chung.

"Sorry it doesn't work like that, you threaten the life, of the most important woman on this planet, so now you're guilty, for the assassination of Jack Cash, and how do you plead?"

"Not guilty."

The Giant stepped in, to say, "From the evidence I heard, this Marisol talked of such a plan, but didn't think she was serious, then there was this so called Colonel, of what I don't know, maybe she is delusional, but she sang about you and how it was you, so you're ready to talk, yet, in my country, we just cut off your heads?" said Ivan, being articulate.

"Yeah, what do you want to know?" said the cocky Chung, with his hands on the bars, looking at the ever so mean Clarance. Who stepped up and began the questions, to step close to the bars to say, "First off, why did you attack, a Chief Justice of the World Court?"

"I didn't know who she was, honestly" said Chung pleading.

Clarance looks over at Ivan to say, "Let me tell you this Ivan, he is lying, and once a liar, always a liar, no you see Ivan, Chung here, hold on I just got word that Jack Cash is alive, and found, he turned to Chung, to say, "Now you really do get to come to face to face with those you tried to co-conspired against Jack Cash, you'll be hearing, from me again."

Jack heard from the relief shift there was a change now all the men are going to the rifle range. Jack was up, and on the move, he showered, dressed, and then paid for his spa, and left, he entered the women's floor, and instantly everyone froze. As Jack just stode there, as instantly Mark the UN advisor was on the phone to Miss Hohlstein to say,"Jack is here and he is alive, Miss Meredith to come down here, please." Jack had a seat in the lounge, only to see the World Chief Justice, for Jack, to say first, "What happen in there, what's going on here?"

"We had a little accident, all will be cleaned up by tonight, where have you been?"

"Where else, the spa, what else is there to do?, so I heard were going to the rifle range?"

"No, actually they were, you're here till you can talk with your President and have him, stand down,"

"I need a phone, got one?"

"Yeah, follow me" said Meredith, now smiling, as Jack walked behind her, in flip flops, and his robe, he made it to her office to see it was all in a disarray, to take a seat opposite her, as she dialed the President, who answered it hot, he was angry, it was in his voice, and he wasn't happy as he was on the rampage, as people were losing their job, till he heard, "Mister President this is Jack Cash, how are you?"

It was all silent on the other end, for Jack to say again, Mister President this is Jack Cash, I have fourteen wives, when can I have a congeal visit?", "Ha, Ha, Ha, was heard as the President was a little more reserved to say, "What is going on there?"

"I have no Idea, I hope all is well with you?, as Meredith hung up the phone, to say, "So Jack, your off till 0800 tomorrow morning, later tonight your room will be ready, for you and Michelle."

"So what happen to Callista?"

"I believe the term is she was washed out, and is no longer here."

"Too bad, I really liked her, oh well, what of those attendants, you promised me?"

"I'll send them over to the spa? is that where you're heading?"

"Yes Ma'am," said Jack as out the door he went with Meredith's phone in hand, went back through the UN, to the rear supply closet, opened the door, closed it, slid the panel open, and yelled, "Jim, Jim, it's Jack."

Instantly Trixie, heard that call out, scrambled down the ramp, and over to the wall, to say, "Where have you been everyone thought you died?"

"Nah, I was hiding out, as Jack hands her the phone to say,"It's hot, I need any live feed, or otherwise, so what's going on."

"Well a lot to tell you, a team of Chinese assassins raided the UN, blowing things up and shooting up the place."

"Why the blue suits in the women's level?"

"Some type of chemical spill of some sorts, they had to bring in a Haz Mat waste barrel in, also, we the US almost declared war over your death with China, as they took credit for your killing, here it is on this phone, as Trixie easily hacked it, to show Jack of the raid, and what Ivan did, it was impressive, for Jack, to say, "Trixie can you go get my phone, I want a private talk with the President."

She left moments later, she came back with it, hands it to him, for Trixie to say,"You should take it, and now go before they discover you missing."

"Alright," said Jack, to hear, "Oh one last thing, Clarance is here he is questioning a prisoner. "Jack slid the compartment door shut, now in the darkness, he dialed up, the President, who said, "It really was you?"

"Abort, the pick up, and coming here, I'm onto a major coup, and from now on, please don't declare war, if I'm alive or dead, remember I'm on a mission, and have so much going on, allow me some space, I'll fix everything," said Jack.

Just like that, Air Force One, was heading home, much to everyone's agreement, especially at the UN, as it was calm again, as Meredith realizes her phone is missing, as she had a tracker on it as it showed it was 20,000 feet in the air. Trixie, deposited the tracker, to a supersonic jet, and hands the phone to Mark to crack.

Jack watched as others in front of him, of the supply closet, then he exited, to go to open courtyard, to his Suite, it opened for him to see that the women were just finishing up the final touch ups and then had cleared out in a hurry. The fresh air was cool, as he said, "Up to seventy please." On the right was the sitting area, and small kitchen, in the middle was six new large pallets, he past them, to his room, and his bed, then on the left was the master bathroom, that led out to a pool, Jack saw his luggage containers stacked up, as he went to the drawers, began to open them, and put stuff into them, to think about Sara, and when would he be back, as he found some trunks, and put them away, till he off loaded, everything, and took it to what was called a supply storage, that was once a suppose bedroom, he opened the door, to see it was empty, and put the suitcases in. Then went through the bathroom, and slid open the door, to the warm pool area, and dropped his robe, and dove in.

Michelle, just finished her own debriefing, for her role as Captain for the remaining girls, she was told of Jack missing status as found, much to her happiness, and that of the Russian girls. Then she was told of what support people they had, and lastly how to contend with the spouses, it was totally different than, being a worker and her position, as she has an extensive schedule to go by, while she exited, she walked proudly, to her Suite number one she placed her hand on it to hear, "Your access granted", the door slid open, and went to the bedroom, she changed into some athletic gear, as what the others chose to do, work out, "Now that's what she was hoping for", she had befriended several women, like Lea, from France, and Nina Toop from Russia, she remembers mentioning on how her friend would love to meet her, she went to the bathroom, to close the door, to see Jack swimming, then exits.

Jack finished swimming, to climb out and into the hot spring tub, to lie back and relax. He sensed someone, he opened his eyes to see Debby standing there, with a towel in hand, dressed as a UN girl, to say, "Do you need someone to wash your back?"

"Sure, how did you get here?"

"I was asked by Erica to keep an eye on you?"

"I got that part, I meant in here, in this room?"

"Well technically, I'm your support staff, I set out all your clothes and deliver your packages, and most importantly I'm your gossip girl".

"I guess I'm the lucky one."

"Yes you are, now Mister Cash how do you want me?"

"I could lean up and have you slid in from behind?" said Jack.

"If you like, you're the boss, shall I undress?"

"Whatever you like, I actually had called for some attendants to help out." said Jack watching her drop the towel she had, to undo her shirt, to show that she wore a swimming top, as she dropped her pants, to see the matching bikini bottoms, she sat down on the edge, then into the hot water, to begin the massage, of his back to say, "What would you like to know first?"

"What's the plan for tomorrow ?"

"About that, they changed the schedule, because of the earlier events in the UN, so who knows?"

"Alright, why are you here?"

"To help you of course."

"To do what, everyone wants something?"

"Well first off, I work for you now, what more do I need to prove to you why I'm here?"

"Fair enough" said Jack.

"Anything else?"

"Why are you still in your bikini?"

"I didn't know you felt that way about me?"

"We slept together."

"True, but nothing happened."

"Where were you at?"

"What are you talking about?" she asks honestly.

"Well let me put it to you this way, you were nude, and so was I, and we went at it and then all of a sudden you had passed out, you were literally in some sort of shock, I dressed you and called in the cavalry, and they gave you a soda, and glucose tablets, you came too, dressed in a night gown, but not before…"

"Alright I get it now, you know, I dreamt of something, but I just didn't know what was true or not" she said as she flung her top over his head, to see it floating, he got up to turn to see her, for Debby to say, "I have no protection, can we wait till later, or do you have a condom?"

It's not about that, besides I'm not in the mood, I just like looking at that incredibly hot body."

"Well in that case here you go", she said as she pulled off her bikini bottoms to show him her goods, he quickly changed his mind, and she didn't refuse him.

In the living area, sat Ivan the Giant, as he sees Michelle, he says to her, "We have a meeting, then off to some sensitivity training, for the spies." said Ivan in a statement.

Michelle got back to the room to see Debby, dressed, and cleaning and tidying up, to say, "You look familiar."

"I should I work for Jack Cash and who are you, oh yeah, that's right Michelle."

"Yes it's me, what are you doing here?"

"I'm part of the cleaning crew, come on in" she said as Michelle went in, as the door closed. Jack was at mess hall, then went to the spa. Jack looked around as a line had formed at the entrance, who were waiting, as the spa was the new, It thing, and they were getting overwhelmed, then as each name was called, then it was Jack's, as he was led to a private room, where he was asked to change, and put on the robe, he took a seat in the pedicure chair, for the first time, for him, as a lady washed his feet, then cut his nails, massaged them, then applied a clear coat, he then slid into flip flops, and was led to the manicure station, where his hands were soaking, then dried, massaged, then clipped, a matte finish was applied, and then led to another room, and went face down, as the robe was discarded, and replaced with a sheet, and the massage began.

CH 3

A new spy's line up

It was 0800, Monday Morning and the door to the Auditorium opened, both Men and Women, were let in, but segregated, Men on the left, Women on the right, as two men and two women of distinction took to the stage, a dapper gentleman went to the podium to begin, by saying, "Thank you for all that is attending the United Nations spy summit, designed to assemble the best available spies in the world today and to allow ideas to be exchanged, my name is Professor, Gustave Goins, I'm from France, my colleague, and main teaching professor, is Claude Benz, of the famous Benz family of Germany, more specifically, Bonn Germany, and on my left, two distinguished women, are Susanna Hill from West Berlin, as she stands to be acknowledged, and for professor Goins, to say, "And the other, is Professor Abigail Watts, from Sweden, she is a liberal arts and attorney, and just then, another figure stood proud, off to the wings, but out of view, for the Professor to see her, to say, "And lastly, I want to introduce the founder, and presiding chair, for the World council, for the World court, please stand, and give a warm welcome, to the Chief Justice, Miss Meredith Hohlstein, she gracefully walked over, to the podium, composed herself to say, "As the presiding Chief Justice for the World Court, I oversee all diplomatic immunity status's, as a spy, that is what keeps you alive in other countries, when your accidently caught, or detained, I will be the one that saves your life." She looks around the room, to add, "If you're like most of us, we have to travel civilian flights, but there are some among you that, has their own aircraft, and are supported in such a way, that isolates you to the general public, and those are called special spies, spies that travel the world, with the backing of its government, now I know, that should be the case for everyone, but it simply isn't like that at all, take for instance Monaco, Prince Jalbert and family, use spies as intelligence officers in its tiny county, our top UN spy Joe Simon resides there and has a small group learning to be spies, but they are not even on the scale of the Russians, where three of the mightiest are present today, Vadim, the current number one, overall, his young Protégé, Alexander, and the old guard, Alexei, although, he just changed his name again, oh well, they have the vast of all of Russia, to watch over, and they were nice enough to bring several up in comers in the spy game, she looked over to say, "Notably, the world's famous bounty hunter, also known as the Ice princess, Rebecca Adams," she stood, to get an applause, even from the men, next is the model, Nina Toop, then Nina Ivan, the hen mother, and partner to Alexei, Raisa Sergel, and lastly an up-in-comer, Kendra Augustus, all have phenomenal backgrounds, in espionage, counter espionage and intelligence gathering, all here in Europe, as for the United States, there is only one man that stands out, his name is Benjamin Hiltz, his adventures in Europe is legendary, and it's good to see at least twelve of the women candidates, come from his selections, so thank you."

"Now let's talk about why you're here, the UN is ever so far reaching in over 175 countries worldwide, from a tiny island of Cypress, to Russia, the oil fields of Kazakstan, ontop of the Caspian sea, to the great Alaskan pipeline, our main focus is World peace, at all costs, and those costs come from you the spy, it's your job, to diffuse, and organize the peace, from those that take advantage of those less fortunate, then ourselves, as we send spies all over the globe, it's usually ones that have a reputation, that will be received well, instead of sending in someone, say like Jack Cash, into Russia, where as he has never been there before, and to some it was a suicide mission, so what does the spy do, he goes on the offense, as most spies do, they go in undected, and blend, to gain confidence, no, but what Jack did, will forever hold a precedence here in the UN for he went on and took on a whole, known terrorist base, with a help from his friends, namely, Rebecca Adams, came to his aid, and the two of them with some support help, attacked the base, and in doing so took out four of the top Russian secret police and known terrorist, then sent in a well-placed bomb, down a smoke stack, which blew and created a shift in the underground plates, thus causing, the largest earthquake in the world, registered at 18.6 on the Richter scale, it was felt in Poland." She waited for an response, then continued, to say,"He did that all because the current set of spies, were un-available", as Vadim, Alexander and Alexei, looked on with admiration, and new found respect. For them it wasn't about revenge and retribution any more, for Jack had singly handed, freed all of them, from the tierney of the secret police, and now they knew it, as Miss Hohlstein continued, "There is no spy greater than yourself, each of you possess something, each can use, when you're in the field, especialy here at the UN, whereas, someone is selected Captain, that person will have a first assistant, in status form, then it will be the Lieutentant, a Master Sergeant, to muster up the troops, and two Staff sergeants to oversee each group, the rest of you will be sergeants, and thus receive pay as such, however, some of you have been asked to participate, and your pay will reflect that, now on to the United Nations, formed after world War 2, in 1945, to effectively help suppress the next global war, but we are more than that, as I will explain, we take a ninefold approach to the world, and the 1st one is World peace keeping efforts, in every country has its own embassy, we too have someone in those Embassy's to regulate visa's and current affairs, those are the places, you will find trouble long before it really surfaces, with the exceptions of the really large countries, that's where the spies, know all and see all with, their band of groups, such as Mustapha, with his group (CFT) Constantly Fighting Terrorism, he and his group control all of the middle east, with Hendon Aziz, and Z'sofia Baptiste, the three of them, combined with countless others maintain peace in that region, which some day, you all may find yourself there."

"Number 2, is Space, namely outer space, anything above the atmosphere, is regulated, and observed, and here at the UN oversee the International Space Station, and other secret efforts to maintain, global peace, in addition we monitor all of the world's satellites". "Number 3, we control the Arms, race, and selling of and to the world's countries, for some just to defend themselves, and for others, we block that sale, to curb, the event of terrorism, next we control all the under the water, military bases throughout the world, as supported by the world's largest countries, as some of you may not know this, every country in the world, has a secret under water military installation, since the advent of television coverage, and snooping eyes, each country had to put its most secret operations under the ocean." "Number 4, is controlling the environment, such as destroying the world's rain forests, which is all but stopped in the amazon, where thirty thousand million feet of top soil had eroded and has change the course of the river, causing downstream flooding, and ruining of the crops, South America, so desperately needed, and all this scalping was done by a Chinese, corporation, and with that comes the oceans fishes, and namely the whales, still to this day, the Japanese's, are killing those innocent creatures, for what for, the fat?" and discarding the carcasses". "Number 5, is fighting hunger, the fight is here, and it's you spies are the future, there is more, fighting hunger, is all over the world, where, a rich man who lives in a huge mansion, and down the street an orphanage of starving children, wait for handouts, now we have communications, with that rich person, to give through a specific charity, 10 percent of net profit, before taxes, to insure, they are eating, turns out, it now feeds the entire city, and that was a spy, who created that". "Number 6, next we provide aid to refugees, and those exiled from countries, in association with World Red Cross efforts, in countries such as Haiti, which cannot support its own self, it's the job of the UN and the spies, to facilitate their existence in time of need, museums, recovery of stolen and looted items, is all about what spies do." "Number 7 is this thing called an epidemic in the United States, and similarly to Europe, Human rights, and more over Human trafficking, sex trade is running so rampant, that it's one in ten women are taken, either through, kidnapping, being lured, or through the drug trade, which it's the spies, that regulate, uncover and diffuse." "Number 8, is really for the Super Spy, and that's why they are such, if your given a title of Super Spy simply means only one thing, you know all about nuclear energy, how it's made, the smell of it, how Uranium, is processed to make weapons grade plutonium, and what the tell tailing signs are, for those agents alone, they are at the pinnacle of all the world's safety, and for that they are the top of all spies, and for good reason, they allow us to go to sleep at night, knowing they are there to diffuse, secure and keep us all safe, current there are three in this world, and their job is so taxing, that's why we hope to promote three more to that position, Joe Simon's case load is around fifteen thousand cases, as is the others, and lastly, Number 9, the governments, politics and world leaders, any questions?", she waited till a women stood to say, "So what you're saying, all of us in this room, have qualified to be an agent for the UN?" said Peleruth Jaizem, from Poland.

"No, not necessarily, you're here to show us that we can trust you to go out and represent us well, for some of you we are aware of that, and are waiting you to show us, what you're capable of, but for the most part, it's you that has to show us, your reliability and integrity, next."

Another girl stood, to say,"So once we do that, how will we know?"

"That's easy, I will tell you myself, and at that time, you'll be given an assignment, and that takes me to another, thing, through your training you will be asked to go on missions, to see you worth and value, perform well and you will be rewarded, perform poorly, and you maybe out, our goal, is that you can pass, and show us, you're really trying to be part of the team, not some renegade warrior, only out for revenge and retribution, finally she said, "So that will be all, if need be from time to time, you may visit me, but talk with a UN advisor, for one will be assigned to each of you, or some may share, in addition, to the UN advisors, there are the UN's SAS to assist you on this quest, they too have the power, to excise you from the program, there are people watching you at all times, so be careful, and for some of you this is all a test, you say something, you gossip it, it may be your last.", she left as the spies stood, and clapped her off. As Professor Goins, went back up to say, "Enough, sit back down, for the sake of training with no distractions, the Men and Women will be separated, so at this time, the Women, will go with Miss Hill and Miss Watts, as they exited, as he said,"For the Men, we are going to room one, on the men's floor, where assigned seating is in place, Dismissed."

Jack got up, and was walking out, as Vadim, stood in his path, to say, "That was the ballsyest thing I ever heard about, that you did for us and the rest of the world, for ridding us of that general, for we are all free, we never knew that it was you, all we heard was it was you that, blew up the compound, not that you actually killed the General, for this I will always be in your debt.", Jack looked at him to see if he was sincere or not, and then said, "Your welcome", as Vadim, allowed him to pass.

At the next door over was the rooms, one and two, as he entered one, to see high back, chairs, all twenty four of them, you had to go to the front, to see the way they were, but on the back, was the complete names, each was different, at the second row of twelve was Jack Cash, as he slid in, to see a table, and a refrigerator, he tried the door it was locked, then used his card, to swipe it open, looked in to was stocked as to what he liked, he saw, chocolate milks, and water, some juices, and fresh fruit, at the large table was a cup holder of pens, and pencils, a ruler, a calculator, and a clip board, a stack of paper, and note pads, on the right on a arm, was that of a monitor, as everyone took their seats, for the Professor Goins, to stand in front, up on a podium, to say, “Each of you are distinguished in some manner or the other, your country has put up a retainer, for your per diem, which each of you received at receiving, so take notes, drink or chew quietly, let’s begin.”

For the women it was totally different, down on their level, was two newly constructed rooms, room one and two, they came in to see standard, classroom desks, but only 24 of them, in three rows of eight, as Susanna spoke,”Me and Miss Watts, will be your primary instructors, and first off, all male spies are off limits, on all levels, from communications to having sex, no physical contact, understood,?”

“Yes, Ma’am, they said in unison. Well that was for some of them, except Chloe, who just smiled, to see one chair was empty, next to her, “We want to talk about behavior and protocol, let’s talk about male interaction, all male spies are off limits, except, Jack Cash, as for some reason, he will be staying in suite one, with Michelle, in his own private room, as so ordered by Miss Hohlstiens, which oversee us all.” “So you, Michelle may see him as for the others, you may see him in your mess, which incidentally, his entire food service staff is cooking for him, so be nice, they will be all watching you, if you do encounter any man on your level, be respectful and courteous, at no times will you engage in kissing or any other lewd acts, your all ladies, so act as one, my colleague is passing out your bible, to go by, the UN’s etiquette book, follow it and live its principles, it will save your life.”

As both the men and women, were going over some orientation, all were at their appropriate room. It was apparent, Jack was alive and well, as for Chung, he cried the day and night, from the extreme torture, admistered, by the master, first the weighted water dunks with a crane, into lake Geneva, some on lookers thought it was a publicity stunt, but for Clarance and the Giant, it was a growing friendship, then to the cell where it echoed, long and hard for hours, the guy scream till no more, but the information, he spit out was incredible, place, acts of terror, people connected to whom, next up was Colonel Tam-Lu, who was screaming, "I have Diplomatic immunity."

"Hello my name is Clarance, and for you information, Diplomatic Immunity ends, as soon as your declared a terrorist, then your open season, for anyone to go after, I'm sure we could release you, but then either some death squad, would find you and then kill you, rape your body, then severe your head, or stay in the confines of the UN, so that I may interrogate you, which shall you have?"

"Be released", she said in desperation.

"Of course you chose that, problem is my boss, would like a word with you."

"Is he right there, as both men looked behind them to see no one, for her to say, "Have him come out."

"Nah, first I need to inflict some pain on you."

"Why, what will that serve?"

"It will allow me to loosen you up for interrogation."

"So you've done this before?"

"Yep, women are harder than men" said Clarance.

"Why's that?"

"A women pain threshold is ten times stronger than a man's weak mind, so this is how it will go, I'm going to allow you to think about what I'm going to do to you, at 1 pm today, first I'll come in there and strip you of all your clothes, then strap you to a fixed chair, your size, using Teflon strap ties, the reason I use Teflon, is as you squirm, you'll cut your wrists, and ankles, thus start to bleed, so by the time were done, you'll have bleed out, and lastly, I allow you to scream, so any questions?"

"What if I tell you everything?"

"What information do you have that I already didn't get from Chung, because once I'm through with you?"

"Wait, I know secrets but I want someone on my side, I want Michelle, Michelle Quan, I can tell this to?"

Clarance looks at her, to say, "Alright, wait here, I'll have to go get her." Clarance went in, down the hall to the World Council chambers, and that of Miss Meredith Hohlstien's room, knocked and was allowed in, to hear, as she was watching and hearing the whole conversation he had with her, to see Meredith say, "Do you think it's worth a try?"

"I don't know, her willingness to talk, is surprising" said Clarance.

"Don't kid yourself, you put fear into anyone, alright, hold off on her, and go after this Marisol, play nice, will you."

He holds his hand up, to say, "You wanted the best, so here I am, how is Jack?"

"For the time being safe, but I think I want you and his support team on the inside rather than on the outside, in the hanger, on ready alert."

"I'll let Jim know." Said Clarance leaving, and out-the-door he went.

Back in the men's room number two, the desks were arranged in a horseshoe, Professor Goins was holding court, to say, "Class sit in the order of first name first, last name last, and state your name what you do, your rank, and your greatest accomplishment.

"You the young, one, stand and start", the Professor sat down.

"My name is Alexander Yashin, and I'm a spy, I go after young girls, well we use to go to the matchmaker, Miss Monica, but someone blew that up." He was looking over at Jack. "Next please", as the guy next to him stood, to say, "My name, is Andreas Stauros, Captain in the both the Greek, Army and Navy, where I'm the principle welder, and I climbed Mount Everest." The next guy stood, to say, "My name is, Andrain Jonason, and I'm an accountant, I'm here"...... The older man was next, he stood, he was the old guard, to speak, eloquently, "My true name doesn't matter, as I go by Avlada Butine."

"Sit down, Alexei", as the Professor was tired, as he got up to say, "You all know each other by now, you can ask yourself whom is the most deadliest, I like to give each of you a name after a snake type."

"Let me tell you, Alexander, being a spy, doesn't mean you are one, it means you have the means to do what others that have come before you, do you know who the most dangerous man in this room is?' anyone?, Its Jack Cash, does anyone know how to disable a man with one strike, or how to kill a man just with his bare hands?"

Mustapha raised his hands, as the Professor said, "I correct myself two men in this room can do that, but the answer is Jack Cash, let me tell you a story, of an East German spy, who defect in favor of freedom, for its country, and that man is Jack Cash, he uncover a coop, to assasinate the President of the time, Parsons, and in doing changed the countries fortunes, and the rest of the economic society for the rest of the world, as he persuade others, to follow Parsons, into freedom, and the wall came tumbling down, now we all know what happen to Parsons, he was taken somewhere and shot, his body was cut up into little pieces, and dropped into the incinary overlooking the bluffs, outside of Austria, or so called eagles nest, as for the savior he had three choices, be shot in the streets and claimed a traitor, defect to another country, or be exiled to a non-party country, and be lost. His choice wasn't his, the CIA wanted him, and turn him into a double agent, so the US government, lost him in the system, in its penal groups, he was in Seattle one year, the next Kansas the next Florida, there was a year, he was being tracked by a female reporter, who said she would stop all of it, for a face to face." Everyone laughed, as they knew what was up, literally, so after twenty years, he got out and went wild, his rage was so untouchable, it took time for him to settle, as he is here in our presence". Jack stood, as Vadim, did a double take, thinking was, he the same guy, looking across at him, for the Professor to continue, "I want to tell you what he has, that some of you may not, correct me if I'm wrong Mister Cash, a support staff of, one former spy himself, and nine others at his beckoning call, a ground force team called Black Ops, of 24-36 men and women all the time, and a ten thousand man force of combined services Air, Sea, and ground force, two planes, and over twenty eight ships at his disposal at any given time, have I let anything out?"

Jack sat down, to hear, "He controls all of that on this here phone, as the Professor tried to touch it shocked him, for that reason and that alone he is call the Pit Viper." Vadim smiled turned to a frown, realizing he had not that type of support, nor resources. For the Professor to continue, to say, "This Pit Viper, is like a real one, waits, to analyze the situation, and without impulse, strikes, and continues, till your maimed, or left for the dead, and of the status of the Pit Viper, it would be the rock star, of today, thousands of women throw themselves at him, so the next time someone has the idea of attacking Jack Cash, beware he is the Pit Viper."

"Now, let's talk about a legend, his reputation is legendary, his ties are worldwide, and his wife and woman count extraordinary, of course I'm talking about, you, Carlos the killer, Gomez, once a top one or two in the world, he is as old as most of your fathers, but his fountain of youth is young women, but for some of you wanna bees these women are married to him, and choose him, he current runs all of Cuba, with ties, to Alexei, oh yeah, you said your name was Avlada, fine, Carlos is a Cobra, cause he will strike you in all parts of the night, and be asleep, in the earth somewhere, his art of concealment is what books were written for, you'd better watch out for him." "Next is Mister Thomas Jones, him and Carlos have had their run-ins with each other, especially on that case in South America, Brazil to be exact." "For Thomas, I give you Python." "Next on this list is of course Hendon Aziz, a landmark in the middle east, and the work, you have been doing to maintain peace commendable, your called a Mamba." "Alexei, you and all your Russian comrades, one of three decisions, set Russia back fifty years, and you can't be touched, nor, are you asked, when we have Jack now, you can still do damage, that is why I call you Copperhead." "The next guy, is no stranger to Hendon, they both work side by side, in the Middle East, and it's Mustapha, and your name shall be the King."

"There is so many great things, as I'm running out of time, as the UN class bell rang, they exited to the next room, as both set of classes meant a change, for both men and women, were on different floors, Jack walked out with Carlos as Vadim, stood in his way, to say,"I want to say, I'm sorry, the Professor was right we had no reason for revenge, you did what the UN wanted?"

"No let me correct you on that, I was asked to rescue a woman who was taken by force, and for what?" for Jack to look at him, to say, "The Professor was right about one thing, I have friends all over the place, if I want someone gone, that's it, you may think you're on the same playing field as I, but you are only one, I represent 300 million." Jack past him, to find a seat in the back, with Carlos, as the younger man sat up front, for the door to close, and on the board was the words, "Keep your mouth shut and listen, when I call you, stand up, answer the question, and sit back down."

"Hello, my name is Claude Benz, I'm from Germany, I teach ethics, so some would say, why would a spy need ethics, well here is one reason, a spy doesn't kill another spy, because what will happen? "Claude points to Andreas, who stood up to say, "Revenge and retribution."

"No, who are you, anyone else, looking around to see the old guard in the back, to point to Jack, who stood, to say, according to his phone, to say, "Compromise."

"Now that is correct, why is compromise so important, as he saw baffled looks on their faces, for the Professor to say, "You know, when you have to settle on what your girlfriend choose you eat?" as Alexander laughed, for Claude to say, "Did you read my board, is it not ethical to talk, and disrupt the class, No, is it rightful to laugh at compromise, if not you ain't going to get that with her."

"I ain't compromising on this or that", said the smartly Alexander.

"You're right, you not, get out of my class, and go see John Phillip."

Alexander got up frustrated to say, "This isn't the last you heard from me, I still get what I want", as Alexander leaves, the Professor says, "Anyone else, let's continue, just like that, compromise is the building blocks for a spy, the greater tolerance for compromise the longer success, you have, I have to tell you, young guys, half of you won't make it, it takes a support team of players, and compromise is number one, it has nothing to do with the situation, and all it has to do is with options, first let's talk about being a spy, a spy is figuring out how to be as tactful as possible, in accomplishing the mission, for most spy's, its secretive work, for some its plenty of violence, and for some it's their reckless behaviors, a spy is like Thomas, and his Son Tad, upstanding citizens, not making the headline news, a spy should have a relationship with other spies, not turn when asked to join another team, or more recently, the whole, I was rejected as a spy, so I will work for a country that has no spy, with a raise of hands, show me who you are," seven raised their hands, for Claude, to throw his hands in the air, to say, "So do you think you need ethics, of course you do, countries who rely on foreign aid stops, because of a spy, I read in the paper recently, Romania lost 2.5 million in aid a month, in food reserves, because a spy, said the wrong thing in a summit, wait, I have it here, "It says, as I Para phrase, American turned, Stephen Moss, kicked out of the CIA for miss-conduct, ethics, and took the offer from Romania officials to broker an agreement with Serbia, and the annex of the Montenegro act, that as one official put it, it was like seeing a lamb go to the slaughter. "That shows to me Stephen, you'll never work for the UN, because of your in ability to compromise, and who is on your arm at the party, in Serbia it's illegal to touch a woman, let alone wrap your arm around her, this is an ethical violation, I believe the only reason why the Serbia's spared your life was the money or food shares, but the UN cannot send you into any of those three countries, as by now, I believe, you're a free agent, and I think you should leave the class, you're out." With that Stephen got up, went past the class, in shame and walk out the door, to see UN guards, escort him out. "Oh and for the rest of you, I have several violations, so if you don't have a backup, you also might leave." "My goal is to get you all ethically correct before you go back out in the field, you see the UN doesn't need but three people, and just like you, the women are under the same duress, so let's talk about revenge, it's really not in a spy's vocabulary, other people take revenge and suffer some form of consequences, as a spy, you do the tasks assigned to you and go forward. Much of your work as a spy revolves around three basic principles, 1st your ask to do something. 2 you uncover how to get to it, using anything or any means. 3 you execute that order to the best of your ability." "Where in that does it say revenge?" the Professor turned to say, "Now Gordon Roderick, I have your file here and it says, you're a deserter of the British ground Army, is that correct?"

"No, when I got the chance to work for the British version, of the CIA, the Army said I could, just transfer."

"Do you have that written order? you know don't you that a written order is required for such a transfer for pay to occur?"

"Yes but Colonel Tom Houser, allowed me to go?"

Claude paused to say, as he held his service record, to say, "Says here from Colonel Tom Houser, Gordon approach me, wanting to go with airborne, SAS, I talked with their group, and they would love to have him, I was fine with the inter-service transfer, but in his best interests I authorized thirty day leave, and a psych eval, before he goes."

"Well it looks like the psych eval was never done, but you did take the leave, and never came back, do you know why a psych eval was ordered?"

"At the time it was some BS thing" said a dejected man.

"No Mister Roderick, it was so that the unit had a legimate excuse to transfer you, and that's an ethical point, you're classified as a traitor, and according to this folder your marked for death, to be carried out by the SAS, but not to worry, your pretty much safe, while you're in Britain, which is where your operating out of?"

"Well No, after SAS, I had an offer to go free lance, and work out of Monaco."

"Monaco, do you know what that even means, it's known as the playground for the rich and famous, but deep down, do you really know what it means?"

Gordon kind of just stared around, this big brute of a guy was getting humbled, very quickly, as Claude continues, to say, "Monaco, is the number one place for Diamonds, deep in its mountains, is a secret diamond mine, ran by Mister Devine Bears, and the Prince took advantage, and stake the claim, at the time in the early fifties, France was the hide out from the war, especially the French Rivera, Nice, and it was Col Tom Monaco, that uncovered the secret mine, and had his troops, enlarge it, then built a fortress over the site which is now the principality hotel, as the Monaco family still owns it today, and with that it's been producing the gambit of gemstones, Prince Emil Rainer, went in on the stake, as you know he is from Manchester England, and set up shop, so Gordon where do you fit in this whole picture, are you and the Princess Catherine involved?", how did you get a title, and where do you even live, as every inch of that place has a camera?"

"I stay at the palace, on the east fork, called the POG club."

"Wait, are you one of those guys?" asked Claude.

"What are you talking about?"

"Nah, I was just being very unethical with you." The bell rang, for Claude to say, "Yes, another day, and you'll be going home, or what is that jail? Mister Roderick."

Alexander waited as two burly UN advisors, were watching him, as the door opened and a stunning drop dead gorgeous woman with an everlasting smile on her face, to say, "Hi

Friend", she uses her hand to carefully graze his face, as Alexander heard, "Next come in", in broken English, to see the young man, to say, "Come in here and stand at attention, as Alexander, came around the corner and stood, at attention, as he clutched his fists, for John to begin, "We at the UN do not tolerate rule violations, nor espionage, you're on thin ice, as one of our recorders caught you having a conversation, with Michelle Quan, of the US, it is my understanding, you have no affiliations with her at all, if it comes out that you're planning a coup, you will be taken out and shot, then they we will go after your entire family" as the Professor looked mean as he got in the young kids face, to say, "You have no backing and here at the UN we invented the famed hit assassination squads, and now your public enemy number one, so go back, to your class, and shut your trap, listen to what is said, and be a model student, if not I will have you and your family killed, do I make myself perfectly clear?"

"Yes Sir?"

"I cannot hear you maggot?"

"Yes Sir", he said a little louder, but wavered as he was trembling, to hear,"Your dismissed, now get the fuck out of here."

The Men went into another room, as a hot looking Model was walking out as they saw a smartly dressed man at the desk, to hear, "Go ahead, take a seat, as Alexander shows up, as he counts 23 to say, "Someone is missing?"

"Yeah, Stephen Moss had to go home, said Gordon.

The Professor, went over and closed the door, to say, "This class is called Women, as I saw most of you were eying my beautiful bride, Natasha, typically, I'm usually teaching a class of students art appreciation, for you super spies, today it's all about women, women possess qualities, that render most men useless, they take your strength and your ability to think straight. Just because it's there for you", looking at Alexander, he had a hard stare at him, to continue, to say,"Doesn't mean it's for you, women are just plain evil. The men went crazy, talking and commenting, Jack just couldn't believe what he was hearing, "Women have to be ridden, to drive the evil out of them, but not to the point that they become wrecked, looking at Jack, in a long stare."

"I have to admit there are a few men in this room, that knows a women, and what to get out of them, but they must know what that line is, if not they could get themselves in some trouble, take for instance Natasha, excellent upbringing, all the fine schools, and privileges, and Men, she could have any and she choose me, she wanted a Man who could command her, not worship her, someone strong enough to stand free, and give her everything she wanted."

Under his breath, Gordon said, "Till the next guy comes along."

They all laughed around him, to hear, "Enough Mister Roderick, just because you're here now, doesn't mean you'll be here later, listen up, this school is a privilege, and with privedge comes responsibility." Jack Cash stood to say, "Listen up Gordon, keep your mouth shut, your ears open and just listen to what this man has to offer, and compromise, your place."

"Thank you Mister Cash, shall we continue?"

Jack was on his phone, to text to Clarance for a pickup and get info out of, at end of class. Send. Carlos who sat by Jack looked over at Gordon who was looking back at Jack. Carlos was giving Gordon the kill sign, when the Professor said, my name is Alfred, so please be courteous in my room, will you?, now why stay away from women, besides them being evil, and elusive, they can just right be down right deadly.

As for the women, down a level, it was alphabetic order, with first name first and last name last, to hear this special lady speak, "I don't care, as you will sit next to one another, for this is spy class 101". Russian Professor Lexine Gobel, holds class, to say, "I have to say, who's ever idea it was to allow women aboard is brilliant, I have to tell you when I found out that women were finally allowed a place, well I was excited, let's go around the room, to find out about each of you, your name, a brief background and who inspired you to be here today?", she points to Cami, who gets up, to say, "My name is Cami Ross, I'm from Detroit Michigan, my inspiration was when I was going to college, and in walked this guy, who took my breath away, strong and powerful, he had a force with him, that was incredible, and from that moment forward, all I wanted to do what he was doing?"

"Can we ask who that was?" said the Professor.

With a huge smile on her face, said, "It is Jack Cash." as Cami looked around as others were smiling too. For the Professor to say, "Yes, I know about Jack Cash, I was investigating the disappearance and capture of our Presidents wife, Victoria, of our Mother Russia, when he just showed up, he talked, and flirted and then he was off, and as I watched from the palace window, helicopters, sent to finish the job, were blown out of the sky, and he ran around all by himself, so yes I know all about Jack Cash, he is truly a super spy, as she wiped away a tear, to say, "Next", a stunning red head, stood smartly dressed, to say, "My name is Chloe Ryan, I'm in the intelligence field, for the British Secret Service, and the SAS, I too am enamarated with Jack Cash, and hope someday of being his wife?"

"Really, so if you were to win, this, and be asked, to be a UN spy, what would you do?"

"Be a UN spy", she said confidently, as she high fives those around her. Next, to stand was, a tall big bone girl, with dark brown hair, she said, "My name is Dana Scott, scuba specialist, I too was inspired by Jack Cash." Next, was a shorter version, who said, "My name is Darlene Lewis, I currently write code, and learning protocol, by Miss Margaret, and I too is inspired by Jack Cash." Next up was a beautiful black haired stunner, who said, "My name is Erica Adams, former Marine, and Jack Cash inspires me." Next up was a littler version, and brunette, as she said, "My name is Esmeralda, Romero, I'm from Spain, but work and was recruited by the US, I work as a translator, and my inspiration is Jack Cash." Next up was a short haired red head, stood up to say, "My name is Freya Lyons, I'm married to my husband Michael of four years, I work as a roaming spy, and inspired by Jack Cash". Next up, was a very mature girl, beyond her physical age, to say, "My name is Jill Hoyt, and from the moment I could talk and walk, I wanted to be a Marine, to follow in my father's footsteps, then all of a sudden, I'll just tell who is, it was Jack Cash, came to my college looking for our missing friend, and he was being tag around by our other friend Austin, so we went with him, it's been a wild ride, and now it's getting better." "Good for you, next please." Instantly stands an outgoing girl, to say, "My name is Joana Celek, I was recruited by Miss Margaret, while I was in the US just from Portugal, to assist a relative unknown agent, who also happen to be Jack Cash, I work as a translator, at Langley, for the CIG, and of course for Jack Cash."

The Professor gets up to say, with a show of hands how many have or been in contact with this man Jack Cash?" fifteen hands went up, to see ¾ of the class, to say, "Three fourths of this class of potential agents have either had contact or worked with him?"

Most of all the women said, "Yes's, Ma'am". "Wow, proceed," a stunning short haired Blonde, stood up, to say, "My name is Kellie Ryan, I too work at CIG in intelligence, and yes it was Jack Cash."

"Next please", a long haired, big breasted woman with a stern look on her face, said, "My name is Kendra Augustus, from Mother Russia, and work for Alexei, he also has inspired me, but I must say, this Jack Cash, for going after Varfolomey, and getting Victoria back, as we all sat on our hands, is my new inspiration, so its Jack Cash". "Next please", a smug looking red head, stands to say, "When can we have a smoke break", as the Professor, motions for her to continue, for her to say, my name is Lea Lucas, and I work for the Prince Jalbert, of Monaco, my inspiration is Prince Jalbert." She sits as the Professor to say, "Let me clear up something, you are not an actual field agent, all you do is work in his office, is that correct?"

"Yes" she said.

"Do you have spies, working out of that office, strike that"

"No I'll tell you, there is one guy, who Princess Catherine, asks us to give some assignments to, his name is Joe Simon."

"Thank you carry on, next, it was their Captain, standing all little less than five foot, solidly built, to say, my name is Michelle, Quan, I work for SIT group, and Jack Cash inspires me." Next up was, a cute dark haired girl, who said, "My name is Nika Kenna, from Romania, and Alexei, is my inspiration." Next up was, a tall brunette, who say, "My name is Nina Ivan, from Mother Russia, and it was Alexei." Next to stand, was a cute short to shoulder length hair, to appear to be the prettest of them all by a long mile, to say, "My name is Nina Toop, I work as a super model, and Alexander inspires me". Next up was a tough looking girl, who said, "My name is Peleruth Jaizem, I work for Poland, I am a boxer, my inspiration is Muhammed Ali Allafourth". Next up, was a frizzy out hair do, of an extremely beautiful girl, shy as she spoke, my name is Protima, and I was raised in a refugee camp, in Brazil, was trained, to be a bounty hunter, and work for hire, evidently I was working for the wrong person as I was trying to kill Jack Cash, and he put me down, he was mere moments from breaking my neck, and let go, I vowed revenge, only to find out spies don't do that, they only compromise, as said so by Jack Cash, himself, If I could do it all over again, I would apologize, as she showed tears, as Raisa, comforted her, for her to say, "Will you Michelle ask Jack if he will, forgive me."

"I imagine he will, "said the Professor, as Protima sat down, and next and still standing was a lovely woman, who said, "My name is Raisa Sergel, I too work for Mother Russia, as a Clears processor, and too believe in Alexander". Next up was a tall skinny girl, with short platinum blonde hair, she said, "I'm known simply as the ice princess, but my friends call me Rebecca Adams, I went to the same class in international bounty hunters school with Jack Cash, he was already a legend then, he is the most fearless man I have ever met, and the thing about Jack, it is all about compromise, so what you're a double agent, his last partner was one, he is someone I'd consider being a double for, he makes a strong argument why not, follow what he is doing, he gets results, so of course I say, Jack Cash". The next girl stood, she was harden, and a beautiful face, smart, as she spoke,"My life was pretty well set for me, I was dating a successful doctor, we were set for marriage, and then all of a sudden, in walks this guy, who turned me completely around, took the state boards in twenty minutes, and has the power to put away whomever he wants, and then there was one night I saw he had sleighed twenty plus women." There was some gasping and some were bashful.

"So you were there?" said the Professor, to add, "That put eight women in the hospital, that was a big topic here at the UN,when I heard about it I thought it was criminal, he went room to room, invading their privacy."

"No Miss Gobel, you got that all wrong, he stood, in this area, as each willing girl, moved into position and bent over, and allowed him to do his work, and after that they collapsed, it was the next and so on, and so forth."

All the girls watched her, as she heard, from Professor, Gobel, say,"Why didn't you participate?"

"Because, we were there for him at first and he was mobbed by all the sorority girls, Tia, asked them to leave him alone, but it was no use, and Jack did what he does best satisfy those that wanted it, as for me, you could say, Jack and my partner, took care of Jack at a later time."

Kellie asked, "How big is it?"

Roxy shows her, about eight inches, and as thick as a salami.

"You didn't tell us your name? said the Professor.

"'Sorry, my name is Roxy Carr, I was a NOLA police detective, and yes, it's Jack cash."

Next up was another lanky girl, short cut, to say, "My name is Simone Bailey I work for the CIA, I run deep cover ops, and so far I've been just before Jack Cash would arrive, and when he gets there, all chaos is released, my Inspiration is Abraham Lincoln". Professor was checking time, as the last girl stood, to say, "My name is Z'sofia, Baptiste, I work for Hendon Aziz, in the middle east, in translation of different languages, we have heard of this Jack Cash, but as of now..." the bell rang, as the Professor, said,"The next hour is lunch, good luck".

Michelle had all kinds of friends, especially now that it was him who was into sport fucking.

For the first time men and women had lunch together in this part of the UN, even the professors were there, it was truce time, as they were in compromise time, as one man put it, the neutral free zone, as the women had a shift in who to have which loyalty to, Alexander, or Jack Cash, as for Jack, he sat with Carlos, as Jack checked his phone, about the rat Stephen, and news about a new organization, details in next class, as Kellie Ryan approached Jack's table to say, "Is there anyway, you could come visit tonight, for a round or two, as she pulls Cami around to see Jack, to say, say room 12 at 9 pm?"

"Perhaps, what will be doing?"

"Your favorite sport?" she said in a secretive manner.

"Use to be, I can't find enough participants."

"Don't worry about that allow me to recruit the reinforcements." Said Kellie. Miss Gobel over heard that, and was going to put a stop to that. As lunch was over and to the lower floor went the girls, and to the east was the men, walked in, to see Claude Benz again, as all the men settled in it was different for the women, as Miss Gobel, just told Kellie it wasn't going to happen, sex was out of the question, and a new curfew will be established at 9 pm, as a UN advisor will be posted on the outside of their suites. Michelle smiled, as she heard, now you can sleep with each other, in each other's room, but for the most part, it should be men free."

For the men class began, and this time it was espionage, 101, the ability to undermine another spy's work, as written on the board.

Meanwhile Jesse and Jim, were summoned all over the UN on cleanup jobs over the last shooting, as Meredith met up with Jim and team, to say, "So Jim who are your two pilots?"

"Bill Bilson, and Ron Wilson, why you ask?"

"Well a stray bullet killed our flight simulator instructor, what would you think of the pair, would they oversee it?"

"Sure that is what Bill does for the Air Force, pilots, of the F-18 and F-22 super hornets."

"Excellent send them in,"

"Is there a reason why you're keeping us on the inside?"

"Because you're whole team is valuable."

"Precisely, that is why we work for Jack, exclusively, at least let us have some communications with him?"

"You do, he has his phone on him, so call him," said Meredith.

Back in the men's class, Claude was at it again, being long winded," Spy's work in parallel of each other, and when you cross into a path of that spy, well there will be some action taken". "Take for instance Jonathon, Razor, that's his MO, he will find a spy, follow him around, see what he is doing, then, kill him, and take over, unfortunately for Jonathon, the UN know this and at some point one of the top three will come visit you and end your life. As the Professor continues, espionage is deadly and there are consequences, and signs to watch for, and the information could be contaminated. As he saw Kyle Devon and Joel Robbe, talking, to say, "If you two are through talking."

"Well actually I'm not", said Kyle, as it was instantly quiet, he got up to confront the Professor, to say,"Yo old man."and just like that Claude Benz struck, he struck the young cocky man, a shot to his Adam's apple, which put him down and for Claude to say, "Looks like you need to go see the doctor, as Claude was on the phone to someone, all the while Kyle is still trying to breathe, he was in a fetal position, and just like that, in walks the Giant, Ivan, to stop, to say, "HI Jack, and pick up Kyle, and takes him out and close the door for Claude to say, "Maybe I don't make myself perfectly clear, Mister Robbe, after this you will become a working UN sanctioned agent, and in doing so, you're going to need all the help you can get, I guess we could just get rid of the old ones over the new ones, then there are those young ones, who behave like a child, for men its 40, and women its 25, is the optimum age to be a working spy, and so far that is why the old guard is still going strong, as for the young guys, not much for you, maybe you should just read the board, listen, and hear what I'm saying, now let's talk purpose for this training, our first goal is to recognize, the top agents in the world, and find three that will manage the world, and the rest of you will fall in line, and provide support, with a show of hands how many would support an older agent?" almost all raised their hands.

"O Kay, how many would support a younger agent?"

Again the same result, almost all, as Jack raised his hand from the back, "Go ahead Jack, as someone else said something, Jack stood up to say, "I'd say, it doesn't matter who it is just as long as we know who he is and his title, were here for one common goal; Peace." And sits down, for the Professor to say, "Jack brings up a good point, if we had in place, operatives, who all of you knew, would it be easier to work with each other?"

Most of the group agreed. The bell sounded ending day one of Nineteen one by one they went out, Claude said, "Could you wait Jack, as he saw Carlos, who said, see you at dinner?"

"Yeah, catch up with you later", said Jack as he faces the Professor, to hear, "I have to say, I believe you're ready to take over here at the UN what do you think?"

"Whoa maybe in five years, I have a Spy Academy I'm building."

"Really, need instructors?"

"Yes, and I'll consider you but I got to go", said Jack getting out of there, he looked down at his phone for a map locator, when out of the shadows, appeared three men, first was Jonathon, Joel and Sean, to hold Jack back, for Jonathon to say, "You ain't no bad guy, and just like that Jack took the outstretched hand of Jonathon's, and bent it back till it popped, and a quick kick to Joel's right knee, and he went down wincing in pain, and he did the same to Sean's left knee, and he too was on the floor in lots of pain, just then Jack walked past, as Jonathon, was winching in pain, for Jack to bend over, to say, "People don't scare me, and I took on a whole army myself, look that one up, farewell".

CH 4

Both teams set, let the games begin, spy vs. spy

News spread like wild fire, it was Tuesday morning, Day 2, on both levels, some agent's smiled, others looked worried, as Louie, sat with Vadim, he said, "I did hear of him, in prison they called him A Parthian Stranger, he could kill you 100 different ways, Vadim, I'd wait till you were on your ground before you go after that one." Said Louie, known as the grand master.

Mustapha has given Jack his full support, and so has most of the old guard, as Jack took down suppose bad ass's, since training day, where Simon was so vocal, he has since been, low key, so much so when it was said by Claude, double agents are dead agents, a line also had been crossed, as young guys versus old guys, as Clarance was the equalizer, and that they don't know he is with Jack Cash, as a new session starts, everyone comes in the room, including the three wounded, for Professor Goins, to say,"Alright, everyone sit down, so some of you got hurt, it seems to me we have what we call Spy versus Spy, since last night's incident, I need to layout some ground rules, all spies are dangerous, especially practicing ones, for some of you, you have never been in the field, especially you Gordon, or shall I call you Banded snake, a snake of no real purpose, I talked with Prince Jalbert last night, and he told me you were the apprentice to Joe Simon, if so, good for you, he is here today, so for now you're safe, I'll let you all on a secret, the higher ups, want you all out, past the twelve, but so much has happened, and so much will happen, that keeping twenty four is the only option, as you can see Stephen is back, and according to this paper, you work for France now, congratulations, what about the US, that didn't want him?" Professor Goins was looking over at Jack and Carlos, and then over at Ben, for Jack to stand up to say, "What are you implying Professor?"

"Well to recruit him to your team?, like Jonathon did."

"I think you're mistaken, I have no power to offer someone a job."

"That's where your mistaken Mister Cash, you do indeed have the power to recruit, train, and add whomever you want to your team, and they become agents for you." Jack sat down as his mind was racing as he thought of CC, and thought, "Yes, I can hire whomever I want, I guess all the details will be worked out, as the Professor started back up to say, "As I was saying, "I want to introduce, Joe Simon, the UN's working spy, he lives in Monaco, but is from the British, who pays him, and gives him support, much like Thomas Jones."

"But I'm still in and he is out" said the smug British agent.

In walked a debonair man, in suit and smart tie, dressed in egg shell colors, short hair and sunglasses, as he struck a pose, as Jack looked at Carlos to say, "Bit of a pussy, for Joe to say, "Hello class, my name is Joe Simon, I'm from Manchester England, I use to love to beat people up as a kid, then through advanced education, I was the bully, I didn't get into firing guns till I was nine, and shot a bird, now all I do is shoot men, men who rob banks, and men who steal things."

"What about women who are abducted" said Jack to interrupt his train of thought, as Jack looked up on his phone, as it said, as this prick, it came across, Dirty and a bad agent, handle with caution, UN approval before killing. Jack, put away his phone, to listen, "I move around a lot, as several agencies are after us, I have a small staff, if you didn't know I have Gordo, short for Gordon Roderick, and a smart woman, named Lea Lucas, for Jack thought maybe he should help others, such as Joe Simon, "Interesting", thought Jack, still trying to figure all of this out, and what he was doing here, as Joe said, "What all of you are doing here, besides trying to kill one another, is to network, ideas, on how to help one another, we are all working towards World Peace and it begins with the spies, so what if a spy is called in via the UN, because when that happens the whole world is watching, the UN is given clearance to allow, the agent they think who can carry out that request, and in doing so, it was discovered that, what ended up happening, was to uncover the largest plutonium building plant in the world by far, who knew the former KGB was still operating, since, its demise at the end of cold war, and for you Russian's that don't believe that, the spies were the ones who set that contract in place, and for them to be doing it all these years violates the agreement, which, is why Alexei has changed his name, as he is one who is named, the penalty is one billion dollars, and exposure to the fine arts building vault 2, for in that vault contains all the secrets of the war, and if its discovered, that Russia had a hand in the undermining of the US and Britain during that war, then all of Russia could be dismantled, which we already know that's true."

Joe continue, to say, "That is why it's so important that we work together, its spies that turns countries, especially the relationships, take for instance Dominican Republic, use to be my domain, I know King Leopold personally, and then recently he told me that his eldest daughter had married, an American spy, that my services were no longer needed, and I was exiled, I lost land, and all my contacts" Jack stood, and Joe saw Jack, as Jack said, "Isn't it true, you possessed over 25,000 women, and most you sampled yourself?""

"No!, what are you saying?"

"Miss Monica explicitly told me, she had a major spy working for her" as others looked at the spy, as did Professor

Goins, for Jack to continue, "Why is it no one suspected a thing, as young women were being deported out of the US, and the Islands, then all of a sudden its stop, as agents, are on every island, and instead of ten a day go missing, it's one at best, so Joe, what is your involvement in that?"

He backed up against the door, even the Professor who had looked up to Joe, saw him for what he was an opportunist, and wrote 100 points next to Jack's name, giving Jack 246 currently, far leading, as Jack continued to press him, to say, "Before, I only knew of Scopus Tyrell, but there was always someone being protected, and that man is you." Said Jack.

"You know of Scopus Tyrell, then you know of Master Mind, he had a far flung hooks into everyone."

"Really, I took his palace down, freed five hundred hostages, and exposed two double spies, named Tatiana and Isabella."

"I know both of them, I trained them."

"No worries, there in custody now, and now for the rest of their lives, perhaps another day I'll take you in, even if you are a UN spy, here let me just ask, as Jack dials and places it on speaker to hear, This is Meredith Hohlstein, how may I help you Jack?", I have a one Joe Simon, here, what's his status?"

"Works in the UN as the caribbean islands coordinator, what has he done?"

"He has been confirmed as a partner to Scopus Tyrell, what is my order?"

"Kill on site, he is armed and dangerous."

The scared Joe was at the door, as all in the room had their undivided attention, till Jack closed up his phone, smiled, as Joe came to Jack and the two hugged it out, and stood before the others, as Joe said, "This was all a set up", as the room calmed, as Joe, continued, "This is a life of a spy, you're in Compromise mode all the time, yes, he got the order to kill, which I will have to talk with Meredith, and for those that don't know it yet, Miss Meredith Hohlstein, is the supreme ruler on this land, for all things spy, she knows who has diplomatic immunity and those who don't, that is the only way a foreigner on any countries soil is protected, and when someone uses that card, check it out with her, because if it's, as the bell rang. "Do they stay here, or what?"

"Stay in your seats I'll talk with Claude" said Professor Goins.

Joe continues, "If its expired, he is free to do as you please, now I myself having been given flax for what Jack is doing in the field, saving and preserving lives, instead of the old days, where you would just put a bullet in the head, but because of the preserver of life, is doing it, so is countless other agents, and now we move into another phase of spy work; Interrogation, the ability to extract information, out of someone, before they expire, that was Carlos Gomez's MO for years in Cuba, him and Castro, would capture and torture their prey, extracting certain whereabouts of some of the largest gold finds in the islands, they did however, set up a martimers museum, to display the bulk of it, the rest who knows, but that's just it we are secrets keepers, the better a secret is kept, the better the chances you have to survive."

Just then in walks both Professors, and the ugliest, meanest looking man ever, for Joe to say, "And Spies, this is world famous, Floyd Henderson, the UN Super Spy trainer," as he takes a seat, to see the man, was and has been wounded, to say, "Thank you Joe, I'm here to talk about Emotions, you have none, you kill who your asked to kill, no emotions, nothing, this is a game, you're a UN spy like Joe, you kill, you put one in the head, although you are right Joe, because of Jack Cash, people like me have a new lease on life as interrogators, however, he himself has the world's best, and I have him with me right now, come in here, "This man is my protégé, his name is Clarance Morey, this Irish lad, is bad, mean and tough, his forte is putting fear into others, as the class looked at the average looking guy, for Andrea's from Greece stand up to say, "What fear did you find in Jack Cash?"

Everyone was silent, even Clarance who wasn't much of a talker, then said," Fear, he is what Fear is." For Clarance to continue, he says, "Fear, is the essence for which all life strives, for animals, that is how they know if they have won the fight or not, and then they are consumed, in the world of interrogation, there comes a point where when someone shows fear, it's over, but the longer, that person stays in fear, they adapt, till it becomes them, and fear, is their partner, and that is what Jack has, fear, with him at all times, so much so, the infection turns on those close to him, and makes men go wild, and women attracted to him, he is a magnet for women, a spy like Jack Cash, there isn't anyone or anything like him, so other spies, if you smell, it, sense it, or see it, for Jack is fear himself", as Clarance looked over at Jack, and then left the room.

"The word to the young ones, Jack Cash is a certified weapon, so I'd stay as far as you can and as nice as you can for what Clarance said, Fear is Jack Cash, and if that is fear, you all better watch out, I will certify all of you, that will be all for now."

The bell rang, for Professor Benz to say,"Its lunch." The class let out early, and Jack and Carlos, walked together, and Vadim, Alexei, were talking, to say,"This is your chance to develop a friendship, if Jack can sway Rebecca, then maybe you should try."

"I could send Natasha at him?"

"That's maybe a start, but you need to give more than that, find out from the attendants what he likes, and do that, really try to be his friend., I'll deal with Alexander, after this I may have to retire." Alexei himself was scrambling.

First to approach Jack was Steven Smith from Australia, who said, "The prime minister from New Zealand, would love to meet you."

Jack looks at him as he finished loading up on his platter, of fish and chips, a small shaker of malt vinegar, and two milks each, and set his platter down and swiped his card, in front of the lady, and then went to a table. This was neutral free zone, and everyone was equal and no pressure. Just then the other bell rang for the women, and just like that they made it up a flight of stairs and flooded the space, while most guy's had their lunches, it was the women, next, twenty four of the hottest girls in the world, beautiful smiles, as each got their food, paid, and made a bee line to Jack's table, where Carlos, sat, a very stunning red head, placed her tray next to Jack's to say, "Is this seat taken?"

"Nah, go ahead", said Jack more engrossed with his cod pieces than the lovely girl, who said, "What would you say, if we went back tonight and go a few rounds? I have reinforcements, Erica and Freya, and Roxy."

"Sounds tempting, but I have been down that road with Roxy, as for Freya, I believe she is married, and very committed to Michael?"

"She said she would forsake all that just for you and what you did."

"She owes me nothing, all I care about is doing my job" said Jack, finishing off the cod, thinking should he go back or, Chloe offered him hers, to say, "I'm not very hungry, for that?"

Jack looks at her, as he takes a piece of her cod, and douses it with malt vinegar, for her to say, "So, we have about an half of an hour, say, we go to the private bathroom, I'll bend over for you and you stick it in, come on."

Carlos said "Yes my brother-in-law, do take them up on their offer, as for me I'm recruiting" as he looked at Jack, only to see a raven of a beauty, who said, "Care if I and my friend sit down?"

Carlos, looked her up and down, to say, "No, be our guests, what is your names?"

"I'm Dana Scott, and this is Darlene Lewis, Jack waves at them, as Chloe was getting annoying, till she realized Jack wasn't going anywhere, for Dana to say, "So Jack, you finally got your wish?"

"How's that?"

"Well for women to be spies?"

"There will always be women spies, it just at what level?"

"What do you mean by that?" asked Dana, seriously.

"Just that, I feel, women have a place, but at what level, you look around the room, and ask yourself this, how many of them will become a double agent by next year, or will they use their body", as he looked over at Chloe, to say, "To get what they want, I want a women, who can be my equal, and show her strength on the field, and then be ready for bed", just as Michelle arrived, and motioned to Chloe, she wanted to be where she was at, so Chloe got up, and allowed her in, then slid in to be right next to Jack, as he was pushed to the wall, Michelle was between Chloe and Jack, as Chloe just sat on the other edge, to hear Michelle, say, "So what are we talking about?"

"About how women should be men equals" said Jack as Michelle said, "You're the only one, I heard Kellie was propositioned by a guy named Sean Calvin, I guess you really messed up his leg, he was in sick bay, when Kellie, had a migraine, and he assaulted her," said Michelle as Jack looked, to see Jonathon, and Sean had his left leg in a cast, to see the only stunning blonde, she saw him, and came over to Jack, leaned over Michelle and gave him a hug and a kiss, to say, "You're sure popular, and from this table I can see why."

"What happen with you and Sean?"

"Oh him, he was lying down, I asked him, if he needed something, and just like that his hands were on my boobs, and falling on me, as he slide off the table, at first I thought it to be weird, but his other hand was between my legs, instantly I backed away, why, will you pummel him, for my honor?"

"Depends, I don't appreciate a guy taking advantage of you, yeah, he will pay."

"Really, as she leaned in and whispered, "If you do that, I'll be in your bed, for the rest of our time here and beyond, hey I heard you're putting a Spy Academy together, can I be in the first class?"

He looks at her to say, "Sure, I'll have Mitzi cut your orders."

"Thanks, as she went off. As Jack slid, pushing Michelle and Chloe out, with Carlos and took his platter, as Carlos and him, left, to the girls waving goodbye. At another table sat the UN's Stud, for Floyd to say to Claude, "He sure has a huge fan base, I'll put an end to all of that, as he saw the clock, as the bell rang.

The girls returned to their floor, and into class, took a seat, as Floyd walked in, all big and bad, his shoulders back as he made it to the front, he began, "Hello ladies, my name is Floyd Henderson, I was asked by Miss Hohlstein, to talk with you, about being a spy for the UN, first off all spies are equal, as he looked around at all the attentive faces, for him to continue, "We currently have over 48 female operatives, serving here and abroad, there mission is everything and anything, but one of those things is not to use your body, to acquire information or secrets, using your mind instead, skill learnt here and through knowledge, will give you the wisdom to be successful." As Lea had her hand raised, "Yes, go ahead?"

"What happens if he is just so damn cute and irresistible?"

"You have to resist temptation", said Floyd wavering, as Lea, opened up her blouse, to show him what she had, to say, "So if I told you to come fuck me, you wouldn't?"

He looked at how exposed she was and ready to unbutton her pants, for Floyd, said, "No, please stop."

"Oh alright, but see my point? you could barely contain yourself, and you're no way close to Jack Cash."

As she buttoned back up, and sat back down, for Floyd to say, "So what makes Jack Cash, so cute, and irrestible?"

"You want me, or the whole class to answer that, as Floyd looked at the teacher, Miss Susanna Hill, who had her hand raised, as well, as Floyd was in disgust, for Lea to say, "A spy of his caliber, is what typifies what being a spy really means, a bad ass in the field, good looks, and he has, HST, get a good whiff of him, and you completely surrender to him, in any capacity, I have never seen one person take on a country's worth of baddies, and slay them all, I'd fight for him."

"So who else would fight for him?"

Nearly the whole class, except Peleruth and Protima, who sat next to each other, bored, of all this Jack Cash talk, so Floyd, took charge, to say, "So, let's talk, about being a spy, and our point system, Miss Hill will be scoring, your work daily, and give you a point score, at the end of the week, you will know who is on top, and who is on the bottom, at the end of the three weeks, those on the council will vote on who they feel who deserves to be elevated to the UN, I can tell you there are at least half of you may make it, so go to the classes, take the tests, fire at the range, and participate in the field, and above all stay away from the men, and especially Jack Cash."

Back at the men, some accountant looking guy, was talking, to say, "As the council all voted, what happen was to keep only the top few, but it has become more apparent, those can learn, and be in the ready and for those that qualify we will be administering all the classes for, we may have an assistant or two, but your overall grade will come from us, first off, I'd like to introduce our system here, you will be sitting in marked chairs representing your current rankings, in the world of spies, and let's begin, in position one, we have Vadim, the Adonis, or lady lover, he is Russian, a master spy, teaches outside of Moscow an academy, he is the one to beat, next is Alexei, the nasty, his gentle smile, signify that death is near, he is from the Ukraine, but works specifically for the red army, he is number two. Number three is "Chu", he is Japanese, intelligence, who works for the US of A, according to the treaty of 1955, and works the Pacific Rim. Number four is Hendon Aziz from Turkey, who works the Israeli circuit, very dangerous man. Next is number five, some called him the second coming of British Spies, from a long line of aristocrats, this gentleman, is atop of all the society circles, his name is Thomas Jones, he sometimes teams up with number six, from France, his name is Jonathon Razor, known for his escapades, excellent ground insurgent fighter, spent time in Iraq, with Hendon. Then we come to the outlaw, from Russia, Alexander, he is the rogue agent who seems to be everywhere. In China, there is only one name his name is Chung, but since his involvement and cover up he was number eight, but he is out". "In America, it was one name for so long, that he is the institution, where everyone else learns from, multiple agents he has sprouted, his name is Ben, Hiltz, currently he heads up the west coast operations, for the United States. Then there is three more, first from Australia, but works everywhere is Steven Smith, a favorite with the UN and its agents, as he loves trouble, and finds ways to fix them. Next is the Italian lover, Louie Bellini, has ancestry roots to the Kings of Rome, once a envoy to the Vatican City, he has more connections than all the flights out of Rome on a yearly basis." he waited for the group to laugh. "Lastly, we have an alternate, due to the unexpected death of another spy, his ranking have soared, in recent months, from the US, his name is Jack Cash. As for the rest of you, right now you're not that important, so make yourself important."

"So, now, let's, open that envelope to your right, but before we do that, take a look at your chair, in the inside is a refrigerator, that can only be opened by your key card, it is filled with drinks you like, a chair massager, and plenty of writing paper and pens, so feel free to take notes. Any questions?"

Hendon raised his hand, to hear, "Yes Hendon."

"Why must we be here?"

"From the UN charter, says if your country gets any type of foreign aid, or needs assistance at some point you must be here, as for other countries, we asked that they send us their best agents, to teach a fundamental language and set forth laws to govern by, in accordance to what are needs are and how it relates to that country."

"Now, let's talk about the good stuff, each of you will be assigned an assistant, tomorrow will be in the field, we would like the women to participate, is everyone cool with that?"

No complaints, as John continued, "Tomorrow morning at 0800, we will be fully loaded, but no live rounds will be handed out, and the only one not going out is Joel Robbe, still on medical leave." "Now let's wait for the Women to arrive, and we will assign teams,

John looked around the room, to figure out what he was going to do, when an idea, came to his mind, to say, "Count off, one, two, one two, after all 23 went through, he said, "Now all the ones, on the left and all the two's to your right" they made the move, looking at some pretty big teams, so then he took a attendance sheet cut it up, and place in half, as he then called out, the following, only to be interrupted by the Women, as they made their way in, and soon, the room was filled with twenty three women, who all found a seat, as Miss Hill hands John her attendance sheet, which he cut up, and placed in his hat, to say, "Who would you care to do the honors, were selecting names to see who is on what team, as we know we have a north and south division, and within that division will be groups, equal Men to Women, let's draw, go ahead, as Professor, wrote, for the South division, team Orange, Stephen Moss, and Andreas Stauros, and for the women, it was on the other side of the hat, Miss Hill pulled, and said, "They will be joined by, Z'sofia Baptiste, and Nina Ivan. "The next team, will be called Team red, and its Benjamin Logan and Simon Jonas, for the Women, Miss Hill, she pulled two slips, to say, "Joining them will be Peleruth Jaizem and Protima." "The next group will be called team Yellow, it will consist of Gordon Roderick, and Sean Calvin, and for you Miss Hill?", she reached in and pulled two more slips to say, joining them will be Raisa Sergel, and Nika Kenna." For the Professor to say, "Next team, will be Team Gold, as he pulled Jonathon Razor, and Alexander Yashin, to say, "Now you Miss Hill, looking her over, for she to say, with two slips in her hand, to say,"Simone Bailey, and Esmeralda Romero.", for the next group, will be called, Team Copper, as he pulled two more names, it will be, "Louie Bellini and Jamal Oman, and Miss Hill countered, with, "Freya Lyons and Joana Celek. For the Professor to say,"This is our last three, for team Turquoise, Kyle Devon and Andrain Jonason, for Miss Hill to say, "I only have one, Nina Toop."

"So the rest of you is the North team, but for formalities, I'll read off the assignments, "Team Tan, Mustapha, and Hendon Aziz, and for the girls, Chloe Ryan and Jill Hoyt." Said Miss Hill. For the Professor to say, "Team Green, is Thomas Jones, and his son Tad Jones, for the Girls, its Roxy Carr and Kendra Augustus, said Miss Hill, as the Professor went on to say, "Team Brown, is Vadim Adonis and Alexei Putin, and for the girls, its, Erica Adams and Cami Ross". For the Professor to jump right in, by saying, "Team Black, is Steven Smith and Ben Hiltz, and for the girls, its, Darlene Lewis, and Kellie Ryan." "Next up was team Blue, Jack Cash and Carlos Gomez, and for the girl's its Michelle Quan, and Lea Lucas", and the last team, is Team White and its Chu, and the two remaining girls, who stood, Rebecca Adams and Dana Scott." "Now that the teams are established, break off into your divisions, and determine, who is the warriors, the spies, who hold the flag and HQ, a boy and a girl, and three teams on the outskirts, do I make myself perfectly clear, both myself and Miss Hill will be there to ensure safety and integrity."

"Your all dismissed."

Meanwhile in the hanger, a UN advisor team, came over to get the whole story about Greg and Jonny, as they was hauled off, as a security breach took place, meant a thorough search of the aircraft, as the UN team boarded the prop plane, which Jim was there to assist, as they demanded to see what was under the security blanket, so the Strike Team helped Jim and Jesse to un do it, they saw the car, it was unlike any one had ever seen, and there was a moment of silence as everyone paused, then the UN advisors said, "Alright put it back on, what's in there?" pointing to the huge pallet hung in the air.

Jim instructs the Strike team outside, as another team, went to open the door, to Jack's room, only to see on the bed sitting was Mitzi, they quickly looked around, as a drug dog came in, and then left, as did the investigators, to the flight cabin, to see Mike and Mark, sitting at chairs that faced them, to see a pilot, to say, "Why are you all sitting here, there is a lounge to watch T V?"

"Or we can sit here and talk" said Mark.

"Who are you guys supporting?" asked the nosey UN advisor.

"You don't know, said Mike sarcastically, to add, "Our boss is Jack Cash."

They said something, then left, Casey came in to say, "Something's up, we need to get Jack some help, if the breach is in the inside, the play could be going on now."

"Alright calm down, I have someone on the inside, I'll call her and see if she has news on what is going on," said Jim. To add, "What on the radar, with was going on, at the UN?"

"That's fine, whatever the team needs" said Casey.

"Well were still on Brian, but according to traffic control, a MIG -28 just flew in, and will be here any second" said Mike.

"That Jet smells, let's bring up the ramp and seal the cargo bay closed up" said Jim, while Casey got everyone in. and up went the ramp. The hanger doors went up, and the huge exhaust fans blew, till the aircraft was taken in, and set in its position, the outside camera's showed a single pilot, carrying a big bag.

"Hey Jim what do you think that is?" asked Mark.

"To me that looks like a payoff" said Mike, to add, "We need to get in there, Jack isn't armed, Jim."

"Hold on guys, wait till I get confirmation, where Jack is at, and what if anything's going on?"

Mike and Mark looked at each other, knowing their position to agree with Jim.

There was a tap on the outside metal door, Casey went to the door, opened it to see the UN advisor, who stepped in, to see him, to say, "We like to thank you and your team for helping us out, and would like to know if you and your team would like to help us out in the field, what do you say?"

"I have to check with my supervisor, but I'd say it's alright, with us" saying it shyly.

"He can go, as for the team, I need a runner, per day, and if we need to move would they be able to come back?" said Jim.

"Yeah, what ever, are you their supervisor?"

"Just in charge, till our boss comes out."

"So you're a team awaiting a spy?"

"Yes, why do you find it surprising?" asked Jim.

"Well you're the only team here, why are you here?"

"Because I told him he had to" said Mitzi, standing at the door way, as Mike and Mark were waving at her to back down.

"Well Mitzi it's surprising to see you here", said a senior UN advisor.

"You're seeing me here because I support the world's best agent, and if….."

Just when Jim, stepped in between them and took her back in, while Mike said, "Don't bother with them you know it's a power struggle, the team is at your disposal" said Casey, as Clark seconded that.

"Great, tomorrow morning at the mess hall, then?"

"Yeah, they will be there" said Jim.

"Oh one more thing, who is the greatest agent?"

"Don't know, who the greatest agent is, but I do know who the world's best agent is our boss, Jack Cash".

He looked back at them, as Casey closed the door.

CH 5

Field ops for fun and a little danger

Jack laid his head back, his body soaking in the mud, he was reminiscing about the time Carlos and Him had spent in the spa, thinking he could be here, instead of him. What makes him so much more important than the next guy or girl, why would Blythe turn on us, for all that we did for her, it doesn't make any sense, why do I have a team that looks out for me, is my support team, it's not like any other job in the world, yet what do they get out of it for their effort?" Jack was in his own mind, when he heard, from one of the Russian's, to say, "I'm the world's number one."

Others were chastising his frankness, as Thomas Jones, said something brilliant like, "Maybe it's a test."

"What do you know British spy?" said Alexander, rather smugly.

"They chose me over all you others" said Thomas Jones, proudly.

"What Mister Jones is saying, is look at your body of work" said Steven Smith, the Australian.

Sitting next to Jack was Jonathon Razor, from France, who said, "I don't know why you don't speak up?"

"Why should I, all I am is a glorified hostage takers" said Jack.

"Yeah, but your resume is impressive, like that extraction of the Russian Premier's wife, that was balsy, where was Vadim or Alexei for that?"

"I don't know probably on vacation or something" said Jack.

"What's that, what are you guy's saying about me" said Vadim.

"Calm down brother, there are some very dangerous people in here, as they looked over at the two Asian's beauties moving closer to Jack and Jonathon, as did Thomas and Steven, on one side was Louie, across from him was Hendon and Ben, leaving the two Russians together and Alexander was missing. There was a division occurring, and Jonathon was the first to notice it, to say "I see why" only to stop in mid -sentence to see a bevy of spectacular looking woman, come in to hear, "There is my man, as a tall blonde bombshell, came to Steven, she bent over and gave him a kiss for all to watch, as he helped her in the green mud soak, Jack opened his eyes to see Michelle standing above him, only to see the two Asian women staring at her, as each of their counterparts came to take a seat beside them. A cute blonde, with shoulder length hair, was a hot item, as she got in and straddled her man, Thomas. Next to Jack was Jonathon, and his girl, went topless, as she climbed in, as Jack laid his head back, to close his eyes, to hear, "I'm back, the King has returned, you miss me" said the ever flamboyant Alexander with Nina on his arm, as they got in to the mud pool.

This was the first chance to see the competition, thinking, "What makes them more special than Jack, who is literally worshipped in some countries, and has a Queen gushing over him, and half these guys are so damn conceited, how can they be so disrespectful, and yet command so much respect."

Alexander stared over at Jack as Michelle watched, that smirk smile as he joked with his other Russian buddies, and here is Jack resting comfortably, she knew, she needed to tell Jack what Alexander was up to, and soon, the guilt was welling up inside, to see and hear a young hot Swedish woman, say

"Alright it's time for your bath's we have twelve rooms, set up for each of you and your partners, an attendant will take you back."

"Mister Cash, its Hendy, it's ready to go."

Jack looked up to see the itsty tinsy little bikini she wore, over that gorgeous frame, by far the hottest girl, careening over him, as he got out, as he was hosed down as the mud fell off of him, and Michelle was the other, when he heard, Jack, can we talk?"

"Sure just follow us" said Jack looking at Jonathon, who wore his bandage proudly, as he was getting hosed down.

Jonathon said, "I think I know her", as Jack, Michelle and Hendy left, each holding hands, Jonathon and his girl were close behind, as other were leaving, Louie said something in Italian, to Alexander then left, as Alexander questioned what was said, to say, "What did he say?"

Hendon spoke first to say, "You're a jackass and a punk kid."

"What the hell, I'll kill'em" said Alex, getting up and coming at Hendon.

"Calm down my young friend" said Vadim, he didn't say that, he said you're crazy or loco, something like that, listen, you need to control your temper or you will get killed, Vadim turns to say, "Natasha, I'll be there shortly", she leaves with her friend Alexandra, and Alexei.

"So listen, I told you before, you were selected because of how you like to seek revenge on others, but within this group, you have to change that thought and be very careful" Vadim says to Alexander.

"Says who, you?"

"Unlike you or me, there are agents that carry a force around with them."

"So what Vadim, once there spy goes down, they will lose the fight, and go home."

"You don't get it, there are things moving about and around you, you don't see it, be careful".

"Vadim, were waiting for you" said his attendant, for Vadim to say, "Just be careful", as he extracted himself out of the mud, to his awaiting attendant.

Jack sat on an opposite table of Michelle, while he asked Hendy to wait outside, so they could talk, as Michelle carefully thought her words out she spoke, "Well yesterday an agent approached me and asked about Blythe?"

Jack looked at her, then laid on his back to say, "I'm listening?" somewhat bothered where this was going, to hear, "He asked me to poison you." There was a pause of silence, then Jack said, "So did you?"

"No, No way, but instead of playing it off, I enticed him along", for her to say,"Too bad for Callista, she must of taken what was for you."

"Really, too bad for her, I kind of liked her, go ahead its sounding a bit more interesting" said Jack getting up, to face her.

"Really, cause I don't know how you would react to someone wanting to kill you" said Michelle, getting use to all this Spy vs. Spy games.

"It happens every day" he mumbled.

"So he wants me to place a solution of something in your bath, and then you would die."

"What was he giving you for that in exchange?" said Jack getting up, to face her as she said, "What, what did you say?"

"How much money was the bounty?"

"He said he would wire a million dollars."

"Ha, I'm only worth a million, that's insulting, who is he?, and when is your payoff?"

"Well that's just it, I told him I wanted it in cash, recycled in yellow ink."

"Good for you, to expose if it's real or not, and that was good thinking, to get US currency, to see where it came from?"

"What are you saying, actually, I was thinking of getting something in return, you act like you're happy about this?"

"Absolutely, In the Spy game, it's better to get the wire of funds, for who cares where it comes from, just as long as you can keep it hidden, it's always nice to know, that someone is targeting you, and to think that they can use anyone of us, you're a spy, this is what spy work is all about, the secret deals, and the outcome, so listen, get that powder over to Debby, the house maid, make sure you use a wet wash cloth to handle it, it may have toxins on the packaging left over from Callista touching it, and then when you get that money also give it to her."

"Is she one of us?"

"She and countless others, now run along and get this transaction over with, and ask Hendy to come back in."

"You seem so relaxed about all of this" said Michelle looking at him like she needed a hug, so he pulled her in, to say "Look you did the right thing, someday you'll make a great spy, everything will be just fine, oh one more thing who is that agent?"

"Knock knock, said Hendy, as she literally pulled Michelle out to say, "I gather she doesn't want the seaweed wrap?"

"Nah it's just the two of us" said Jack with a smile on his face.

"In that case let me lock the door", she said as she turned the deadbolt, and undid her bikini, to say who gets to go first?"

Michelle briskly walked, through the huge spa, the canoe like windows, showed off the windows, for which to look at the lake below, but it was her contact that was waiting for her, with duffle bag in hand, that was until, and arm pulled her into a room, he was alone as he said, "Michelle, what are you doing here?"

"I don't work for you anymore, leave me alone, I'm an American Citizen."

"You're always going to be a Chinese, so what are you his wife now?"

"Yes, so you better leave me alone, or I will tell him everything?"

Chu let her arm go, looking at her, to say, "I'm sorry, for the way I treated you, I had no idea, you wanted to be a spies wife."

"This is not the time and place, I got to go" she said, and left, only to see Alex was gone, she routinely checked each room, to finally see he was in the last one alone, to hear him say, "Come in and close the door, she did as she was told, and stood by the door, to hear, "I had you checked out, and your clean, you're a Chinese nationalist, and Chu, was your sponsor and mentor, and lover, so why did you leave him, to be with Jack Cash?"

"Many reasons" she said gaining confidence to deal with this monster.

"So are you wearing a listening device?"

"For what, this is just between you and me?" she said with reservations.

"So you won't mind if I check you for myself?"

"No, by all means" as she had no idea what was going to happen next.

"Well then strip" said Alexander, smiling.

Without hestatation, she pulled off her bikini top, and slid down her bottoms, as he reached in and inserted a finger inside, as she stood like a soldier, waiting, till he was through, he pulled it out to say, "You can dress?"

"I'm fine, where is my money?"

"In the bag", he said pointing over at the duffle bag, with Russian markings, for her, to say, "Can I have the bag too?"

"Yeah, that's where the money is at? Looking at her as if she was dumb."

She looked at him, to think, "What is he gay, maybe I'll have fun with this one, as she turned to face him, she launched herself at him, catching him off guard, and pinning him on the bed, to say, "You just paid me a million, how about we go a round or so."

"No, as he cried, as he tried to get up, he threw her off of him, to say, "Please leave, and get dressed."

She looked at him, in shame, as she dressed, to realize, he was not on her level, to think, "He is a coward", she grabbed the bag, and was going out, only to hear, "I expect to have the job done tonight?"

"Yeah right, you loser" she said mumbling to herself, as she left his room, thinking what an idiot he was, only as she touched the door to the UN, was a team of security people, and from what she heard, it was all about the bag. She was on one side of the door, and they were on the other, she ducked into a room, to keep the door, slightly open, she placed the bag on the table, and pulled a sheet over it, and quickly undressed, and hopped up on it, just to see the door open, she waved, to say, "Hold on, you want to be next Mister?" as she saw it was a spa table, she sat on.

"Nah sorry miss, were looking for Alexander, you seen him?"

"You try his room, he is the third one down on the left?"

As the door closed, she dressed, and waited, to see, a group of UN advisors passed her, to come up with an idea, she took the bag, and rolled it up using a sheet, giving the pencil look, she took off her top, and placed it inside, and her bottoms, on the other side, to look like laundry, she went out, barely covering up her front, to open the door to see the two guards to say, "They wanted me to bring their dirty clothes to the laundry room."

"Sure they do?" said one of them looking at her behind.

As the other one said, "Here let me lend you my jacket, you'll catch a cold" as he placed the jacket around her body, as he zipped it up, "See you in two" she said as she was back on the move, as the hallway was filled with carts, for housecleaning, to see one she said, "Is Debby around, I have a load, exclusively for her?"

"No, she works a floor down, in Suite number one, but I think she is done, we could call her?"

"Please I soiled myself, I'll be in Suite one, my floor?"

"Yes, hold on, as she paged Debby, and said, "She will be there shortly, as Michelle waddled into the freight elevator, with the cart, she went down a level, and onto her floor and into her room, using her hand, the door opened, she stepped through, and it closed shut, she tossed the sheet down. And went to the drawer to see the vial, then into the bathroom, and ran the water, cold or hot, then choose cold, she wring out the cloth, to take it back to the vial, she placed it in and around it, then closed it up, as she began to think, what to do with all that money, then it hit her, cut newspapers, arranged, as she saw what appeared to be a bundle of papers from Latvia and Belarus, so she cut the ties, the half dozen or so on the table, the door slung open, as Michelle was naked, she looked up to see Debby, come in, and the door closed.

"What is going on?"

"Jack asked me to give you a vial of poison."

"Ssh, as she put her finger to her mouth, to say, "They could be listening, let me see it?"

Michelle looked at her, then led her into the bedroom, to pull out the drawer, to point at it.

Debby looked at her, then to the covered up vial, to say, "Good, this should diffuse the spread of contaminates, does he want a report, as she placed the container in a box from her cart."

Michelle just looked at her, for Debby to say, "Alright, I'll get him a report on what it is, anything else?"

"Oh yes, I have some money he wants you to keep for him" she said as she unfolded the sheet, for Debby to say, "Had anyone from the UN seen this?"

"No but there looking for it?"

"Come lets pile the money into my hamper, I'll get it to Jim and Mitzi, as she pulled out her phone she took a picture of the duffle bag, to say, "You better, put something in there, hold on I got an idea" wait here and I'll be back, in the meantime you may think about getting dressed, there are camera's all over this place."

"What's the big deal, I really don't see what all the fuss is about, I like being naked."

"Well I will tell you, it's that your body is near flawless and it intimidates others."

"Thank you, that's all I wanted to hear" said Michelle.

Debby wheeled the cart out, and down the hallway. Into the maid's quarters, and down a path, using a secured sat phone, she dialed up Jim, who told her that the Strike team is out in the field, doing some training, and that he would meet her shortly at receiving, with a bag.

He saw her, as the two worked together, then gave him the box that contained the vial, she smiled at him, as he ditched the box inside a duffle bag, and carried it back to the plane.

Meanwhile, Debby went into another maid's quarters to see a another duffle bag, which she pulled up, and pulled out her bag, and opened the bag, to allow all the contents to fall into the duffle bag. She took both with her, as she wheeled it back to number one room on the girl's floor, the door slid open, and there was Michelle dressed waiting, the two of them re-rolled the contents of the duffle bag, and out went Michelle, and Debby went back to the waste and disposal department, where an American worker, took the Russian marked duffle bag and threw it into the incinerator.

Michelle wore the jacket back but open, while she carried the wrapped up duffle bag, the guard took his jacket back and she went back inside the room.

Inside the first room, she pulled the duffle bag out, and slid it under the bench, and discarded the sheet, she opened the door to see the UN team advisor, to say, "Are you all through in there Miss?"

"Yes Officer" she said passing them, as they rushed in to say, "Here it is I found it?"

Michelle turned to see the duffle bag come out, and then they opened it, then dropped it, but the Advisor picked it up, to allow Michelle to see what was inside. She saw a bag full of sex toys to say, "Those aren't mine?"

"Well see about that" he said with a smile, to say, "Come with me".

Jack was thoroughly entranced in sleep oblivious to what was going on, but could feel the seaweed extracts working, as his body felt reenergize and alive, he turned his head to see the lovely Hendy doing the same thing, enjoying herself, Jack began to reflect on his life, when he realized he was living in the moment, and went back to sleep, about an hour later, he was awaken by the sound of water, looking over he saw Hendy showering off in the middle, her perfectly nude body was a turn on, but he kept his mind focused, as she helped him up, she washed him off, to say, "The spa is closing, we need to get you out of here."

Hendy acted all business, as she helped him into his robe, and slippers, unlocked the door, and Jack left. He continued past no one else, to the guard, who said "Ah you're the last, Mister Cash, there has been a change in the program, we will muster at 0700 in room number one, don't be late?"

"Yes sir" said Jack. Comedic, then took a huge yawn, as he walked back into the high speed elevator, then back up the hill, he got out, to the right, he showed his pass, and went into the food court, and down the hall to his suite, he went in, as the door slammed shut, took off his robe, and stepped out of his slipper, into the bedroom, as he lifted off the covers, and slid in, and went to sleep.

The next morning, was Wednesday day 3, it was Michelle, pulling on him, to wake up, he stumbled out and into a shower, afterwards he toweled off, to pause to watch Michelle dress, in military gear, he too had something in the same form. Jack was out five minutes before 0650, and rushed to the mess hall, for a sandwich to go, and out to room one for all to muster.

On one side was the South division, and the other the North, as Jack slid in where he was at, evidently Alexei and his team held the company flag, as he spoke, Vadim and I will man HQ, with Erica and Cami, the warriors, will be team Black led by Steven, Darlene, Ben and Kellie, for our spies, it will be team Blue, Jack, Carlos, Michelle and Lea, on our outskirts, will be the remaining teams." Said Alexei, as the Professor said, "Alright, for the South?" Jonathon stepped forward to say, "It will be team Gold, with Alexander, and Simone, and translator will be Esmeralda, our teams, Warriors, will be team Red, led by Benjamin, Peleruth, Simon and Protima, as for our spies, its team Turquoise, led by Kyle, Andrain, and Nina, for our field will be the rest." The Professor showed everyone on a map, the location, as he said, "There will be a massive tent, for your HQ, and a place to hang your flag, once a flag is caught by opposing division, the game resets till everyone has had a chance to play out each role, does everyone understand?, and oppose", there was none, for the Professor to say, "Go load up in your appropriate truck, and get set up the game will start at 1500 hours, understood?" Jack got into the mess truck, as it headed out, about five miles in, the convey stopped, as Team White Chu, Rebecca, and Dana, went into the hills, as the convey continued on, five more miles, when it stopped at a ridge, whereas two teams got out, one went up, and the other down the hill, to set up camp, as the trucks went on, a short ways, to a clearing on a hillside, to park, to hear, "End of the road, set up camp", as Jack hopped out, to see the massive tent was folded up, as he looked at Carlos, Steven Smith, Ben, Alexei and Vadim, and six girls, as Jack looked up the model number on the tent, on his phone, and it showed him the fastest way, and said, "I know how to set this up, any objections?"

Not from anyone, as Jack assembled the center pole, as he was showing with his hands what to do, as the others stretched the tent out, as it seemed pretty easy, around them stood referees, as, a path was made, held open by Alexei and Vadim, as Jack went in with pole in hand, thinking, "Ivan the Giant, could come in handy about now.", as he went in, found the center, and drove the pole straight up, and in the ground, as everyone had a side, and put a pole in, and Ben and Steven, drove the stakes, and set to stabilize the huge tent, Vadim, came in, and set down the center base, as he helped Jack secure the pole, to say, "This is vast, it will be a good HQ."as the two went outside to grab tie ropes and the pair worked together, as Carlos and Alexei, set the new stakes, for Steven and Ben, Headquarters was up, and inside they went to lay the floor, and put up partions, as furniture went in, a desk, a switchboard, and a make shift mess, food was also brought in by all the women, stacked it up off the floor, a side flap, was raised, as Vadim said, "Now, we need crew quarters, as Alexei and Carlos unloaded the cots, and sleeping bags, and set them up as a pot belly stove was brought in and set up by Steven and Ben, and they both ran a pipe up and out, outside, Jack and Vadim, were assembling, another tent, this time it was smaller, it went up fast, as Vadim said, "This will be our arms room, and armory.", as the rear flap was secure, and roped in as pegs from the outside by Carlos and Alexei drove them in, as Jack and Vadim, worked well together, and undid the opposite flap, on the other side, as Vadim, helped Jack with that tent, as the girls went to firing up the stove, and easily got it started, it was Erica, as she brought the temperature up and took the chill off, as the other tent went up fast, and Carlos and Alexei, secured the outside, as Vadim, said, "This will be our storage tent, as the rest of the supplies were loaded on empty cots, and off the ground, several more tarps were brought in, for the flooring, when complete, all twelve stood around the bot belly stove feeling the warmth, as a SAS field officer, said, "All will get 100 points, you put this tent up in record time, so now run your comm lines, send out your warriors, the spies can go too, to provide back up?"

Vadim took it all under advisement, as he and Alexei, agreed, to break up the warriors, so Vadim, said, "Steven, You and Darlene, take a reel, and go to the right, Ben and Kellie, take a reel to the middle, and Carlos and Lea, go to the far left, bury the line the best you can, under boulders, and take a shovel with you, as for you Jack and Michelle, I want you two, to survey, the area up to the safe zone, and if possible cross over and give back Intel." said Vadim, as he looked over at Erica who took upon herself to do mess, and Cami, was the radio operator, as she with Ben's help tied off the comm lines, Steven held a stick as Darlene helped to slide the wheel in place, and out the front went Steven, as Darlene trailed, to set the line down, and off they went to the right or west, as

Jack went with them, down the middle was Ben and Kellie, she buried the line, as Ben took off running, and for the left side, it was Carlos, spinning out the comm line, followed by an enthusiastic Lea, and Michelle, went with them, as the SAS guy, said, "!00 points for you, good job of delegating."

To the South was far different, the only one who could put up a tent was Simon, Kyle helped somewhat, as Nina Toop sat, with Simone, tried but it was no use, then it started to rain, and all went into the trucks to wait it out, Jonathon, and Alexander were baffled on how to set the pole, that they decided to send a messenger to the other teams to see how to raise a tent, as the rain died down, to see the women, Jonathon, asked, "Do I have any volunteers to go and fetch someone who knows how, other than Simon, to raise a tent?"

Three women volunteered, as Jonathon, sent Peleruth to the right, to team Copper, and Protima, to the middle, and Esmeralda to the left to team, orange. Two hours went by, and the tent was still in the same place, as the convey was ready to go, the North had sent theirs away, as the South was way behind, so much so, Jonathan asked the SAS guy, "Can we borrow one of theirs to assemble our tent?"

"No, figure it out yourself" said the Guy, who looked angrily at them, for not trying, as Simon, put up the smaller tent and secured it himself, as he went after the large one, all by himself, he unfolded it, and set the smaller poles with it, as Simone, helped him, as Nina Toop looked on, as Simon, built the center pole, and found, an opening, and went in, he himself, hoisted it up, and just like that,Simone, and Nina secured one line, then another, as Jonathon, and Alexander, were just facing the opposite way, as the tent went up, while Kyle and Andrain, waited as well, with Benjamin, sometime had past, as one runner came back walking, it was Esmeralda, with Stephen Moss, who came to the group, to say, "What gives, it's up, what the hell man," said Stephen turning around, as did the others, as they saw Simon, and Simone did all the work, even though Nina was there somewhat, as the others came back as well,

Protima had, Gordon and Sean, who was visible limping, to give Simon a hand, Stephen helped too, till it was done, and the other tent was up and secure, the desk went in, with the pot belly stove, and it was assembled, and lit, to warm what was pretty cool outside, as the switch board went in on a table, with a chair, comm lines, were secure, as Stephen took his back with him, and Gordon took one and Sean, really was fighting the pain, took the other, as it was two o'clock, something, as three was close by, at one point all three lines were tangled amongst themselves, as Jack, on his point with Tad, showed him his vantage point, both Roxy and Kendra were happy to see Jack, as they both gave him a hug and a kiss, Kendra was infatuated with Jack, as Jack saw they needed to get going, with their shelter, as Jack said, "Where are you going to sleep at?"

"In the bushes" said Thomas.

"What about cover and concealment?" asked Jack.

"What do you suggest we do?, then."

"Dig a hole, partially underground, and that way, if it rains, you'll be protected."

"Really, that takes some work", said Thomas, not going any further than where he was at.

"Precisely, that is what the SAS advisor is here for to award you all points, just ask him" said Jack.

"Yes Jack Cash is correct, and no one from your group will get anything except Jack Cash, fifty points." said the SAS agent.

Jack took off, much to Kendra's disappointment, as it was nearing the start of the event.

With the South completed their HQ, the SAS guy, said, "Alright, Simon and Simone, 100 points apiece, and fifty to Nina Toop, all others failed." As Jonathon puts his hands up in the air, to say, "So I couldn't build a tent."

"That's not the point, find a way, and accomplish it, never give up or you will die, and the game starts at 3, 2, 1, it's on." Said the SAS advisor, as the trucks rolled away, and towards the center, as Kyle hung on for dear life, it slowed, as he rolled off the back, and made it to a clearing, then up a hill, to a ridge as he pulled out a pair of binoculars, to scan and take a look, as he stopped to see a rifle pointed at him, as Tad, waved him back, as a SAS advisor, said, you're dead, you're out, follow me. At South HQ the report came in, Kyle was shot and killed. For Jonathon, to say, "Send in Andrain, with Nina."

"No, I want Nina here with me, send Simone, she seems tough." Said Alexander.

"I'm fine with that, I'll be a spy"' said Simone, gearing up and was ready to go, to see Nina come in and flank Alexander, instantly Simone knew what was going on, to say, "Alright, this is how it will be."

Except, the SAS agent, stepped in to say, "This is a foul, Nina Toop, is assigned as a spy, and thus must be in the field, there are people watching your every move, and if you were to send her out before her time, then it would constitute a fraud."

"He is right, let's take him, and just like that Jonathon and Alexander subdued the SAS agent, and zip tied him up, and even his mouth, and pulled him to the other tent, and on a cot. To take the radio, he had, they could monitor progress, as Simone saw the writing on the wall, and left.

Jack and Michelle made it back to HQ, where a hearty meal, was presented, as Jack took a plate, courtesy of Erica, the twelve of them ate, as even fresh baked bread was prepared, as Erica said, "I took all the rations, broke them open, to make a hearty beef stew, and dumplings, I had some staples so I made fresh bread, so enjoy."

As Vadim said, "This is what we should do, the Warriors, go establish a position, in a roving pattern, with two on and two off, throughout the night, as for the spies, go do some of your spy stuff and capture some troops, with that Jack, Carlos, Michelle and Lea, pulled it together, for Jack to say,"Alright, you two, Michelle and Lea, down the middle, while Carlos, you're on the left, and I'll be on the right, take down and zip tie them up, as a call came over, that Tad, just assassinated Kyle, he is out, "So down to 22, our goal by day break is the Flag. All put their hand in to say, "Goooo North." Jack took off and he was running, as was Carlos and the other two girls, as they, easily worked to the free space zone, as Jack caught up with Thomas, and Roxy, who were dirty, and digging in the dirt, while Kendra, stood support for Tad, as a SAS advisor, was close by, as he said, "Someone standing, smoking a cigarette?"

Tad, made the motion, and said, next to her, another female, in the head, dead, confirmed, as he said, man's head, shot, is he dead?"

"Yes, confirmed", said the SAS advisor.

On the other end, the SAS advisor, said, you three down, you're out, as Gordon, pops his head up, for Tad to say, "Shoot, confirmed dead." Dead confirmed, all down and out."

In the South, the SAS advisor, spoke out, your all dead, a sniper rifle shot at all of you."

Jonathon tried the switchboard, to get Team Yellow, on", as he kept saying, "Team Yellow its HQ over."

Jack made it down past Tad, as Tad kept Jack safe, as he made it through the woods, as Michelle and Lea made it to the Yellow's position, to see all is dead, and into the half dug out hole, where a ground radio was, as it kept ringing, Lea answered it, to hear, "Good, Rod what's your status?"

"They're all dead, and honey we are all coming for you" said Lea.

"Who is this?"

"The enemy."

Jack made his way over as the group in front of him had a camp fire, as the first one, was Z'sofia, said,"I need to take a leak."

"Go over there, we would like to watch" said Stephen, as she said, "Go fuck yourself, as she made her way, into the brush, right in front of Jack as she loosened up her trousers, and pulled them down, and did her business, and afterwards pulled them up, is when Jack dove on her, and pinned her down, as she fought a little, as Jack was an expert at keeping her mouth shut, and zipping her up, and then turned her over, as her pants, were down, a bit, as Jack used a zip tie and cinched them tight, and then her mouth, and finally her, ankles, as she smiled at him. He watched her as he waited for his next victim, it was the other girl, Nina Ivan, she too walked into the trap, as she squatted and let it out, only to rest a moment, and that's when Jack got her, and zip tied her wrists, as he held her face, and was wrestling her down, as her pants were at her ankles, as she peed all over him, she smiled as he zip tied her mouth, pulled her pants up and then did her ankles.

Jack made it around to the fire, where Andreas was as Stephen was in their somewhat made lean to, to say, "Come on Andreas", that was till he saw, him go down, and you would have thought someone was getting murdered, as Stephen began to whelp, and Jack pounced on him, subdued him. Meanwhile Carlos was in trouble from the beginning, as He took Nina Toop, face to face, and it was hand to hand combat, as Nina was taking Carlos to task, and beating him up, that was till, Michelle was on the scene, and Michelle easily took out Nina, then Carlos and Michelle went after Louie, he was a brute, as Carlos had enough, as he succumb to Louie beating him up, Michelle took out his legs, and Louie went down, as Michelle put him in a hold, which he tapped out and he was dead, then from behind their shelter, she took out Jamal, as both Freya and Joana, were asleep. As Michelle was racing towards the flag, as the South's Warriors, were the hand to hand fighting machines, as Jack took out Benjamin, and zip tied him up, as Michelle took out Peleruth, as she went down but Michelle won easily, meanwhile, Simon and Protima, were in their racks, when Jack stormed the HQ, by pulling up the stakes, and all went dark, as the flag, was in Jack's hands, as he and Michelle, went back.

Next morning, was Thursday, day 4, Jack awoke, to hear, "Alright switch", Jack got up to see, Steven in command, with the commander's jacket on, to say, "Jack, Team Blue is on the left flank, hurry up, you don't want to be late." Jack was squirming, in his sleeping bag, when all of a sudden, a girl appears, with the striking face features, to say, "Jack I want to be one of your wives?"

Jack stopped, as she pulled the zipper down, she sat on his cot, to say, "Let me explain, ever since you freed Annabel from her captors, My Mom, Miss Samantha, and I have agreed, to allow you to marry me, exchange for securing her safety."

Jack looked at her, as she was serious, to say, "Alright after, this is over, you could be picked to be a UN spy, then what?"

"Then I shall talk it over with you, and if you think I shall do that, then I will, and then when that is over, I will find you so that we may have a family, that's what you want right, lots of children, so do I, "Let's make lots of them" as she bent down for that eagerly awaited kiss, to hear, from Steven, "Chloe Ryan, not now, allow Jack Cash to go out to his position." She let him pass, as he dressed, and went out, to see Carlos who was beaten and battered, for Jack to say, "What truck ran over you?"

As Lea was attending to his wounds as she smiled up at Jack, for Jack to say, "What's gotten into you?"

"Oh, I'm having the time of my life, usually, I work at a desk, processing the spies work, and this is been so much fun, when will we start fucking?" Jack did a double take, as they were waiting Michelle, she came, and they all went, to their GPS coordinates, it was a valley of sorts, for Jack to say, let's climb up to that ridge," and low and behold a cave, he checked the GPS against his phone, as the phone quickly mapped and it still showed it was alright, as Jack asked the SAS guy with them, "Is it alright, to set up on that ridge, and still be where we are at?"

"The rule states, in a five hundred foot area, so yes, this is within five hundred feet, actually its straight up from here."

"I get the point will you shut up" said Jack, as he looked back at Lea, who had a smile on her face, as they made it up to the cave, as Jack went in deep, he found a ledge, and saw, but a slit, and enlarged it a bit, to see the other side, and thought, great place, under rock and under cover, as Lea, made her way up, to stand by Jack, to say, "You were taken back, when I said I wanted to Fuck, so what's a girl has to do?"

"What of Roderick?"

"He is of only a boy, with a boy's dick, I want a man to fill me up, touch me, and see that I am ready to receive you, as Jack reached in, with his finger, and it was wet, as it explored much to her liking, as she said, "How do you want me, from behind, in front, on the side or in the rear?" Jack moved her around, as he was ready, from all her talk, as she undid her trousers, he pulled them down, to see her perfect sized butt, and he un zipped, and placed on protection, and it went in, it stuck at places, then it cleared, as she held on, as he stroked her from behind. Meanwhile, someone else was looking for Jack, as it was still daylight, in the valley below, she was trying to find Jack was Chloe, just as the lamb was led to the slaughter, so to was the spies for the South as they easily caught her, as Alexander wanted her to strip, as she resisted, they tackled her, and begun to rip at her clothes, only to feel a hand on their backs, as Carlos captured both of them, zip tied with or all of Michelle's help, as an echo of passion could be heard, as Jack was wrecking Lea, till he realized it, and pulled out, as she finished him off, she was exhausted as two hours had past, as she said, in between breath's how long do you normally go?"

"Oh, about four hour blocks?"

"Are you kidding me, I feel like I'm wrecked, I need to call in reinforcements, I know several good girls, who want to be bad, as she was trying to get up only to collapse, for Jack to say, "So who, would be interested?"

"Well namely, Nina Toop, she is merely eye candy for Alexander, you know he is gay?"

"Who cares" said Jack intrigued, as she continued, "Well my roommate, she says she is married, but she is so pinned up, a good drilling like that, and of course you know Kellie, she was ready day one, and Kendra she is the hot Russian girl, one more possibly is Joana, but she is really into Raisa, and you know about Chloe, if I could only tell her." While Jack went up to the observation tower, part, as he called down to her, to tell HQ a small party of two, as Jack saw Michelle subdue Simone and Esmeralda, the two were captured. Jack and Lea were first in their sleeping bags, to sleep, while Carlos and Michelle were on guard. Jack, slept side by side with Lea, as she got up and lit a cigarette, for Jack to turn over, away from her, as she said, "You don't like that I smoke?"

"It lessens your value to me, that's all" said a sleepy Jack.

"Well no one ever cared to say anything to me, and just like that I'll quit", as the night wore on to the day, three, Jack and Lea were up while Carlos and Michelle slept.

A message came over comm, as it was Friday day 5 and the game reset, the North won, last night., and Chloe did find Jack especially when Lea, told her what she took, but was apprehensive as she choose to stay with Jack, as Michelle went elsewhere and Carlos, still sore, went to HQ. Jack, Lea and Chloe, went to the front bunker, climbed in, and waited, as Chloe said, as she looked at the two of them, "So how does it all work, as Lea took the lead, to say, "Well, you drop your trousers, and bend over and in goes rover, I mean Jack, and he will work it out of you till you have no more, and then some more, Chloe seemed alright by it, as she undid her trousers, and pulled down her white panties, as she faced the bunker front, and bent over, to rest her head on her elbows, and waited, she saw movement along the front lines, as Jack did the rest, he put on protection, and slipped it in, and it took a little time but was in, and working it, when instantly Lea grabbed his balls, really hard, and he went flaccid, as Jack fell back, with Chloe to say, "I'm waiting Jack, as the jealous Lea, was bottomless, and sat on him, as he was trying to get up, she grinded against him, till he was risen, and much to her delight, as it went in, and she rode it while Chloe watched, as Jack unbuttoned her blouse, and to see her tank top, he pulled it up, to see the littlest tits he had ever seen, she was flat, as she continued to grind him, till she was done, and he pushed her off, and was at the ready for Chloe, who turned, once again to assume the position, and Jack went in, only to feel a surge of pain, as Lea once again had a lock grip on his ball sack, and he went down, clutching them, he was crying, it hurt so bad, as Lea said, "Call me Mistress Lea, you bitch." standing over him naked, except her trousers were at her knees, and top was off, all Chloe could do was to watch, but crouched down, out of sight. Jack laid in a fetal position, as Lea stood naked for all to see and they did, when all of a sudden, the North charged, as hand to hand combat, was going, on, Carlos, came to Jack's aid, to say, "Come on brother, let's go, as Chloe, helped her man up, he walked gingerly, and rolled out, and was helped along, with Chloe, all the while, Lea's diversion, turned the tide, as a UN advisor said, "Miss you can get dressed now the war was called as SAS advisor, to say, "It's over come forward, to assemble, Chloe, Jack and Carlos had captured others as the North took the South by surprise. Lea came up to Jack, gave him a kiss on the cheek, smiled, to say, "Sorry Jack, I was role playing, can we pick it up later?"

"Perhaps" said Jack with Chloe's help, to the assemble area, and took a seat, with Chloe, holding her man's hand. Lea was on the other side, as Jack was thinking of a way to wreck her and her dominatrix ways, also smiling was Kendra, who came by to say, "Lea asked me, and I'm down with that." Kellie was all smiles, but the surprise, was Freya, as she asked Jack for a word, he gets up to walk gingerly, to another chair, as she said, "If we do this, it has to be from the rear?"

"Nope, for you I want to see everything?"

"Alright, I can't deny you, when tonight?"

"Yep, coordinate with your team, wear only a robe, as he turned to see Kellie as excited as ever, to say, "So tonight's the night, I could recruit, but I guess you have a line up, of you and me, Chloe, of course, Kendra, she is pretty big up front, and Freya, finally, she needs to get laid, Lea, who knew?"

"I did" said Jack, and "Finally Nina Toop, what a wild card, who knew she was just arm candy for a gay guy, what a shame."

The SAS instructors, came out to say, "This was far more eventful than we could ever imagined, Team North won all three times, and it didn't matter who was the spies, and we almost had a rape, I say this in the kindest of ways, had this been real, things would have been different, above all only one was injured, Louie Bellini broke his arm, as he went off a cliff", as Jack looked over at Carlos, who smiled, to hear, Dismissed go back to room one, a Professor awaits you." Jack got up as the trucks, were waiting, and into the back, with Chloe at his side, in the truck was Protima, and Peleruth, both looked concerned as Protima asked, "Why haven't you asked us, if we would like to participate, in your adventure?"

"The last you and I saw each other you were trying to kill me, remember?"

"All I remember, I was hired to guard you, you escaped, as I was trying to keep you safe, from that sinister Kimberly, then you were on top of me, and I didn't do anything, since here I've gotten to know you and would like to join in, Me and Peleruth, we can bring Raisa, who is infatuated with you and Z'sofia, you know the one, you snuck up on and pinned her down, she was ready to have you right then and there", said Protima. To continue, to say, "What do I have to do to prove my loyalty to you."

"Nothing, not now, but some day when I trust your doubt, then show me how loyal you are," said Jack.

They all arrived at the UN, as advisors were separating the men from the women, the UN it was different, as the women were led away, Jack, followed them in, as they were led to the conference room, as Miss Hill was sternly telling the girls that the boys, were off limits, as Lea, topless was featured as the example, to hear Miss Hill say, "So who and why were you topless, as she came back cleverly, to say, "To distract the enemy" said the confident Lea, for Miss Hill to say, "Actually it did work, your warriors captured all the advancers, for that your awarded 200 points, as for the rest of you it will be posted, now let's talk about the sport you will all be participating in, the

UN has chosen Soccer, as the game you will be playing, the games will start on Saturday morning, to Saturday afternoon, then a qualifier will be on Sunday, so let's decide on teams, and that team will be flown in, for you to play, center, an additional field position, inside the striker, as some of you might have played it before, a single designation, per a special color you will wear, as the team will set you up, all you do is run down the middle of the field, and only you will score, now let's pick our teams, now because the US has over sixteen loyal agents, its recommended that one take the US and all the others chose a different team to represent, this is just being like a double agent, so here is the top Women's World Cup standings, as each team has agreed to come to participate, and for those of which you represent your country, well, let's look at our current top agent spy rankings, Captain Michelle Quan, is leader with 570 points, so choose, she thought about her homeland, and thought about others, and said, "I choose China." Next at Two at 364 points, on that list was Lea Lucas, realizing, being with Jack was thrusting her up the leader board, to say, "France." Next was Darlene Lewis, Third, at 205 points, choose, "Canada.", next was Kellie Ryan, the blonde blue eyed girl, at Four, at 196 points, wasn't going to let the US get away, and said proudly, "US of A of course." Next up was Cami Ross, at Five, with 194 points, she saw the next best team as and choose, "South Africa." Next up was Simone Bailey, at Six, with 175 points, and followed suit, and said, "Chile." Next up was Erica Adams, at Seven, with 162 points, she choose, "Honduras." Next up Dana Scott, at Eight with 130 points and saw the next available team, and said, "Argentina." Next up was Roxy Carr, at Nine, with 125 points she choose, "Australia." Next up was Kendra Augustus, at Ten, with a tie at 120 points, to say, "Russia of course." Next up was Jill Hoyt, at Ten, with 120 points said, "New Zealand, Next" it was Rebecca Adams, at Twelve, with 105 points, to say, and thinking of Jack's upcoming wedding, to say, "Latvia." Next up was Nina Toop, at Thirteen, with 91 points, she too was thinking of Jack, and choose, "Belarus." Next was Esmeralda

Romero, who was at Fourteen, with 62 points, said, "Spain". Next up was Freya Lyons, at Fifteen, with 50 points, who had some contacts there to say, "Mexico." Next was Joana Celek, from Portugal, at Sixteen, and with only 46 points, so she choose her country. Next Z'sofia Baptiste, at Seventeen, with 44 points, she choose, her country, to say, "Turkey." Next up was Nina Ivan, Eighteen, and with a mere 38 points chose "Croatia." Next was Protima, who was at Nineteen, at the near bottom limit, of 32 points, who choose, "Brazil." And last on the list was Peleruth Jaizem, at 30 points, took her country, and said "Poland."

"Listen up ladies, those at the bottom need to find a way, to Sixty, by next week, each game you win, will give you twenty five points, so dismissed, for now and tomorrow I'll have all the teams here early Saturday morning."

The Women exited, as some went to clean up, and ready themselves, for tonight's events as others went to the mess, as for Raisa, it was chow time, and consumed a huge meal, as her friend Kendra said, "That won't be good, later."

"Oh I'll be fine" she said cautiously.

CH 6

It's a free for all; a traitor is exposed

Jack went up a level, and met with the other men, went to the room, number one, and found their seats, everyone else was doing something, Jack swiped his card, looked in his refrigerator, to see chocolate milk, he took one out and placed a straw in it, and took slow sips. Meanwhile he pulled out a pad of paper and a pen, to see Mister Benz come out and count the seats and all of the agents to say, "Alright everyone is accounted for, let's begin, now I know, I was told you that you could have today off, but a fantastic offer came to us, for tomorrow, and that deal, I will keep to myself, but let's talk ethics, and strength, each and every one of you are spies probably highly decorated and carry a rank within the military, and in such a case that occurred 3 mos. ago, when an agent was abducted, blindfolded and bounded, they flew a short distance and the plane blew up."

The Professor scanned the spies for a reaction, only one shook his head., then continued, "And that person was Louie Bellini from Rome, he jumped out of the plane, after he cut the line, and pummel to earth, and escaped, with only a top sheet, so we thought we would try that on you guys, but in a more controlled atmosphere, so after class today, were going to recreate that scenario."

The Professor waited for another response, there was none, either half were still asleep, like Jack or just didn't care, but he continued let's talk about strength, there are about only five of you that has a support team, take a look at the monitor." Each and everyone, had small video pictures on the right side of their desks to view, it was of the plane and the strike team, of Jack Cash's that was featured, for the Professor to say, "Can anyone tell me where this is at, anyone, anyone?", the class was still silent, that was irritating the Professor, to say, "Alright, number one, Vadim, tell us about your strength, in relations to how many do you have in reserve, what ground forces are at your expense."

Vadim got up, to say, "Well I have none that I know of?"

"Wrong, every agent in here has their government backing them, allocating the flights and travel arrangements, gone are the days of being rogue, and doing as you please, today we are in the world of accountability, so each and every one of you has some form of support, it is your job, to know what that is, and how to utilize it."

"Little do you or all the other agents in here know, but there are other agents around you either working for you, against you, or just in different. Double agents are the common place now a days, maybe even in here, a government may ask you to work for them for say ten million dollars, and you'd probably do it, if it goes along with your beliefs, because it's really all about the money, power and sex, that is the basis for being a spy, if that's not the truth, just look around the UN has allocated the finest world class chef's to prepare your world's cuisine, then let's look at the women you have and brought with you, and for some of you they represent hired help, for others they are loyal followers, and then there are those that could have anyone of them as he pleases."

As the Professor looks over at Jack, smiles and continues,

"Let's talk about another issue, but let's break for lunch take two hours off, get cleaned up and we will meet back around four, dismissed."

Inside the prop plane was a special team, Jim and Jesse, carefully tested the poison, under a watchful eye of Mitzi, while Jared, was tasked with stacking the money in the security locker, for which he saw the jeweled box, he shield himself, as he lifted the top of the box, the mirrored top, showed glitter of gemstones, he reached in and pulled out a green emerald cut gem.

Inside the flight cabin, Mark watched over what Clarance's, was doing for the UN through the inside video feed. Mike was monitoring the progress in the field with Brian, and then that of the rear cargo hold, then the armory cage, when he said, "What the hell, take a look, Mark?"

"Let's go get him?"

"Wait let's see if he hides it?" said Mike.

"And if he does?" asked Mark.

"Then it's an attitude adjustment" the two high five'd each other, when Mike asked Mark, "So how do you like the rooms, the UN has provided us?"

"Well Mike, you know it's far greater than any other place I've stayed in, let alone, the food, now I know where all the celebrity chef's go."

"What do you have?"as they both watched the monitor.

"Looks like he put the gemstone back, but"

"But what my friend" asked Mark.

"He doesn't respect Jack's property."

"No, he doesn't, I still think he needs an attitude adjustment" said Mark.

"I agree with you, Mark, but we can't leave our posts or Jim will kill us."

Jim took the final steps, to say, "Its cyanide, totally clear smoking gas, and no residual effects, let's seal this up, and leave it in the chamber, pull out your hands, Jesse."

Jesse did so, to turn to see Jim was ready to contain it.

Jim turned to see his helper, for Jim to say, "Clear out, I need some room here." Jesse leaves the armory, for Jim to finish off the containment process. Jim finished and placed in in the chute to the small barrel, whereas Jim slid the top shut, vacuum sealed it, as the edges pressed together, for Jim to say,"Its safe now."

Jim went out, and washed up, with Jesse, for Mitzi to say, "Wait Jim, come in and close the door." As Jim walked into Jack's cabin to hear, "First I want to say, "How right you were to be here, if that poison contacted Jack, and died, I'd been guilt ridden for the rest of my life" said Mitzi.

"I just received a call on a in bound flight with Jack's new sniper weapon is ready and was flown by a super hornet, also some surveillance gear for Jack for night ops, it is here." Said Jim.

"Then we will keep this to ourselves" said Mitzi, allowing Jim to go, to say, "Yes, I will and if Miss Hohlstein asks about him, then we will tell her him and the rest of the base is safe, I was able to pull a particle print, the other two were Michelle, and that of Calista, now the jet is on the ground, and I will guide them in."

"Have Mark and Mike help you, then we need to get ready for night ops." Said Mitzi, concerned.

Meanwhile back inside the UN, was alive for the upcoming night ops, as UN was on high alert, as teams swept though both levels for the Men and Women, as two teams readied themselves, the ones who never jumped before and those that have, to support the agents. Both floors were on lockdown, as SAS agents stood guard at all doors, with weapons set, for Kellie to comment,"There goes the fun, abort, abort abort."

They all went to dinner, so did Jack, it was a light meal, as he ate with Chloe, who has since been inseparable with him, since professing her love for him, but so has some others namely Lea, his other companion to him, as she has proclaimed, she is going to be with Jack, forever, but not as as a wife. Michelle has troubles of her own, as Alexander and Raisa is pressuring her to kill Jack. But Raisa was the force behind all of this action, to show her loyalty to Alexander, and Alexei. Jack and Chloe, went off to his room, to showered together, as she washed him, of dirt, and made sure he was clean, he did the same for her, as he was hard, and she bent over, and allowed him inside, it just felt right as he did all the work, her near perfect body reminded Jack of Blythe, but Chloe was a red head, and fierce, she showed him her appreciation for him, as he allowed her to come, many times over, till Jack was done, or so she thought, as he was a monster, they got out he toweled off, to show her how big he really was, for her to say, "That thing is dangerous, you're gonna put someone in the hospital."

Jack opened the door to his pool, and dove in, as Chloe followed, she jumped in, and then came over to him, as he held her in his arms, the two felt safe, just then sirens, went off and men were running all over the place as the chase was on to find the traitor.

Alexander was on the move, then hiding out, from the roving UN patrols, he moved place to place, as in the UN HQ, they received word, from Miss Hohlstein who's print was on the vial, as she ordered a lockdown, and for her troops to come in and protect the spies, they were watching his every move, contemplating their next move, seeing it was close to four, and assembly, as the announcement went off, on all floors, for general assembly.

Jack left Chloe in the pool, and dried off, changed back into his gear for tonight, and left suite one, with an SAS agent in tow, through the women's level, and went one up, turned the corner, and into room one, he was late, and took his seat, to see Alexander come over to him, to lean on another chair, to say, "So your still breathing, not for long, I have a message for you, Varfolomey wants to play, a game of cat and mouse with you."

"I know" said Jack pulling out a piece of paper, to say, "Listen I know you're a terrorist like him, and know that you influenced one of my best agent Blythe, who is in custody."

"That's too bad, she seemed weak, but smart," said Alexander.

"Really, I wouldn't have said she was the sharpest tool in the shed," said Jack.

Alexander looked at him, to try to get a read on him, as Jack handed him the picture, for which he looked at it, to say, "What is this?"

"Oh that is what happen to Blythe" said Jack with a smile.

"You beheaded her, she was so pretty."

"Run along punk, tell Varfolomey, that will be his fate."

The Professor said, "Alexander please take your seat, so we may get this class underway, now that Jack Cash is here amongst us." as the other agents all took their seats, "As, I was saying before the break, now that I have your attention, were going to talk about ethics, among spies, to be gentlemen, is to let another agent know that your challenging them, and then the two will square off, that is the right way, the wrong way is to be secret and using others to do your work, and in the end they fail as will you, one of the oldest form of treachery is using poison, as he looked at Alexander, who turned his head away. "It has been discovered that someone was paid off to poison another agent, as Hendon, squirmed, as he looked around to say, "I'll kill the one who is behind this, I told them I wanted my gun, and I want to protect myself?"

"Calm down Hendon, the poison has been recovered, and accounted for, we have a pretty good idea, who it was" as Alexander was now squirming, to hear, "In addition we have called in 100 troops to help with our next week's Global games, and no none of you will have a personal weapon, other than I guess, your hands and your support personal, let's talk about that, for that person who was behind the poison incident, let me show you, what consequences you may face, watch this" said the Professor, as the video played, first Music, then came on a rear admiral, of the Navy, of the United States, as Alexander saw the picture, and the picture Jack drew for him, he was sweating, as the Admiral said, "We just got word, from our President of our United States, that we are on the verge of war with the country or individuals involved in the attempt on any agent there at the UN, at our disposal is this Aircraft carrier we have over 300 hundred fighter aircraft, and 24 other ships in our battle group, and four nuclear subs, also five thousand of the elite forces are on minute standby, ready to put down any of you that are involved in this plot, so I ask of you to confess now or suffer the consequences later, make no bones about this, have your Professor switch over to the flight field and you can see the troops coming in, and they are locked and loaded. Thank you."

The video went off, as the Professor, said "Now this is why we don't have a day off, because of this plot."

"One or more of you bastards confess or I'll kill you myself" said Hendon, who stood up and was threatening anyone.

"Hush up, no threats are needed, does that person, or person's want to come forward, the Professor waited, then said, "No, alright, from this time forward, a special forces person will escort you everywhere for your safety and those around you."

"Is that at night too, make sure she is pretty" laughs Jonathon.

"Laugh all you want, I expect someone to come forward, over this, by the nights over or else, we will be on lock down."

The Professor waited, then clicked a switch, and big men came in, to stand against the wall, for all to hear, "At ease soldiers, now agents, when you leave here, you will have an escort, they will have all access, and follow you everywhere, any questions?"

Everyone was quiet, Jack was jotting down some thoughts, as he looked over at Alexander, who was swaying back and forth, and sweating, to hear, "In addition, to that video we saw, when that American battle group isn't supporting us, they follow and support Jack Cash.

Louie looked over at Jack in his corner seat, as did others, as they were realizing that the ranking was false, as they knew they didn't have that kind of support, nor the resources, Jack continued to write, to hear, "So no one is confessing to this action against the team, I say we will go on to our today's challenge, upon dismissal, were going to the hanger, for some night ops, so go to your rooms, and change to camo, each of you will have a pack and a compass, there is a course you will follow, and one more thing each of you has their own course, and this is timed, the winner, will move up one spot, the rest of you are losers, dismissed."

One by one, they exited, with a Ops man behind them, and lastly it was Jack, and the same guy before waited, who was silent, and held his weapon up, Jack got to his room, and went in, to see Michelle, dressed nicely, to see him to say, "Everyone knows now", then see the burly guy to say, "Who is that guy?"

"Pretend he isn't there, he is my bodyguard."

"Will he be here tonight?"

"Why, where's this coming from?"

"I had some nice classes on etiquette today, this is so helpful...."

"That's nice, so what does that mean?"

"Means you'll have me tonight and as much as you like?"

"Really, no more rejection?" asked Jack.

"Of course, never, I'll do whatever it takes, besides it isn't like you haven't had me lately?"

"That's nice to know, even if I want him to join us?"

"Sure I will welcome that too." The guy's eyes grew big.

"Well I'd love to sit and talk about all the things I'd like to do to you, but we have our first challenge tonight, so don't wait up for me, and tell Chloe she will just have to wait."

"Oh I will, let me give you a kiss" she said as she made an affectionate gesture towards him, as she kissed him passionately. All for the fact that the guard stood there silently, as the two parted. Jack was dressed, in night scout gear, and boots, a camo jacket and cap, he went out, into the large hallway, to see his new friend from Belarus, who didn't look happy, as he came closer, the soldier was moving as Jack said, "Stand down, or I'll put you down", as the Giant came close to Jack, to say, "I failed you?"

"No you didn't, everything is fine, come with us."

"He can't," spoke the man behind them, to add, "It will be breaking the rules."

"Sorry Ivan, go see Michelle, and she will tell you what's going on" as Jack went away from him, and towards the rest of the agents in the line, and away they went, all in order, up the stairs, into the squadron bay, where more troops gathered, Jack looked around, to hear the smart looking Frenchman Goins, speak, in good English, and translated by the near guard for each spy, to ask who has never jumped before, about five raise their hands, Jack watched, but wasn't about to volunteer, as they were divided, to hear, "For those who have jumped before, it's on to the remedial center, which the two Russians led, followed by the two British, two American's and the Frenchmen, Jonathon walked by Jack to ask, "How many jumps had you had?"

"Enough to know not to spend the next few hours on learning" said Jack.

The doors opened to sunset, and the cool weather, as the two Russians were first, Alexei didn't look so good, but slowly went up to the tower, as the jump turbine went into action, it was deafening, the noise, as Jack put in some ear plugs, as each agent stepped into a flight suit, special forces members were all over the place, except for any of his black ops guys, they all were wearing the UN patches. Jack looked up on his phone, about this and what to do, a video showed a brief five minutes instruction, as he zipped up his suit, each received a helmet and goggles, gloves were offered, but no one took them, except Jack, as it was a test.

The strong seven were ready, and they climbed up to the finishing tower, to the top, Vadim, was first, as he dove head first into the fan, his arms out and legs up, he held his head and rode it out till the horn sounded as he made the chute ejection gesture. He was pulled out, and next was Alexei, who struggled, but completed it, as he was led out and collapsed. A medical team came to his aid. then Thomas, then Jonathon, Ben, Steven, then it was Jack's turn, he knew he had never done it before, but he was ready, and took a leap of faith, he leveled off his momentum, and moving his hand he could feel a turn, he pulled back, to adjust the cruise speed, he put his hands on his butt, he took a dive, deeper, as he tested the machine, to level off, he gestured the pulling the cord.

He was pulled over, by the lead instructor to say, "This isn't your first time, good job, you're the best so far."

Jack smiled, as he stepped off, as the machine was shut off. Jack stepped back up the tower, to see Vadim, with Alexei, being carted off, then it was Vadim who was first on the chute ride, moving the parachute through its course, as Jack watched all the others, to touch down, it was Jack's turn, he was harnessed up, he lifted off, using his hands to guide the parachute through the paces, he took the outside course, using long swings, he acted like he was a pro, as he swooped in, to a perfect landing on the spot.

"Agent's listen up go in and rest up, have dinner, and we will get you when were ready for you. The agents fell into the line, and went in.

Four hours later, an agent came to suite one, on the girls floor, and summoned him to come, Jack was contemplating going back for some more with Michelle, but got up and followed the agent out, up to the men's floor where they picked up the six others, they were all wondering why was it taking so long, there was no answer, as finally they were escorted to the hanger, where they saw a weird sight, five agents were all laid out, Jack thought, "Are they asleep, or what?"

The French Professor, said, "Alright, get up rest time is over, as they staggered to get up, for him, to say, "Do you want to quit?"

"No" said Hendon, looking at the other agents, who looked at him in disgust, for having to wait.

"Alright other agents put on your flight suit, they did it quickly, to be ready, to hear, "Now we're going to repack your chutes, each of you go to a table that has a UN member, Jack fell in with his group, while the five others took their time, as Jack watched Steven, but was assisted by a jump pro, till it was set, then he had help putting it on, it wasn't so bad, until his hands were tied from behind, he cliched his fists apart, as they tied it tight, as the ambush took affect all agents went down quickly and then their ankles, lastly was a blindfold. Jack was hit and kicked and beat up then placed on some machine, whereas he and the fellow agents spun around for about a hundred times, Jack felt it to be like a massive washing machine, he and others fell into each other, then rattled, they were led into a cargo plane, and Jack fell over someone else, guys were getting sick, but it calmed down, as the plane, taxied, to hear, "There are three drop zones, aim for the furthest one from your escape point, to the southwest, each drop zone has your directions, futherest away is the hardest, closer to the base the easiest, good luck."

Those were the last words spoken, except Steven the Australian, who was lying on Jack, to say, "Sorry mate, good luck to you".

Jack turned his wrists, to wiggle out of his restraints, as has his blind fold still part way on, as other guys were about the same. Jack noticed the plane was going back and forth in the air, the ramp was down, as the first guy was the example, they lifted him up, cut his hands, and then pushed him out, as others were launched out the back, as Steven was pulled off of Jack and out he went, Jack sat up against the reserve chute, as he could smell and then see fear, as men were fighting to stay on as they were thrown out, there was a pause, as the plane turned around for another run, this time a hand grabbed at Jack, to hear, "Leave him to the last, get the stragglers, as Jack watched as Alexander was not wanting to do this, as he held on for dear life, to hear, "Leave him be, get the gun."

Jack watched as Alexander went to the ramp door, "hold him were past the jump zone".

Jack looked around to see three others and Alexander, being held at the door. The plane turned around again, on the final run to hear, "This is it the best of the best all of you get out."

A hand helped Jack who was free, sent him outward, he collided with Vadim, but got his bearings. Off to his right he saw something go straight down in a hurry, as his chute was open, thinking he won't make it, out of the corner of his eye he saw a beacon of light, it was faint, but pulled hard to go left, and he went upside down.

On the ground, troops were scattering as sirens went off, Casey sat with Paul Clark, to say, "Thank god it wasn't Jack, did you see that the guy did a cannonball to the ground, I don't want to go over there it must be some sight" said Casey holding binoculars to his face following Jack, to say, "Did you see that he just done a loop to loop, he is gliding like a pro, after he is on the ground retrieve that beacon."

"Already on that, Kenny is up the tree, and when he passes by we will pull it."

A radio squawked, to say, "We need your troops down here to pick up the pieces, a lot of these volunteers are in a disarray."

"Yeah, we will be there" said Casey.

"What do you think it's a trap" said Paul Clark.

"Don't know, but were obligated to help them, call in everyone, have Kenny pull it and meet up with us, what about his partner?"

"Keep them together, let's go" said Casey.

Meanwhile Jack was having too much fun, gliding around, after the upside down move, he knows he was being watched and tracked, he saw the beacon getting closer, but a little too far, he kept moving left to right, trying to keep up, and go farther, as others in his group, were landing below him, he was just above the tree line, he felt a push of wind, that carried him to the beacon.

Down below his team looked up to say, "He made it, he is incredible" said Paul Clark.

Jack saw something, someone, as his feet was at the tree, he held it up, to soar down in the clearing, to the round target, and the bull's eye. He put it down, he turned and was pulling in the chute, he rolled it up, as he pulled off his pack, he set it on a metal stake, then gathered the chute, and rolled and folded to pull it back together and back into the pack, he detached the reserve, and attached it to his pack, then placed it back on the metal bar.

Jack looked around for the clue pack, it was near where he landed, he counted eleven other packs, as he opened one up, knowing people were watching him, he decided to move easterly, as his first clue suggested, Jack was on the move, he was running, behind him, he could sense he was being followed, he picked up his pace, his compass was on course, he calculated how far he need to go, he was still running, to his point, where another clue was on a wooden stake, he grabbed it, and doubled back, as he ran, that it was north to the road, cross over the road, and up the hill to the coordinances.

Jack was a stud. And those behind him, were way behind, as others came over to watch Jack, in UN,HQ.

Meanwhile, Casey's team, arrived on scene, as trucks and lights were brought in, Gia with Drew, Craig and Paul, Casey met up with the ground commander, who said, "You were referred to us, that you work with this all the time, most of my ground forces are green, take your time, you have seven right?"

"That's right Sir" said Casey.

"You don't have to call me Sir, you're a gentleman."

"Yes, we will find the parts, any leads?"

"Yeah, check down by the stream, they say he hit and went in every direction, does your team have night vision?"

"Yes, we will put it on, if you can kill the lights."

"We will and we alerted CIS, to assist you."

Jack was coming close to the road, as he slowed, to see trucks coming and going, when it was clear, he sprinted over it, and down into the stream, he hopped over rocks, he cruised up the hill, to the stake, he went up to it, grabbed it, and then, went back to the bushes, to read the clue, the clue said, go due south, to the road, catch a truck and back into the base and you will win this challenge".

Jack was already running, down the hill, across the stream, along the road, to see an oncoming truck, it past, and he ran behind it, to affix to the bumper, and held on, they came to a stop, and then through the gate, it went to the hanger, it honked, the door went up, and in it went, past his plane, as Jack waved to Jim, Mark and Mike, just watched him, as it turned the corner, it parked, two men got out, and when one came around the corner, Jack looped his arm around him, to hear "Bravo, you got the base commander, Jack let him go."

The Base Commander looked at him to say, "Did you cheat, it's only been an hour?"

"Jack you're dismissed, put your packs on the table" said the French Professor, to add, "We will contact you when we will meet tomorrow, good job."

Jack said, "Where's my escort?"

"That's not needed anymore, we know who was behind it, so go relax."

Jack pushed through the door, he steps down, to see an empty food court, but decides to see if his place is open, he swiped his card, and the door opened, to see it empty, he turned to hear "Hold on were open, come on in" said a food service worker.

Jack entered, to see the chef, who said, "Is training over?"

"Don't know, doesn't look like there is a special."

"Don't worry about that, we have anything and everything, from prime rib to pizza what do you want?"

"Prime rib, what's that?"

"The best cut of meat, how do you want it?"

Jack looked at him, to say, "Like with a baked potato, and all the fixings."

"Yes, with all the fixings".

"Alright, I'd like to have that made, with a beef dipping sauce, minus the salt, like au jus, a baked potato, with butter sour cream and chives, eggs poached, can I have six?"

"Absolutely."

"Oh, one more thing, can I have a couple of artichokes?"

"Peeled and cored?"

"Nah, just whole, can I have it with melted butter, and a lobster tail?"

"Hungry?"

"Yeah, could I also have oysters on the half shell?"

"How would you like them?"

"Um, with some fresh lemons and limes, jalapeno's julienned, mustard and horseradish sauce." Said Jack.

"Yes sir, it will take about twenty minutes."

"Make it thirty, I'll go clean up and see you soon."

"You got a deal, but we do have room service, shall we just deliver it to you?"

"Yes fine whatever." Said Jack, leaving with four milk's as he swiped his card.

Casey scanned the area to see Kenny and Gia approach, to report, as he handed Casey the beacon, to say, "Jack took them for a ride, and ran the course, a couple of the special forces thought he was going to walk, and left them in the dust."

"Good, put on your night vision, and I need you in a tree, use your ear piece, and keep me informed."

"What will I be looking for?" asked Kenny.

"Oh, sorry, we got a man down."

"Does this have something to do with it" said Gia, pointing to the severed man, at the waist?"

"Yeah, do you have a poncho?"

"Sure" she said as she pulled it out and placed it over the body, to hear, "You're pretty strong about that?"

"You get used to it living on a military base, and I always wanted to be doing this."

"Well you are, and you're doing a great job, where do you think the rest of him is?"

"Probably in the stream, or downstream." Said Gia.

"Your strong."

"Yes I am, thanks." said Gia.

Jack entered his room, to see Michelle attack him, as he held her, he said, "It's alright, you can let go, I need to take a shower."

"Here let me help you" she said sweetly, as Jack undressed, to hop into the shower, to hear, "You were right, it was poison, and Debby was so helpful, we heard, that there was an accident in the field."

"Well I'm alright" said Jack as he finished, dried off, and dressed to the clothes Michelle set out, she said, "Debby wants to see you later?"

"That's fine, do you want to have dinner with me?"

"Sure let's go."

"Nah, it's coming in the form of room service," said Jack.

Inside the prop plane, Jim was watching the field maneuvers to see men crossing themselves, some were working together, to remark "Jack you did that in record time, congrats man, Mark sat next to him, as Mike and Jesse, went out into the field, with the base commander, Mikes credentials recognized him as a Medical examiner, or so as what Mike put in the UN system. To get out of the plane and help out, knowing Jack was in and safe.

Mike and Jesse, with a body bag, took the hummer out to the war zone, people were all over the place, as the two men rode in the back, as the Commander turned to say, "You guys are way to efficient, whomever you support is one lucky agent, usually we get agents that get dropped off, and are left on their own, so who is it?"

Jesse looked at Mike and back at each other to say "Jim"

"Jim Carmichael, the former UN spy, he is here?"

The two just sat quiet, while the Commander just talked, till they arrived, Mike got out, to see Ben Hiltz, who went by, for Mike to say, "So how long does this usually take?"

"Usually four hours to all night, but tonight, the record was shattered, to a staggering one hour and four minutes, or one hour thirty four minutes."

"I'd say that record was destroyed, and by who?" asked Mike.

"By Jack Cash, you know him?"

"Yeah I heard of him" said Mike as Jesse said, "Me too".

Casey saw the Commander, and then Mike and Jesse, but held his tongue, to hear Captain Casey, this is Mister Mike Adams, Medical Examiner, and his assistant, sorry I didn't get your name?"

"His name is Jesse" said Mike as he shook Casey's hand, as he passed the beacon over to him, he put in his pocket, to be led over to Gia who had collected the top and bottom, while Mike looked at the body minus the legs below the knees, to say, "Any idea where the lower legs are at Miss?"

Mike looked at her as she said, "Is there anything else?"

"Just wondering how's Jack?"

"Jack who?" she said kiddingly.

She threw her hands in the air, to say "Fuck off", as she went over by Casey to get away from Mike.

Casey saw the Commander take off, then approached Mike to say "What's going on Buddy, what did you say to Gia?"

"Just asked her about Jack?"

"Just leave her alone, and get back to work."

"Yes Captain" said Mike, innocently.

CH 7

A son finds out the truth and a father finds a son

Next morning, it was Saturday, day 6, Jack awoke early, with Debby on one side, and Michelle was in the front, he was resting comfortably, after a night of passion, and fun, with no stress or games. Jack felt good, he got up, dressed, and went out to the lobby, then up the stairs and around the corner to room number one, on the men's level, where he saw Professor Goins, who said, "Class and all schedule events cancelled for the day, due to the scandal, and were still missing men from last night, I wish they could all be like you?"

"Really?" said Jack.

"No, as for the rest of the day, take it off, and go out and support the girls, today they start the soccer matches."

Jack left, and went back down, the stairs at the bottom, was two glass doors, as he swiped his pass, they opened for him, as he was back on the women's floor, and into the morning mess, which was full of familiar faces, from yesterday, as they all ate, as Freya, said, "So what do you have to do today?"

"Nothing as I know, I was thinking of watching you all play?"

"That would be great", said Kellie, and you can root for the US of A, I mean us," as Jack took the line, to order, "Three egg white omelet with scallions and parmesan cheese, with a side of four pieces of bacon, and crispy hash browns." It was made for him, as he made it to the milks, he took two each, white and chocolate, swiped his card, and took a seat surrounded by his fellow admirers, namely Lea Lucas, a changed woman, with Kellie, and Roxy, Jill smiled seeing him, she took a place where it was empty, Jack looked at the clock, it read 06:50, and just like that all the girls cleared out, not a soul was around, so he went back in the room, took off his clothes for another round with only Debby, as Michelle was dressed in all yellow, and was leaving.

Meanwhile Jesse, went back into the UN to help assist Jim, work on the damaged flight simulator, as Miss Hohlstein, came in, to see the two of them working to say, "You look very familiar, what is your name?"

Jesse gets up, to wipe off his hands to say, "My name is Jesse James Rogers."

"And what of your mother, who is she, and where does she live?"

Jesse says, "Her name is Natasha Rogers."

"The investigative reporter?"

"Yeah, I guess you can call her that" said Jesse.

Miss Hohlstein ran this information on her I-Book, to see that it was indeed his biological mother, and that his last name was Rogers, to say "Who is your father?"

"Colonel Tom Rogers, of the Army, but was killed in action, when I was very young."

But when she ran his information, it came up with a match, as she saw Jack Cash, a perfect match, she kept that to herself, to say, "I want you to visit Clarance he will come by and visit with you?, is that alright?"

"Yeah sure."

Some time had passed as Clarance walked up, to say, "Can I have a word with you?"

"Yeah sure" said Jesse. Not knowing what was going on.

As Clarance led him to a private room, and to a table with a desk, as Jesse took a chair, as Clarance closed the door, to say, "I have been asked to acquire a time line of why you're here and why?"

Jesse was very cooperative, in saying, "Well not much to tell really, where do you want me to start?"

"At the beginning", said Clarance, looking him over, as he set the recorder on play, to hear, "Well I was born, in Seattle Washington, and then, from the earliest time, we moved every year."

"Why is that?" asked Clarance as he sat across from him, to hear, "Well it was my mom, she told me my father was killed, so we were searching for something, I just don't know?"

Clarance looked at Jesse to see he wasn't lying, and that there was something going on, to say, "Tell me of your mother?"

"Not much to say, she is a journalist, and now lives in Mobile, Alabama." As Clarance looked at last known whereabouts, was Washington DC, to say,"So what does Washington DC mean to you?"

Jesse shakes his head, to say, "I don't know?" Clarance knew he was sincere, and realized that Jesse must have been brainwash, as it appeared to be some sort of block, to say, "So when was the last time you saw your mom?"

He thinks about it for a minute, to say, "My graduation from MIT.

"That was some time ago, where is she at now?"

"I think Mobile, she told me she had discovered a conspiracy, and she was going to get to the bottom of that."

"Fine, were done", said Clarance, who turned off the recorder, to hear in Clarance's ear, "Can you come by my office later, after your done with all that."

"Yes, Ma'am." said Clarance.

The two exited the room, as Jesse went back to work, and Clarance went to see Miss Hohlstein, he was let in, and he took a seat, to hear, "So what did you get?"

"He had been brainwash, no real memory of his early life, none at MIT, and only to see his mother occasionally, no, we need to un wash his brain, do you know anyone?"

"Yeah a doctor, and a machine" said Meredith.

"I'd say that would be your next step, as for being a double agent, doubt full, he is just too loyal, it's like he was a calmer version of Jack."

"Really, alright, so how is it with the Chinese, their country is asking their return, get anything?"

"Just about there with Col Tam-Lu, give me another day, then she should be able to go."

Jesse came back to see Jim, who said, "What was that all about?" asked Jim.

"I don't rightly know, but maybe something to do with my mom?".

Inside Suite one, on the women's floor, Jack rose, got dressed, to see it said it was 10:05, and out the door he went, and out of the UN, to the field, where, the huge field was broken up into four fields, a running clock, was moving, as another set of games he had many places to stand, as he was on the field, seeing, both tough girls, Peleruth and Protima, running up and down the field, and then over he went, to the other two games, Honduras, led by the sexy Erica Adams, versus the ice princess, Rebecca Adams, as she scored to make it 1-1, tie.

On the tarmac, at the UN was a single Lear jet, with CIA markings, it taxied, then went inside, and parked. A Doctor with distinction was whisked inside, and taken to a secure room. After a break, the curious, young Jesse, asked to see Miss Hohlstein, and was led down to a secure room, where he was led into a chair, restrained to say,"Hey what is going on here?"

A doctor, was sent in to administer a cocktail of mind numbing drugs, while they waited word was sent up to the upper observation room, where Miss Hohlstein was waiting for the drugs to work. Wondering "What his story?"

"You're going to love this, he is the geek, who tunes the super car?" said Jim, what's his story anyway?"

"Says here", as she shows Jim his folder, "He is of only two in history to graduate first in his class at M.I.T, with a perfect grade point average."

"Yeah, so what?" said Jim.

"Well he is was only seventeen."

"Really, so how did he get here?", for Jack."

"He was recruited to be a technical designer of his car, as he quickly worked a prototype, as he was in California with Ben Hiltz, it was there he excelled, but according to Clarance the young Jesse has mind blocks, and the crazy part, he didn't even know that where he lived at, or his friends, he says his mom asked him to keep her name quiet, we picked her up, but she escaped, something is going on here, and I'm going to get to the bottom of this," said Meredith.

"It's getting better and better"said a new visitor it was Lisa Curtis, as the two acknowledged each other.

"So Jesse took leave, from California, and goes to Florida, for a day, to Quantico, on base, then he goes to Mobile, to meet his mother, only to fly back to California, and back to work" said Lisa as a report.

"So he is indeed looking for something or someone" said Meredith.

"Yep, that's about it."

"Did you check to see his credentials?"

"Yes, the base commander, told me he wanted to transfer, to Quantico, for a new assignment, to work for Jack Cash."

"So Mister Jesse Rogers, why are you in Mobile, and at the house of Jack Cash, whom you just transferred to his team to say out loud,"Ramon, can you get on the sat phone and get in touch with Mitzi Long, and find out why she is not here?"

"What shall I do with you" said Meredith, out of respect to Jesse, especially if in fact he is Jack's son, only to see the doctor, who said, "He is ready."

"Good move him into the white room and hook him up" she said loudly, to add, "Then let me know, I want to be there."

"Yes Ma'am," said the doctor below.

To herself, she said "What are you holding, and why risk your career to go to Jack's house, and who is your mother" as she opened the file for Jack's wives, and known mistress's, not a single one was near the age to be his mother, just what is going on."

Lisa was called first, as she summoned, the others, Meredith and Jim and she went down into the control lab, to see Jesse was confined to a single chair, arms and legs bounded in a sitting position, and an old looking hair dryer on his head that resembled a helmet, that had hundreds of leads, coming from, it.

The doctor started the process, as the information streamed in. deep in the sub- conscious, The guard said, "Come on in ladies, who were you here to see today?"

"Oh I'm Brenda White from Oklahoma, and this is my friend Marie- Elizabeth Duke, the socialite."

"And who is she here to see?"

"No one, she is just along for the ride" said Brenda as Marie leaned up against the wall, to hear, "You can join them if you like?"

"Nah, I'm fine."

"Really, from where I'm standing, your super fine."

"Thanks but not interested."

"What would it take?"

"More money than you have" she said annoyed.

"Listen Miss, I wasn't asking for me, I'm married, but maybe for another prisoner?"

"What do you mean" she said as she came closer, to see him, she smiled.

"Well just like your friend, we try to recruit college girls, who want to make some extra money, to be with a harden criminal."

Instantly Meredith knew where this was heading, and it intrigued her, as for Lisa, she was just listening to the audio tape play and hit record.

"Wait are you telling me, that my friend, is not seeing her boyfriend, but a harden criminal?"

"Yep."

"Whoa wait, that's disgusting, what does she get out of it?, some disease?"

"On the contrary, most of the criminals are disease free and live a clean life, so actually they may be cleaner than the local guy you might meet at a bar, or you're social club."

She looked at him, to process what he was saying, to say, as she was thinking about it, to say, "So how much does she get?"

"Five thousand.dollars."

"Five thousand dollars, you're kidding me?"

"What does that appeal you?"

"A little prostitution is illegal, the last time I checked."

"Now this isn't what this is about, it paid community service" said the guard.

"How's that?"

"Well in our efforts to calm down our male prisoners, were allotted the ability to allow congeal visits, and for your time and service we will pay you a professional wage."

"Really, and how long would it be?"

"Depends on the person, and what they're in for and how dangerous they are?"

She stood thinking about how her mom would kill her, and was starting to like the deal, to see the guard, who said, "Look I can see your thinking about it, how about I sweeten the pot to Ten Thousand, you look like your worth that and much more."

"Alright" she said with a smile.

"Great, step up, and let me see your ID, for pay purposes."

"What are you paying me with a check?"

"Nah, just cash, untraceable, it protects you and us."

"Good, now there isn't any camera's in there or what?" she asked.

"No, how it works depending on the prisoner, but, you will, leave your coat, and purse with the guard at the end of this hall, and wait in a room, that you can see the head of the watching guard, for your first visit, the prisoner will be sitting in a chair, locked down."

"Sounds private?"

"Yes, for your security and that of the prisoner, do you want me to choose who is next or do you want to decide?"

"I'd like to know who is the most feared, and the biggest, baddest of them all."

Together Meredith and Lisa, said, "Jack Cash."

"We have one, but he is in special lock up."

"What's his name?"

"We call him Jesse James the outlaw."

"Sounds fierce, I want him."

The guard looked at her, to say,"That will require the wardens sign off, it may take some time?"

"I'll wait, if he is the biggest and baddest, what's he like, what's is he in for?"

"Well all I can tell you is that he is most feared when he is out on the grounds, he is into the mediation crap, all about mind and body control, as for baddest, I saw him take out ten prisoners in a riot, and subdue them to avert the riot, if he isn't in isolation, he is fighting."

"Sounds like a saint in here."

"You could say that, as for where and what he did to get here, well it says its military related, and that's it."

"What is he like?"

"What do I know lady, he is no Dali lama, all you're doing is screwing the guy."

"You're right, sorry", she went and took a seat, thinking "Wow, there on to something here."

An hour went by, when her name was called, as the guard motioned her to go through the doors, she was feeling very excited, with all the danger, and being with a bad boy, maybe he will be like some tattooed, huge giant, who is hung like a horse" she thought, as she saw her friend coming to her she said, "Now I know your secret" said Marie.

"As I do yours" said Brenda, to add "I know, it's been a while go easy on him, both of you."

"Coat and purse, any loose items" asked the guard.

"Are you going with me?"

"No Ma'am", as another guard, looked her over, and led her down to a room, to yell, "Open Twelve."

"Shall I undress for him now."

"If you like, but not necessary, most girls just remove their panties, like you're wearing a skirt, so you can keep it private from watching eyes", as he points a round.

"You seem alright."

"I'm married too, but some are just pervert's, so watch out for them."

"You're talking about the guards?"

"Yeah the guards, the prisoners are harmless, they just sit in the chair, and let the girls have their way with them."

"Really, and what about the prisoner I choose?"

"He is the bad of the baddest."

"No I mean how many girls visit him?"

"Oh, none, this is a special circumstance, as you can see we doubled the guard."

"What should I do?"

"Just like I said, there won't be much conversation, you could talk with him, but it's useless, he knows you're here for one purpose only, so there won't be much chit chat."

"How long do I have?"

"Depends, the warden gave us two hours for transport and delivery, but I'd say you're new to all of this and he has been celibate, perhaps thirty minutes?"

"Sounds fair."

"Go have a seat in the chair, and when you hear, "Prisoner ready, get up and go to a corner, then we will cuff him down to the chair, and take off his hood, then you have thirty minutes to have your way with him, as for his clothing leave it on, all you have to do is unzip him."

"Wait, before you looked me over why?"

"Because you're probably the prettiest girl that has ever come down here, so I can see why he was granted this visit, normally it takes three years of good behavior and lots of bank to have a girl, so I'd say you're making his world, oh and one more thing, if at any time you feel threaten, just call or scream and the guards will come in and subdue him."

Marie, watched as the nice guard closed the door, as she sat, thinking about her decision, she was single, and tired of the rich boys games, maybe this could be what she needs, besides sounds like his has a reputation, and she liked that, in some ways he is like he is society, all the prisoners look up to him, and the guards all fear him."

She awoke out of her day dream to hear, "Prisoner ready."

"Open the door."

Marie went to the far corner, to see a medium sized man dressed in all red, with the zipper flap, he was of medium build, his exposed arms were small in size and bore no tattoo's, that she could see, as he waddled in, he sat down, the black hood covered his head, she felt bad for him, but her excitement level rose, like never before, to heights that far surpassed any other experienced she had ever known, to see the final cuffs were in place on the firmly secured chair, the last minute the hood came off, to hear, "He's all yours."

She saw a beautiful face, shaved head, and beautiful chin line, he was beautiful to look at, his eyes were closed, as she knew she was dripping, as she came closer to him, she said, "Hi, my name is Marie, you are so handsome."

No response, he acted like he was a zombie, she came closer, to see that the guard was looking in, she faced the guard's view, to pull down her very wet panties, the anticipation was overwhelming, as she said, "What would you like first a kiss" she said as she got closer, to feel his breath, it increased a bit, to kiss him on the cheek, she lowered herself back to the guard, to rub her breast against his bounded hand, as she said, I'll take them out for you to touch if you like, still he was silent, eyes closed, realizing the guard was right, he justs sits there, so she went around and knelt, unzipped him, and went in, and found it, she wiggled it out to look at it in amazement, to say, "You are hung like a horse, oh, my god?"

She began to work on it, as her excitement overcame her, as she worked on it, placed on protection provided for her, as she stood up and turned around, and lowered herself onto him, slowly as he stretched her out, but her enjoyment level was so severe, she erupted, trying to contain her excitement, half hour was over just like that, as she heard, "Guards coming in."

She got off of him, to turn to see the huge purple monster throbbing, as did the two guards, as she backed up to the corner, to watch the guards try to put it away, as one said to the other, "Do you see the size of that thing?"

"It's huge, you're not going to be able to get it back, let's let her get it off."

The guard turned to say, "Alright Miss you have another hour, good luck."

The guards left for her to regain some composure, she was totally turned on, and wanted to tear her clothes off, only seeing those perverts in the window, calmed those idea's, she looked at what he had going on, and it was like nothing she had ever seen before, she touched and tried to put her thumb, and fingers around it, it was so large, to think, "This is every girls dream", this time she faced him, and knelt inside the huge chair, and re-inserted him into her, as she did all the work, but this time Jack awoke, as his eyes were open, she leaned in and kissed him, he tried to kiss back, she did it again, this time parted his lips to touch his tongue, she felt as if he was seeking love, and passion, as she slowed the momentum, to feel each stroke, and as he went deeper he hit the right place, and she flooded him with fluids, as she let it go, to saturate him, to think, "That's, my first real orgasm", she was beaming, as she continued to kiss him, trying to be more intimate, and enjoying the moment, as another hour went by, to hear, "Guards coming in."

She held onto to him, to the very last second, as the guards had to pull her off, to hear, "I think it's worse,"

"He'll just have to live with it."

"Shit look at him, were going to have to hose him off."

She was clutching herself, thinking of going after him, feeling sorry for leaving him in that manner. She collapsed, to the floor, her panties were useless to put on.

Over the next couple of month's her and Brenda came to visit, like clockwork, every Saturday, she wanted to visit, more but he was in isolation, it was always the same results, two hours and he still was stiff, this next visit everything changed, instead of sex and put him through that misery, she brought him a book and handed it to him, a classic Sweet Endeavors, he said, "Thank you."

She leap up from her chair, and hugged him, and kissed him to say, "You speak?"

"Absolutely, when necessary."

"Excellent, My name is Marie, and your name is Jesse, I'm of society and principle, I could put money on your books."

"No, don't do that."

"Why honey, I want to take care of you, I love you, and I want to marry you."

"No don't do that."

"I will and you can't stop me, now, you're talking when is your birthday? how old are you, you must be my age?"

"Stop, with the questions" said Jack.

"Listen, my boyfriend, I have a surprise for you, on my next visit, next Saturday, I'm bringing a friend of mine, and I promise you that we will solve your erection problem, you need to stop being in your head so much, and focus on the pleasure of touch, will you do that?"

"Yes, for you" said Jack.

The next week came, right on time, this time he was led into a bed, and they tedered his wrists to the ends to allow for four feet of room, he was stripped, for the first time Jack felt good, and somewhat free, the door opened, and Marie and her friend Mercedes, came in to see Jack was ready lying on the bed, both girls stripped, Jack showed he was ready, foreplay was quick, as each girl was extremely excited, Jack twisted the lines, to enter each of them from behind, he liked the tight suppose virgin blonde, who was far from that, to Marie who was ready for him, the two went at it like rabbits till he erupted inside her. Marie rode him out, till he collapsed on her, and still was throbbing inside of her, he slept on her stomach and breasts, as a guard watched, but at this point she no longer cared.

The next week she came to visit him, and she was told he was gone, she spent the next twenty years searching for him, only to track him to Mobile, where he lives now. Along the way, she became a free-lance writer and a champion of prisoner welfare and causes, and of DNA testing.

Along the way, when she was close, he was moved, that's when she set out on a crusade, with a son in tow and an absent husband, she even changed her name.

Lisa saw the data she needed and told everyone to clear out, namely Jim, to see Meredith as they looked at what it said, Marie-Elizabeth Duke, legally changed her name to Natasha Rogers, when she married Captain Tom Rogers of the Military police of the Army, who was killed in the line of fire, now receives his pension, she bore a single son, named Jesse James Rogers, he grew up to be a very smart kid, that went on to MIT, at age fifteen, and graduated by the age of seventeen, with an impeccable record, and was recruited to spy research and development, while having no idea his biological father is Jack Cash, super spy."

Outside, of the UN, for the women, it was the soccer field as the first round games had concluded, it was the surprise Protima with nine goals for Brazil, and Kellie Ryan of the US over Kendra's Russian team, 3-1, in addition, Joana, Z'sofia, Peleruth, Erica, Nina Ivan, Lea, Dana and Simone Bailey as the first round winners, as they all headed off to lunch, as Lea caught up with her new man Jack, to say, "Did you see that goal?"

"Yeah, it was a tough one you or Jill, who seems somewhat out of it?" Jack went to lunch with the girls, they all walked in together, Jack went upstairs to check on the status of the others, as Professor Goins, said, "It's still the same, we have some missing?"

After lunch it was game two, it was a tough battle in game one, Portugal, Joana, playing like a pro player, her pastimes, game, and beat Protima's Brazil, 4-1. Mexico, Freya, bounced back from a morning loss, to beat, Simone, with Chile, 11-4,the closest game was the US 1- and South Africa 0, Kellie, loved to boot the ball, so did Argentina's Dana Scott, the large woman was a Diva. In addition to them, Canada, and Darlene picked up her first win, The model Nina Toop, won with Belarus, 10-4 over Poland, Honduras was 2-0, with a win over Latvia, 5-2. France and Lea, inspired by Jack beat Croatia, and was 2-0. Spain took New Zealand 7-3, thus thrusting Esmeralda, into the spot light. And finally the game of the day, was Australia, Roxy Carr, versus, Kendra, with Russia, as Australia, won, 3-2 in Overtime. Jack and the girls went back to their suites, as along the way, Kellie said, "Let's go some rounds?, I'm really into to this new sport, yeah, I know, who are my reinforcements, anyone?" no one commented for Kellie to continue, to say,"No, what I was going to say, was "I'll come to you, so either it's you and I or?"

"Nah, I'm just going to rest up, see you tomorrow?" said Jack.

The week ended, its Sunday Morning, day 7, all the men were finally accounted for, and time for change, it was uncovered that Alexei and Raisa were behind the plot to poison Jack, and if it hadn't been for Alexander, apparent suicide, he was the man behind it all. The super spy ranking were out and posted, on the top at number one was Jack Cash, at 846 points, followed by Vadim, the Russian, at 325, who escaped any involment in the scandal what's so ever, so much so he distanced himself from Alexei. Tad Jones, the sniper did well in the games, to get 310, for third. Carlos Gomez was fourth, at 295, and fifth was Steven Smith, the Australian, at 212. As for the bottom, it was determined, that a minimum of thirty points was necessary, to stay in the Academy, so, with 26 points, was Stephen Moss, and at 22 points was Sean Calvin, both spouting off that France was their new place of work, to include Joel Robbe, he was to injured to continue, plus he was holding up further training as he was lost, somewhere. And his point total was a dismal 4 overall. On to the women, with 12 points total, it was Nika Kenna, as Romania, was excluded to play in the tournament. And thus she was sent along her way. As for the spouses, a real favorite was Alexandra Lucien, who was Alexei's protégé, and wanted to stay, with anyone, but she too was radioactive, in that she only spoke Russian, so she was out. The remaining Russian women all said, "No", as for the Nina's, "No", as for Rebecca, she wasn't having anything to do with her. Now on to Louie, who beat up Carlos, and Carlos, took him out by breaking his right arm, thus putting Louie in a cast, it also required two weeks of immovability, so he is bed ridden, and thus decided to go home, but his girl, Alessia, wanted to stay, and Gordon Roderick, took her in.

For Chloe Ryan, she wanted out, and become a wife for Jack, it was approved, so she was out. She was going back to England to pack.

For the first time, Jack gets to visit his team, he escorted Chloe out, she was tearful, in her goodbyes, he was a pro at getting around.

Jack led Chloe out to the squadron, to the supersonic jet waiting to take off. Jack entered the place where his plane was and the strike team intact and his team lined up, the team leader Mitzi was first, she hugged and kissed him to say, "Nice to see you, boss."

Next to her was Jim, with a smile on his face, the two shook hands, then it was Rick Teal, to whom Jack said "Where's Brian, and where is my rifle?"

"He is in the field, and yep its inside, if you want to see it?"

"Sure in a minute, as he hugged Trixie, a little more than Mitzi and she returned the favor as well. Next was Tami, who also hugged and kissed him.

Jack next shook hands with Mark, then Mike who he just waved to, to say, "Where's Jesse?"

"Oh he is in the UN working, said Mike, proudly.

"What's going on here?"

That's when they all begin to talk at once, for Jack to say, "Hold it, Mitzi, you first."

"Later in your cabin."

"Alright, so he turns to the strike team, to shake Casey's hand, to say, "Are you guys bored yet?"

"Nah, this has been a very interesting week, to say the least."

"Well that's good to hear, is the UN feeding you well?"

"Yeah, too well" said Paul in his deep southern accent.

He sees Drew, and Craig, then he stops at Kenny to say, "Didn't I see you in that tree out there on Friday night?"

He shakes his head no.

Then on to his newest team members, it was Gia, who embraced him, then kissed him as well, for Jack to say, "Is the team treating you with respect?"

"Yes, and much more?"

"Good, and you like it?"

"Yes, it's what every girl dreams about."

"That's nice to hear," as everyone broke up, and Jack followed Jim in, to the cage, which Jim opened up for him, to show him, on the table in a newly built frame for the two sniper rifles, for Jack to say, "What a beauty, and I gather the ammo box is full?"

"Yep, straight from the United States."

"Nice, thanks for getting it back, what did you do with the million in cash?"

"It's here in the lock up, with your sword, and jeweled box."

Jack left him talking, and went into his room, to close the door, to see Mitzi, to say, "The flight simulator was broken, and Him and Jim are fixing it in the UN."

"That's great and know he will do good. To add, so any news on the home front?"

"Other than the bomb you dropped in Moscow, is now being claimed as an earthquake, to keep it under wraps what really happened, oh, and one more thing, Belarus, and Latvia, and western Russia has allocate forces to track down Varfolomey, and the terrorist agent Fyodor, also escaped, but as like everyone else, their waiting till you get out for a showdown."

"Here I thought I was courting a new bride?"

"Is that still a possibility" asked Mitzi.

"Sure why not, I have my wives blessing so I'll make it happen, I'll make her number seventeen, as for Miss Ryan, she is number sixteen."

"What's going on the inside" asked Mitzi.

"Oh you know, after the apparent suicide of Alexander, and the scandal of the poison, Alexei was taken out, leaving us with eighteen solid, with two weeks to go, how does Trixie feel about going in?"

"She is ready, and from that hug and kiss, I hope you saw it too."

"I did, it was pretty clever of you getting Debby to be inside for me," said Jack.

"Actually this is not her first go around, she was here for the President," said Mitzi.

"Alright, run along I need to check my phone, and send in Gia."

"Yes sir."

Jack opened his phone, to see all the calls, he changed it to text form from voice, to read those from all of his wives, who were anxious about coming home, and if their invited to the wedding, he responded and sent a quick message, to read "I love you, miss you and when possible will be back soon, and sent it to each of them, changing it up for each woman, he saved all the rest, none from Clarance, he closed it up to hear a knock on the door, for him to say, "Come in."

Gia walked in, and then closed the door, to face him, she stood at attention.

"At ease, first off the Commander of the base wanted to commend you for the collection of the body parts of Alexander, here is a medal, do you want me to pin it on you."

"I hope so, don't worry I won't report you for sexual harassment?"

Jack stood up to look at her to say, "What are you talking about?"

"Oh nothing. I was just thinking of how, I'm tired of boys, when I can have a real man, I saw your show on Saturday, I'd like to jump with you someday."

"We can make that happen," said Jack fumbling with the pin, and touching her left breast.

"Now your acting like a scared boy, just pin me or bend me over, sorry did I just say?"

Jack pushed it in as he reached in, to secure the two clasps.

"There that wasn't too bad, you only fondled one side, you have to work on the other to even them out, as his phone was ringing, he looked at it on the bed, to see it was Lisa, to say, "Look, maybe later, I have to take this call."

"Sure, you know how to work up a girl" she said as she left.

Jack answered to hear "Jack, this is Lisa, I want to tell you some news, now if I could I would have waited till you were through, but I wanted to let you know, that Jesse is alright and he is your biological son."

Jack looked at the phone, thinking how, when, where.

"Your silence must be that your processing the information, so what would you like to do?"

"Who and where is the mother, is she married?"

"Hold on, one question at a time, the mothers name is Natasha Rogers," said Lisa.

"I've heard that name before."

"You should, her real name is Marie-Elizabeth Duke, she is the upper class of society."

"Is she is danger?"

"No, but were having some time at locating her," said Lisa.

"Where is she at?"

"In the bayou's of Louisiana."

"Don't worry, I know the right person, to find her, and to answer your next question, yes I want protection, on her."

"What about Jesse?"

"Send him back, it's time we get to know one another."

"Really," said Lisa.

"Yeah, the way you made it sound, is that you had some doubts" said Jack.

"Well I'm afraid to tell you is that we used some methods to extract that information."

"Understandable, I forgive you, you were just looking out for my best interests, he does act weird from time to time."

"Thank you that is a relief to know."

"Oh, can you coordinate with Queen Ana, of Latvia, the wedding and have my wives out there after I get out."

"Absolutely, we will do whatever you like," said Lisa.

"Bye" said Jack, trying to process what was just said to him, that Jesse is his son, he did kind of look like him, wow the ugly truth is hard, I have a son, and oh that Marie was a spectacular looking woman." Jack cleared his mind, to get up and wipe away the tears, to say, "What am I crying for, he sat back down as the title wave of emotion hit him, he began to cry, out loud, as Mitzi was at the door, she came, in to see him she closed the door, and went to him, to say, "We just found out and were very sorry, come rest your head on me, and let it out."

Jack cried in her arms for some time yet, feeling the same emotion for losing Samantha, thinking of Marie, to think it would be nice, to see her again.

Outside a UN advisor came to the ramp to see some somber faces to say, "Is Jack Cash ready, to come back in?"

"There has been an event that has occurred in his family, can you give him some time, we don't know if he wants to fly out or not?"

"It's that serious?" said the UN advisor.

"Yes it is "said Jim, "Go along and let us be", as the advisor acknowledged that, he left, for Jim to say, "Assemble inside, and lets close up the ramp."

"Yes Sir" said Casey.

Jim went back to the flight cabin, to gather up Mark and Mike., Commander Bill Bilson, was in the UN lounge, when he got a beep to come back to the plane. He arrived, through the side door, as he saw Casey guarding it, as he saw Jim, and went into the flight cabin and closed the door, while Jim spoke, "From this point on, we treat Jesse as one of our own, but a part of the team."

"Yes Sir" they said in unison.

Jack opened the door, after he washed his face, he was ready to go back in, Trixie had already gone, as he stepped out to see Jim, and the others, to say, "We will be here two more weeks, stand down, Mike I want to speak with you."

Mike past him, to go inside, as Jack followed and closed the door, to say, "I know we haven't been on the best of terms, since Dominican Republic, but that doesn't mean you're not good at what you do, with that said, "I need you to go to Louisiana, and find a woman named Natasha Rogers, and bring her to me, here."

Mike looked at him to say, "Absolutely, as he was saying something."

Jack over spoke him by saying "I want her un hurt, have Carly Curtis, a C I, I have in New Orleans, Mitzi has all of her contact information, she will help you, bring her to me once you have located her."

"I understand shall I go now, is it that urgent, or can it wait?"

"Wait for what, you'll go, check with Mitzi she will arrange, for her return and take Gia with you, she wanted to stretch her legs."

"Yes Sir" said Mike as Jack moved in to hug him, he was caught off guard, but took the embrace well, for Jack to say, "Thank you my friend."

"You're welcome, see ya."

Jack leaves his room, as he pushes out Mike, as Mike said, "He is in a good mood".

Mike gathered up Gia, to say, "Wanna take a trip to Lousiana?"

"Sure, let me get my stuff, how will we be flying?"

"By supersonic jet," said Mike watching her pack her pack, to say, "All set."

"Jack wants you and I to find a woman, named Natasha Rogers, in Louisiana, we will have help from a woman named Carly Curtis, do you know her?"

"No, should I?"

"Yes, all girls know one another, well come on then, we have a flight to catch," said Mike, waving her on.

CH 8

Kelly Kline and her candy company

Jack showed his pass and went right through the security, then down to his room, onto the girls floor, to suite one, the door slid open, and he went in, undressed and went into the pool, to relax, a little time passed, and then Trixie came in, looking good, dressed in her uniform, she saw him and came over to the sliding glass door, she slid it open, to see him, to say, "Looks like you started without me."

"Nah, just waiting your arrival, get comfortable and come in."

She dropped her luggage, to say, "Alright I will" and with that she undid her top, to let it fall, she unzipped her skirt, she let that go.

Jack looked at her near flawless body and her small panties, and her full figured bra, which she popped off, to let breasts out, she pulled down her panties, to say, "Do you like what I did?"

"Yeah it looks nice" said Jack, standing up to help her in.

He sat down, and she straddled him to say, "This week I hope you give me that individual attention I need."

"I will just as long as she can join us" said Jack pointing to Debby, who was already undressing, for Trixie to say, "Do you have anyone else?"

"Perhaps" said Jack as they were joined by Debby.

Jack took Debby from behind, and Trixie was in front, with Jack's arms were around Trixie. Trixie rose, and went in to take a shower, while Debby dressed and kissed Jack goodbye, as he quickly dressed, it was five till eight, Sunday morning, as he left, go upstairs to room one, just as everyone else filed in from the mess hall.

"You ain't had breakfast mate" said Steven.

"You mean dessert?" said Jack with a smile, taking his seat, the huge chairs were moved around according to the new position, and the room was larger as those that were cut were taken out, to the up-front in the number one position, according to the board on the wall, as the Professor Benz came in, to say, "Pop quiz challenge, Vadim, come here and pass out the tests."

He distributed it to each agent, as the harmony continued among the agents after his comrades left, one by suicide and the other disgraced, who threaten to kill Jack at some time, but now everything is calm, as the Professor said, "Go", the hundred questions, took about fifty minutes, to hear, "Turn over your tests, and let's get up, were going on a field trip, so if you need a jacket go to your room, and meet back here."

The women, were on the field, at it was Sunday, it was the qualifier, for the finals, the third game, first up was Canada versus Belarus, Darlene Lewis showed her dominance and the score was 4-2. Next was Mexico, Freya, was on a hot streak, taking out Australia, 8-4, the top team was Argentina, led by Dana Scott, easily put away Poland, 6-0. Brazil and Protima, knocked off Joana, who seemed not to be in the game, as Brazil, took down Portugal, who was Number 3, overall. Russia, and Kendra, won, 9-3 over Erica and Honduras. South Africa, led by Cami Ross, scored 11 times, to defeat Croatia, who Nina Ivan was hot at 5. Latvia, and Rebecca Adams, over China and Michelle, who was way into her own mind, at 0-3, she was out of the finals. The next strongest team was the US, led by Kellie Ryan was high flying, doing a wheel kick, to a victory over Lea and France, 4-1. Spain, Esmeralda was strong, as Turkey, Z'sofia, put on the best show, as it ended in a 6-6 tie, then it was Esmeralda, scored and Spain won, lastly it was Chile, Simone Bailey, dominated, Jill Hoyt, as she twisted her ankle, her pain was bad, as she limped off the field, with New Zealand. The day was over for them, as they all made it back, to see the following posted;

ELIMINATION GAMES, AS FOLLOWS;

1. Argentina	3-0 18 pts.	vs. Turkey	1-2 6 pts.
2. US	3-0 8 pts.	vs. Poland	1-2 7pts
3. Mexico	2-1 19 pts.	vs. Croatia	1-2 8 pts.
4. Spain	2-1 14 pts.	vs. Russia	1-2 9 pts.
5. Brazil	2-1 11 pts.	vs Belarus	1-2 10 pts.
6. France	2-1 11 pts.	Vs South Africa	1-2 11 pts.
7. Portugal	2-1 10 pts.	Vs Canada	2-1 7 pts.
8. Honduras	2-1 11 pts.	Vs Chile	2-1 8 pts.

Jack went back to the room, and looked in a drawer, to see a protein bar, and grabbed a jacket, he caught up with the group, as all eighteen men were mulling about, as all fit in the elevator, it went down, and opened as it said B, Jack and Steven brought up the rear, as they walked on an ancient pathway, up a hill and then back down, for Steven to say, "Hey Mate, have you ever been to Australia?"

"Nah" said Jack.

"You should come visit, we could have fun?"

"Perhaps, depends on where we finish in the standings?"

"What do you mean?"

"Well the top one or two, will be going around the world," said Jack.

"What is your take on Ben and Tom" asked Steven.

"I think their sandbagging it, so they can go back to what they had, then there is you and I who are seeking some adventure" said Jack.

"Where do you think we're going?" asked Steven.

"Will see when we get there, and here we are" said Jack.

A large door opened, as the agents walked through. Standing on a platform stood a stunning dirty blonde haired woman, with a very large chest, who said, "Gentleman, leave your jackets by the door, grab a white coat, put on a pair of booties and a cap, then single file step up the stairs."

"Hey what do you think of her Mate?"

"Who, what are you talking about?, Mate?" asked Jack, looking around.

"Her", points Steven.

"The one on the railing, you can have her, give me some room, either stay way back or get in front of me" said Jack already annoyed with all of this and that god awful smell, it was something like sweet, or something.

"I know, you want to be in back to learn from others, alright Mate, I'll be in front of you" said Steven.

They all stood on the platform, when all of a sudden it raised up to the top floor, two workers pulled the gate open for them, to hear "This way, keep up, come in here and take a seat."

Jack went to the back, to take a seat, as he saw Steven sit up front who smiled back at him, then he had a frown on his face, just as a door opened, and then a voice whispered, in Jack's ear, "Don't like the presentation, or the presentor?" she waited for an answer, where there was none, to add, "Neither, you should turn over that sheet?"

She slid in to sit next to him, to egg him on, to turn it over, till he finally turned it over, to see the name Kline family candy company, to hear the woman in front say, "Take this with you as we will sample each area, so fold it up, and when you see something you like, check it off."

Above her talking, this girl next to him says, "Check off whatever you like and I'll fill it?"

Jack looked it over, then sets it aside, for her, to say, "You didn't see anything you liked?"

"Nah, not really, there was no sandwich on there."

She laughed, as everyone got up, to say, "If you want I can make you a sandwich if you like?"

Steven comes back to Jack, to say, "Who is your friend, my name is Steven."

"Well my name is Kelly, please to meet you, as Jack walked off.

"What's wrong with him?"

"Oh, he gets bored easy, I think he is hungry, but he did say he was looking for some dessert?"

"So are you an agent?" asked Kelly looking him over, his eagerness, was infectious.

"Yeah, I'm from Australia, why?"

"Well, I was having some trouble and needed some help, do you think you can help me?"

Steven looks her over to say, "Sure, what can I do for you?"

"Well the reason I agreed, to allow the super agents in, was maybe someone could help us, we had a break in, and"

She was still speaking to him, totally out of his element, he knew it and was looking for some help when he heard, "Hey buddy, what are you doing, everyone is waiting?" said Jack. As he came back in, to say, "Are you done flirting, we need to go" said Jack.

Jack came to him, to say, "Miss we need to go, can you actually let my friend go?"

"Actually, I just hired him?"

"To do what, you know he is confined to the base for the next two weeks."

"He didn't say that, he said he could help me out."

"What was he going to do for you" said Jack, as Steven bugged out.

"Well it looks like he left, so do you think you can help me out", pauses, now he was getting in trouble, for Jack to say, "Depends on what you need?"

"You sound like a more causous spy, are you a spy?"

"That's what people have said about me, what is your issue, that you need a super spy" said Jack.

"How about I fix you that sandwich you were seeking?"

"Sure lets go?" said Jack as he followed her through some doors, to a mass gathering of people, mainly women, as she led him to a kitchen, and pulled out lunch meat, and quickly made it for him, as she smiled at him, to include a pickle on the side, to say, "Do you want some chips and a pop, we make that too", she gave it to him, he ate while she was talking, he heard only what he wanted to hear, as he got the just of it, as he finished his sandwich, to say, "Hush I'll take the job."

"I can pay you whatever you want?"

"Not necessary, consider it a gift, can you catch me up with the group?" said Jack, seeing candy and chocolate.

"Take whatever you like, come on" she said getting a bit annoyed, with him, they took the stairs down, to pop out, at the group, to see Steven, and he got away from her, as she talked with the Professor, who pointed at Jack, to say "I'd like to introduce our host, this is Kelly Kline, the owner of this company, and has welcomed us to continue, our tour but she has asked, if anyone can help her out, please come forward?"

Steven looked at Jack to say, "I thought you were helping her out like you said."

"So did I, maybe she needs a contract or something?"

Not a single agent came forward, as Jack raised his hand, as the other agents turned to see him, she saw him, to whisper something, for the Professor to say, "That's alright she isn't interested?"

"Suit yourself "yelled Jack back.

They all passed her and Thomas stopped, to say, to her, "You must not need help that bad?"

"What do you mean, someone stoled from my safe."

"Doubtful, probably an inside job" he said in passing, the tour was somewhat fun, as Jack began to rethink his attitude, and so what if he doesn't get a job, who cares" thinks Jack.

A frustrated girl ran off, to hear Steven say, "She is probably a trust fund baby."

"Hey I got a good idea, why don't you Brits take the case" said Jack.

"Sorry we can't, we have to fall in behind the best" said Thomas respectfully.

"Thanks' guys for the compliment" said Jack as he hugged the father and the son.

The three of them, entered into a batching room, when out of the shadows pops that annoying girl, who puts her hand up, to stop Jack, to say, "You didn't tell me that you're the famous Jack Cash, who took down the entire Russian secret police, so why didn't you come clean, with me?"

"Not interested, like we all told you were locked up, so how can we do it anyway?"

"Come on, why didn't you tell me, I made you a sandwich, so you owe me?"

"I owe you nothing, I don't even like candy or chocolates, except chocolate milk."

"We make the chocolate that goes into the milk."

"Listen I know you're this all mighty girl here, I'm not interested, leave me alone" as Jack was getting annoyed with her, as he passed her to hear, "Alright what will it take?"

"Let me think about", as Jack caught up with others, to hear from Steven, "Sounds like she likes you."

"Doubtful, when is this over?"

The tour was as boring as paint drying, the guide spoke some form of German, and she wasn't very nice, after two hours, what was thought to be fun, turned out to be a desperation attempt to hire an agent to recover her lost documents, everyone was ready to get out of there, not a person, filled out a request form, they left was a relief, as the huge door closed, the agents all jogged out of the tunnel, to the elevator, as they stepped in, it went up, to their level, and everyone went to the mess hall, that's when the Professor pulled Jack aside, to say, "We at the UN would have let you help her out as her family is a big contributor, to this place."

"Are you asking me or telling me?"

"Which would you prefer?"

"You're the boss, I'd hate to miss any pertinent information over a rude girls wishes."

"Would you think about it?"

"Could I take another agent with me?"

"If you wish, but you'll have to talk with Miss Hohlstein."

"So it was her they say, but I'd like to spend some time with my friend Steven."

"Well we would love if you'd help out" said the Professor.

"I might under one condition, that I investigate it at night, and continue the classes during the day?"

"You got it."

"Oh one more thing, I'd like to have my gun on me, while I'm in the classroom?"

"I'll have to get clearance, then I'll let you know."

Jack went to his room, he went in, over to his kitchen, to grab a water, he turned to see her, standing at his doorway, with the Professor, as she stepped in, the doors slid closed, for Jack to say "Why can't you leave me alone?"

"The Professor told me that you have the ways and means to help me out."

"If you had listened to what I said in your kitchen."

"You said you would do it" she said.

"So which is it, are you listening or are you talking, I have to tell you, I'm really not interested anymore, I don't care to whom this benefits, cause it surely doesn't benefit me."

"Why, I need your help."

"What did you do before we came along?"

"Well my father handled it, and we had a security force, but with the economy we cut it in half."

"And that's my fault, listen why don't you take off, and I'll send someone in, to get some data and information?"

"What's their names?"

"You don't get it, leave me alone, get lost, I don't care about you or your company."

"Do you want me to go?"

"Yes, get the Fuck out, you stupid bitch" said Jack in a hurtful tone.

Monday Morning was day 8, Debby was in front and Trixie, well she was in the back, or simply discarded, over the incredible Debby, who turned out to be a another Melanie, with whom, Jack was missing, but knew he had her for the rest of his life. They both got up together, showered together, and practically, dressed each other, as Jack was rested enough to go, to mess, where Dany the chef was, and was flirting heavier than usual, to say, "What would you say, to a night on the town just you and I?"

"I'd say, maybe, but I can't find the time?" as he tried to diffuse the incident, as he received his platter, his four milks, swiped his card, and took a seat, as his girlfriend, came to him, all dressed up, but nowhere to go, as, she cozied up to him, her heavy red lip stick, was evident as she halved hugged him, to say, "I hear, you're going out at nights?"

"Yeah, that's the plan."

"How about you take me with you?"

He looks at Lea, to say, "Perhaps, something comes up, I'll ask you, I saw you on Sunday, which was a pretty spectacular goal you kicked, at first I thought soccer was boring, but I think you elevated the game, so that I may really like it."

"Thanks, but I think you like watching, me in those oh so ever short shorts."

"Alright that is true, as she leaned in to straddle him, and hold his head in her hands, and proceed to kiss him, he was surprised how sweet she smelled and tasted, long gone was that cigarette smell, and taste, as she pulled back, she wiped off his lips, to say, "Come by sometime, lets recreate what we had the other night?"

He thought about how Trixie was off to the side, to say, "Will you play with another?"

"Of course, why would you even ask?"

"Well I was thinking of that fox hole, and Chloe."

"That was different, you're going to have her for the rest of your life, you and I will just play now, and then, I'll go back?"

"Or you could come and join me at my spy academy?"

She looked at him as he was serious, for her to say, "In what capacity?"

"Whatever you want, like being a spy, like your training now for."

With that she instantly hugged him, to say, "Yes, count me in, I'd love to be there, she whispered, "There are people out there that don't like you, but from now on, I will help you out in any way, just its hard to get in touch with you."

"That's alright, I'll get you a phone, as the bell rings, for both of them, as Jack slowly gets out, as Lea sees he wasn't finished, to say, "Sorry next time I'll let you eat."

"Don't be, I'd much rather, be in your arms any day, I can eat this in class.", as the two kissed for Trixie to see that and immediately left."

Jack went up the stairs to room one, and sat down. As others filed in, to have the Professor say, "Today is Dive tank, I need all of you to go get changed into swim shorts, a robe, and some footwear, be back in fifteen, minutes., Diss-missed."

Jack went down stairs, with empty plate and tray, to drop it off, and went to his shared room, went in quickly changed and put a shirt on, then his robe, to hear Debby was there, he saw her, to say, "I'll be leaving in a moment, for Jack asked her to come to him. She smiled to say, "Yes dear", as the two kissed, then she hugged him. For Jack, to say, "Can you get a message to Jim, I need him to act on this immediately."

"Sure but I won't see him till four, why don't you text him on your phone?"

"The darn thing is all locked up, can't get a call out nor receive one."

"Alright I'll try," said Debby, a bit flustered.

"That's fine, give me a minute, to write something up, do you have an envelope?"

"Here you go", she pulls it from her lavish cart.

"You have a lot there" said Jack.

"Yeah, do you need writing paper and a pen?"

"Sure it would help."

"I could write it if you like" she said smiling.

"I'd rather have you in bed" said Jack kiddingly.

"Give me a minute and I'll be ready." she said seriously.

"No, I was kidding" said Jack, as he finished writing, he stuffed it in the envelope, licked it and closed.

"Don't be teasing a girl now."

"I won't, you be getting it later" said Jack liking their whole arrangement, not Trixie as she despised her.

"Where are you going?"

"I have to dive today, or swim or something, Hey, how would you be if I had another join us?"

"You don't even have to ask?" said Debby.

"Just make sure Jim gets this as soon as possible." As Jack leaves his phone, on the counter and walks out the door.

"Yes sir" she said as she picked up things, thinking he is a pretty clean guy, nothing seems out of place, as she looked in the refrigerator, to see a single bottle of water missing, she put a new one in, looking around, to see it was perfect, she pushed her cart out, with the letter in her pocket, she pushed her cart to her restocking station, in the room it was designated, then went into the break room, to pick up the sat phone, she punched in a code, to bounce the signal, then made the call to Jim, he answered immediately to say, "How are things?"

"Good, Jack wants you to come pick up a letter, I have for you, can you have someone pick it up, I only have ten minutes."

"Yes, Mark is outside and running errands, he will pick it up, are we still on for four."

"Yes, I'll see you there" she said as she hung up, she watched the clock, to know that her ten minutes was being watched, as each minute passed by, she was losing hope, till at the last moment, a tap on the trap door, she slid it open to see Mark, smiling, she hands it to him, then slides the door shut.

Mark folds it up, to get back in his Hummer, and continued his trip around the base, collecting, and dropping off work orders and requests, checks written by Mitzi for food and resupply basics, till he saw, it was three, and knew he had to get back, he drove in the receiving and stationary place and parked the UN vehicle, they at the UN has treated them very well, as he waves at other UN personnal, he was even asked if he wanted to become a UN inspector, which he was really thinking about, as he made his way up the ramp, to see Jim who said, "Where's the envelope?"

"Here is your love letter" he hands it to Jim, who saw it was Debby's handwriting, that said Jim, as he unfolded the sealed envelope, he felt a little weird, as he opened it up, and pulled out the paper, to read, Jim, we have a new mission, prepare the plane for takeoff, and have the strike team on ready alert, next I need you to have Mark go to the Kline family candy company, in Geneva, before four, and begin the investigation of some missing documents, I need you to have my clothes and gun, ready, and I need several phones or ear pieces, for the inside, as soon as possible, Jack.

"Oh shit", he yelled, as he grabbed Mark to tell him, he needs to go, in turn, he just took off, Jim, thought an bout his reserves, so he pounded on Jack's cabin, to see Mitzi, to tell her the news, meanwhile the strike team was working specifically for the UN, were scattered all over the place, doing different jobs, from the running course, to swim operations, to the rifle range, Jim knew he would have to send Tami in, with a message, so he went to her, as she was reading a book, to hear, "I need your help, will you help me?"

"You mean inside?"

"Yeah, can you do that?" asked Jim.

"Well it depends on your tone, what are you not telling me?"

"Well once you go in, you'll be subjected to a strip search, and a cavity one as well, nah, I was just kidding, go through the center door, to say, "You have a message for Jack Cash, and they will let you through."

"Really, well if I get to see Jack, I'll do it."

"Great thanks" said Jim relieved.

Tami was no dummy, she met a flight captain, who said if she ever need to see her boss, he would get her in.

Tami left the plane, with a message, in the envelope, with her ID and she went to the squadron, and went inside, to ask for that Captain, someone said he was in the air, and that she could be escorted in, she said "Sure, thanks."

Tami walked right in, no metal detectors or nothing, her guard was a big brawny guy, up to the guard's station, at the cafeteria, where they looked at her, and him, to say, "Allow her to go, we don't want any trouble with any spy she is connected with" said another.

Tami, marveled at how beautiful and luxurious everything was, and came to the number one door, and knocked, the door opened, to see a lot of high backed chairs, as Jack turned to see her, he asked permission to go, and the Professor waved him on, as Jack went to her, to say, "Boy, it's nice to see you?"

"You sure have it nice in here" said Tami.

"Yeah, it's alright, as he and she embrace for all to see, Jack whispers, "Tell Jim thanks, and to have the car ready to go at five."

"I will, boy I wished I could have come in."

"Another time and another place, but if you want you can accompany me on a mission tonight?"

"I'd love that."

"Great be ready, and dress a bit more provocative?"

"You mean show some skin, where to?"

"All I can say, it's a night club."

"You got a date."

Jack and Tami embraced for all to see, as she kissed him, it was a passionate, as all watched, as she handed him the envelope, and was off, then Jack went back inside as the door closed.

Jack sat back down, thinking, "They were underway, only to hear, Professor John Hughes, come up to the podium, to say, "We have just found out we had a secret agent among you all, she works for what they call the WTN, or what we like to further call the World's Terrorist Network, it was uncovered, that, how to tell a spy or not is the branding of a tattoo, of some number and letters, on the inside of their pelvis, as he flashed a photo of a picture of a star, for which Jack took a picture, as it scanned the data base, till it came up with one name, Raisa Sergel, for Jack to say, "So that is why she is out?" thinks Jack, as the Professor continued, to say, "All women, and men have been screened, and we found, four women, and two men, all confessing to work for this terrorist group, thanks in large part to Clarance, and his efforts, at extracting information, now when you see one, what shall you do?"

Jack raised his hand, he was called on, to say,"Just kill them."

"Precisely, because, unless you have an interrogator, on staff, it's going to get interesting on what they will do, now on to another matter, we are all in this together, as in all for one, one for all, as it pertains to you in the UN you see folks, someday, your brother may help you, and you will reciprocate the same, we need to all fight this terrorist group together, with that Class dismissed, now let's go to the pool."

Jack got up, and went to the Professor, to say, "I'd like a word with Miss Hohlstein?"

"Wait a minute, to fulfill that request." A moment later, after a private phone call the Professor, said, "She will see you now, a UN advisor, will escort you there, as Jack saw, his UN advisor, Christina, with clip board in hand, as he followed her out of the classroom, into the elevator, down, and then over, and out, as she led him to the Chief Justices door, and knocked, he went in and closed the door, Jack came around, as she said, "Please have a seat, what can I do for you, is it about the job we asked you to take?"

"Yeah, I want to know if I can take another agent with me?"

"I'm fine with that, anything else?"

"What ever happen to Raisa Sergel?"

"She is out, due to the involvement over your suppose poisoning?"

"It wasn't because she was a suppose agent of the WTN?"

"What are you talking about, perhaps, how do you know about this?"

"Just now in class, Professor John Hughes, told us about it."

"I know that, and the picture taken was similar to the tattoo of the others, Raisa did pass the interrogation, with Clarance, as the others buckled, so what are you saying, you'll personally vouch for her?"

"Yes, either she will be here working for you or one of my field agent, she will be a spy, I think she has something to offer."

"So why is it important, she come back in?"

"Because of how she was let go."

"Oh, because of the rules violation, I see what you're saying, as you could have had your hand in there literally, alright she is back in, but she must have that tattoo removed, and play by the rules."

"Where was her standings?" asked Jack.

"No, that doesn't matter, you're up to something, so I will allow her back in, get what you need from her, even if you have to pump her for the information, then do what you must do, but here at the UN she is through, as of yesterday, Anything else,?"

"Yes, I want my outfit and gun?"

"No way, you have been given access off the base at night, and during the day, as you have amassed more points, than any other agent in twenty years, so whatever you do, you'll have the number one spot, afterwards will you be a UN agent?"

"Yes."

"Really are you kidding me?" as she almost fell back in her chair, stunned she got up, to say..."

"Why not, I like you, were working together", she was so excited, she came to him, hugged him, and said, "You have made me the happiest woman ever."

"And all I said was I would work for you, so what's the big deal anyway?"

"O it's the commitment, which is really huge, it means, I have you to go on missions, see that stack of folders that is all the unsolved cases, and of other agents, but that would all change?"

"Why's that?"

"Because you will oversee all of this, and some hundred plus agents, what do you say?"

"I have access to the 2500 plus girls?"

"Absolutely, and more, that was just ones I was able to screen", her excitement was rising, to say, "I'll pay you a million per day for the rest of your life, and for the next hundred years thereafter, and of the women, I know about you and your sex parties, you can have as many as you like?"

"Whoa, it doesn't work like that, it's always been them that, has initiate it."

"Wait, what are you saying, it's not you that asks them the when and where?"

"No, I just show up?"

"Interesting, so it was the women who initiate it, and then what you agree to it, do you have to see them first?"

"What are you getting at," asked Jack, looking at her, for Meredith to say, "No, not me, but I have had some inquiries from with in."

"Sure, let me meet them, and if they say the right things, it maybe Go time."

"Well one is you advisor?"

"I don't mean now, all I want is my own room, just like I have on the girls floor."

"I'm already a head of you, the pool is about done, you'll have number one, on the men's floor, and be by yourself, I see that you have an companion, another potential spy?"

"Nah, she is my air traffic controller."

"Oh, one more thing, the flight simulator, was broken, since the earlier shoot out, I have your son Jesse and Jim working on that, is that alright?"

"Yeah, there here to serve you as well" said Jack.

"According to your manifest, you have a commander Bill Bilson, is it possible, he could oversee the flight simulator?"

"Sure, do I still have access to the girls' floor?"

"Yes, your pass, allows you everywhere access, in addition if you need a supersonic jet, you can have one of them."

Jack left Miss Holstein's office, with a smile on his face as he saw Christina, and her cute face and very voluptuous figure, to admire her as she said, "It's not nice for you to stare at me, Mister Cash?"

"Oh sorry, I couldn't help but admire the view?"

"What view, what are you even talking about?"

"Oh I was thinking of your request?" said Jack as she led him into the elevator, and off to the spa, but, down a different corridor, then it opened to a huge facility, a three platform dive board, and massive deep pool, and off to the right as they came in was a dive tank, huge. As Christina, said, "The dive tank has a replica sunken ship, on the weekends the employees, are allowed to go down there."

"So you dive?"

"Yes, a lot of the Advisors have to do the same things you all have to do."

Off to the left all the men sat while the women were in the water, most wearing one piece swim wear, as they were finishing up, in the open pool, a stunning red head, also in a one piece, walked past Jack, to say, "Hi Mister Cash." In her best English, as she was a Russian, for Jack to say, "He-low." And went over to take a seat by his friend Steven, who said, "Who don't you know?"

"I met the Professor in Saint Petersburg, Russia.", only to hear, shred you robes, and into the water, screamed Floyd, with his arms crossed, to yell, "Alright, tread water, till I tell you you're through", with that Jack tilted his head back, and rested, as he kicked freely, as others were floundering, and growing tired, below were several divers, watching, as Floyd, was yelling, "In order to be an appropriate spy, one needs to know how to float, as he says, look over at Jack Cash, now tilt your heads back, calm your fears, and relax, and just like that all was calm, and it was peaceful as they all did it, for Floyd to say, "Now go to the bottom and hold your breath, the longest one wins, and is out of the pool, ready 3, 2, 1 Go."

Jack took a moderate breath, and went down to the bottom, he saw others immediately go up, till there was three, Gordon, and Tad, but then, Gordon, followed by Tad, went up, as three minutes, past, seeing no one else around, Jack went up, to breathe, and to hear, "Alright Jack Cash, your out of here, you're the winner, 100 points, next will be the top three, 3,2,1 Go."

Jack emerged to see a young SEAL, team mate in Scott Mackenzie, who kept to himself, knowing the Commander, as he said, "So have you ever dived before?" for Jack to think about it, to say, "Yes, a while back."

"Well over there is gear, check it, as Christina was watching Jack, she came over, to say, "Here let me help you, she adjust the pressure, and squeezes the breather, to say, "Its ready for you to dive, each set has a belt, as she helped him, with the pack, and a pair of goggles and fins, as he waddled over to the edge, where the Professor Gobel was at, as she helps her last girl out, it was Protima, who looked simply amazing in that one piece, so he thought, Jack was given the O Kay, to go in, only to hear from Scott, "Find the star, and you can come back up, and your through."

With that Jack jumped in, and quickly went to the bottom, a real ship of epic proportions, from its appearance, seemed to be a WW2 ship, old metal bucket, with a huge hole in the side, he swam in, to turn on his above head lamp, as he went further in, through doors, up passageways, he turned to see, another, he instantly though ambush, when he saw who it was, Lea, waited and embraced Jack, and led him into a room, and then, turned and closed the door, she pulled the handle down, turned to face him, when she began to pull off her suit, as he watched, till she was naked, as he had risen watching that, he came over to her, as she bent over, he easily went in, and the two went at it. Meanwhile up top, Scott was supervising the others, as thirty minutes had past, the girls were gone, to lunch, and Scott and the professor Hughes were contemplating, breaking for lunch, and he asked Scott, "We have anyone down there?"

"No I believe all is accounted for?"

"Then lets break for lunch", as the Professor, gathered, up the rest, and led them out, Scott and two other divers, donned their gear, and together jumped in, armed with a knife and a spear gun, the went in through the hole, and began the search, for Jack, who was still having fun with his girlfriend, as the three came up empty, they tried one door, but it was locked, so they, came back out, and swam to the top, discarded their gear, and Scott turned out the lights, as Jack finally let loose, as she took him all the way, he pulled out, to see her, pull her suit back up, and went to the door, tried it, it was stuck, as she motioned for Jack's help? He swam over to her position, tried it, it was jammed of some sort, it was stuck, thinking of a way out, he saw his watch, so he undid it, and it went to the bottom, he waited, nothing happened, high above him, number one Super hornet, received the faint signal, and without hesitation, fired, the smart missile, the missile, went up down, and around, as it was trying to find the best path to the watch, it crash through, a glass window, went down a corridor, through an open door, as others were, coming back, they hit the floor, as Scott and his group stopped to see the missile slow and take a nose dive in the water, it hit the side, and blew, the missile went off, and rocked the pool area and the whole of the UN.

Miss Hohlstein got up from her meeting to say, "Was that an earthquake?", she sent others to go investigate, as UN advisors, took Scott and his two accomplices down, as Jack and Lea floated to the surface, and was helped out of the tank, by Tad, and Jonathon, and Jamal and Hendon helped Lea, as Jack was calm, to see Miss Meredith, enter, with others, Professor Benz, Floyd was anxious, as she said, "What just happened?"

Jack said, "Sorry it was me, someone, locked one of the rooms, I was in," as he showed the missing star, for her to say,"Sorry, you could have been killed?"

"I had some help, but I do need to call off reinforcements or all of the UN will be under attack."

"Alright you two," she looked at Lea, who had a smile on her face, to say, "I guess you can go too."

Jack and the concerned Christina, who was gushing over him, led him out. As Meredith, saw the three that were bounded, to say, "Don't you think we have surveillance, in here, and down below, as she showed the Commander, on her Tablet, what he did down below, as he pinned the door, and for her to say, "Take them down to Clarance for questioning." As she looked at the larger rather bigger hole, the missile made, and the shrapnel it created, for Meredith, to say, "Now we actually have authenticity, a real missile shot at us here in the UN."

Mark drove his Hummer, off the base and in a hurry to the candy factory, he knew he had blown it, by waiting a good three hours to get back, as a text message came over his phone from Jack, that said pump her with questions on the who, what where how and why's, tell her you my assistant, and lastly keep it professional, I'll be heading your way at five, have her keep the plant open, till I arrive. Mark sped up, down to the main gate where a single guard was stationed, to show his ID, the gate guard called it in, as he sat, for fifteen minutes, till finally, the guard let him pass, he drove, around the curve that surrounded the huge fountain, and parked in VIP, he walked across, and went in, where a receptions sat, then standing by the elevator was Kelly, who said, "Who are you?"

"My name is Mark, I work for Jack, I'm his private investigator."

"Are you a spy?"

"No Ma'am, once special forces, and that's about it, how can we help you?"

"Your nicer than him, my name is Kelly, and I'm the owner, I guess if Jack Cash sent you it must be alright, let me see your ID, he gives it to her, as she swipes it at the main station, to see it was who he said he was, to say, "That's what I like someone that tells the truth, are you single?"

"No Ma'am."

"Well she must be a lucky girl, and don't call me Ma'am, call me Kelly."

"Alright Kelly, as Mark pulls out a note pad, to begin taking notes, for her, to say, "And you take notes too."

"Why don't you just help me" said Mark, getting fed up with this girl.

"I am, I mean without the famous Jack Cash?"

"No, I work specific for him, I'm only here for him, He will be here shortly", looking at his watch.

"It will be our secret?"

"And no one else" said Mark, condesendly.

"You don't have to be that way with me."

The elevator doors opened, to a whiff of a lovely fragrance, as she led him into the office, as he scanned the room, to see half the desks were empty, to say, "Do you run split shifts?"

"Yes and No, we just recently let go of half our administrative staff."

"Can you get me those names, and while you're putting that names together, can you also provide a list of all visitors and vendors, you don't mind if I ask the remaining staff questions, do you?"

"No be my guest, do you like chocolate or candy?"

"Sure both" said Mark, not thinking what he just said.

"What's your favorite?"

"Anything gummy" said Mark, hoping to get rid of her, she's a bitch, she won't like Jack, nor I imagine Jack won't like her."

Mark saw some interesting things, like an irregular wall, now he wasn't a trained thief, but knew what he saw, as he went right to the hidden safe, touched the wall as the other girls watch, and presto the secret door opened, he tried the handle and the door opened as others looked at him, he looked over the bank statement to realize it was a dummy safe, only to turn to see Kelly with a box of candy, to say, "How did you get that open?"

"It was unlocked, and turned the handle, actually, there is a trick to these old safes, spin the wheel, then use a combination of ten-ten-ten, and it usually opens, no usually I would work with CIS but we already know it's an inside job."

"How can you deduct that as he was opening packages of gummy worms, and stuffing his face, to say, "Well ninety percent of espionage is insider knowledge, and probably some disgruntled secretary who lost her job, called in some pro to steal the secrets, in exchange for a retirement fund, and that's good place to start."

"Then where will you go?"

"Next tell me where the other safe is?"

"That's it I swear, I know of no other?"

"This safe is where you kept all of the family secrets?"

"Yep, as far as I know?"

"No it's too easy, who do you bank with?"

"Geneva International Bank."

"Then there probably in there."

"How do you know all of this, your good, I'm sending you a case of this forever?"

"Let's not get out of hand here, remember I told you I work for Jack Cash, please don't send me a thing anywhere, there is still the manner of how or who had the knowledge, do you have surveillance cameras in here?"

"No they were too expensive."

"That's alright, there is another way, can you get me the plans for the building as he saw it was nearing five, to say, "What time is the office closing?"

"Usually at five, Why?"

"I'd like to talk to each one?"

"I don't know, I wish you would have come earlier, I hate to pay overtime?"

"Listen, I wish I came earlier too, believe me, but its life, and do you want to find out what happen here or not?"

"Well I already asked them and they said they knew nothing."

"Which usually means something, but did you ask the right questions?"

"Which is?"

"Precisely, then on to the ladies mulling around Mark said loudly, "Listen up before you leave, come to me, I need to ask you a question, so form up a line, looking at the eight girls he took a rest on a desk, to see the first one, to say, "State your name, alright, who is the office manager, alright, when did the crime occur?" really, Do you have access to the safe, really, how long have you worked here?" really, that's all next,"

Five o clock came and went as Jack was on the move, out the squadron, and into the flight area, to see his plane, as he was on his phone, with Mark, while texting to Mike that he needed a room, with a bed and amenities, available to him, on the inside the plane, for Miss Rogers." Jack saw his car, behind the plane, and the strike team that surrounded it, a cover concealed it.

Jack past them to go inside, where Jim, and Mitzi stood, Tami was over dressed in her trench coat, as he went into his room, he quickly changed into his normal outfit, to have Mitzi come in, and help him with his badge, and slid his phone in, then his holster and gun, which he checked and loaded it, next there was a knock on the door, Mitzi opened it, to see a smaller than average guy, walk in, open the box, took out a cool blue looking watch, and placed it on Jack's wrist, to say, "The UN has authorized that you wear this for the rest of your duration, as authorized by Miss Hohlstein." As he pulled out the pin, as Jack said, "Can you set it to countdown to zero seven hundred?, he did so, as he showed Jack how to do that, and several other features, and left. Mitzi helped him on with his coat.

"Thank you, I got to go" Jack took Tami by the hand and led her out, of the plane, to the car that was unveiled, the door opened to his command, he helped Tami in, as Jared looked on, but stayed at attention. Jack got in, and it fired up, as he drove it out of there, as the exit door went up, to a rain soaked night, to say, "Traction on, Tami sat quietly, and tried not to look at him, while she glanced over, to see him pull out a laptop, which she couldn't tell if he was driving or not.

Jack let the car travel in stealth mode, while he was down loading the conversation between Mark and the secretaries.

Jack saw the plant in the distance, to look up and say slow down, off to the right he noticed something, he took the wheel, and put on the brake, turned right, and slowed down, he parked the car, kitty corner to a white non-descript van, he said "display, J", release, using his laptop, he took control of the pigeon, he let it soar, then level off, as it headed straight for the van, as the pictures came streaming in, to see men in suits wearing headphones. Jack was on the move, as he let the pigeon, glide down. He ran over to the van as Tami watched, Jack pound on the van door, it open slowly, as Jack pulled the first one out and drew his weapon, to motion four other men out, he lined them up, had them put their hands behind their back, as Jack heard, "What are you doing man, we have done nothing wrong."

"Then you have nothing to worry about."

"Who are you have no right to tie us up" said the blond haired guy, as Jack said, "Turn around."

Jack stepped back to see all five men dressed in black, to say, "State your business?"

"Were with the CIA?"

"What is your purpose here?"

"We got word that there was some illegal activity around here."

"Who do you work for?"

"You wouldn't know him?"

"Try me, step a foot towards me and I'll canoe you" said Jack looking at the guy on the end to hear, "Stand still Tom."

"Name ", said Jack holding his gun still, as he pulled out his phone to say, "Who is it?"

"Agent Carter" said the blonde.

Jack pulls up three names, to say, "I need first name and where he was born?"

"Wait how do you know all of this are you CIA?"

"No, what is his first name?"

"Tom, he is from Daytona beach, Florida." he said with a sigh.

Jack dialed him up to hear, "Who is this?", so that his team could hear, Jack said,"I have five of your men in the proximity to the UN, thus violating the international treaty, for this they are under arrest, by order of the UN, deputy director, you have less than two hours to turn yourself in to authorities, or I will come see you personally."

"Who is this?"

"I order you to do this as an order from the President of the United States, for I am Jack Cash international Super spy."

The phone went dead, as Jack checked the area from which the call came from, and dialed up the local FBI, to say, "This is Jack Cash I need a rogue operative picked up at the following address, his name is Tom, C Carter, CIA Ops manager, by order of the UN, when you have picked him up and placed him under arrest, call me back on this line, thank you." Just then Tom made a rush towards Jack and Jack shot him in the head only to see their buddy go down.

"Wait you said your Jack Cash, the champion and preserver of life, why did you shoot him in the head?"

"Just like I may take all of you out, your trespassing on a neutral country, land, in my book, that's called for to shoot and kill, as Jack was on the phone, to say, "I have a hostile party need a pick-up and a tow truck."

In that next moment two police cars closed off the end of the road with weapons drawn, they came closer, to put the men on the ground, as Jack holstered, to hear, "We got ourselves a listening van, directed at the UN, as Jack came closer, to look in to say, "Can you pull up the listening tapes and put them in a long reel, and over to my plane at the UN?"

"Yes sir it will be taken, and accomplished as you wish."

"You know if there is one, there must be others" said Jack.

"I'll call our boss and it will be dealt with" said the Chief.

"Everything good here" asked Jack.

"Yeah, you'll get the credit for all five."

"Hey, what can you tell me about the candy theft?"

"That one's a tricky one, I sent two detectives, you know it occurred at the beginning of the month, so your three weeks out, I could get you everything we have, but we have come up with nothing?" said the Chief of Police.

"What is your gut telling you "asked Jack.

"It's an inside and pro job."

"That was my impression, I'd think you would know what is going on, and who could profit from that knowledge?"

"I don't think they're the real ones?"

"Why's that" asked Jack.

"Because the old man and I were friends, and he told me that the recipes were intentional dummy's, the real ones are in the bank vault, if you want I could get you in to the bank tonight, there still there till six, and available twenty four seven", to add, "And for you any time."

"Let me think about it, I'm going back for another visit."

"Good luck, the grand daughter is a real pain."

"Don't I know, hey do you think it's a setup of something bigger, like you said, they have dummy recipes that probably won't work, telling them that their fools, so a bigger thing is happening?"

"That could be true, what are you thinking about?" asked the Chief of Police.

"Something you said, dummy files of recipes, what if those recipes, were codes for something else, you been in there right?"

"Yeah, what do you mean?"

"It's not set up like a candy factory should be set, in my opinion," said Jack.

"Do you think it a cover, wait, you think the accidental deaths of the parents is really the cover up, to allow the immature girl to run the factory to the ground?" said the Chief of Police, to add,"God, you good."

"No, I'm Jack Cash."

"Of course you are, but to us your god."

"How so?"

"Simple you have the license to kill, on my report I write killed by Jack Cash, usually your known as the preserver of life".

"Sometimes you just have a bad day, and she isn't helping matters."

"Just shows that you're not perfect. "The two shook hands, for the Captain, to say, "Call that number were moments away, and we will take care of the rat problem, do you want to interrogate them?"

"Let me think about that, I'm on a date."

"Then you better get going" said Police Chief Aaron Winters, who stepped out to see Jack pick something up and walk over to the shiny silver car. Jack leaned over to the launcher and reloaded the bird, to look over at a smiling Tami, who said, "You really have an eventful time out, when can I participate, and what is with this?"

"What do you mean?"

"It seems like you know everyone" said Tami

"Really, I guess I do".

CH 9

Surprises, Surprises and lots of fun.

Jack and Tami waited in the lobby, for Kelly, as the annoyed receptionist, kept calling her.

Tami stood still, confidently, as the receptionist kept staring at her, Jack paced, to finally see his foe, at the elevator, she stepped out to say, "Oh the big man is here, who is that your wife?"

"Nah, she is my assistant, I can see you're your same ole self," said Jack, mocking her.

"What did you think I would change since the last time we were together", she was winking at him.

"I was hoping you would have became more respectful since you knew I was helping you out" said Jack.

"Why should I, you're not charging me, so you're not working for me."

"Your wrong about that, I work for the UN now, and oversea, the entire world, and you're in that World."

"So what, you still should charge me a fee?"

"Alright, you want a number, how about five million dollars in gold bricks."

"Whoa you're serious."

"Sure, you wanted my fee, and that's it, but if it takes more than a week's time, you can expect to double that, come Tami were done here."

"Wait, you have a man upstairs, don't you want to go up and see what he is up to?"

"Nah, everything he does is sent to my phone, I already know, besides if you could help me get into the Octane night club, you know the secret part? I'm listening." She didn't say a thing for Jack to say, "When you have the gold, call me otherwise, wait till you hear from me, Good day" said Jack thinking of Steven, as Tami took his arm and they walked out.

The frustrated girl, went into the elevator.

Mark saw the message Jack sent him, to allow the rest of the girls to go, he waited for the elevator, he put his notebook away, to see Kelly as the doors opened, she stepped out totally frustrated, she vented on Mark who took it in stride to say, "So do you think you can show me around, you know a private tour?"

"Hey if that's what you want, how dare he talk to me like that."

"Like what?" asks Mark earnestly.

"What do you care, all you do is work for him, you have loyalties to him, is he listening now?"

"No, he is going to some nightclub."

"Why didn't he ask me out, I'm pretty, don't you think I'm pretty?"

Mark looked at her, to say, "Yeah, you're nice, but you being so overbearing, ruins any chance that you may have."

"What are you saying, sounds like your being dis-respectful to me."

Mark, knew now, what Mike went through, acting like Jack Cash, this girl's a real duzy, to add, "No not at all, but most men have a huge ego and when you crush it, they hurt."

"What about you, do I hurt your ego?"

"Nope, I have none, I do what I'm told."

"So If I told you to take me out you would?"

"Sure, if you give me a tour of your plant."

"You got a deal", she led, as Mark text to Jack what to do, Jack responded by keeping her happy, will you do it?"

Mark responded "Yes" and closed up his phone. And caught up with her, to hear, "Did he allow you to come with me?"

"Yes he said it was fine."

"Why do you put up with it?"

"I like him and the pay is good."

Mark kept the real reason to himself, sense of duty.

"What do you get, I'll double that, how much is it?"

"Oh about two fifty" he vibed on the number, he said calmly.

"I'll pay you a half a million dollars for ten months with two month's off, plus benefits."

"Let me think about it?"

"Where do you want to go, first" she said as she pressed herself upon him, as he said, "How about in the back."

"Oh that's research and development."

"That's fine, let's check it out" said Mark as she felt him below the belt. She seemed to be warming up to him, and now he now knows what Jack feels like.

Mark followed her past, a few mixers, to a flour and sugar room, as he tried a door that was locked, to say, "What's in there?"

"Private."

"Great, let's go in there and be private together."

"Really, you want to be with me, as she was fumbling for her keys, she inserted it, and swung the door open, as Mark got a whiff of the scent, as the private place was home to some pretty powerful contaminants, as he said, "What do you keep in here?"

"I don't know, I never had been in here, Mark was getting light headed, thinking there is something going on here, but his headache was killing him and for her to say, "I'm getting a headache, do you want to leave. She said motioning for him to come with her as she pulls him towards her as they enter a kitchen as she is stripping him and he has his hands all over her. Mark picked her up and put her on the table, as his hand were pulling her pants off, then he just stopped as he placed his hand on her mouth, to say, "Ssh, do you hear that?"

She shakes her head, No.

"Listen", said Mark as he was looking for something as he ran down towards the East door, he opened it, to see men loading something on a truck, as Mark was looking for his phone, to think it was where he dropped it.

Jack and Tami arrived at Octane night club, in downtown Geneva that lined the west side of the lake, he parked the car, along the VIP entrance, where a parade of expensive cars sat. They exited, to a fan fare of those in line waiting to get in, at the front was a girl who smiled, as a bank of photographers took their pictures, only to be discouraged to see he was nobody in particular. Jack gathered Tami's hand, and went to the front of the line, no one objected, as they were let in, and walked into the club, to the right was coat check, as Jack helped her out of the trench coat.

She appeared over dressed for Jack, to say, "Who dressed you Mitzi?"

"Yeah, it was short notice" said Tami, looking up at him, to add, "What do you suggest I do?" she asked.

Jack looked her over to pull out his wallet, and his credit card, to hear, "Are you going to buy me something?"

"Nah," said Jack as he went along the shoulder seam, and cut the stitching, down on both sides, to see the sleeve fall away, then the other side, he looked at the front cut.

"Wait before you cut it, let me take it off", as she pulled it off, to show a silver camisole, that looked nice, as he said, "Toss that aside."

"I agree with you, you know Mitzi, insisted I needed that."

"Nah, you don't." said Jack. Watching her shimmy back in the dress he just cut the sleeves on, to lead her along, he saw a bar area, and whispered in her ear, "Go out on the dance floor, till I come up with a plan, enjoy."

Jack strolled over to the bar area, to sit on a stool, watching Tami dance, to hear,"Rumor has it your coming to Washington D.C. I hope for your sake that ain't true."

"Why's that?" asked Jack, not even looking at the guy.

"Because if you do,I may have to harm you and your family?"

"What about you, don't you fear for your life?" asked Jack.

"Nah, you can't do anything to me" said the cocky guy.

"That's where you're wrong?"

"What are you saying?"

Jack looked at him, to see the guy made a quick mistake, as Jack said, Hands behind your back, as Jack had his pistol out and pointed at him."

"Whoa wait, who are you" asked the guy, to add "I thought you were Tom Moore."

"Who's Tom Moore?" asked Jack.

"He is a terrorist, that comes here to party with the elite crowd look around, there is the playboy Gustave Renoir, the party girl from Spain, Maria, and that hot mama over there, is the music producer Gloria Thomas, and watch out for that one she is from Russia, her name is Katarina Lett."

"So how do you know about them?"

"I've been following their crew."

"Why's that?"

"There a ring of thieves."

"So arrest them" said Jack cinching up his wrists with a zip tie.

"I can't, I have no evidence and no justification here in Switzerland."

"Precisely that is why I'm relieving you of this burden, said Jack.

The Police Chief came through the door, to meet up to Jack to say "I know I should have followed you, this one too" as he grabbed the agent who said, "Wait what are you arresting me for?"

"Because Jack Cash said so."

"Wait he was Jack Cash, I thought he was in school?"

"They let him out on good behavior, now shut up".

"Where are you taking me?"

"Your next stop is the UN, then on to the World Court."

Then he was silent, as the Police Chief saluted Jack, to leave a police car behind.

Jack goes back to watching Tami dance all sexy, to see a stunning Spanish looking girl, who's dark complexion and piercing eyes, is being shown off by a weird looking guy, Jack's first instinct was that this guy was a predator. Thinking she is totally out of his league, but then, he thinks what if Tami was there to compete with her, only to hear, "Now she is of your equal, you know she is like that Madame you shut down in Puerto Rico."

"Really did you know her?" Jack was looking at the Chief's top assistant, Ricardo.

"Yeah, she was a regular recruiter here, till you came along and put a halt to her operation, half the men in here were hurt over it."

"Like who" said Jack looking at the Police chief, already back, to say, "It was a few blocks away, besides I didn't want to miss this encounter."

"Well now that you're here, show me who I affected and I will go arrest them."

"I thought you were going to say, "Get some information out of them."

"That too, so who do you have in mind?" asked Jack.

"First what are you drinking?"

"Nothing, not really thirsty, as I am hungry."

"Upstairs is a four star restaurant, I could get the chef to cook for us personally?"

"Nah, I'll wait till later thanks anyway" said Jack.

"You know what your problem is," said the Chief of Police, looking at Jack to add, "Is that you need to lighten up, but I know you have lots of pressure on your shoulders, especially when I had the President of the UN tell me to cooperate with you, that was impressive to get a call from him, you must have some clout."

"What's her story?" said Jack.

"Like I was saying she is your equal, she is from Spain, her name is Maria, from a very rich family, like the rest of these people, a true trust fund baby, she has a villa just south of the candy factory, on the edge of the lake, you can't miss it, the east road dead ends at her villa, it use to continue around the lake, but she had it blocked it off."

"That's a shame, so who's the guy that's with her?"

"A rich wanna be, she isn't with him, he wishes, he is a rich playboy from Paris, you want me to pick him up?"

"Nah, I'll send in Tami, but your cramping my style, give me some room" said Jack to see the Police Chief, go to the end of the bar to sit, next to Ricardo his number one, as they waited, to see what unfolded next.

"Can I buy you a drink?" said a sophisticated looking lady, as Jack looked in the mirror behind the bar, she smiles at him for her to say, "Your quiet, and handsome do you mind if I sit next to you?"

"Nah, help yourself" said Jack.

"What did our Police Chief want from you?"

"Oh, you know, just checking on those who cause trouble, does that offend you?"

"No, it actually excites me, to think your that strong and suave, I like that, so my name is Gloria, can I buy you a drink, what will you have?"

"What will it be sir" said the bartender.

"Whatever the lady thinks I should have?"

"Your quite a charmer, haven't seen you around?"

"Oh you know, I just flew in, been cooped up for a while, and this is the spot to let loose and have fun."

"Yeah, that's what a lot of people do" as she volunteered the information and then became the reporter, to say, "What do you do?".

"Who's asking?" asked Jack.

"Well the girl, who is getting wet with anticipation."

"Your quite forward?" said Jack who turned to see the woman, then back over his shoulder, to see Tami. who smiled back at him, while she was dancing on her own.

"Oh this and that, I'm retired. Then looks at her, to say, "And for you, you must have been successful."

A mixed drink was set in front of him, he placed his watch by the glass, to see a normal, fade away. Jack took a drink of it, to test it, then set it down to hear, "Why would you say that, you could have assumed I was married, and received a huge settlement."

"Or been a famous record producer" so said his phone, said Jack taking another drink.

"So you recognize me, now that's impressive, what's a suave guy like you doing here all by yourself, surely you must have a woman at home?"

"Or two or more" said Jack.

"So your married, let me see your ring."

Jack shows her his ring, proudly, for her, to say, "That's too bad."

"For who?" responds Jack. He was looking at her.

"Well you can't cheat on her."

"Coming from a woman who just ended your 5th marriage, but you still wear your ring?"

"Well what are you saying, men can cheat, and get away with it, like you?"

"I married a lesbian, who wanted me to have multiple girls come home."

"Ha, your such a liar, you talk like you're a playboy, like Gustave over there, I want a man just for me."

"You mean you want a slave to you, let you be the one in charge and he has no say, I'd say you were selfish."

"How do you figure that I'm still here, ain't I" said Gloria.

"It's not like I asked for you to come over here, but wait, I enjoy talking to you, I'm sorry" said Jack.

"That was hurt full, I was beginning to believe you."

"Alright here me out," said Jack to talk with her, as he saw Tami waving at him, and smiling, to say, "This world is filled with a lot of amazing people, like yourself, and take me for example, If I meet a lot of people around the world, there is always a chance to be intimate with them, I could hide the ring, be a totally charming guy, and say whatever you wanted to hear, but I'm not, I don't lie, and say if I told her, and she was alright with it, that's fine, but listen we are all our own individuals, we either meet someone we like or not, we either have sex with them or not, but ultimately it's our own decisions, and most importantly, you find someone you can live with, cheating is a state of mind, and actually an interpretation of all parties, you're a possessive person, your seeking to possess someone, the longer you believe in that principle, the longer you're going to be alone."

She looked at him, to smile, to say, "Your right, Let's start over, I'm Gloria Thomas, famed music producer."

"There you go again, being possessive" said Jack now getting annoyed with her, to hear, "And I've been married five times and the last time, and who are you?"

"I'm Jack Cash, I work for the United Nations, as a security advisor, I have fifteen wives, no sixteen wives, two mistresses, and fiance, and countless lovers."

She looked at him like he was crazy, to finally say, "For that knowledge I could get you in trouble."

"Depends on what country you live in."

"What, are you saying?"

"Just that, depends on your citizenship" said Jack.

"It's forbidden in every country in the world?"

"I don't believe you have all your facts straight."

"Where's that it's legal?"

"Cuba, Dominican Republic, Belarus and Latvia, as far as I know, and the US."

"Whoa wait, your saying that those countries allow multiple marriages, to one person or more?"

"Yep, And I know first-hand, in Cuba, multiple men have more than twenty five wives and over a hundred mistress's, his kids runs a whole village."

"Whoa where have I been, I didn't know that?"

"Obviously you lead a sheltered life."

She looked at him, using his words to hurt her, to say, "I'd say I was possessive but now I know the definition of a playboy, it's you jerk, as she throws her drink at him, he pulls away, for her to run into the Chief of Police, who she shoves away, and he wheels around, to handcuff her, as she is fighting back, Jack goes over to them to say, "Aaron it's a misunderstanding, she has had too much to drink, can you drive her home?"

"Yes Sir" said the Chief.

He hauls her out, into the door that was open, as the Chief of Police says, to Ricardo, "Double the guard, and give him support in there", he sets her in, the car and shuts the door, and gets in, to hear, from her,"Why are you taking orders from that jerk?"

"I should lock you up, sit back and shut up."

"You know me Aaron, why are you taking orders from him, some security advisor."

"That's true he is, but he also saved your life tonight."

"What do you mean by that?"

"While you were here, thieves were waiting at your house to rob you, from his tip, we found out about a group stealing and killing home owners, you usually get home by 8pm, like clockwork, its, 9 pm, and we have the thieves and killers in custody, however their boss was in the nightclub."

Jack went on the dance floor, to take Tami's hand to walk over to Gustave, to say, "My friend, how would you like one of my women?"

The guy's eyes lit up, seeing Tami, especially that she was showing off her cleavage, she was sweaty from dancing., she took a seat next to him, for Jack to feel his phone ringing, he turned, to answer and see it was Mark, for Jack, to see Gustave's men had pulled their weapons. For Jack, to hear, Gustave say, "You're in with the Police here, so turn around, and as Jack did he heard "Alright drop your weapons, Jack dove for Gustave as his men opened fire on the police, as Jack missed Gustave, to cover up Tami, as he pulled her off the seat, as bullets rained all over the place. Gustave and his group exited out the back. Jack's only concern was for her safety, as the bullets were coming in closer, Jack wasn't one to back down, as he kept Tami safe, Jack stood, gun ready, he shot to wound, first one to their hands, then to their thighs, in that mere second, the shooting was over, the music was off, the place cleared out, as police rushed and secured the injured men, as the Police Chief, walked in, to yell, "What is going on here, I leave for a moment and this is what happens?"

Jack helps Tami up to say, "Can you go out to our car?"

"Yes", she said, wiping her tears away, for the Police Chief say, "Is she alright?"

"As can be expected" said Jack, dusting himself off.

"What happen here?" asked the Police Chief.

"It wasn't me" putting up his hands, ask your boy wonder."

Jack watched as the Police Chief belated his top assistant who said,"That once he saw the guns drawn, he moved in" as he referred to Jack.

Jack looked at his phone to see it was from Mark, he was trapped in the plant, can you come and help us out?"

Jack went over to the Police Chief to say, "We have an issue at the candy plant, now we can do it my way, or do you want it?"

"No, it's your lead, were suppose to follow you."

"Alright let's go, you going to follow me?"

"If I can keep up."

"Don't worry I'll be slow", said Jack looking out to see his only car, that was left, he saw Tami sat inside, as he joined her, to hear, "Oh my god, it's been a while to be part of that, it's not like the spa?"

"No its not, its reality, so listen, I need to go help out Mark, can you wait till I'm through?"

"Yes, of course, sorry to be so emotional."

"No, don't worry about it, just sit back and relax, and let's go have some fun."

Jack programmed the car, as he pulled up his lap top, he punched in Gloria Thomas, as a cross reference to Gustave

Renoir, and they were connected, surprise, thought Jack. Jack dialed up Jim, as he texted what he wanted with Mitzi, and then disconnected, he knew he needed to handle her, and changed his mind, to mentally change the cars course, to do a 180, and he thought about a few options like missiles or guns, the car slowed then came to a stop, at the richly styled villa on the south of lake Geneva. Jack was on the move, as he hopped over the fence, into a courtyard, he was on the move, he pulled his gun, he hugged the wall to hear that she was on the phone, talking to a friend, as she was talking about Jack. He listened to her talk with a girl, he used his phone, to ease drop on her conversation, thinking, "Forget this" he was already to move, when she stepped out on the patio and Jack cracked her on the back of the head, she fell flat, on the patio floor, he pulled out a zip tie, and hooked up her wrists, to hear a voice from her phone, he picked it up and placed it against his phone, to say "Hi, the person you talked with is not who you think they are, Surprise" said Jack.

"Who is this, where's Maria?"

"She is getting ready for bed, do you have any last words for her?"

"No, what is your name?"

"Jack Cash" he said, and the phone went dead.

Jack took her phone, and hoisted Maria on his shoulder and carried her through her gate, to see his car, the trunk opened, he tossed her in the trunk and it closed. Jack got in to hear, "What was that all about?" asked Tami.

"Oh I just took care of a mistake, Jack drove out of there, to get back on the road however he was on the west side of the lake going south. Even though he had programmed in the car's GPS system, he saw the map, as he pulled it up to see, that there was a blocked road ahead, yet the car was speeding towards it, something was telling him, either the car knew something, even though they were going seventy. Jack surveyed the probabilities, and what the alternatives were, then he saw what the car was doing, as it slowed to think, how smart is this car, as released L two front missles took off, hit and blew out an opening. They went through now open road. Jack thought. He hit the J button, and the pigeon shot out, as it soared above the huge paneled chain link fence, as the video feed stream, showed a drilling operation, just south of the lake, he pulled up the plans, for the county and which was the city, it was the city, which was illegal, first but why were they digging, so close to the lake?", he allowed the bird continue the right hand turns to hover, till the bird was shot out of the sky, and the screen went blank. Jack kept the car going, down the road, which turned to gravel, he hit the letter S tire traction spikes, and the road was easier, as he dialed up the UN, inspector service, Identified Jack Cash and where the target is at and what property that needs to be recovered, tomorrow morning?" Jack took the road south of the villa.

He took the long way around the villa, and then back on the road south of the factory, as the road was firm. There was shops and a small town, as he sped through, then a huge sign that read "Kline Candy Company, receiving", Jack turned, in through the open gate, as the car was going where Jack wanted to go. It came to a stop, as he said, "Stay here and whomever you see stay put, and don't get out you will be safe." Tami nodded in agreement.

Jack was on the move, into the open receiving door, and north he went, through doors, then as he saw the steps up he took that to the bridge between buildings, everything was quiet, but slowed, to look at the building north of his position, as it was built into the hillside, looking like it had been like that for a while. He continued on, to either go down, or hear voices, talking about the two, down in the kitchen, he used his phone to translate the words spoken, to translate to English, he concluded that they needed to take care of them, Jack hid along a support beam, till one went one way and the other guy came towards him, he held his position, till he was close, then Jack jumped out to scare him, the guy jumped back in a defensive stance, Jack pulled his weapon and shot him in the leg, the guy went down screaming, that was till Jack zip tied his wrists and one for his mouth.

Then one for his ankles, Jack pick's him up and carts him over to the wall to be placed face down.

Jack followed the other man, who was shouting out his friends name, Jack saw him, then fired back and that guy went down, cursing and crying about being shot in the leg.

Jack jumped down, to wrestle the man's hands behind his back, then zip tied them, the same for his ankles, then a fatter zip tie for his mouth. Jack drug the man over to a wall, and out of sight.

The smell of a heavy fragrance was present. Jack looked around, to see a respirator, there on the wall was the breathing apparatus. He put it on, then donned a hood, then some long gloves, he went into the mine, a switch on the post, flipped on the lights, then a light by light went on till you couldn't see. He took two steps and hit his head, fell down, he rolled on his side to see the steel raised bar, his hand was on a rail, he rose up and went into the mine, he controlled his breathing, he went further in, as even though he had the breathing apparatus on, the intoxication, was overcoming, as he could feel the heat and the strength getting stronger, till, there was a door, then he could hear a light wine, of machinery, he opened it to see a huge mine car, to his left, then a huge machine that looked like a reaper, Jack moved closer to the machine, when someone said, "It's about time".

Jack jumped back, to see the huge guy, who said, "Where's your coveralls?"

The guy points over to the wall, Jack went over to, only get hit from behind, sending Jack into the wall, he hit, then fell back to see a shovel come at him, and he used his foot to kick out, the guy's knee, then hopped up and used his knee to the guy's head, and watched him go down. He moved over to zip tie him up, wrists, and ankles, then going south, he saw a huge driller in operation, a small front end scooper, he walked back over to the mine cart, to pick up a handful of powder, and placed some in his pocket, then zipped it up, then went out, away from the door, to see on the right was abandoned tunnel, he clicked on a light, he took out his phone, to take a picture, then sync'd it up with directions, and depth of tunnel, two miles dead north, and it is under the UN, "Interesting, I wonder if the UN knows that?", so he thought, took a picture of that reaper, he went back in the room, to see the reaper, he began to snap pictures, only to have his arms grabbed, he held onto his phone, he took a picture, and held it down. Jack was pulled over to the guy he knocked down, Jack heard, "Stretch him, across, the front of the driller."

As they waited, for the driller to back out, it was taking too long of time, as the men grew tired of holding Jack, that Jack, used one foot, to one guys, inside knee, and all three went down, Jack got up with his gun out, to see two men backing away with their hands up, as Jack side to the side, and sucker punched the guy, he earlier put down. Jack decided to end all of this, as he motioned for all three to the wall, and to turn around, he zip ties them up, then marches them out, down the way he came in. The main door was open, the UN was all over the place, as well as the Chief of the Police, as Jack pulled off his breathing apparatus, he saw Mark, who was cozied up to Kelly, Mitzi was all smiles, with a disc in hand. Police Chief Winters, said, "Come let's get you dusted off, then out of the corner of his eyes, he saw the South Atlantic team of UN inspectors, Garp and Myers, to have the woman come over to him to say, "It's good to follow you."

"I thought you work the South Atlantic?"

"Nah, we are assigned to you, and where you go we follow."

"Funny I didn't see you in Russia, or Belarus?"

"Those two countries are out of our jurisdiction, but this place is in our backyard." said Roberta Myers, smiling at him.

"Then you won't mind taking a prisoner off my hands?"

"Well we have five, are you hiding one?"

Jack thought about it to say, "Yeah, those two inside."

"Yes, and with that bird that was shot out of the sky, your girl Mitzi has that, where's Lisa?"

"On vacation, besides you'll be dealing with her from now on" pointing to Mitzi said Jack.

"That's fine, her and I are cut from the same agency, oh and to let you know, we let your stubborn girl out?" looking over at Jim, who was smiling.

"Who's that?" asked Jack as the police Chief finished brushing him off to say, "I can't take you anywhere."

"Her name was Claire, Claire Montfork?"

"Oh ya her, well whatever, so listen, can you have your agents go into the tunnels, especially under the UN."

"Don't worry, if it goes under the UN, we will get to the bottom of it, listen do you have a moment, asked Roberta, she said sweetly.

"Sure let's take a walk" said Jack.

She leads him over to the north fence away from everyone, to say, "I know, no one has told you yet, and I gather your figuring this out, but, this is how it works, you do whatever you want, on your phone, is a blue button, in the middle, that button activates us, to come in, when we arrived you weren't around, our sole job is cleanup only, were not here to assist you in any way."

"So does that go for you?"

"What do you mean?' she asks.

"Simply that, if you're in trouble, you won't call me to help you."

"No, were the UN, we have our own forces, not of course like you."

"Alright, so you're mad at me, I get that, and so I accidently pushed the blue button, believe me it won't happen again" said Jack as he began to walk away, only to feel his sleeve being pulled on."

"Do you mind" said Jack.

"Wait, let me clarify our position, you sound upset?" said Roberta.

"Why would you worry about that" said Jack walking away from her, to Mitzi, and Aaron, who he said, "Chief, can you hold someone for me?"

"Sure what did she want?"

"What you know her?"

"Yeah, she's a power hungry bitch" said the Chief.

"So You do know her."

"We have had some run-ins, but you're here now, no troubles."

"What does that mean?" asked Jack.

The police Chief used his hands to explain, to say, "Think of this place here in and around you, is your area, you're the main guy, then you have support people like me, and your group, then lastly, the UN team, that comes in to clean it up as you leave."

Jack looked at him, to realize what he did, to say, "You mean, where ever I go, I hit the blue button, and she has to come."

"Yeah why?"

"I got an idea, listen can you have your trusted available for the next eighteen hours?"

"Yeah, sure, I'll do it myself, this is fun stuff."

Jack thought about disagreeing with him to say, "All right, let's go."

"Where to?" asked the Chief of Police.

"Back to the police station, do you have a back entrance?"

"Follow me I'll lead you there."

"In a moment, as he looks at Mitzi to say,"Did you find what I was looking for?"

"Yeah, you were right the place was wide open, it's all on disc, can you take Tami back, also I want Clarance relieved, can you have him picked up, and brought back here?"

"Yes of course, anyone you want out there?"

"See if Casey or if Mike is back yet?, will do it."

"In that order?"

"That's your choice, I'd like Clarance here."

"You got it boss", as the two went around to help Tami out of the car, it was near midnight, and over to the UN hummer. Jack got into his car, to place the disc in the laptop, he fired the car up, and backed out as the UN moved their cars, to allow Jack out, he waited for the Police Chief, to pass him, he went out on the road, as he passed the entrance to see Mark and his passenger Kelly, the Police Chief, slowed around the back of the station, he parked, as Jack did the same thing, he got out, as Aaron went to see Jack as the trunk opened, there Maria was pissed off, she began to yell at him, as Jack went to touch her, as Aaron said, "Wait a minute, he pulled his weapon.

"Wait I want her alive."

Aaron, adjusted the gun, then shot Maria in the leg, as she shook and momentarily was out, to say, "Now you can get her out. Jack just looked at him, to hear, "Do you want to help me get her out of there, wow you got it padded, this isn't your first go around" said Aaron.

"Nah it's my prisoner holding cell.", as they pick her up, as Jack says, If you get the door I can carry her myself."

Jack adjusted the woman on his shoulder, as Aaron, unlocked the steel door, and then led Jack to an open cell. Jack put her on the bed, as he said, "Do you have bolt cutters?", thinking about his new tool, in his lock pick set.

"Don't worry, we will take good care of her, you better go rest, you got a major run tomorrow?"

"What do you know about that?"

"Week two is the fitness and rifle shooting week."

"Interesting, I guess I need to talk to you about my training."

Just call me, as Jack pulled his dusty phone to say, "Go", he punched it in, as he left out the door.

Jack got in his car and pulled out to see it was 0100, in the morning, he let the car take him back, he went through the check points without any problems, his UN pass was solid green, with red stripes indicating VIP, the hanger door, went up, as he drove in, at the door, was the strike team, Jack drove to the plane. Jim was there to say, your dirty, let's get you inside."

"Listen, I want you to send Clarance out to the police station, there is someone there I want questioned."

"Yes, yes, we will as soon as you're back inside."

"Excellent, I have some powder, in my pocket can you analysis it, and lastly have Clarance talk with Police Chief Winters, and get some info out of woman and her relationship with Gustave Renoir."

"Will do, same time today?"

"Yeah, I'll have my phone, said Jack pulling off his holster and gun, he unloaded it to say, "Hey Jim, what would be the chance I could get a Taser?"

"Nope, not for you," as he hands Jack four ear pieces to say, "These work better than a phone up to three miles, they speak, you listen, as he hands him one to put in his ear. said Jim adamantly.

"What do you mean?"

"Listen, your no police officer that has to worry about people lives, you're an agent who puts his life on the line, I don't agree with that."

"Agree with what" said Mitzi.

"Jack want's a Taser to carry."

"No, I agree with Jim, absolutely not."

"Alright I will see you guys tonight."

CH 10

Paris 101

Next morning, it was Tuesday, day 9, Jack and the other agents stood at the start line, his strike team, and other UN advisors were administering the run, as they were off at 0600 sharp, after thirty minutes of warm up. Chu was next to Jack as he said, “Where were you at for breakfast? Seen Michelle lately?”

“No, she has her own room, besides I slept late.”

“Too bad, now I’m gonna kick your ass in the run.”

“Doubtful” said Jack but watched as Chu took off, he was right he was tired, as Jack faded, to where Andrain was keeping a slow pace, so Jack fell in behind him, only to hear, “Hey what happen to you last night.”

“What do you mean?” said Jack still running but not looking back at them two.

“We had boys’ night out” said Jonathon.

“It’s cool, we can do it tonight” said Steven.

“Who’s we” asked Jack.

“You, me and him, said Steven.

“Alright If I can pick the place” said Jack, to add, as he fell back to them, to say, “You’re going to have to see Professor Benz, to get an overnight pass, how’s your wrist?”

"It's better, since the surgery, my carpal tunnel has cleared up, so it was a good thing, you did that, it hurt at the time, but I'm a 100 percent better."

"What do you have in mind Mate" said Steven.

"He probably means going out to Geneva, and club Octane" said Jonathon.

"How do you know about that place" asked Jack.

"I heard all about it" said Jonathon.

A voice on a bull horn said your halfway there", yelled the voice when all of a sudden, men dressed in all black attacked Vadim and Chu", as Jack and his line took their attackers head on, the ambush was well planned, as it took some agents off guard, Jack, Jonathon, and Steven subdued, their attackers, they got back out on the road, ahead of the rest, as Jack realized it was all a game, it was real, but continued on with the game. They went a ways, then down the hill to the squadrons, obstacle course, they came to the rest station, as they asked who was first, they looked at the pair, as Steven, said, "Yeah, I know the drill, I'll go first, then Jon, then Jack."

The UN advisor said, "Is that the order you all accept?"

The three shake their head, as Jack found a protein bar, and juice, as Jonathon, hands Jack his, for Jack to say, "Are you sure?"

"You gotta stop skipping breakfast."

"You only say that because you don't know what I got I'm working with."

"True, I'll my girl wants to do is eat, did you get your case from the candy factory?"

"Yeah, I don't know, perhaps" said Jack.

"Who's next?" said the advisor, as Jonathon sees Jack still eating, to raise his hand.

Jack continued to eat and drink, feeling his strength back, stood in line and waited, as a group of three come over the hill, Chu, Andrain and Vadim.

Jack took off, over a few obstacles, then over a hill, to stand on a log, as he jumped to the next one, then down a zip line, the course was easy, but it was gradual as it was cut in the hill side, just his momentum carried him up and over, Jonathon, was way ahead of him, and down below, Steven was near finished. Jack noticed he still had his watch on, but that was the last of him thinking, at each obstacle was three soldiers, Jack noticed them as mere spotters, as an advisor walked the course with him, Steven was through, and told to go, he looked back at Jonathon, then trotted off. Jonathon finished the course, next and was told to go, but ran in place instead, waiting for Jack, who was closing the gap quickly, behind him he saw another agent on the course. Jack finished the course with the rope walk over water, then down, the plank bridge, to hear finish up your race, Jack pickups' Jonathon, and the two took off, Steven was on a slow pace home, on the horizon, the sun broke the day, and they both saw Steven tiring, and then they decided to kick it into gear. Steven was looking down, as the pair caught up with him, for Jack, to say,"Hey boy wake up, see ya".

Jack and Jonathon blew past Steven, only for him to pick up the momentum, as the road took a turn, towards the UN, where a car sat and a young girl had the hood up, Jonathon pointed to Jack to stop.

"Suit yourself, I don't know her, do you?"

"I will" said Jonathon.

"I wouldn't" said Jack, as Jonathon stopped, to talk with her, as Steven past him only to see the UN soldiers ambush Jonathon, and he was done, Jack cruised through the finish line, next was Steven. The UN advisor said, "Meet in the meeting room at one pm sharp." Jack ran past him, to the open door, which, soldiers held the doors open for Jack, as he went in, the cool air felt good, he went right to his old room on the women's floor, realizing it was Michelle's, he turned back around and went upstairs, to his room, using his hand, and the door slid open, it was 0923, and then saw two huge boxes of candy and chocolate from the candy company.

An hour later, he had showered and dressed, he picked up his phone, to see the missed calls, he scrolled down, to see a print out of the white powder. It was called Calcamite, it was discovered, and kept secret, except for a patent, under Joseph Klein, the grandfather, of Kelly, is an addictive substance, used in the candy to lure and keep the patrons to continuing to buy their candy, however the by-product that which is refined, becomes an oil, which is used in perfume making, in Paris, France, by the Renoir industries, in addition, the refined powder from the Calcamite is a strong attractant used in a multitude of drugs to enhance their dependency.

Jack closed up the phone to say, "Looks like the boys night out will be Paris, tonight." said Jack as he finished dressing, phone in place the door opens to see a stunningly beautiful blonde, it was Trixie, who had her hand on her hip to say, "This was supposed to be our time together, half the night your off and, all I do is sit here and wait, will you be here tonight for me?"

"No, I'm off to Paris" said Jack.

"Can I come? She asked.

"No, you need to stay here and brush up on whatever they teach you, and receive Debby."

"I will under one condition?"

"Yes, I'm waiting?"

"That you're in my bed at some point."

"Perhaps" said Jack, as Jack collects her up and left as the door closed.

Jack takes Trixie to the mess, where he orders up a steak and fries, with blue cheese, and an artichoke, with melted butter, she is fine, as he takes four milks, two chocolate, and sits down, with Trixie across from him, while he ate, and drank, to say, as she reached for his hand, to say, "What would it take for me to go with you to Paris?"

"Nothing really, I guess I could use you as a decoy."

"Yes, use me as a decoy, this sounds like fun."

"Well get to the plane and chart a course to Paris?"

"Will do, as she got up, went over to him, took both of her hands, and placed them on the sides of his head, and gave him a kiss, it was wet and juicy, as she bit his lower lip, to say, "Tonight you and me lover, when do you wanna leave?"

"After five PM, or whenever I get out of here."

"See you later."

As the jumbo jet, flew in, taxied, given prior clearance, the hanger went up, and taxied in next to their plane, lowered the ramp, and out stepped Erica Meyers, and Miss Samantha, with Chloe Ryan in tow, Jack's soon to be wife. they escorted them over to the plane where Jim was holding court, and they all welcomed Miss Erica, who had a wild look in her eye. Clarance was back from the police HQ, and was ready to go back into the UN, but as he passed Erica, he noticed something different, but past her and she caught up, and the two went through service entrance where her credentials let her pass. Debby was first to greet them, as Clarance said, "See you all later" and went back into the UN.

Erica acted like something's up, but Debby was unsure what it was, didn't know what to say, and she realized, it wasn't her place, to further say. As Erica had a troubled look on her face, to say, "I need to see Jack now?" Now Debby knew something is up, as she said, "Currently he is in class, but I can get word you want to see him, in the meantime, let me put you in his suite?"

She agreed, and followed her to the Suite, Debby swiped her card, the door opened to a room, that six pallets sat, with two additional candy ones, for Debby to say, "Make yourself comfortable, I'll tell him you're here waiting."

Jack sat in class, along with his new mate, Steven, who was sitting in Vadim's seat, on the first row of luxury seats, high back, with a refrigerator as which Jack pulled a soda from. The order was as post; Jack Number one, Vadim, number two, Tad number three, Carlos, number four, and Steven number five. Next row, behind Jack was Ben Hiltz, number six, Thomas, number seven, Hendon, number eight, Jonathon, number nine, and Mustapha, number ten. The last row, in regular existing chairs, was Simon, number eleven, Chu number twelve, Jamal, number thirteen, Andreas, number fourteen, Andrian, number fifteen, Kyle, number sixteen, Benjamin, number seventeen, and Gordon was number eighteen. Jack, leaned out to say; "Did both of you get a pass from Professor Benz, yet?"

"I was just going to wait till class, was over" said Steven.

"No, it's a secret, you need to do it before class, we don't want the others to know what we're doing?"

"Oh yeah, I gotcha" said Steven, slipping out to get up.

"You're taking your tray right?"

"Yeah" Jack said looking at him, then looking around at all the others left behind, to say, "Yes Dad" said Jack.

"If that is the way your…."

"No, no sorry, I forgot your sensitive, sorry, said Jack.

"Hey have you had your candy yet?" asked Steven.

"Nah, I'm not much into the sugar stuff, said Jack, to add "You better go with him." Jack said to Jonathon.

"You got it boss, as a familiar face shows up for Steven to look at her, with his hands up, to hear, Trixie say, "I'm Jack's mistress."

Jack looks at the two, to say, "Do you mind getting her tray too."

"Of course not" said Steven smiling at Trixie, who said, "My name is Trixie."

"Sure you are" said Steven leaving, for her to say, "Tell me something Jack, how is it you already have made good friends?"

"It's not hard, I'm likable," said Jack as he guides her to the men's mess and took a seat, she sat across from him.

"Yes you are", as she began to eat her chef's salad, to say, "I have a whole new respect for you now, these classes are wonderful, and your bodyguard Ivan the Giant, he wants to go to school."

"So he will, he deserves it," said Jack.

"This place is phenomenal, everyone is so nice, and all they have is nice things to say about you, do you know your activities for the week?" asked Trixie.

"No, not really" said Jack as a chef came over to drop off a bag to say, "Here, you go Mister Cash?"

"What's that?"

"Your evening meal" said Dany.

"Are you wearing make up?" asked Jack.

"So you noticed, I was wondering what time you'll be back tonight?" asked Dany the chef.

"Why? Asked Jack finishing up the last rib he had.

"Well, I want to give you something."

"For what, you don't owe me anything?"

"Oh you'll see" she said leaving, and for Trixie to say,

"These classes are amazing, I just realized, the position I'm in," she looked at him, as he wiped off his fingers and his mouth.

"What I'd like to say is that it is true everything revolves around you, but, you could have anyone by your side, as a trusted employee to you, I must give myself to you with free of mind, and give you the pleasure, that Debby does without commitment, even though Jim and her have pledged to be together, when this is all over," said Trixie, adding herself to him.

"What's that" asked Jack.

"Well maybe I said too much" said Trixie digging.

"No you haven't, are you saying Debby and Jim are together?"

"Well yes, sort of."

"How long has this been going on?"

"Oh about a month ago, but anyway, I learned, either were in or were out, so I want to let you know that I'm in, forever."

"That's not what they mean?" said Jack looking at her, she looked at him to say, "What do you mean?"

"Well what they're talking about, it is being on the edge, and knowing that the decisions you make are the right ones, cause if there wrong you could get killed or simply be left behind.

"Oh" she said looking at him. She was pretending to listen.

"I didn't bring you here because I wanted to have sex with you, I wanted you to enjoy yourself, take in what the UN has to offer, and really have fun, now if you choose to lay in my bed, like maybe Debby wants to, but maybe she is doing it because she thinks she has to, I'll go ask her."

"Wait" she said, as she pulled on his arm, knowing she went too far with him.

"What are you doing, all she has to do is tell me what is going on" said Jack pulling away from her, with his tray in hand, he deposits it, and with his Chinese dinner in hand, he heads to his room.

Jack enters to see Miss Erica Meyers, for Jack to say,"Hey Boss what's up?"

She came to him in somewhat of a desperation, to say, "Its over?"

"What is it, are you talking about?"

"It's official, the Supreme Court, is turning you and Ben over to the UN to regulate national and international work, so I'm out a job?"

"What about your position at the spy academy?"

"I was only a liaison between the Supreme Court and your actions" said Miss Erica, nearly crying.

"No, you're not listening to me, you work for me at the spy academy, I don't care that you have lost your job at the Supreme Court."

"Well I've chosen another job."

"What about you becoming a wife?"

"I told you I don't like to share, I want you all to myself?"

"And I told you I had wives before and I'll have wives after you."

"So what you're saying is that, I'm just a number to you?"

"No, I didn't say that, just that you're my boss, and I'll do what I can for you?"

"Then why didn't you go after Varfolomey when you had the chance?"

"Who cares about him, he will get his due, I have bigger issues than a kidnapper," said Jack not even looking at her, as she had tears in her eyes, as she wept, knowing it was over between them, finally, as she kept her secret, as she left, she stopped at the door, to allow it to open for her, then she was gone.

Jack was on his phone, sitting at the large table, with a map of Paris in front of him, to see the door slid open, there was Debby, with her cart in hand, sees Jack, to say, "Hi, how have you been?"

Jack just waved to her, she noticed that, but began to pick things up, to constantly look at Jack who was busy, on his phone, then jot down some coordinances.

She felt like he was icy, as she went into the bedroom, moments later she came out to say, "Hey that isn't like you, what's up?"

Jack turns to see her holding a towel up in the air, for her to say as a joke, "This was on the floor?"

"So hang it up, what's up with you" said Jack.

"What's up with me, how about you?"

Jack turns in his seat, to see her, as she tosses the towel away, steps forward, to part his knees, to stand next to him, to say, "Now what were you saying?"

"When's your boyfriend getting back?"

"What, what are you saying, I have no boyfriend?"

"Come on I know, you need not lie anymore."

She unbuttoned her apron, to let it fall away, then started to un do her blouse, to hear from Jack, "Stop, not now, not ever."

"Wait, where is this all coming from, I have no boyfriend, you're the only guy for me, who told you this", to add "I want to know", as she continued to unbutton her blouse to let fall, and before Jack could respond, she popped her bra, for her to say, "Now look up, these are for your eyes only, if someone told you different, there mistaken, I choose to be here, one to be close to you and second to rekindle what chemistry we had in Arkansas."

"That's what I always liked about you, head strong and self-determinate, so if that's the case what's your relationship with Jim?"

"Jim, where did that come, oh wait, I know who told you, it was Trixie, she overheard a conversation between him and I as he tried to pick me up, and told me he loves me, I told him, as I have told at least every other man that has been my boss, but as I told him, there is only one man for me, and that is you, and here touch these" she said pulling his hands to her breasts, to continue, "As I told Jim, if at some point if you don't want me ever, then I may consider my options open, but its highly doubtful that will ever happen, besides I'd consider myself your mistress, what do you say?"

"I'd say, I don't trust that source anymore, as he unbuttons her pants, to get up, and bends her over the table, to announce, "Lock down", then drops his pants, he was ready and inserted into her, her willingness was very evident. With each stroke, he held onto her hips to grind it out, he noticed the clock was nearing the One in the afternoon, to pull out and dump on her butt, he zipped up, to say, "So officially you're my mistress, if I ask you to be a wife what will you say?"

"Yes, she moaned, turning to see him, but I can't have any children?"

"That's too bad, I'll take this, if you're alright with that?"

"Forever, absolutely, she said as she turned to hug him, the two kissed, as she whispered "May I seek revenge on her?"

"No, but make sure she gets plenty of candy, and leave her alone, also, I want you to end it with Jim, just you and I?"

"Yes sir" she said, as he picked up his phone, and said "Do you want to participate in some action tonight?"

"Absolutely." Said Debby, coming to him.

"If you do, that means you will be out."

"Then no, I'll stay here and wait for you."

"Good answer" said Jack, leaving, as the door opened leaving Debby nude for all to see, but she didn't care, as she knew she just moved up the chain, as the door slid shut.

The last hour of class was concluding, as Professor Benz said, "Before I forget, let's talk about protocol, when dealing with the UN Inspectors, now some of you, may not even know that they are there, some of you have relationship with them, and some may not get along with them, Overall, the UN is your friend, however, at no times will they be insubordinate to you, on some of your phones is a button, if you push it a team will be at your disposal, except in Communist countries where we are not respected, but in the event that we find out that occurs then action will be taken, in this such action has occurred quite recently, to one of your fellow agent's, he was confronted by the inspector for accidently calling them in, what that Inspector said was illegal, and incorrect, each and every agent that is assigned to us, is protected and therefore they are at your disposal, for anything, in addition, you the agent is in charge, not the inspector, and at no time will that ever occur, there will be times when you need them, do not hesitate to call on them, where ever you are at, there is supposed to be a UN team covering your every move, in addition several of you already have a support team, that does the same function as what we do."

Jack rose his hand, he called on him for Jack to say, "So what happens to that agent?"

"She or he will be taken off active duty."

"How can she be placed back on?"

"Only if you want her back."

"And that's it" said Jack, wondering if he was talking about him and Roberta.

"That's it, however let me tell you this, and this goes for all you rest of agents, you have the power to save anyone, or dictate what you want to happen to them, like say you want a prisoner to be held, you can instruct how and when where and what you want from them."

Jack looked at him, thinking, "This information would have been helpful last night, but what about this whole agent thing, and what challenges do they have in store for all of us."

Jack looked down at his watch, to see that it was slower than the one on the wall, the huge chalk board revealed tomorrow's actions, called the mud run, because it was beginning to rain, and the outdoor cameras were showing it to be so, while Jack and the others listened to the Professor ramble on, Jack thought maybe he was right, I could have missed it he thinks."

Debby, finished her shift, and went to the exchange center, where she saw that it was Jim this time, with that boyish smile and rugged looks, she knew it was over and he was going to have to be let down easy, as she saw him come close, for her to say, "Hold it right there."

"Hey what's going on" asked Jim.

"He knows about us?"

"What, how, who?"

"It was Trixie, she overheard your confession of love, which then she told Jack, and now I may be out if you don't leave me alone."

"Okay let's think about this."

"There's nothing to think about, it's totally over."

"What, why, I love you" said Jim.

"Yes and I told you that my first love was Jack, and once he says it's over, well then we may pick up things."

"Well I told you that I was cool with that" said Jim, to add, "Anything I should know about?"

"Nah, from now on, I'll send Trixie to handle the communiqué's, so you can deal with her lies."

"Alright, what is Jack's plans?"

"I think he is going somewhere to where he will need to fly."

"Thanks for the info, you need anything from us?"

"No, he is in the UN building, he has anything and everything a man could want," said the frustrated Debby, with a tear in her eye, for Jim. She left and closed the door.

Jack looked at his watch to see that it was five past five, and the Professor said something about a Rugby game, Switzerland is holding a tournament, this weekend, and each of us gets to participate in each game, the one team that advances the furthest wins a prize."

Jack was ready to go, when the Professor said, "Let's see what player goes with which team, as he motioned for all to get up and over to the leader board, there was Jack, at the top, for Professor Benz to say, are you taking our home country of Germany?"

Steven moved closer to his friend, to whisper, "Choose New Zealand, and impress everyone?" pointing to the top teams on the opposite board, that showed New Zealand on the top, for Jack to say, as Jack looked at the Professor, who said, "Choose and you can go?"

"New Zealand," said Jack, and next was Vadim, he took Russia, Steven was next, he choose Australia, Tad Jones, choose England, Carlos, choose Cuba, Ben Hiltz choose the US, Hendon choose Turkey, in following what Z'sofia, was doing, Simon Jonas, thought about North Korea, but saw it wasn't available, and next available under New Zealand choose, South Africa, Thomas Jones, choose Wales, Mustapha, choose Israel, Kyle Devon, choose, Egypt, Chu, said, Japan, Jamal, choose Saudis Arabia, Jonathon choose France, Andreas, choose native Greece, Andrain, choose Norway, Benjamin Logan choose Columbia, and lastly it was Gordon, he choose Italy.

"Dis-missed."

Jack checked over his phone to see his number one message was from Clarance, who said, "How can I help you out now, boss." Jack thought to himself, "Just be who you are".

Jack broke away only to have the Professor stop him to say, "Try to keep an eye on them, their like lambs, I hope you don't lead them to the slaughter."

"Nah, were just going to Paris."

"That's what I mean."

"They will be fine" said Jack, to add, "What time is that course start?"

"When you guys get back?" said the Professor.

"That's what I like about you, "You're so understanding", said Jack on his way out.

Jack went to his room, picked up his leftover Chinese food, and picked up all his papers, to stuff in a pouch. The door slid open, there was Debby at the door, she walked in like she owned the place, dressed to the tens, opened her mouth, to begin to say, "Are you going out again?"

"What do you want from me?"

"Just what, you want, you know inside of me?"

"Well I doubt that will ever happen again?"

"What do you mean?, what happen to earlier, remember I'm your mistress?" she asked as she began to undress, for Jack to say, "Don't bother, I'm leaving, A mistress to me, is someone, who keeps it a secret, and the surprise is the best part." said Jack on his way out to hear "Jaaack".

Jack picked up the pace, to see Steven and Jonathon, was waiting at the guard's station, with passports and passes in hand, sees Jack, who waves to the guards, who allows him to go.

Jack says, "There with me", and they picked up the pace to follow.

Jack passed all check points as the other guys were on his heels, Jack pushes the door open to the hanger, the strike team was on the ready, with weapons drawn at salute, as Jack passed by them, and held their position, till the guests were on board.

Jack was greeted by Mitzi, for Jack, to say, "Can you have Jim get some guns for our guests, and send Trixie in."

Steven and Jonathon, stood by Jack's cabin, to see an older beautiful woman, who said, "My name is Mitzi, and would like for you to take a seat forward, I'll have Casey get you some helmets for the trip."

Jonathon looked at her to say, "Whose plane is this?"

"Oh, it's Jack's plane, we all work for him."

Mitzi went into the flight cabin, to get things moving, Tami and Trixie got up, as did Jim. Then the pilot Bill, fired up the plane, the ramp went up, Mike looked at Tami, to see her close the cabin door.

Mitzi went to see Casey, to let him know they had guests, he would send Clark and Bauer up.

Jim, went in to the cage, to pull out two .45 Cal pistols, he loaded them, with two clips, one in and one on a sling arm holster.

Jonathon watched in amazement how Mitzi was talking with the one soldier that appeared to look like a woman, she nodded and agreed, then, Mitzi knocked and waited, the door opened, she went in, to shut the door.

"Where to boss?" asks Mitzi.

"In between bits of egg rolls, he dipped in an orange sauce to say, "I want Jim to fly us into Paris International airport, while Mark, who is babysitting Kelly, at her family's candy company."

"Have Clarance find out Gloria Thomas role in all of this is? Good, be on your way, have Tami, get with Jim on making up an ID for our two guests, said Jack. Jack continued to eat.

Jonathon, watched a gorgeous girl leave Jack's suppose room looking at Steven, who said, "Calm down, it's only a girl, only to see Trixie leave. Bauer, in front of them, to offer a helmet, only to see a tough looking guy, open the hatch, and then, close it up, to say, "Who was that?"

"A tough guy" said Jim, looking over at the two agents, to see Tami close by, to say, "What's your names and where are you from, are you in the system?"

"Whoa wait Miss, one minute why do you need to know all of this?" said Jonathon.

"When we land, and in case you get into trouble, will be able to find you?"

"Fair enough Mate, my name is Steven Smith, I'm from Australia, and of the other thing I don't know."

"Perth or Sydney?"

"Sydney" said Steven.

"And what I was referring to is the International Spy Network?" said Tami.

"No, don't know about it."

"That's alright I'll check?" said Tami, to add, "What about you?"

"Names, Jonathon Razor, from Paris France, and I think my ranking is 126, nationally."

"How do you know that mate?" said Steven.

"It's simple, someone dropped out and I was added at the last minute" said Jonathon.

"Listen up boys, I want both of you to sit, here, for the entire flight, put on these helmets, when Tami has your ID's ready I'll get you your guns." said Jim, going into the flight cabin.

As Casey and Bauer took a seat, on each of the boy's sides, for Jonathan to say to Bauer, "What do you do for Jack?"

"Support and assistance" said Craig.

"Really, what about her, pointing to Mitzi "he asks.

"She too", said Craig.

"Wait you mean anything?"

"Sure, why not he is a super spy?"

Jonathon's preoccupation, with Tami ended suddenly as a huge guy, with a stern look on his face, ordered, silence. All four looked at him, as he sat beside Craig.

"What's his problem" asked Jonathon.

"Ssh, you'll get us both killed" said Craig.

The plane taxied, as Jack's instructions, from his room, was given the clearance to take off, to hear, "If your hungry, I'll serve you up a meal?" said Mitzi.

"Maybe on our way back." said Jack.

As he finished dressing, the plane took off, to hear Mitzi say, "We have another problem?"

"What's that" asked Jack.

"I believe Trixie life's in danger?"

"How's that?"

"Well, it has been kept secret for some time, but, she and Mark are still having an affair?"

"Really, and how long has this been going on?"

"Don't really know, however, when, they both Mark and Brian were asked to relieve Clarance, well Brian stepped up to prove his worth, leaving Mark behind."

"Brian didn't need too, he is my armorer, I'd much have preferred, Mark over Brian, in the field."

"Yes, but Brian was covering for him, and besides he is a better sniper" said Mitzi.

"That is true, as you were saying?"

"Well, she may have said something's that other people may have found offensive."

"So what are you saying?"

"That once she gets out that she goes home?"

"Perhaps but who will watch over Natasha, when she arrives, and how come Jesse isn't here?"

"Well Mike will be watching Natasha, as for Jesse, he is here now, you just haven't seen him, shall I go get him?"

Mitzi left, and moments later, in walked Jesse, to say, "Yes sir, I hope I haven't failed you?"

"No, you haven't, but I do want you to keep up the good work, that will be all," said Jack.

Jesse leaves, as Mitzi came back in, to say, "So did you tell him?"

"Nah, I couldn't, I don't know what his response will be."

"That's not for you to decide, just let it play out, said Mitzi, for her to say, "What do you plan on doing with Debby?"

"I don't know, I'll have Clarance get to the bottom of this, somehow and some way, in the end if it jeopardizes the mission, she will be out."

"Wait, why, what has she done now?"

"It's just the way she acts, send her home, I'm getting a bit tired of her pushiness anyway?"

"How so" asked Mitzi finding another problem, with a greater existence, to add, "What has she done?"

"She just wants to play house, and act like were married."

"Whoa, don't worry about that, that won't happen again, I'll talk with Debby and get to the bottom of this, and adds, "Anything else?"

"Yeah, could you give me a moment and send my friends in."

"Sure, right away".

She leaves and moments later, the two men step into, the room, and close the door, to see Jack dressed, in kind of a teal outfit, for Jonathon to say, "Boy, you got it made."

"What do you mean "asked Jack looking at him finishing his egg rolls.

"Just that, this is your own plane, and the girls here are hot, I mean super-hot."

"So, there my trusted friends, don't you have a plane?"

"Heck no, I flew coach from Paris to Geneva, then bussed up to the UN, and what you just flew in."

"Yeah, I fly everywhere, or hop out of a plane whatever it takes, what about you Steven?"

"I don't even know what you're talking about."

"How so" asked Jack.

"Well first I don't have a plane, nor a vehicle, let alone a support team, how did you get those two hot girls?"

"On one of my last missions" said Jack, to think which one is he talking about.

"How many missions have you been on?"

"I don't know, really lost count, but along the way, I seem to collect both men and women."

"I noticed your handle is white, can I see it?"

"Nah, it's a mood gun, basically, it's designed for my hand only, some call it a smart gun."

The door opens, to hear, "It's called a signature weapon," said Jim, to add, "Jack we have a problem, can we talk?"

"Steven and Jonathon, meet Jim, he handles the plane."

They wave to him, as Jim, came close and whispered, "Their not agents, nor any true classification of being a spy, Jon from France was a replacement bounty hunter, and Steven from Australia well he, let's say he is a volunteer, lastly I don't feel comfortable giving them weapons."

Jack puts his hand up to say, "Alright, give us a moment?"

Jack waits for the door to close, to say, "Alright out with the truth?" asked Jack, to see blank faces, to add, "This is a Super

Spy, forum, it was supposed to be the world's best spies, so out with it, why are you here and what do you hope to accomplish?"

"Well like I said, I basically volunteered, because the regular guy was hurt" said Steven.

"Same for me basically, but I was an alternate" said Jonathon, to add, "But I did get surgery, for free?"

"To me it sounds like, you have no idea what you're getting yourself into, both of you.", now knowing what the Professor was talking about now.

They both shake their heads Yes, for Jack to lay out the law, and what he does on a daily basis, he was still considering allowing them weapons, but will decide when they land, he now was thinking, they may have to stay on the plane, till Jonathon said "I heard were going to Paris, I could show you around?"

"Perhaps", thinks Jack but would rather have someone who could fight, to say, "Have either of you been in a hand to hand fight? as they look at one another, to say "No".

"Great", thinks Jack to himself, he was thinking of turning the plane back, time was ticking away, they were about an hour away, as he had an idea, but decided against it when he pulled out his phone to see all that he wanted from Clarance and much more, to hear, "I stepped in, and she told the whole story". Jack thought about a three hour flight to Paris by helicopter, and sent out a text to Clarance to bring Mark and Chief Winters to Paris, and to leave her there, still intact?"

"Yes understood, A.S.A.P." said Clarance.

To say out loud, "Alright, so you guys want to be spies?"

They both shook their heads to say, "Yes", for Jack to add, "Alright, I will help you, the first order of business, ID a motto I picked up from the Marines, Swift, Silent and Deadly and be Discreet."

"First thing a spy needs is his feet, to run, to evade and to defend, next your silent, at all times, observing, seeing what's around you, like a tracker, and never make a sound and lastly be deadly, with your fists, feet and knife, lastly use deadly force as needed and never kill to kill, always injure, so that you can question later, and that's all you need to know to be a spy," said Jack, as he continued, "But if you want all this, you need to build a reputation, and to do that you need to participate in missions, where you interact with others and see how well you perform, there will be people who will lay down their lives for you at all costs to them first, because in some cases, you are their mission, do you understand?"

"So what you're saying is the people on this plane, have a mission to take care of you at all costs, and nothing else matters" said Steven.

"Precisely, so from this point forward, remember those three things it will save your life, as for coming with me, I think I will go alone?"

"Had you ever been to Paris before?"

"Nope, but it can't be hard to get around."

"Trust me there are bad people out there and I could help you out" said Jonathon.

"Precisely" said Jack to add, "Now take a seat on the sofa, we will be there soon."

Clarance went to the police station with Gloria in tow, after a dance at her home in Geneva, he looked over at the Police Chief, as they put her behind bars, earlier Maria was released, her ankle cared for, for Clarance who looked at his message from Jack to say, "Know anyone who has a helicopter?"

"Where do you need to go?" asked the Police Chief.

"Jack wants us in Paris?"

"You need something faster than a helicopter, you need a jet."

For Clarance to say,"Know anyone who has a fast jet?"

"Yeah, she is in the cell?"

"What her, really?", to say, "Open it back up" said Clarance.

Police Chief Winters stepped in to unlock the ancient door, Clarance stepped in, to see her, for her to say, "I get it, what do you want now, I told you everything I know, you know I'd like to get out of here."

Clarance looked at Aaron to say, "You have another option?"

She stands up to say, "Whoa wait what are you going to do to me, look mean man, I'll give you money, do you want money?"

"Shut up, I want you to be quiet" said Clarance.

"Alright what do you want from me, I will give it to you, just don't hurt me."

"Will you shut up, and no right now I won't hurt you but I do need something."

"What is it, I'll help you out?"

"Shut up, and let me speak," said Clarance.

She backs down, to allow him to be more articulate when he was speaking, to say,"Alright, you have something I need?"

"And you have something I want" she said coyly.

Clarance looks at her then to the Police Chief, to raise his hands to say, "I heard you have a jet, can I borrow it?"

"Under one condition."

"What's that?"

"That you take me with you."

"That would require me, to go against what my boss wants."

"Take it or leave me alone."

"Let's go, but stick close by" said Clarance, resigning himself to her.

Mark and Clarance passed the slower plane, of Jack Cash, as they veered off to avoid the jet wash, as the jet came ever so closely to Jack's, as Gloria was warming herself up to the mean man, to say, "Ever have a girlfriend?"

"No," he said sternly, as the Lear jet made it, in 30 minutes, as they landed at Paris International Airport. Clarance was first up and out of the jet, only to turn back to see Gloria, to say, "Go back in your seat, when we leave, you can leave yourself."

"Oh, no, you're not getting rid of me that quickly, I'll wait for you, don't be long."

Clarance looked at her, to have Mark, pat his arm to say "Come tough guy, leave the girl alone, we need to get ready to receive when Jack finally gets here."

Jack, was pacing, as the plane was on the descent downward, into the airport. The plane taxied, into a hanger, where Mark guided the plane in and Clarance was at the hanger door.

The plane stopped and the ramp went down. The strike force ran out, to their positions, except for Jesse and Jim, and pulls out the Mercedes, McLaren, super car. Jack exited the room, with his two friends, Jack stood on the top of the ramp, to say, "Mark, Clarance, I want the two of you, to handle the outskirts, and work your way into the destination, and that place will be Renoir Industries, and Renoir castle, I want three teams of the strike team, of two."

"Steven and Jonathan, I want either of you to work with some of my seasoned members, meet Mark, and Clarance. "Trixie come with me, were going to catch some criminals."

Trixie was ready, as she slid into the car, Jack got in, and sped away.

Clarance looked at Mark to say, "The company or the estate?"

"If it's my choice, it doesn't matter" said Mark.

"Then I'll pick the place you pick the rookie, and I'll chose the company" said Clarance.

"Then I'll chose the Australian," said Mark.

A parade of SUV's arrived there courtesy of the French secret police, who were the drivers, Clarance and Jonathan slid into one, as Clarance with his raspy voice, spoke perfect French, and off they went.

Jonathon saw how fast this officer drove, but he had questions, to ask, to say, "Who asked these fellow countrymen to help us out?"

"Jack did" said Clarance.

"Yes, but how does he know to call them?"

"It's a spy thing, he knows everyone."

"Why do you work for him?"

"By reputation, I guess, I actually just joined the team."

"How does one apply?"

"I don't know?, it's a bit of luck, knowing the right people, and having the right attitude."

"Would you take a bullet for him", said Jonathon.

"Why would you ask that?" says a calm and composed Clarance, thinking why he was there, because Jack Cash asked him to babysit him.

Meanwhile, Mark and another driver was off to the Manor, but noticed Jack's car was up ahead, and so they followed him, to hear, "What's it like Mate to work for Jack?"

Mark turns in his seat to say, "Fun, I guess why?"

"Does he have a reputation as some may have said?"

"Yes, and much more, it actually saved, another agent from certain death."

"Wow, so his reputation, was so great, it saved lives, why are you working for him, and not out on your own?"

"It's a thing called the edge, Jack is in, and everyone else is out, and I'd like to be in" said Mark.

"What's he like to work for as a boss?"

"It doesn't work like that, were like his eyes and ears, and behind the scenes, and he is out front facing the enemy, he is first to get shot at, and the one who gets the big payday."

"Are you married Mate?"

"Nah, not while Jack is out traveling, were always on the move, how bout you why did you choose to be a spy?"

"For the fun of it all, and besides the Australian government is paying me hundred thousand per year", Mark looked at him, to think he was making ten times that a year, plus bonuses.

The dress was riding up high on Trixie's thigh, while Jack allowed the car to drive itself, while he was on his lap top and monitoring police chatter, he had been talking with the Chief of Police, from Geneva, who was working with the Chief of Paris police force, and word out there was a huge party at Oslo Inn, downtown, Avenue George V, the car slowed at the night club, he pulled into a diplomat spot, he Hit N, and the plates turned Diplomatic. They both got out, he held her hand, and saw a line, he went right to the door, and they let him in, the night club was hopping, he was near the dance floor, to see some of the familiar faces from last night, on a pole was the Spanish beauty Maria, who's ankle was heavily bandaged, in the corner was Gustave Renoir, whom had a very hot blonde on his one arm and a brunette on the other, while Trixie gathers the drinks for them, a man dressed in traditional Police gear, says, "For a man of your stature, why spend the evening here, Mister Jack Cash."

"I'm here for Gustave Renoir."

"And that's it, how about the famed pop queen from Spain, Maria?"

"Nah no use for her, I have her, this night" said Jack pointing over at Trixie.

"Yes, a fine choice indeed, however, when you want the capture, do allow me an advance notice, but next time you come to our fair city, please stay longer, we always like to celebrate a hero", said the inspector, as he tipped his hat, and strolled off.

"You know he's right you could have any woman, here you want, why choose me?" asked Trixie.

"True, because I like you, and trust you, I'll see you in a minute, try not to get into trouble" said Jack as he walked onto the dance floor, he made the first move, young bodies gyrated around him, as he saw the two girls flee, and Gustave get up, the same cast of characters were also moving, when he felt a hand across his butt, he quickly grabbed her wrist, to turn her towards him,to see it was the blonde, he pulled her close, to say, "What's a nice girl doing in place like this."

"Trying to make money."as others crowded them.

Jack was pushing her backwards off the dance floor, into a wall, as he put leverage on her weak arms to hear her cry, he said "Tonight is your last night doing this, if I so hear of you doing this again, I'll track you down, and do you myself."

"What's this about sex, Mister, Gustave sent me over to entertain you."

Jack let go of her arm and she fell to the floor, got up and went off.

"Now as I was saying, do you want to put me into that position, I'm sure I will enjoy it more" asked another blonde.

"What is your name?" asked Jack looking at her, while turning, his back, to face her, as two arms grab him, and haul him back, into a quiet room, to a chair, the dark, room becomes light as Gustave is there, waiting, to say, "Ah, the famous Jack Cash, super spy, how an bout you tell me why you're in my club, and please don't leave out any details."

Jack looks at him, only to feel his hands being tied down, and a hood over his head, to hear, "In a minute I want to watch him die first, to add, "You have had way too much time to think about what you need to say, off with his head."

Jack at that moment realized, it was no fun and games anymore, he was serious, as at that last second he ducked to feel a waves of air above his head, using his jacket sleeve, he slid a knife out, to cut off the restraints, and as quickly, he was out of the restraints, he fell forward, rolled, pulled his gun, and fired two shots, he pulled off his hood, to see two direct kill shots, for Jack he knew it was time to end all of this now.

Jack came out of the room, with his gun out, as he saw a guard and fired, direct hit, he was moving with precision, he saw Gustave, and fired, but saw that he ducked, and his guard went down, they had a door open, Jack fired again, as another guard went down. Jack was at the door, to see a black car sped off. Behind them was a big black SUV fast behind them.

Jack went inside, to see that blonde, who was fast at work, lifting a wallet, she turned as Jack gave her an uppercut, and she went up and back and to the ground to release the wallet, as Jack stepped over her, stopped and decided to zip her up, as he turned her over, and bounded her wrists, then lifted her up, and met back up with Trixie, who held the door open, the trunk went up and Jack laid her down, then zip tied her ankles.

The trunk closed as Jack got in, the car was running, as he took off, to see his phone rang it was Clarance, who said something is going on at Renoir Industries, and Jack texted his response at 125 mph, the car was on stealth mode, to instruct them to hold position, and wait for him. Jack punched in the exact coordinances. Trixie looked over at Jack, to say, "I don't know how you do it."

"What's that?"

"All of this?" she said with a smile.

"That Jack was a thinking, to ask, "So why are you causing trouble for Debby?"

"What are you talking about?" Jack was punching in info, as he adjusted the computer. "Just that, you're stirring up some trouble for her, all she is a house maid, and works supply for our base, what's the big deal?"

"Well, to be truthful with you, she kind of scares me, she is just so beautiful, and her so willingness threatens me."

"It shouldn't, you have a job to do, so does she, gossip like that could get you killed, especially with Lea or Kendra, where they take this form of espionage seriously."

"How did you learn all of this" she asked.

"Evolution, of needs, I was asked a few questions, and the only one new is you, so be care full and watch out", as they came to the place the car slowed, as he saw the lited sign said, "Boulevard des Invalides", the car saw an opening, it turned left into the business park, until, the huge iron gates were visible, as the car came to abrupt halt, behind them, another gate slid shut, Jack saw he was boxed in, then off to his right a huge forklift was coming at them, Jack looked at his display, to see I and instantly, left side guns erupted in time to throw a figure eight, but the huge forklift hit with such force, it drove the car back against the wall, Jack saw O, and dialed in the position, and off went a rocket, to loop around to impact the seat and the man on the lift to see it explode into a million pieces, some deflected off the car, the upper building rattled, then both gates fell down, and Jack drove forward, to see the huge glass building, on the other side of the courtyard. Moments later, people poured out of there, as Jack was heading straight in, glass broke and cascaded, around them, Jack was out, running, as people fled around him, Jack was using his phone as a guide, as he went up the stairs, to a secure door, he pulled off his belt, he placed a piece on each key hole, then a blasting cap for each, turned his back on the opposite wall, and tuned in the frequency, and press the hit button, the doors shook then imploded, Jack was on the move, he was looking for the safe, his GPS, was showing him the way, while scientist, scattered, gave way, to the security force, armed and opened fire on him, he dove for a desk unit, as the bullets shredded above him.

Jack pulled up his display, to see what was available, he hit O, and off went a rocket, as he targeted the one with the grenade launcher, as the rocket hit him and exploded. Silence overcame the long room, as Jack got up to see a bloody mess at the door. He was on the move, to the safe, he stopped to see the huge door, its glass surface, showed a huge safe. Jack stopped to see the imposing structure, to hear, "Did you need something out of there?" said a sweetly voice.

Jack turns to see a young woman, who held a gun on him, she motioned for him to put his hands up, he raised them with his gun held high, she said, "Drop the weapon, over to me."

Jack gladly was ready to do it, except he said, "Why did you ask what I wanted from the safe?"

"Because what you were probably seeking isn't even in there."

"How do you know what I want?"

"Because this happens once a week, but I have to say, looks like your better prepared, now throw me your gun."

"So I gotta know, where is what I'm looking for?"

"The patents, are kept in my office, bear bonds, in Tiffany's room, and well Lisa she has the gold reserves, now toss me the gun."

"Right" said Jack, as he hit the safety and let it fly, to her feet, he somewhat felt sorry for her, not really, as she admired the pearl grip, she touched it, she short circuited to drop it, he went to her, laid her back, to massage her heart, her fingers were burnt, he performed CPR, then thought about his phone, whereas he dialed up Trixie, to ask her to come up stairs with the Emergency pack. He continued the CPR, till Trixie got there, she pulled the portable unit, and Jack administer, adrenaline into her chest, then zapped her, once, she was still motionless, as behind him was Clarance, and behind him was Jonathon, admiring the wall décor, from behind the desks was Mark and Steven in tow, moments later the strike team all showed up, while Jack continued to do CPR, her chest was open as Clarance got in there, to say, "Let me help you out?"

Clarance took the paddles, and turned them all the way up, to say, "Clear", he applied the pressure, and it went off, her body shook her back to life. Clarance put them away, for Jack to say, "Take her with you and have the strike team, look for the Klein family candy company folder, through there" points Jack, as Jack, Trixie holding the pack, Clarance, Jonathon, Mark and Steven, followed Jack down, Jack and Trixie was in the Mercedes, he backed out, and sped off.

Craig was helping the girl up, who seemed to be alright, gave her a lift up to say, "Are you alright?"

"Who are you, you're not security?"

Craig held her arm, as her breasts would occasionally show, to say "Did he do this to me?"

"Well actually, he was the one who saved your life?"

"What do you mean?, all I remember, was touching his gun, and then I blacked out."

"Precisely, you probably fainted" said Craig.

"Yeah, your right, what are they looking for?"

"The file to the Klein family candy company, in Switzerland.

"Yes I know of it, it's on my desk, why do you need that?"

"Because that's what my boss wants and he shall get it."

"Who is your boss?"

"Jack Cash, ever hear of him?"

"No can't say I have, come with me I'll show you that file.

Jack reached the Manor, to slow, a single car, was at the front door, he got out, with weapons drawn, noise was coming from the upstairs, as he made it up the stairs, to see the huge master bedroom, the place was a mess, everything dumped over, even the fish tank, had bullet holes in it, for Jack to yell, “Drop the weapon, or I will shoot it out of your hand?”

Gustave turned with the gun, Jack fired, hitting the gun, and bloodying his fingers, he let out a yelp, and began to cry, to say, “Who are you, and what do you want?”

“My name is Jack Cash, International Bounty Hunter, and Spy to the United Nations, you’re under arrest, for the murder of Mister Klein, both of them.”

“On who’s authority, I want my lawyer.”

“Unfortunately, you don’t get one, My classification is that I’m license to Kill, no questioned asked” said Jack as he closed the gap, to hear, “Why are you doing all this, it was Rose - Marie idea?”

“Who’s that?”

“She was the girl who was the office manager, who was fired by that bitch, everything was fine, till she took over the company.”

“So what you’re saying, is that you had nothing to do with their car crash?”

“Nope, the son was doing business with us, why would I want him to go.”

As Jack pulls Gustave’s hands back and zip ties them, to hear, “Now what, and how did you find me?”

“Your IT guy from America, name Henry James, gave you up, and we have the file from your company, too bad the UN and EPA is shutting you down, as well.”

“You were there?”

“Yeah, and you won’t like what I did” said Jack as he pulled him along to hear, “Look Jack, I could give you some money?”

“How much were you thinking, one million, five hundred million?”

“One hundred K.”

“That’s an insult, right now your life’s worth ten times that.”

“You mean, you make one million to bring me in?”

“Yep” said Jack.

CH 11

Rest and relaxation, while being worshipped.

Jack, Steven and Jonathan stood at the beginning of the course, it was Wednesday at 0800 sharp, day 10, having slept two hours, and eaten a protein and carb rich diet, they were last, as the rains were cold, and the course was muddy and extremely wet.

Steven said, "Mate, how do you do this every night?"

"It easy, you have to condition your mind to keep alert and focused."

"All I know is that your one cool dude, you took Paris to school, and cause some pretty heavy damage, how do you know where to go and who to focus on?"

"It's simple, I have an ear piece and someone tells me what to do." He said kiddingly, only to him.

"Oh" said Jonathon.

The course was carved out of the hillside, as they were off, Jack ran the course, with the other two following, it was up and under things at specific places the mud was so bad, it weighed him down, at a rest stop he saw others, and just kept going on, as the rain was something fierce, others were struggling, as he passed them, going from the rear of the pack to near the front, then he came to a lake, as it read, "You must swim under the water undetected, hold your breath for up to five minutes,

Jack eased in, and propelled himself like a dolphin, under the water, easily covering the distance, he eased out, with not a shot fired, from a gun nest above, it was a bit different as Steven had gunfire above his head, and Jonathon, well he was as others having trouble, Jack was on a platform, he saw them, but decided to move, that took the advisors by surprise, as they were all off in a tent, and before they could respond Jack was past their harassment, he was in the lead, as he made his first hill climb, no one was there to harass him, as he kicked it into over drive and up the next two hills, his lead was daunting, as he came to the last stop, a zip line back to the UN.

Jack waited till the two men had their backs to him, and he lept up and pushed them over, grabbed the sling and away he went.

Jack took the long trip back to the UN, down the mountain side, as it took a good fifteen minutes and landed safely at the finish line. As a team from the UN, took him in to the warmth, he stripped off his clothes, thinking this is what Jim does, there for him, thinks he may have to treat him better. He washed off his body, showered, to get back some warmth, dried off, and put on new clothes, another mission done, another tyrant put down.

Jack went through the doors of the UN first again, to see Debby outside, who smiled, to say, "How was your mission, I missed you last night?"

"Did you stay with Michelle?" said Jack.

"No, I have my own quarters, I'm not here for her, I'm here exclusively for you. She leaned into him to say, "If I could I'd kiss you."

"What's stopping you?" said Jack smiling.

Debby placed her hands around his neck and kissed him, it was slow lingering and with an audience. As she let go, a group of women had been watching, as Debby said "I'll see you tonight?"

"Hopefully sooner" said Jack, as he sees her go elsewhere, to see all the women of the men, who were still out on the course, each of them very pretty in their own right, with Trixie missing, as he went to see why they were mulling around, to see a big television screen, with the current action, on Jack's far right, was this tall blonde bombshell, her name tag said "Natasha", she had a very cute smile, she was some form of Russian, then about as equally cute, was an older yet sophicated blonde version, who was British, and her name was Dana Jones, probably the wife of the distinguish gentleman Thomas. Alone, but next to Dana was Tessa, she had short brown hair, cute to look at she was American, in the middle was three Asian girls, the real long haired dark skinned Z' Sofia Baptiste, he remembered seeing that name in his phone, she is some ruthless spy, double triple, whoever pays the highest price, next to her, going from right to left was the two distinct Asian women, next was a Japanese women named Misaki, she looked articulate, and then there was the one who was staring at Jack, the very lovely Michelle, definitely Chinese he knew all too well.

Next to her, but at some distance was probably the most recognizable person in the room, she was a bitch and a supermodel, who she was with was a total guess, it was the famed Alessia, from Greece or something like that, then off to the far left was two of the sweetest looking girls, probably his two friends, both turned to mouth the words Hi, a stunning brunette similar to Mitzi, but skinner, her name was French, Lea Laplanta, and the last girl was Cari Holmes, who was a bleached blonde.

Jack was ready to leave when Michelle came up to him, smiled to say, "Someday I hope you come and visit me in our room?"

"What of Chu?"

"Oh, you know about him? Well he is the chosen one, but he is not like you, for you will always be mine."

She came closer, looking like she was ready to strip, when a another group of men past them, for her to say, "I have to go, but we will talk later" she left.

Jack got up to turn around to see at the door way Cari Holmes, who said, “Sit back down Mister, we need to talk.”, she stepped in, and closed the door, as Jack sat opposite her as she stood, to say, “You better leave my man alone, he was talking like he worshipped you or something, like he wants to go to America and work for the famous Jack Cash, and I don’t like it.”

“Why not, I might have mentioned to him that I’m forming up an academy for spy training.”

“I won’t allow him to go.”

“Why not, he is a free man” asked Jack.

“We have a wonderful life together, I want children.”

“So have them, what is stopping you, you shouldn’t have to put your life on hold.”

She looked at him funny, then said, “Your right, I should start having children right away.”

“Absolutely, if that’s what you want” said Jack.

“Well I do long to have him in my bed at night, but he is away a lot.”

Jack thinks, “What does he do, whatever” to himself, he looked up to see that she was gone. He was getting up when Alessia walked through the door, and closed it, to face him, to say, “Victoria Ecklon, asked me to rely to you a message, if there is anything that I could do for you, I will, in thanks for saving her life, so Mister Jack Cash, what of me do you want?”

Her tone was manful, yet she was offering herself up to him, but Jack decided to cut his ties with them and say, “When you see her, let her know that she doesn’t owe me anything and that we are even” he said looking at her body, the way she stood, she was evil, pure evil.

“So this is the way you want to play this, I offer myself up to you and you refuse this?”

“No, I’m refusing the messenger, if she feels like she wants to repay me, then it needs to be on her terms not a messenger’s, and no I’m not refusing you, I’m just respecting you.”

She looked at him, thinking, "Respect, indeed", to say, "You're a very clever man, Mister Jack Cash, someday, I feel I'm going to ride you wildly" she said in a smile, as she opened the door and left.

Jack got up, to see Tessa at the door, to say, "How is everything for you, your making quite a name for yourself?"

"I'm doing alright" said Jack.

"You know you're the number one agent in the world?"

"Hardly, what about your husband, he is the legend, he is the true agent."

"He is confined to the west coast only, your International."

"Really, that is where the criminals take me, it's not my choice" said Jack.

"What's your plans after all of this?"

"Why are you asking me out on a date?"

"Maybe, you know Erica Meyers and I are good friends, and she told me about that encounter she had with you, and well I thought well we are here, why not?"

"How does Ben feel about that?"

"Who cares what he feels like, he has his mistress's and now I want one of my own?"

"I'd love to accommodate your request, however, I have my own set of principles, never mix business with pleasure or a fellow agents wife, sorry" said Jack passing her.

Jack went to his room to relax, the morning turned to noon, he got up and went to have lunch, with such a diverse menu, he had a club sandwich, and sweet potatoes fries, chocolate milk. He sat at a table, to see Natasha, who placed her platter across from Jack, she sat to smile at him, as he ate, she ate slowly and seductively, then Vadim, came over to sit next to Jack to say, "How did you do it."

Jack looked over to his left to see the big hulking Russian, to say "It was easy."

Vadim looks over at his girl then back at Jack to say, "You like her, she is yours, you are a warrior, and Varfolomey hopes that you are safe, so that he may kill you himself" he said in a serious tone.

Jack leans in to say "After I kill Varfolomey, your next, your wife and kids in the little town of Tula."

Vadim looked at him, took a deep breath, knowing that secret if leaked out meant certain death for them. He kept quiet, while Jack said, "You just threaten me, and I don't take kindly to threats, just ask Alexander, oh that's right he is dead, and so will you, the rifle range is next up."

Vadim knew he was serious, he wanted to get away from danger, as he left his girlfriend, and Jack alone, as he know knew Jack was extremely dangerous, and from the looks of it he wasn't happy. Jack finished off his sandwich, to see the time, he went out, and into room one. He found his seat, and sat down, he pulled out his phone, to punch in Tami number, it came up, as he dialed, she answered, to hear her say, "Yes, darling?"

"How is Trixie, is she back in?"

"Yes, and with an attitude adjustment from Mitzi, this morning." Chu, who was off to his right, as the class was filiing up, till all were in, with Steven and Jonathan coming in last.

Professor Benz came in to say "There is a change of plans, the rifle range and sniper course has been cancelled", Jack raises his hand, to say, "But, this is perfect conditions."

"For you maybe, but the UN advisors, can't control the situation, so we will wait another day, now let's begin today by talking about espionage, it is the practice of spying on industrial companies, and then exposing their wrongdoings, as in the case of the Klein Family candy company, the Calcamite, was used to enhance the formula of the candy to attract and dope people into buying more, thanks to Jack for discovering all of that, and capturing everyone involved, the sum of your net worth has been transferred into your account, as others looked down and around at Jack, to hear, let's Identify footage from the scene of the crime, as a video played, for all to see, for the Professor to say proudly,"Under French law it is forbidden for a company, that does public business to have locking gates in place, nor as you can see, the forklift attacks the car, so now deadly force is possible, either way, when the trap was set, he could use any means possible, he chose to use guns, then a missile, as the gates drop, he goes into the lobby, then it becomes a race against time, as he blows a locked door, he get retaliatory fire, from men that resembles commandos, he then ends their life with a well-placed missile, and all of this occurred last night, calm down, this is a clear example of what we're looking for in an agent, who is not afraid to get his hands dirty, and what the UN has uncovered is startling, here is a list of all the finds, as he hands them out, to Vadim, to pass out, to add, "In addition, if you, as the agent, this is yours, like this is Jack's, Jack Cash's everything in a circle, and its value, and current price the UN will pay, if a piece of art, found along the way, and that country owns it, the country will pay the agent a finder's fee, like number twenty one, a painting stolen from the queen's royal castle, at Windsor, valued at 1.3 million, Jack will get one hundred and thirty thousand dollars, or ten percent the value, Hush down, this is why you're here, to confront, capture and rescue, people, places and things. Your reward is the money you acquire, some countries offer property, others offer powerful women and men to marry, and you as agents can have as many women as you like, especially, when trying to unite countries, this is common practice, among the best spies, means a longer survivability factor, and longevity, as others will protect you to the final end, also, if you have not had that support the UN has made a room available, a retirement community for those who provided service to the UN." he pauses to say "Let's talk about the UN, we are a mere branch of the World Court, our actions have a prior approval, even before, you set foot on a country, such as Somalia, we sent a spy in, he brought peace by using the US Marines and the Royal Air Force, then as he left, and his forces pulled out, the Army took over, and they made a movie about the blunder, the loss of life, it was a shame that people hungry for power do the things they do, but this is 2010, and thing are different, no more are the days of the mercenary going in and taking a country, if it's not UN approved it just doesn't happen, this is where all of you come in, as a UN ambassador, your job is to maintain peace however you see fit, with as support as you need, while in your own country, it is usually the highest court that places the order for the action, as a result of some case brought to them from someone else, overall we all work for the people, and in such a way, so do you, but you only answer to yourself, now your all probably thinking I have all this power, I can do whatever you want?, well your wrong, just in another case, when the Russian Premier Vladimir Ecklon's wife Victoria was taken by the spy's, he called in Jack Cash, to find her and bring her back safe, both fellow agents Alexander and Alexei were behind that, and both are gone, she is safe, and rescue also uncovered the nuclear weapon base under Moscow, and the arrest of the secret police, which the UN and US is still on site."

"Gentleman this is only the beginning, the winner is among you, so now it has been determined, each of you will be out there, doing some of the things listed here, it will be your job, to handle the details, for your survivability, remember you're not above the law, now let's talk about procedures, wait why don't we take a break."

Jack was out the door, before everyone else, he went down the corridor, to the support teams training area, as classroom, lined the hall, he pulled his phone, to look in the window of the door, to see all the women in one, as they all turned back to see Jack, led by Trixie, who came to the door, she opened it to say "Hi, stranger, as she hugged him, she kissed him, he was looking for someone or something? They finish the kiss, to say, "I'll see you tonight lover." and went back inside.

Jack walked slowly, He came up on another room, to see the Ivan the Giant, learning basic systems, to say, "I guess he'll want to go to college next?"

Jack went back to room one, where Vadim was waiting for him, to say, "Jack I'm sorry man, I had no idea, it was you?"

"Who do you think it was?"

"A force of thousands, some said a whole division of your American troops."

"Nah, just a handful of my most trusted, what you're getting cold feet?"

"No, no, I want to make an alliance with you?"

"How so, Vadim, your known as a playboy, not a fighter, are you saying you want to go a few rounds to get out your anger?"

"I have no anger, I was miss-led, by Alexei, and see that we could be brothers, you know help one another, you know he is with Varfolomey, as is Fyodor, they are all after you, I can help, will you let me?"

"I may consider it, I'll let you know when were through here."

"Fair enough, and in the meantime you shall have my girl Natasha."

"How does she feel about all of this?"

"It was her idea, and she is fine with it."

"Then it shall be" the two shook hands, as the Professor Benz saw it to stop by to Jack to say, "Diplomatic relations or?"

"Two men getting to know one another," said Jack.

"In addition, your two men, Mark and Clarance have tied up the loose ends, we were going to pay them a share, or is that something you don't mind?"

"What do you mean Professor?" asked Jack.

"To tell you the truth, you have at least ten that could fill that room, of agents better qualified then these men, most of them had a glazed over look on their faces, like this was the first time they saw blood."

"That's because were living in the fantasy world here, you instruct us on what the UN wants them to do, but not how to practice it in real life, I'm more of a hands on guy, enough of the rhetoric, let's go mingle with people whose lives have been affected, let's say for a field trip we go to Turin, and drop us off, and then we have to find a way back."

"Interesting, I may take that under advisement."

All came back in after a short break.

"What makes a spy, going out and being tested, in real life situations, instead of a protected environment where nothing is real, how does one learn, when everything is planned out for you, anyone wish to comment?" said the Professor.

Jack rose, to say, "The first mission was cool, with being thrown out of a plane, the ambushes, all except we had nothing to defend ourselves except what we could find, so Professor, where is the realism in that?"

"Your right, and I'm sorry I just teach what is given to me."

"Sorry is right, you do what you must, oh one more question who decides when and where I go, is it the UN or my country that supports me, or am I free to do as I please."

"Good question, I'll answer that" as the Professor held on to the podium. Jack looked back to see Natasha past them, with a smile, and a wink.

Jack was going over his phone, while the Professor talked, to say "I have a question I'll answer now, it was brought to my attention, by an agent, and it was asked who tells you where to go?"

"Well that one is tricky, with hundreds of field agents out there doing the work of the UN, you're bound to over cross, think of it as a means of discovery, like take Jack for instance, he captured a huge thief, as you can see by the inventory list, for him, he could have stayed around a week or so at a spa to relax."

"Or sit in class" said Jack out loud as the whole class laughed.

"Calm down, here is the best answer, after this council is over, each of you will be given an assignment to carry out, a teaser per say to see what you do with it, then as you finish, the UN will check with your country first, to see if they need something first, if not, we will call you, you have two, actually three options, first accept, second refuse to say you are working on something else, as then a UN inspector will be assigned to your movements, lastly your on vacation, well that's not really true either, a spy is a spy always 24/7 forever, or in this lifetime, when you walked through that door, you gave up your personal life for that of this world's fight for peace, everything you do, will be monitored, and reported back, when you leave here you will be given a number as to your ranking, and each year, you'll come back for a refresher, a week before 356 new candidates come in, which of you will recommend, exclusively, there will be no other way, someone becomes a UN agent, unless one of you vouches for them, honestly this is your club, I do recommend you bond with one another, before I forget, I want to talk with you about this upcoming rugby match, starting tomorrow beginning matches will take place, we have an indoor field set up, we have called all the teams you selected, they will be on the other end of the squadron, you may even work out there, as there has been some trusted established among yourselves. The Professor writes the teams schedule on the board to show the three game line up, talk amongst yourselves, I'll be right back.

Steven came up to Jack to say, "Sorry mate, about my girl, she thinks I need to be home with some kids, on some farm raising chickens, hey just a heads up, the team you choose is a fast team the All-Blacks are the best, what about you Jon, who is your first game with?" as they peered to look at the list.

"Vadim, and Russia."

"That's gonna be tough, good luck."

"I guess it depends on the picking order" said Jack, seeing the Professor come back in, to say, "Upon some recommendations we are deciding to change some of the training, so anyway, let's begin with Jack Cash, and his New Zealand team versus, the US and Ben Hiltz." Tad Jones of England, versus, Turkey and Hendon." Carlos Gomez of Cuba, versus, Israel, and Mustapha." Steven Smith of Australia, versus, Thomas Jones of Wales." Jonathon of France, versus Russia and Vadim."

Simon Jonas of South Africa, versus, Greece, and Andreas."

Chu of Japanese, versus, Saudia Arabia, and Jamal."

Andrain of Norway, versus, Columbia, and Benjamin.

Lastly, Kyle of Egypt versus Gordon of Italy."

"Now that the teams you choose, is here, and you saw the first round, let's go meet your players", they all followed the Professor, into an elevator one floor down, and on a escalator, a good mile, to pop out to a huge dome, where a field was laid out, all eighteen teams were summoned, each dressed in spectacular outfits, each held a sign up signifying who they were, as Jack saw his chosen team, all twenty members, a grumpy looking older guy was the coach, Jack came up on them, the grumpy looking man said, "Hi, my name is Magnus, this is the A-team as requested."

"My name is Jack."

All the players shook his hand, prior to them walking out there he looked up on his phone the concept of Rugby and what position to play, to hear, "How much do you know of the game, and had you ever played, we were told, it would be you only scoring, that was the only catch?"

Jack said, "Well I know about the game, as you advance it in backward passes, and you can kick to advance, or for goal, run in and use a downward motion, to score a try.

"Excellent, what position do you want to play?"

"Either Fullback or Number eight" said Jack.

"A man after my own heart as he laughed, to say, "Come in here boys, so Jack wants to play full back, let's get you kicking for accuracy, while the rest of the team and I will make up some plays for you to score try's.

Jack and the fly half, set the ball at different angles to the posts, as Jack changed into kicking shoes and shorts, he kicked for accuracy and distance, while others had quit, Jack wanted to practice the plays they came up with, meeting opposition, he rolled off them, and drove the ball down, as the coach called them in, to say, "Tomorrow we have our first game, then we play the US, in round one, it's a three game set, then on to single elimination, to the finals."

Jack walked off the field, to see Steven was waiting, to say, "Can I talk with you, I really like the idea, of going to your academy, mate."

"All things work themselves out, besides change is on the horizon, maybe we can get out of this whole plastic thing, and make it more real," said Jack.

"I'd say it was real, wait till Friday you're going to get the crap beat out of you," said Steven.

"I don't think so, I heard the Professor call us VIP's and that the teams were there for our protection" said Jack.

"Believe as you will, you'll see what I'm saying, Friday."

Thursday morning, day 11, Jack awoke very happy a good night's rest with Debby and Trixie, each fulfilling his every desires, only problem was he couldn't remember a thing, he slept so peacefully.

He was up, showered, dressed and off to the cafeteria, only to see Michelle as excited as ever, she hugged him, to say, "You're a blessing."

"What's this all about" asked Jack standing in line to say "six poached eggs on a couple of those buttermilk pancakes, and whipped butter, and some links."

She walked with him, opting for the breakfast special, to say, "Next week your all flying to China to visit the world's expo."

"Yes, that's right, how did you know?"

"An advisor told me so?"

"It was the President's idea," said Jack, "Among things."

"Can you take me with you, or our entire class?"

"Possible, I'll ask Professor Benz."

She kissed him on the cheek, and went in front of him.

"Jack, he picked up his plate, to add some strawberry syrup, and set his platter down, and went back for some chocolate milk, to see three girls at his table, Michelle, Cari and Natasha, in deep conversation, as he went about his business, just letting it all soak in, the moment, the fact that three girls were sitting here with him. He thought about how this course was run, here at the UN and knew he needed to make some changes, with his academy. Jack sat down with them, and ate quickly, The days seem like a blur before, now he knows its Thursday. He left the lovely girls, to head towards another day of lectures, role playing, and observation of his work, actually he meant to say Vadim, and his kind, what about the rest of the group, well he knows Steven and Jonathon, have no field experience, and Mustapha, well now that Alessia, knows Jack is here, well she has shown considerable interest in him, his reputation is far greater than the former Louie could ever think about, but it was interesting what the Professor said, "That this is only a snap shot of a moment, this time next year, it will be totally a new batch of hopefuls, yet a week prior, the world ranked will come back for refresher material, and awards like, what Jack didn't know, till the Professor said that Jack was considered for a Nobel peace prize, given to the best UN agent, it was Vadim, who's work in Afghanistan, that won him that prize, last year and he received that in class, they all stood and gave him an applause, somehow this group has become, closer, more trustworthy, a separation line has formed, one the upper level is Vadim, and Jack, in the middle is Ben and Thomas, Hendon falls in there somewhere, then the rest all look up to the others. The day dragged on, till it came to an abrupt end. The Professor said, "Now for something, a little different, normally, I'd dismiss you for Rugby practice, but we here at UN, we decided to change it up and throw you all a party, so exit the room, and into room two."

Jack followed the others out, and into room two, where a party was in full swing, the women, were having the time of their lives, as the rescue was being played, each agent was handed a drink, Jack put his watch up to the glass, it was fine, so he drank it down.

Later that night, Jack awoke, in a weird position, upside down, his hands were binded, eyes covered, and ankles were restrained, he hung by his ankles, thinking lets start the spin, he used his momentum to begin to circle, in a figure eight move, to which frayed the rope, he crunched and dropped onto the bed, slipped his wrists past his ankles, and then pulled off his blindfold, he looked around to feel the sound of the nightlight outside, the room was lit up, he undid his ankles, he got up off the bed, to see on the back of the door, that read, "If you're reading this, then your eligible to continue, you have ten or so hours, depending on how long it took for you to get out of the bindings, to be back at UN HQ, by ten AM sharp tomorrow, use any means at your disposal, no help from any of your support teams, unless your life is in danger.

Jack looked at his watch, as he set it to count down to 0930, he also spun the raised ring, on his watch, which easily cut through his bindings, he let fall to the floor, he was out and on the run.

Jim looked at his watch as Casey was screaming down his neck, to move the plane towards Turin, Italy, to hear, "It's right there on the screen, what more do you need to know."

"Maybe it's a trap" said the newest member of the team, said Jesse.

"Maybe he is right, and maybe it's a game, but it's our job, to protect him at all costs" said Casey.

Jim looked at him, to say, "You're the hired help."

"Yeah, that's my job, but you're the support team, it's your ass" said Casey, as they began to laugh and hug, to see the young Jesse, who looked at the two of them, putting him on, to say, "Your dad is alright, the UN, has a special operation in place, were told to stand down, he will be back shortly.

Casey, comes over to Jesse, to put his arm around his neck to say, "Come on kid, it's my turn to watch over you, you're our new priority."

Jack was out on the streets, cobblestone, it was late, and he was hungry, so he saw a restaurant, Jack walked in, went up to the large older woman to say, I'm hungry, may I work for some food?" he said in a somber tone.

She looked at him, and smiled, to say, "Have a seat and I will serve you."

A plate of spaghetti, fresh asparagus, in a butter sauce, and a warm bruschetta, a glass of Chardonnay, was set down, to hear, "Eat my boy, you'll need your strength".

Jack slowly ate, till he was done, he picked up his clean plates, and went past the mom, into the kitchen, to the dishwasher area, which the dishes were stacked high, he rolled up his sleeves and went to work, he was a machine, he ran the dishes through a small machine, as he prewashed the plates, and in another sink he was scrubbing the large pots. Behind him in the kitchen, the Mom and Dad were arguing, as Jack turned, to see the two they stopped, to smile at Jack to say, "That'sa good", here you go, as the Dad hands Jack forty dollars cash, in lires.

Jack was out on the street, as he ran downward, past the churches, down to the train station, he looked at his watched that read 0125 in the morning, the last train, was 1125 PM to Aosta, but Jack had another idea, as he looked over at the airfield, where airplanes sat, to hear a voice behind him, "Hands up Mister, or I'll shoot you?"

Jack raised his hands, and began to turn, to hear, "Don't turn, just give me your wallet."

Jack brought up his foot to the guys groin, as he turned and struck him, to see a very pretty girl, Jack took the gun away, to say, "Now your wallet, Jack waved his gun at the guy, to see the guy wet himself, as Jack knew it was a plastic gun, to say, "The keys too", the guy waved them up to Jack.

Jack spoke, "I know your showing off for your girl here, but you choose the wrong man to mess with, my name is Jack Cash, International Bounty Hunter, I'd suggest you walk yourself to the local police station, and turn yourself in, for I will have one of my associates come looking for you."

"Wait I didn't know?, take my car, and my girl."

"Sorry I don't work like that, do you have a plane?"

"How about a Lear jet?"

"That will be fine, lead the way" said Jack.

"Nah I was just kidding."

"Show me this car of yours, get up" said Jack helping him up, as the two walked together, with the pretty blonde following behind. The guy led the way to a pristine BMW, to toss the keys to Jack to say, "Here you go hot shot, you drive."

Jack shrugs his shoulder to say, "Alright", and hit the key fob, and opened the door, and slid in, to see the girl take the passenger seat, to smile at Jack as she placed her seat belt on, for Jack to say, "Where's your boyfriend?"

She shakes her head, to say, "He isn't my boyfriend, I just met him back at the club."

"Have him get in."

"Let's forget about him, and you and I say get together." said the girl.

"What's your name" asked Jack. As he fired up the car, he set the Nav to Geneva, to hear, "My name is Claire, Claire Williams."

"That's nice" said Jack, as he turned the car around, to slow he put the window down to say, seeing the guy walking, "Get in, Claire was looking all over for you", the guy got in, as Jack took the BMW through its paces, using the gear levers, to open up the BMW, he launched it out on the highway, doing turns at 120 MPH. The guy in the back was getting tossed back and forth.

Jack was focused on the road and feel the road under him, while Claire was moving closer to him, placing her hand on his leg. Jack looked down to see where his speed was at when he blew through a speed trap, which he looked up, to see the above lights were all flashing red, Jack changed his Nav for Chambery, the last minute, as it went into the tunnel, the car was screaming, he then noticed something in his rear view mirror, it was another BMW coming on strong, for Jack to say, "We got company, do you know who they are?"

The guy shrugs his shoulder to say, "I don't know", maybe they want their car back? as he was looking back.

"What do you mean?" asked Jack.

"Well this is a borrow."

"What, this ain't your car" screamed the girl.

"Calm down, he probably did it to impress you, are you?" asked Jack.

"No, definitely not, so what are you doing later?"

"Getting us out of here" said Jack.

Jack looked over his dash board, to see what he was looking for, as he clicked off traction control, it was squirrel for a moment, then it kicked into over drive, and he opened the gap. Jack was weaving in and out of traffic, then off to the left he saw, a caravan of three BMW's, and with the roads so lite up, he could see men with guns, as they literally had them mounted on the side of their vehicle's, but as he calculated, their position, and his, he decided to have fun with them.

Jack slowed the car, to a stop, to get out, and went to the trunk, as the guy followed, Jack saw a tire iron, and in that instance, he threw the guy in, and closed the trunk, got back in to hear?"

"Where's Jim?"

"Who cares, he decided to take a nap, besides I thought you were into me?"

"I am, so what is your plan with that thing?"

"Even the odds" said Jack as the three BMW's flew by him, as Jack and his tail picked up with the other three cars, as Jack was behind them, he picked up speed, they saw him, to slow, but Jack did something unexpected, and hit the rear of the BMW, sending it into the wall, as Jack was tapping the next one, it went squirrely, but he held it, he came next to Jack to show his phone, Jack looked down to see the cell phone, he picked it up, to hear a heavy accented man, to say, "Alright you can have the car, if you let me have the briefcase, in the back seat."

"Get the briefcase, from the backseat" said Jack as he sees Claire, lean over the seat, to see her dress is hiked up, to see her panties, she sat back down with the huge case on her lap, for Jack to say, "Open it up." to say "Wait, I have one just like it, turn the levers outward, then pop them together, she did that, to hear it click, then she lifted the top, to show the contents.

A single smaller envelop, it sat within a cut, place for it, for Jack to say "Pull that out, and open it up and let the contents slid out."

She did so, as she tilted it on its side, to a single small item landed, in that space, for Jack to say "hold on, don't touch that, tell me what is on it, wait do you have a cell phone?"

"Yes, why?"

"Does it have picture text function?" asked Jack still driving, next to the other car, as Claire pulled out her phone, then got close and took the picture, to hear Jack says, "Now place it as close as you can and take another picture."

Claire did that, to say, "Now what?"

"Now lift up the case and let the item fall back into the envelope, whatever you do don't touch it."

The phone rings, Jack answers it to say, "Yeah, what do you need?"

"What will it be your life for the briefcase?"

"Well let's see, I have what you want, why don't you let me have what I want?"

"You're in no place to negotiate, its either you live or you die?" said the guy.

"Here, here, I don't take to kindly to threats, allow me to consider your offer." Jack cut him off, to say, to Claire, "Let me see your phone" she hands it to him, as he suddenly slowed to a stop, immediately he dialed up his phone, to reverse its use, he sent the pictures, to get a response, it came back as he was confirmed it was a WW 2 inter-postal stamp depicting Adolf Hitler, its current value, is 79 million dollars, current status, stolen, possible leads a Italian financier Arnold Cohart, suspected bank fraud and wire transfer agent. As he looked at his E-mails only to have Claire say "Jack look at what's coming at us, duck," as bullets rattled the BMW, as the car drove by, followed by another, as bullets riddled them again, tires were blown out, as the car went down, while Claire was crying, Jack continued, to check his E-mails, then used the phone, to the support group, he put in his password, to text, that he needs support ASAP, he texted, three targets, running a line at the car disabled.

In that next moment two super hornets, buzzed their area, painted the picture, and launched the three missiles to confirm with Jack the each targets. Three explosions, and three BMW were blown, up.

Jack pulled the tire iron into his sleeve, to hold onto the handle, to toss her phone at her to see that it went blank, to take the case from her, he got out, of the car, to see the other BMW, behind him, as three other men exited their remains, Jack strolled over to them, but before they could speak, Jack used the case to club, the first one, then, drew out the tire iron, and struck one, and then the other, Jack saw the guy had power locked the tailing BMW, as the guy was panicking, Jack raised his hands to the air, to point down to him, only to see the door locks unlock, Jack opened the door, to say, "Alright step out, I thought you wanted this case for my life, or was that, I keep this case, and take your life, now get out, let me see your phone, get in behind the wheel, as Jack took his side arm, as he hit the trunk button, Jack set the case down, and saw how big the trunk was, and placed the driver in, then the opposite way, he placed the other guy in, the other guy, he helped him into the back seat, after he zipped tied his wrists behind his back, as Jack with Claire waited, as Claire, said, "My phone is dead, what did you do to it?"

"Sorry, I'll get you another one" said Jack.

"What about Jim, in the trunk?"

"Who cares, if you want him, go wait by the car, someone will be by to help you out?"

"No, no, I'm with you" she said.

"Then get in, and sit up front."

Jack went around and got in next to the girl, as she scooted over, for Jack to say, "Start it up, and set your Nav for Geneva."

Jack eased back, with gun in hand, he set the briefcase, on his lap, while he checked over the phone, to link up to his phone, to hear, "Are you through with my phone?"

"Just drive, I had to call off the air support, we can always stop, and I'll let them give you one more missile."

"Nah, that's alright, but I have sensitive stuff on that phone, make the calls you need then give it back."

"Oh alright" said Jack as he had his phone pull off all of his information, only to see the phone go blank, it went way to quick, to toss the phone in the back. Jack turned to the guy next to her, to say, "You got your phone?"

The guy produced his phone, from inside his pocket, knowing Jack knocked his gun from his hand, his head still ached, to surrender the phone to him.

Jack took it to say, "Thanks, I hope you don't want it back?"

"Nah, just keep it" he said holding his free hand on his head, the other on the wheel.

Jack dialed up his phone, to connect the link, only to hear "Hey what did you do to my phone?" asked Arnold.

"He did to my phone too" said Claire sitting halfway in the front seat, as her dress was hiked up, she caught him, to adjust herself, for him to laugh, he said, "So you have air support, what do you have on the ground?"

"Just you and this car, just drive, and the air support, well that was a friend I knew who owed me a favor," said Jack.

"That's what you call it" said Arnold.

Jack nodded, then dialed up the police Chief Winters in Geneva, to expect a reception. He ended the call, to check his GPS, to see that they were on track, he then checked the car's schematic, and on board systems, to close it up, to look at his E-mail, to see a message from, Lisa, he opened it to see, requests from all the branches of the special ops community, to help with the training of the new recruits, what do you want to do?"

Jack replied, to say, "Send all the recruits to Marine Corps Boot Camp, at Camp Pendleton, in an open call, for officer training, and get back with me when there done". the phone went dead, he closed it up, to toss it back, the ride was fast, as Arnold kept trying to get information from Jack but he didn't answer, but his companion, was a willing person, who answered all of Arnold's questions, like, "So how long have you too been together?"

"Why are you interested in dating me?" said Claire.

"I might, that is if your man approves" he said kiddingly, as the car Nav system, drove to the outskirts of Geneva, then down a back alley he slowed to say, "What is going on with the car?"

The car shut off, as police were at the doors, and out they pulled him, Jack exited to say, "The cars all yours, see ya."

"Hey where are you going" she said.

Jack went into the police station, to see his new hire, the tough and mean Clarance, for which Jack said, "Do you have a car, can you drive me to the candy factory?"

"Sure, it's out front, what do you want me to do with these guys?"

"Get whatever information, you can out of them, after you drop me off."

"You mean us" said Claire at the door, as everyone turned to look at the stunning beauty.

Jack takes Claire by the arm and out the back they went.

Clarance waited a moment to hear, Arnold say, "Who was that guy?"

Police Chief looks at his other deputies to say, "What the guy at the door?"

"No the guy who just left."

"Oh, his name is Jack Cash International bounty hunter"

Arnold said "Aw shit."

"Yeah, and that is his interrogator" said police Chief Winters.

Clarance drove the hummer, while Jack was up front and Claire rode in the back, to say, "What are you two love birds up too?"

"Ah, nothing, just out for a spin, how has it been tonight in the city?"

"Quiet, heard you had a bit of a reception yourself?"

"Nothing a little support couldn't handle, hey before I forget, I got two bodies in the trunk, of the BMW."

"Sure you do, and your girl is back, waiting to see you again."

"Thanks for the ride" said Jack getting out, with Claire in tow, for her, to say, "Where are we at, don't you want to go get a room at a hotel?"

"Nah, I got a room, we just need to scale the fence first."

Jack led the way, up and over a chain link fence, he helped her, seeing he couldn't get rid of her, to the dock, he tried the door, he forced it open, it was dark, he found a flashlight, and a mask, and gave one to her, as they went into the mine, to the left was the abandon, shaft to the UN, they walked a mile or so, to a ladder, Jack went first, up to the top, where a wheel was, he undone it, then pushed it up, a wave of cool air, overwhelmed them, then he climbed up, into a room, of sorts, he helped her up, then closed it down, to see Debby, with lock in hand, to reseal it, to say, "It's nice to see your back, come let's get you cleaned up."

CH 12

Let the games begin

Jack awoke, Friday morning, day 12, to feeling a firm bottom on one and another behind him, the one in front, turned to smile it was Claire, the stunning blonde, and Debby in the back, who he felt her naked body, he turned and laid back in the king size bed to see both girls adjust themselves, to lay partly on him, for Jack to say, "Where's Trixie?"

"Oh, about her, she was asked to leave, so now it's just the three of us" said Debby smiling and looking at Claire.

Jack looked at his watch to see that it was 0930, or so, so he got up, to take the covers away to see that they were both nude, and exposed, he hit the shower, then, finished up his business, dressed, to find his phone, he slipped it in his pocket, and out the door he went.

Inside the mess room, it was empty, till he came in, then saw someone, he order steak and eggs, Texas toast and pancakes, he grabbed four chocolate milks, sat down, and consumed all of it, he place the tray away, then, went across the way, to see that it was empty, but took his seat, and waited, he waited till noon, when a UN advisor came in to say, "When did you get back?"

"Oh, about four something, in the morning?"

"Really, how did you get in?"

"I have my ways, what's going on" asked Jack.

"This whole thing is a mess, we have agents scattered all over Europe, some still where they were left."

Jack followed the man, to the side opening where UN personnal, were tracking everyone including Jack.

They saw the bleep come up to them to say, "How did you get here, in here?" asked the another Advisor.

"What didn't everyone get back?" asked Jack.

"Nope, you're the only one, and when did you get back, we tracked you to Geneva, at 0420, this morning, how did you get in?"

"Alright I had some help."

"I'd say you do, look over at that hanger, you have a whole plane full operators, not to mention, who knows those around us, especially, your ground force, who I have to say has been very helpful to us."

"You're welcome, now what?"

"Actually, today was supposed to be flight simulation and aerial combat, in addition to some helicopter awareness and training, wanna go through it?"

"Sure, run me through the paces, let's do this?" said the eager Jack.

"Well to be honest with you, were not really ready, but go to your room, or the library, or the spa, I'll let you advisor know when were ready for you. Oh by the way the girl you brought in, well let's say she has been escorted out?"

"It's a good thing we had some fun together, but then thought about what Debby said, was that Trixie, or Claire?"

Jack eased away from them, down a different way, to see a sign that said "Archives."

So he tried the door, it opened, he saw the stairs down, as the dimmed lights brighten up, to a door that read "Library", Jack tried the door, it was locked, he saw the hand print block on the wall.

Jack placed his hand in it, and the door slid open, a bank of lights came on, to show tables, above them, was the titles of the books below on the shelves, he stood beside the first line, to see it must be pretty small as darkness, was five aisles long, as Jack turned he heard, "Do you need some assistance, Mister Cash".

Jack turned to see the overdressed man to say "Nah, I was just looking, for a big place like the UN, has such a small library, no I think I'll be fine" said Jack looking over the five aisles, to decide which one to go down. Then bank by bank lights went on, and continued, as far as Jack could see, to hear, "There you go Mister Cash, the entire library at your fingertips, all five million books, so if you would like any book, for here or in your room, I have a slip for as many books as you like, shall I accompany you, Sir?"

"No, not right now, but what is your name?"

"Sir, my name is Alfred."

"Great, do you happen to have a cart?"

"Absolutely, wait one moment, Sir", he said as he scurried off, and Jack went the other way, when he saw a sign that said "New Zealand royal archives", he went down to that aisle, to turn to see, a case where a single book stood upright, Jack saw other books of different degrees of depth, from language, architecture, and the people, among all the books, he noticed a small book, as he pushed the other books away, to see the title called "The form of people".

Jack pulled the delicate book away from its place, and opened it, to read, "This book contains the secrets of how people work, how to interpret what they have to offer and how to use it in everyday life. Jack took a quick spin of the book, to stop on one of the last pages, to see, that the translation, was a bit out of place, but Jack read out loud, to himself "There will be those out there, that stand for justice, regardless of the circumstances, and if they stand for good will prevail, when all else looks like it will fail, a single figure will stand alone, and carry the torch to victory".

Jack closed the book up, then slipped it in his pant pocket to hear "You can borrow it, but you can't keep it, if you would like a copy, we can get one for you?"

Jack handed him the book, to say, "Can I see the book behind the glass?"

"Of course, but we may have to step back".

Out of no where two burly men, past them, to the case, Jack went elsewhere, to another aisle, as he saw something else that caught his eye, a book on Eastern European defenses", he looked up to see he was standing under the War banner, he saw all kinds of books, he pulled off the shelf.

Jim stood next to Casey, for him to say "I don't know how he did it, when all these other guys are struggling."

"Because he is the best, hell he could be dropped anywhere in the world, and make friends, and in some case lovers" said Jim.

"Then why are we here?" asked Casey.

"Because the President asked us to support him, and I said where we go, if you got a problem, you could easily be replaced."

"Whoa, that's not what I mean, I would never."

"That's right, you will never know, Mister Morales," said Jim.

"Wait what are you saying?"

"I think your right, I'll ask the President to take you and the team off of this?"

Casey looked at Jim, then at his team, who were watching the UN advisors, to say, "Look I'm sorry, I said anything."

"Let's say, you and your team needs to prove to me and especially Jack that you belong, now go along and keep your mouth shut, and send Clark to come here?" said Jim.

Casey walked off the ramp, over to the hanger door, to say "He wants to see you", Clark left to see Jim to say, "What's up?"

Miss Hohlstein needs the team inside to patrol the stadium, will you take charge of this?"

"Yes, sir" said Clark, as he collected up the strike team, and went into the UN.

Mike and Gia, made it down to New Orleans, Mike had a companion, while he was getting all the arrangements set, as they made it outside to the hot weather, for them to see a bleached blonde somewhat attractive woman, who said,"You must be Mike, and you are Gia, Jack told me to be at your disposal, so get in, as she went around to drive, Mike took the passenger seat, as Gia was in the back with their two carryon bags, as they were off, she drove in silence, as Mike said,"So you look familiar, where have I seen you before?"

"The fishing boat."

"Oh right, when Jack was luring criminals to the boat, that was very clever of him, so why are you here?"

"To get back in his good graces, so right now I'm doing some small jobs."

Mike looked over at her, to say,"Like what, maybe we could help you out, as your helping us out."

"Yeah, that would be great, I'm so stuck on this one problem?"

"What's that?"

"Well Jack asked me to search for some plans, and I have 800 more cargo containers to search?"

"Alright, how do you know their even in them?"

"What do you mean?"

"Well all cargo containers have a manifest, as he pulled his lap top open, to say, "Name the ship?"

"The South Pacifica, from South Africa"said Carly.

"Ah here it is, said Mike, as he zoomed the manifest, to stop on 736, container, to say,"This is probably it."

"Why do you say, that?"

"According to the manifest, it was last to be loaded, with a mobile office unit, and under notes, says, building plans."

"Are you kidding me?"

"Nope, and that is what I do for Jack."

"Do you mind if we drive over there and I get what I'm looking for?"

"Nope, I just got word, NOLA has detained Miss Natasha Rogers, awaiting our visit, so let's go get those plans for Jack."

Back at the UN, Jim, came over to Jesse to say,"Care to go to the rifle range with me, and fire that sniper rifle you had been eying?"

"Yeah that would be cool" said Jesse, finishing polishing the car.

"Then after lunch we will go," said Jim.

Back in NOLA, Carly arrived at the slip as federal agents were all over the place, as she was waved in, she parked, as Mike exited with her, to see the huge container ship, she was waved on, by the FBI on scene, who saw her everyday, as one said,"Another hundred today, looks like you got some help."

"Names Mike."

"My name is Carter, so far our girl here is down 1200, when ever your ready, said Carter with bolt cutters in hand, as he fell in behind them, into a crane elevator, as the three were hoisted, and moved to the top, as Mike said, "The location, should be down this aisle, and down two, to here, cut this one open Carter, he did, and swung it open, to see a portable office, she went in, with a flashlight, for Mike to say to Carter,"If this is for Jack Cash, why can't we have the whole container?"

"You can, Carly mentioned she wanted some plans, and that was all."

"Yes, but why didn't you show her the ships manifest?"

"She never asked."

"So you have helped her the whole way?"

"Yep, pretty much, when we got the call that this ship is for Jack Cash exclusively, we began to catalog the entire ship, while she went looking for those plans."

Mike looked at his motive for himself, for Mike to say,"You know, she is his, don't you?"

"What do you mean?"

"Simple, she is his, you know Jack cash's girl."

"Oh, I didn't know" said Carter, who was guilty, for Mike to capitalize on this knowledge to say,"So what else do you have that your hiding, cause one call and I could have him down here."

"That won't be necessary, here are the valuable containers, worth millions, in paper currency, as Mike wrote them down, number 265, and 266, to say,"Get those and put them on the dock, I'll call a couple of armored trucks to take it away."

"Yes sir", as Carter left, for Mike to see Carly, to exclaim, "Here it is, the super secret plans.",she hands them to Mike who looks at the markings, CIA, Samantha Kohl.

He looks them over, to say,"Now could you do me a favor?"

"Sure what ever", she said with a smile.

"Can you go and pick up Miss Rogers, watch over her with Gia."

"Sure but aren't you coming?"

"No not yet, I have to sort out some things" said Mike, who was on the phone to Jack, but no answer, so he called Mitzi, who answered, to say,"Yes Mike?"

"I can't reach Jack, but Ive discovered a huge find, where shall I take it?"

"Wait one, as she checked the place, to say,"Mike take it to the Coast Guard, NOLA, I have a James Watkins, commander on the line, and he says, they have a whole armory, available for sortment and storage."

"Will do, thanks."

Carly drove, while Mike's companion was laid over and out, as she approached the station, and went in, to see a giant of a man at the desk, to say,"What can I do for you Miss?"

"I represent Jack Cash, and was here to escort a Miss Rogers to him."

He looks her over to say,"That man is revered here, allow me to call my boss."

Moments later she appeared, with a form that Mike sent, for the new police Chief Andrews said,"Here you go Carly Curtis, as authorized by Jack Cash, as Miss Rogers, went along, as CC picked up the paper, and out the door she went, as Natasha took the passenger seat, Carly got in, to hear,"Who is this Jack Cash, and who is it the secret President to have the seal of the President of our United States, ask for a visit?"

"In due time, all will expose itself."

"Who is that in the back?"

"I don't know, a passenger."

Back at the docks, In a instance ten armored cars appeared, as the two containers, were cracked open, first one had bags of gold coins, as Mike took a picture, as the teams were loading, and then in the back was paper bonds, as a container opened up, and they all slid out. It was placed in an awaiting container, as Carter said, "You won't tell him will you?"

"Nah, just as long as any more finds, you call me, and the next time you work with a girl, you better be on the up and up, or I will tell Jack of this miss-conduct."

"Yes sir,' said Carter, as Mike supervise the first cargo and then the next one, was a single item, as it was set in neutral, and rolled out, a prototype experimental car, looks to be Russian in markings, fully loaded, with missles, guns and defense mechanisms, for Carter to say,"Your not going to get that thing in the armored truck?"

"No, but it will fit in that dump truck" he said as he pointed to it, to added,"Assemble some pallets, tie them together, in that instance he changed his mind, to say,"Hold on, Carter, I have another idea. Mike sees Carly pull up, park as the two girls got out, and came up to Mike, for Natasha, to say,"So are you Jack Cash?"

"No, I'm your escort, my name is Mike Adams, Jack Cash asked me to come get you and bring you to him, while he was still on his lap top, to say,"Could you two please wait in the car?"

She looked at him, and stormed off, with Carly in tow, and back in the car, as the car that was covered, was pulled onto the awaiting pallet, till it was centered. Mike still though that the dump truck would be the best, especially when the operator, agreed with them, and the car was strapped down, and hoisting arm in place, the crane lifted it up, and was guided down into the back of the dump truck, then the top screen was set in place to hid it from the air, as the operator said "Where to?"

"NOLA Coast Guard base," said Mike, still on his lap top.

"No problem, I'm over there a lot, they know me well."

"Take off, and the armored cars will follow you, a reception awaits you", as Mike printed out the manifest list and authorization, a printed signature for himself, and one of Jack Cash, he hands to the driver.

With that Mike said goodbye to Carter, and went over to the awaiting car, got in, the back, moving Gia to the upright position, to say,"Drive to the airport." As they waited till all trucks were out of the way.

Inside the UN, the strike team was led to the field, to hear, "You all need to supervise the rugby matches, we need to watch for terrorist activity, and anything out of place, split into teams of two, said the advisor, to Paul, oh and one more thing, your agent is playing in the first game."

Jack got the summons from the UN Advisor, Christina, that the Flight simulator was on hold, due to a technical issue, at 1 pm is an exhibition match between Japan and New Zealand, as they just flew in." Jack sends Christina off, to see all the pallets of stuff, he snooped, a bit, to see a box of gummy worms, it said, 64- 2oz, and set it on the counter, he saw the pool, and thought, "Why not?" as Debby, entered to say, "I had to take Claire to the spa, to keep her safe, during the day."

"Wait you said Claire, the UN told me they escorted her out of the building."

Debby looked at him, to say, "Oh yeah, that's what happen, I forgot, when that was?"

Jack looked at her, as he opened the door to his pool, she asked, "Are you going swimming?"

"Yeah, are you coming?" asked Jack looking at her.

"Nah, I really would but I'm suppose to meet a dignitary for a tour, and get her settled in, per the UN's request."

"Isn't that what the advisors do?"

"Yes, but she asked for me personally?"

"Well if you gotta go, go", Jack took off all his clothes, and dove into the cool waters, as Debby, watched to admire the view, as she closed the door.

Debby stood in line, waiting the new arrivals, as these big buff players all the same size, big, really big to her, was led by a woman, of medium build and looks, short blonde hair, similar to Debby, as she said, "So are you my guide, I'm the President of New Zealand, Andrea Anderson, and you are?"

"Debby, supply and house maid."

"Precisely, so where can I find, our star player, Jack Cash."

Now Debby knew why she choose her, to say,"He is in his suite, swimming?"

"That sounds fun, he has a swim pool in his suite, I need to see that?"

"Come this way, as she led Miss Anderson, as the other players were escorted to their places, near the field. Debby breezed through security, with the dignitary, with diplomatic authority. As they came out on the men's floor, other agents were returning, some handsome others not so much, as she past the mess, to remark, "It's nearing eleven, time for lunch?"

"Nah, the mess is open 24/7, they eat when they want, true there are some hours of the day, but they can have room service, anytime, come on he is over here, as they saw several huge pallets, being set down, outside of Jack's new room, for Debby to say, "Jack just received another shipment?"

"Where do they come from?"

"Oh from secret admirers, and this one says, the city of Geneva, namely a one, Manager, Tom Atkins, contents say, candy, fruit, jewelry, and furniture?, as Debby, looks that over, to see cards, in one bundle, as she picks that up, for her to say, "Do you want to meet Jack, now?"

"Yes", she said, as Debby, swiped her card, and was let in, as the President saw five more of the same, to remark, "And this is all his?"

"Yep, he just had a seafood, order come in, with lobster, crab, and oysters, with two crates of mud bugs, chef Dany, is going to cook them all, for the entire staff, there is over two hundred pounds, with twenty reserved for Jack."

"Really, I should of brought something, I feel so out of place?" said the smiling President.

"No worries, he isn't like that at all, all of this is so overwhelming to him, just like these cards, you can see, as she opened one, to see a check fall out, as Debby picked it up to read, in the memo, Daughter's back, and to say, the amount, is 20,000, dollars, to show her, as she put it back away, and sets on his counter, as the President looked around, to see the frosted glass, and the clear, well placed, above the knees and above the head.

Debby, slid the door open, to the pool, to say,"He is in here."

The President entered a bit over dressed, as Debby, left, to close the door, as Jack came up for air, to see her, in her long sleeved blouse and striped skirt, nylons and high heeled shoes, for Jack, to say, "Hi, who are you?"

Standing at waist level, obviously nude, for her to see, she gushed, to say, "Maybe, I ought to come back later, when you're dressed."

As she stared at him, to say, "It's sure getting hot in here,"

Jack said, "Take off what you feel comfortable with, you're wearing a bra and panties right?"

He said, nonchalantly, to add,"Maybe I could ask, Debby, to get you a swim suit if you like?" as he was walking towards, the steps, for her to say,"No that won't be necessary, I guess, I could just take off my top and then my skirt, but can you turn" she said somewhat excitedly, as if she didn't want to say, what she just said. She began to unbutton her blouse, and her cuffs, as her blouse was open, for Jack to view, as he was rising, he bobbed the surface, as the President was giggling, a bit, to say, "This is like when I was a school girl all over again, as she pulled her blouse off, her large bra concealed her big boobs, as she undid her skirt, to show him, she had panty hose on, so, she slipped off her shoes, and in that moment, pulled her pantyhose, down, along with her panties, for Jack to see a nice bush, and at that point, they were tangled up in them, so, she further exposed herself, by lifting her leg up, to really show him, as she peeled one down, and then the other, to show him she wasn't shy any more, thinking, now wasn't the time, and then in that instance, she popped off her bra, and with momentum jumped into the shallow pool, feet first, realizing he was on his knees, as she stood, dripping wet, in three feet of water, as she lowered herself, and crawled over to him. With idle chit chat over, the President was all smiles, as her breasts, were on the surface floating, her huge diamond wedding ring present, to say, "So when can you come to our country, I'll personally give you a tour, we have our own geothermal sanctuary, where we could swim nude if we want."

"Looks like you're already doing that" said Jack.

"Well what I meant was in a cavern, just the two of us?"

"Sounds fun, we could practice in here?"

"We could, as she comes over and mounts him, to feel how big he was, she touched it to say, "This is the biggest I've ever seen, there is no way, your putting that inside of me, but I'd like to watch you do someone else, is that possible?"

"Perhaps, say after the game today?"

"Nah, I was thinking later tonight, as she whispered to him, "I know all about your sex parties, I could bring over thirty reinforcements, all I want to do is watch."

"Is it because your married, or what, as she shows her his ring, as she takes his hand, to say, "I would have thought it would be diamonds encrusted, as she allows him, to touch her right breast, he cupped it, and touched it, even squeezed her nipple, when Debby returned, to say, "Miss Anderson, there is a delegation happening in the auditorium, and their requesting your presence."

Debby left, as Andrea gave Jack a surprise kiss on the cheek, then the mouth as they, explored each other, as Jack repositioned himself, and just like that he was in, and she worked her hips, as he held onto her boobs, as she rode him out, till she let loose, and fell against him to say, "Thanks I needed this, as she extracted herself off of him, to see it was still hard, to say, "Didn't you come?"

"Nah, I usually last four hours."

"Wow, wait, I feel really bad, if I leave, and you're like that?"

As she turned around, and said, "Do me from behind, and get it off', as she held onto the other side, as Jack slipped it in, and held her hips, as she clamped down on him, and just like that, he dropped his massive load, for her to say, "I think I tasted that" He collapsed on her back, as he went soft, as she turned, to give him another kiss, to say, "I hope you can keep this a secret?"

"Only if you deliver on that promise tonight?"

"No, we don't need anyone else, it will be just you and I for an all-night session."

She stepped up, as Jack fell away, to see her towel off, and get dressed. And out the door she went as he saw the time as it was nearing noon.

Jack was on the field, kicking the ball in the air, back to another player, on the other side of the field, Miss Hohlstein smiled at him, as she took up her position, Jack was dressed in all black outfit, and wore number fifteen. They huddled up, then kicked off, the game was somewhat unfamiliar to her, and although she watched some of it, her attention was elsewhere, as two fans in an upper row was getting obnoxious, she summons security as they left her position, to march up two sets of stairs, to their landing, and they were gone, only to doubled back, and run into them, to hear, "Where are you going Missy?"

"Names Carla, go back to your seats, or"

"Or what you'll hit me with your stick" laughed one, then the other grabbed the one, while Carla drove her foot into one' groin, and watch him go down in pain, while the other ran off, only to hit someone and fall back and run back their way yelling, "Here comes a Giant", she tripped him, to see him go down, as Ivan the Giant turned the corner, who swooped in and hoisted both men up on each shoulder, and said in a deep voice, "They won't bother you anymore".

Carla turned around to see a flood of people come at her as it was announced it was intermission, she made her way to the railing to see that the field was empty.

One by one Men staggered into the UN, first was Vadim, Carlos, Steven, and Ben.

Jim was in constant contact with the Jet, as Mark and Clarance were waiting its landing, the jets were rotated down to allow the harrier, to land, a roller step was set in place, as the cockpit was set back, in the rear seat was the package, Mark and Clarance helped her out, she was a stunner to look at but both men, paid her a huge amount of respect, allowing her to walk on her own, a golf cart was waiting, as Jim drove it, she said "Hi" to him and asked when she could see Jack, Jim said, "In due time".

Over in the woods on a huge limb, laid Varfolomey, with his partner Fyodor, who said "Is she the one, which one I'll take the shot tell me it's her" said Varfolomey.

"I'm getting no face recognition, you're going to have to wait."

"My chances are dwindling, who is this guy who has so many visitors."

"Well the guy driving that cart was once a handler."

"And you know this how?"

"Because I killed the agent he was suppose to guard."

"Nice job, now get me into that Rugby match, and lets go kill this Jack Cash." said Varfolomey.

Jack came back out onto the field, the lightweight body armor, he wore on his chest was cumbersome, but it meant he was alive, the second half started, with his team kicking off, he was playing against the other only agent to come back, Chu, and Japan, but right now they had zero, and Jack's team, Jack scored twice, and kicked two extra points, to make it fourteen. Then he hit someone head on, fell back, and was seeing stars, he was helped back up, and just continued to play, for the rest of the time, Chu's team, tried valiantly to get back but fell short, the final score was fourteen, to ten.

Jack walked off the field, and back into the UN, and past everything to his room, using his hand, he got in, went to his room, their still in bed was Claire, naked and asleep, Jack took a shower, dressed, and went to the table to see the huge book from the library, he carefully, opened up the ancient book, only to see that it was in broken old English, bordering on Latin, he placed his phone on the page, to hit the written word translation, to English, but it was no use, it was lost in translation.

Debby walked in to see him, with a smile on her face, to say, "Now it looks like it's just you and I and her, shall I get undressed?"

"Nah, not right now, but could you tell me if you know how you can get Claire out of here, without detection?"

"What about our threesomes, she is much funnier than Trixie was."

"So can you tell me what happen to Trixie?"

"Sorry it's confidential."

"Enough with the games, I know you don't like her, but she is my air traffic controller."

"I'm sorry, it's not personal, but know where to find her."

"Great, could you do that, and ask her if she would come back to stay with me, it's only Thursday?"

"Sure anything for you", she left with a smile.

Jack review the whole book to see it must have over two thousand pages, in the large two foot by a foot book. He closed it up, to pull out his phone to look up Professor Benz number, and called him, that moment he cut off the line, for Jack, to say, "What an idiot, I can't do that, he will probably take my phone away, as he scrolls to his E-Mails and first up was the General from Camp Pendleton, who said, "Thank you for the opportunity to train your spies, each will be given, individualize assistance, and looked after with a guard detail."

Jack stopped the endless text, to send one himself, that said "Stop, treat them as you would any other recruit, the idea is to weed out those that can't handle it, no exceptions, eight weeks right?"

And sent it to hear a voice say overhead, Trixie West here to see you?"

"Yes, allow her in" said Jack, as he closed up his phone, to see her smiling, for Jack to say, "You seem unhappy?"

"I am, I hope you have good news for me."

"I don't follow you, what good news?"

"You know about Debby get thrown in jail for what she did to me? Said Trixie

Your feud with Debby must stop, this instance, and on another note, how did I do in the challenge last night?"

"Good I think you were first." She smiled at him.

At least you had Clarance keeping you company."

"True, he was nice to me, and after I was able to produce who I was he let me free and I came in right after you."

"Come on Clarance wasn't that nice to you, you will be fine, so do you wanna join or go home?" said Jack.

"I want revenge on her, and for what she did to me?"

"Then you're out, see ya." Said Jack as two UN advisors were at his door, to say, "Take her to our plane, and let Jim know she is out and off the team."

Just then, she began to cry, as Jack had a change of heart, to say, can you change?"

"I'm working on it" said Trixie in between sobs, as Jack sent the advisors away, for him to say, "Let her go, she will be with me." For Jack to say, "Say, do any one of you know who can translate this book for me?"

They nodded, for one to say,"We will have interpreter be here shortly."

Jack waved them on, he began to think, about how everyone wants something, why can't someone just come in here instead of wanting something, but rather giving something, would be refreshing, to hear, "There is a visitor outside the door, her name is Francesca, is she allowed in?"

"Yes" said Jack, as he rose, to see the door open, and a young impressionable girl walked in, with a cute face and long flowing brown hair, to say "Hi Mister Cash, my name is Francesca, and I can translate that book if you like?" she said with a smile as she eased in next to him, to say, "Ah, the New Zealand's Royal's book." As she looked at him, as he slid the book, over to her to say, "Is there something on that war chant the new Zealanders do?"

"So Mister Cash what would you like to know, other than that?"

"Why's that?"

"It's not in this book, it's an original aboriginal Indians that served the Auckland area, and in their tribute, the chant was created."

Jack pulls out his phone to say "Page 1111, top to the middle"

She pulled out white gloves new, placed them on, then, went to that specific page, to the top to read, "As the armies advance towards us, we discovered, that if we can band up smaller groups of warriors, and ambush them, will result in a lower casualty count, and demoralize, the advancing armies", or so I paraphrased, as she continues, "That, as it was my understanding that the use of spies, with extraordinary abilities that could evade capture, defend themselves and profit from this venture, then we could win the war, and claim victory. Spies are a special breed, they are not born, they are made, with constant contact, and operate on the highest level, almost like my alter ego, and allowed the same privileges I enjoy, they will assume the highest military rank and gain a profit from the surplus of the gains, they are loners, seldom do they rely on anyone, however, there are those that follow, and those secret men, are loyal to the end, no exceptions. They too are self-reliant and need no support, as they act only to defend the spies actions, but always in the rear, never next to him, my spy we will call is Clarance, his name is of no matter, he is merely a figure, a name the enemy knows of him, and he is more deadly to them than my whole army, they won't attack until, they are positive, they know where he is at, he may be back in Takapuna, as of this writing, but his loyal followers are here, and have been in contact with him, to attack, ambush style, at passes and valleys.

"It stops about there, shall I continue?" she asks Jack.

"Yes, go on" said Jack listening.

"Were back in Auckland, Clarance and his loyal followers most of them intact as we lost half of our army, but we overcame them, and killed Samuel the third, of England, the year was 1823. Clarance is back at his residence, in the northern providence of Takapuna. Where his massive fortress, overlooks the harbor, and the Welso river, to his families land of Takapuna (Clarance), is elevated as the families principle caretaker and overlord, to his followers, some estimate, 20,000 and growing with our win, but he told me, he seeks no position, alongside me, he wants to be left in secrecy, to live a life of freedom, rather than the constant pressures of public life, I write this to praise his work only, but to keep his true identity a secret, although when he passes, someday somewhere, someone will know the true story and be satisfied with that, or know the true secret.", it ends, and goes into a bit of philosophy, will that be all?"

"Yes, and you can take that book with you, tell me is this all you do?"

"That and among other things, but yes the Library is a full time job, I live in Geneva, if that is what you're asking?"

"No, not really, you can go."

Jack recorded all of that on his phone to replay it, to say "Now I know my real purpose".

Jack got up, and put his phone away, to go out into the hallway, then down to the offices, to see Professor Benz, who was in a deep conversation with an Advisor, to say "How may I help you Mister Cash?"

"How is all the other agents making out?"

"Well to be honest with you, not so well, I still have the Frenchman and the Australian, still trying to find their way back, one went one way and the other is in the Mountains somewhere, so what do you need?"

"What ever happen to the Aerial combat training, do we actually get to go up in attack aircraft?"

"Well what do you think, yes that was the point, I'm still working out the details, most of everyone is back, to get a game of Rugby in, so be on the alert, Ben is here, so I think you play again at five pm, good luck."

Jack left and was on his phone, but, immediately sensed something was wrong, as the phone flashed a warning sign, to go black, he put it away, to look around to see no one, he went to his room, and went in.

He pulled out his phone to see that it was normal again, got him to think, outside of these walls, especially the hallway is bugged or someone is watching him, but he went on and made the call.

Jim picked up the phone, to hear Jack's instruction, he looked over at Jack's support team, who both were monitoring Brian's position, in Russia, and the Belaruan troops were mobilized for an attack. Although Jim has a new priority, as Mitzi came to him, when, Jim finished the conversation, he whispered in her ear, where she said out loud "I'll take care of the arrangements, what I need you to do, is arrange for a refuel in the air above India."

Mitzi walked around ordering those that would listen. She saw Bauer to say, "We got a new mission."

He looked at her to say, "You seemed delighted by that."

"Why aren't you?"

"Yep ready to go."

Jack realized he was living in a fiasco of biblical proportions, and decided to go out to the field and meet up with the team, up on the board, it read "The top sixteen teams to advance to the next round", Jack scanned the board to see New Zealand was next up to play US, to see that his buddy Jonathon of France, was scheduled to play Russia but was post poned. Jack walked the field, over to the executive's seats to see the very young Francesca, who smiled back at him, while a younger man took a seat next to her, then he saw Alfred, the librarian, then he saw Debby, who waved and smiled, he knew Claire was gone, and too bad, she was nice.

Jack made it into the locker room, to see his team, cheer him on, they rallied around him, as the coach separated the players from him, to say, "Are we ready to go out and win another game?"

Jack followed his team out, to a full stadium, and the cheers went up, on the rail was Francesca, who was waving at him, Jack searched the seats around her to look for the young man with her, with no avail, to wave back at her. She smiled at him. The coach places his hand on Jack's shoulder to say, "See you got an admirer."

"Yeah, her and pick any one else look up in the stands." said Jack.

Debby eased down to the rail, to see the other strike team members, taking their places on the railing, to see Jack and the other New Zealanders, after a traditional dance and chant in their end box. Jack stood on the side line waiting. Then he joined his team. As the Americans took to the field, The first twenty minutes ended in a tie, 24 to 24.

Jack was running the field in the next half, every time Jack picked up the ball, he got crushed.

The coach came over to say, "Listen Jack you need to employ a kick and run game, like Johnny showed you, kick it up in the air, then run after it, no one will touch you, get it and run for try, you got that?"

"Yeah, I'll try, you know I'm getting crushed out there."

"We know, but we were all told to lighten up on the hits, or end up in jail for the rest of our lives, the UN put it this way, consider it like tackling a President of their specific country, so believe me, you might think you're getting hit, but really its quarter speed, and when that guy hit you and knocked you over, he was taken out and sent away, so don't worry about being crushed, you are protected, cheer up, our job is to respect your position, and support your efforts." Jack looked up at the drink cart positioned in his area, exclusively, while the other team, was on the other end.

All of a sudden, the place went quiet, Jack looked over to see they were all at a upright position looking at him, he gradually got up, to see an older woman, wearing a fashionable hat, she walked in, with a staff of bodyguards, she spoke eloquently, as she stood in front of Jack to say "Mister Cash, my name is Andrea Anderson, I'm the President of New Zealand, and our country would like to thank you for your efforts, you're an honorable man, we will support your enthusiasm, and would like to extend an offer to come to our country for a visit, a formal letter will be given to you on your graduation day, thank you."

Jack bowed, to say, "Thank you, your welcome."

She left the room slowly admiring her national team, they were at attention, not a single man moved, showing her huge respect, till she was gone. Even then things changed, the line separating him and them was well respected, and a reverence was shown to him, it was a serious attitude adjustment, seeing their President, made this serious for them, even the coach, changed his tone, as a man came in to watch over them, he stood at the door, Jack surveyed the drink cart, that had every beverage under the sun, on ice. Jack took one, to turn to see, his teammates had their eyes lowered at him, and the laughing and horse play was over, a seriousness was felt. The coach went to the chalk board, to discuss the plans, and put Jack's name in the middle, then circled his name to say, "We know what we need to do, we do this for Jack and we do this for our President, Miss Anderson, let's go." The guys stormed out, and Jack followed.

Jack walked out on the field, this time with a renewed purpose, from when they kicked off, till half way through, the score was 40-30, Jack fumbled the ball forward, and Ben picked it up, only to get crushed. Now it was Jack's turn to shift the momentum, on a side out he reached up and stoled the ball, his backs followed him down, till he got the ball back and scored. Five points, then he kicked the extra point for two more, to make it seven. The game was coming to a close but the New Zealanders, made it doubled in scoring down to the very last minute charge, with ball in hand, and led by Jack, who took the ball all the way to the goal only to get hit from his side, he landed and out came the ball for touch. A roar from the player's red carded that player, and Jack's team was awarded a penalty kick or ball out for a scrum. Jack took the scrum on the 22 meter line, in went the ball, they wheeled the scrum, for the scrum half to pick it up, who tossed it to Jack, who scored a try, outside the posts. With the game ending 60-30. The gun went off, and the ref called the game done.

Jack sunk down to the ground to take the win in stride, but his players helped him up, and they went into the locker room. Jack finished showering and changed back into his UN clothes, to say goodbye to his new found friends, and left.

Jack was inside the UN complex, to see Steven and Jonathon had returned, they waved to him, going out to the field to play in their games, in the food court was Francesca who said, "Do you need me to translate anything else or do you need me just to come over, she said playfully.

"Sure how about around nine?"

"Then it's a date" she said. smiling.

Jack entered the chef's dining room, to see that the line was nearly empty, and stood as next to go, to see the specials board, he read, "Steak and potatoes anyway you like it, behind him was a familiar voice who said "I know what you like, so how about we actually have an adventure tonight." Jack turned to see Kellie, to say, "Are you coming out to see us play tonight?"

Jack looked at her, as he held up the line, but no was complaining, as he turned to say "Steak, med rare, six eggs poached med, hash browns, with onions and peppers and an artichoke with clarified butter on the side, any king crab legs?"

"Absolutely Mister Cash, just flown in this morning, from Latvia."

Jack looked around the room, to search for her but to no avail, to say "and a side order of jellied cranberry sauce."

Jack moved along, to the end, took four glasses and poured out two chocolate and two whole milk, and swiped his per diem card and went to take his favorite seat in a booth.

Kellie, re-appeared, sat across from him, she was all smiles, as she ate her salad, a chef, delivered Jack his platter of food. Jack waved his watched over the food, it showed it was free of poison, and went to work, on those succulent crab legs, he dipped them in a vat of his butter, while he pulled the leaves of the artichoke off, others watched him, eat the vegetable.

Kellie said "If you will allow me to show you around the field, maybe you and I could go out into the town, and all the wonderful foods it has to offer, then I can show how much of a good time, just you and I can have."

In between bite, he said "That's fine, I'll let you lead the way, as he spoke to soon, as other girls came in, especially, his long lost fuck buddy, Lea, who gushed over him.

For her to say, "Come on Jack allow me the pleasure to please you, the only way I know how, right now?' she said as she was pulling on his arm to go.

"Your beginning to bother me, why don't you get lost, now that you're finished with your food."

"I like to watch you eat."

"The UN is only a phone call away," he threaten her with that, she left disappointed, for Kellie to say, "All she wants and talks about is you to do her, that's all she talks about how you and her will live comfortably in Monaco."

"Your still here?" Jack said to Lea, as he offered her a seat next to him.

"Alright I get it I'll leave" said Lea, but Kellie scooted out and left as well.

Jack finished eating, to pick up the tray, and deposit it, and out the door he went.

The door to his room, opened, to see several brown boxes, and there was Debby, pulling tin cans from them to say, "You just received a huge seafood order, half went to the kitchen, the other into your cooler, it was all from Queen Ana, from Latvia, its royal caviar, packaged exclusively for you."

Jack watched as she opened the huge walk in, to place the tins on the shelf, he stepped in, to see a stock of beers, wines and some foods, to say over the fans, "What is all of this?"

"It's what appreciative people send you all the time, it's just that you're here, and everyone knows it, so you get a package a day or so, each box is opened and tested if necessary, unless they know who sent it, these came by jet from the queen herself."

"So all this stuff is mine?"

"Yes, but this is only the reserves, I stocked the refrigerator first, go check it, if you like?"

"Nah, I feel like a swim, and relax in the hot tub."

"Go ahead, I'll join you as soon as I finish."

Jack looked her over, then went out to think of the very young Francesca, but wished Claire could have stayed longer.

Jack stripped out of his clothes, and went out into his pool area, to dive in, then over to the shallow end to rest his head on a pillow, as he laid his head back he closed his eyes as his feet tendered to the bottom, and drifted back and forth, to rest.

The last match was over, and the strike team was dismissed, Casey was still missing after the hit that put Jack down, he was hot, Paul and Kenny tried to hold him back, Casey was ready to kill the guy for the cheap shot.

Jill was pretty excited to see Jack was so active among those giants, it impressed her, which she plans to show her appreciation for. The UN advisors escorted Casey to the plane, and to Jim's care, as they left Jim said, "Now, now, calm down, it's over."

"Really how so?"

"It will be dealt with, when their plane lands, he will get what he gave out, but tenfold, you and me, and Mike and Mark, even the young Jesse, said he would avow that hit back, come in, we got a case of the finest Caviar, and champagne."

"Wait where did this all come from?" asked Casey.

"From Jack of course."

"No, who gave you all this?"

"Lighten up, it was Debby."

"That's what I thought, this is all for Jack, it's like stealing from our boss, regardless of money, his food is equally sacred" said Casey, pulling up the Champagne, to put into the cage, and ordered Kenny to watch over them.

"Wait, what are you doing that is expensive fish eggs" cried Jim.

"That's right, it is, and it's all for Jack, do you see this seal on here?"

"Yeah, so what" said Jim.

"This caviar, is for Royalty exclusively, like the stuff only the Queen of England would eat, you and me and everyone else together couldn't afford" said Casey seeing Mike chomping down on a cracker of the red eggs, to see Casey was mortified, to say "What", to finish it, to walk past Casey.

Craig spoke up as well to say, "He is right, everything on this plane is Jack's, so why is it any different if someone steals money or his prized rifle", they all stood to see one of the two long rifle's was gone, as the frame was still intact, there was a silence and a storm was coming as they all went their separate ways looking for that prized rifle.

Jack sensed a presence, as the lights were lowered, he put on a smile, to open his eyes, to see it was Queen Ana, standing there, all dressed up, with a smile on her face to say, "I hoped you liked my gift", she began to undress, in the background Debby, looked disappointed, as she exited the room, to see Francesca waiting outside his door, to say, "Sorry he doesn't need you tonight he has his own interpreter."

She looked at Debby with confusion, as the door closed shut.

Ana, slowly lowered herself into the cool water, in between his legs, to place her hands on his stomach to say, "You played admiralty well today, I watched from the Presidential box, that Miss Anderson, was envy of us, if she only knew", she continued to talk, as Jack watched her fondle him, thinking she was nice, but Francesca would have been better, the older woman, was slow and dilbert, as any woman of power acted, like Debby, she knows what she wants and how to get it and she shares, unfortunately the Queen, isn't one to share, let alone she tires way too early.

Jack felt somewhat bored with her, the excitement wasn't the same, yeah, she was alluring,with that Jet black hair and that pale white skin, and seductive eyes. Then she did something unexpected, and hugged him, she rested her head on his stomach, and wrapped her arms around him, to say, "I think I can love you for the rest of my life?"

It felt good to be held, to feel her body pressed up against his, was nice, the water around them was heating up, till Jack got up, and lifted her up, and carried her to his next favorite spot, the hot tub, and set her down, as he turned on the jets, he sat and she came to him, she put her arms around him, and began to kiss him, for the first time he held her in return, as she strattled him.

This was an erotic moment for him, as he felt her in a different way, it was nice, he thought, her warmth and tenderness was nothing like he ever experienced before. Jack savored the moment, and just held onto her, and he liked it. She placed her hands on his face to look at him, to say, "So are you still going to marry me?"

"Sure If you'll have me?"

"Of course, you're my lover, I hope my friend and"

"Hush up, you're talking too much, let it rest" said Jack opening his eyes, to see that she was disappointed, to say, "Did you try anything I sent you?"

"What do you mean?"

She readjusted her position, on him, to say, "I've been sending all the seafood for you, and the royal caviar?"

"I think it's in the cooler, as for the seafood, I don't know where it is, I had the crab legs, they were great, as for the others thanks."

"For you it's nothing, and that is just the start of the gifts."

"You don't have to buy me any gifts?"

"Now listen here, Mister Cash, a girl does what a girl wants to do, besides I have a country to show you, and then there is this dowry, we need to talk about."

"What are you talking about?"

"Well I have no heirs to pass on the crown to, so basically It's mine till I die, but now that you're in the picture, well we need to discuss how you want to divide it up."

Jack looked at her to say, "You mean, a pre-nuptial agreement, well I'll sign anything, I don't want a thing, except your love."

"No,That's not what I'm talking about, let me tell you what is really going on, the countries of Latvia, is divided into two, the separation is for those that support our free trade that I negotiated, when we broke apart from the Soviet Union in 1991, however the country's government wants to dissolve the whole royalty aspect, and keep it all in house, but now that I marry you, and with your stature and reputation, may change everything, it may even bring us all together, I digress, this is all about your role as my King, and if I could only have a child?"

"That's what we all hope for" said Jack.

"But you know I'm sterile?"

"Let's get you to the US for a second opinion?"

"Maybe I'll try that, but let's get back to this dowry, I talked about, first off, as Queen of Latvia, I pledge my allegiance to you and all that I have, and later next month, you'll see what I'm talking about."

"Alright let's go to bed, and discuss it further" said Jack lifting her up, he carried her out.

CH 13

The shooter is hit, and surprises follow

Saturday morning, day 13, opened up to new beginnings, the Queen left late last night, saying she was waiting till he would be there in a week or so, a huge wedding was planned. Debby entered the room to announce, "Got, great news for you Jack, Jack looked at her, from the sitting position, as he continued, to do sit-ups, to hear "You have a match today, all the boys are finally back, so the rest of the first round will be played, then the afternoon, game two, for you is, Saudia Arabia, you're a twenty plus favorite., aren't you excited about that?"

Jack stopped to look at her, to say, "Not really, I was hoping to get out of here for the weekend."

"You always want to go somewhere, well I got even worse news for you, your request to go to Shanghai, has been cancelled, due to some terrorist activity, or a trap or something like that." You're going to have to wait till your done here, do you have any plan to take me with you?"

"Sure if you want to go."

"Really you're cool with that?"

"Sure why not, you're my supply girl."

"You mean person."

"Yeah, that too, so when is this game I need to go to?"

"I, imagine it would be in the afternoon."

"You would think that someone would have told me" said Jack finishing out his string of crunches, to get up, he felt a difference from Debby, to walk past her, and out the door he went.

Jack got to the field, to see it was empty, on the board showed the corrections, and the upcoming matches, he saw New Zealand plays Saudia Arabia, where he knew his friend Jonathon Razor would be playing?" From behind him, he heard, "I missed you last night."

Jack turned to see it was Francesca, wearing as little as possible and said, "I thought we could go to the spa together, that is till your next game, at 1 pm."

"Sure why not lets go, I know someone down there" said Jack, who led her down to the spa, however, it wasn't like he remembered it, it was packed, with lots of pretty women, men and children. Jack was ready to go till he heard "Jack you should of called ahead I would have gotten you a private room" said Hendy, the cute hot French woman.

Jack allowed Francesca to go first, as he followed, to say, "How about a soak, in the mineral pools."

"You guys could do that, I have to warn you it will be crowded."

"That's alright we will blend right in" said Jack, as Hendy hands him a yellow swimsuit, as he leaned in to say, "And for my friend?"

"Looks like she does'nt need one, Later I'll come get you for a one on one massage."

Jack went in and changed, and put his stuff in an empty locker, that had a thumb print key mechanism, and went out to the pool areas, and walked to an open spot, and slid in, he rolled up his towel, to lay his head against it, as he sat on the bench to rest. Some time went by, when two guys were talking to say, something, Jack wasn't really listening, till they said his name, then he awoke, to hear, "Yeah, that Jack Cash is some punk, If I could face him I'd put him down."

"Yeah but what about his suppose support team, they say their all over where he goes."

"Doubtful it's probably lies" said the cocky guy, to add "Besides I got my own watcher over that guy,"

"Who would double cross Jack Cash over a security guard like you?"

"Thanks friend, my girl tells me everything, he is a punk."

"What if he were here?"

"Doubtful, he has a match in a couple of hours, why would he relax, besides my girl would tell me what he is up to".

Jack tilted his head up to see the guy, who was looking around for someone, to who wasn't in the mineral baths, so Jack went back to what he was doing, resting, and tuning out the two guys.

It was peaceful, till a hand awoke him to say "Jack, Mister Cash, wake up, Jack awoke, to see everyone that was in the pool, was all closed up in a tight area on the other side of the pool, the two guys heads were down, as Hendy helped Jack up and out of the pool, as she guided Jack to the other side Jack said in passing "Really, I'm not that bad of a guy, but you won't see your girl ever again", to be helped into a private room, to say, "Where's the girl?"

"She has been dealt with, who is exposed as a double agent, she said, added, "She had some help."

"So do I, can I borrow your phone?"

She hands him, her cell, he punches in a code, then it links to his phone, he dials up Clarance, who answers it, Jack says, "Two on the run, for pickup, two security guards, with badges, with bad intentions."

Jack closed up the phone, to see he killed another phone he tossed back at her, she looked at it, then tossed it in the trash, to say, "I needed a new one anyway."

Jack got on the table, as Hendy locked the door, to say, "Were safe now, don't worry about the phone, the UN will get me another, when were done here, you can go out through those doors back to the UN, did you want to see my touch pad?"

"For what, I'm here for a massage."

"Don't you want to see who is after you?"

"Nah, I already have someone working on it, too bad about Francesca, I really like her."

"Over this" said Hendy, taking off her top and slipping out of her bottoms.

"No I take that back, come over here."

Clarance and police Chief Winters waited outside the spa, Clarance had his arms crossed to hear, "If you ever decide to leave Jack, I'll hire you in a heartbeat."

"Sorry, this is my lifelong dream, to work for a world renown spy, I'll do anything for him", as his phone rang, Clarance saw it was Casey, he answered it, to say, "What do you want?"

"Were leaving out on a mission, do we save a seat for you?"

"Nah, I have my own mission."

"What's more important than going with Jack?"

"It's a job, Jack asked me to do, we all don't have a confined space to work in, I take care of the outside remember?"

"Yeah, good luck on that, would you rather be here or in the field?"

"For you guys, Imagine you better find that rifle, or you will all pay."

"You mean, you don't have it?"

"Why would I,I have no access to the cage, besides, if I were you I'd talk with Jesse, I'm sure he is behind it" said Clarance. He closed up his phone, to recross his arms, and sure enough two security guys came out, as two SWAT members jumped down on them, to cuff them up, all the while Clarance didn't move, as the men were lifted up, both saw Clarance, as one said, "Who is he and why are you taking us into custody?"

All was quiet, as a waiting van, as they were put inside, as the door shut, Clarance sat next to the Police Chief, in his car, as they went to the police station.

"What do you plan on doing?" asked the Chief.

"Have fun, first, then get information out of them, to see there connection to Jack, and if their non-corporative, then the real fun starts."

"I like a man who takes his job seriously."

"You haven't seen Jack in action."

"Yes I have, and you're right he is very dangerous."

"You think he is dangerous, I'm ten times tougher, he is more lethal, he has twenty or so ships off shore at his beckoning call, I have myself."

They arrived as the very serious Clarance was in no mood, as the men were placed in separate rooms, as Clarance unclipped his weapon, and holster, to give it to Aaron the Police Chief, as the door opened he walked in, to hear it close, Clarance said, "Stand up" the guy looked coarsely at him, to say, "Are you Jack Cash, I'm sorry for talking bad about you, it was my friend Josh, and his girl Francesca that was recruited by Varfolomey and Alexei, the Russian connection."

"How do you fit in this picture?"

"I was his friend, please don't hurt me."

Clarance flexed his hands, he was ready to go, he clinched his jaw, to hear, "Listen, I can tell you that there is an assassination attempt at the stadium today, by a shooter."

Clarance calmed down, but he was ready to pounce, yet he pulled out his phone, to dial up Jim, then waited to say out loud, "Repeat that one more time."

"About the shooter is going to assassinate you in the stadium during your game."

"What else, all of it" said Clarance in his Irish accent.

"That's all I know, look man, please don't kill me, I want a lawyer."

Clarance closed up his phone, to say, "Ready to step out?"

The door opened, he stepped out, contemplating what he just heard, knowing he would love to call in reinforcements, but had no authority, he knew he couldn't talk with Jack, he knows it doesn't work like that, as he went to the other cell, the door opened to see the cocky guy was on the bunk, Clarance went in and strikes him in the head with his fist, to see the guy roll out of the bunk, he crowded into a corner, crying, to say, "What did you do that for, I have rights, I want my lawyer?"

"Sorry, your classified as a terrorist, and therefore, you're being held without that opportunity but if you like Josh, you can talk with me" said Clarance standing over him.

"Who are you" said Josh.

"The guy who is gonna carve you up, like I did on your friend."

"Doubtful, you tough guys are all the same, hit me around a bit."

Clarance dove on him, and wrapped his arm at his throat, he was choking him, from behind, to whisper, "You have no idea who your messing with, I'm not here to play any games, I'll I have to do is pull my arm in and I break your neck, now hot shot, answer my questions and I will consider you to live, who were your associates?"

Barely able to speak he mumbled, Clarance let off the pressure, and stood up, to say, "Answer the question?"

The guy turned to look at the very mean man, to say, "Alright, go Fuck yourself."

Clarance kicked him in the groin, as the man went down in a heap, for Clarance to say, "I don't care for poor language choices, I'll just go get it from your friend."

Meanwhile back at the spa, Jack was looking over at Hendy, after receiving the best professional massage he has ever received, to say, "Thanks I need that" the door was open to the UN, as Jack slipped on his sweat pants and tank top.

Jack reached the top of the stairs to see Professor Benz, who said, "Your right we should have went to Shanghai."

"Why?" asked Jack.

"Seems like the walls are tumbling in around us, the UN is on a lockdown, I thought we were as safe as Monaco, but I was wrong."

"There is a huge difference from a country, and the UN" said Jack.

"How so?"

"A country maintains peace, here we are the authority that causes pain, and were a holder of very thing bad, that's why I'm always on the move" said Jack.

"Well next year, it will only be a week long refresher."

"Yeah, if we all make it to next year?"

"Well if anything I'll at least see you, oh and your match has been post poned indefinitely till the shooter is found?"

"I already know who it is, let me go and I'll take the shooter out and restore peace" said Jack.

"You can do that?"

"Sure, that's why I get paid the big bucks, my name is Jack Cash, super spy."

"Alright I will allow it?"

"In that case, I want Francesca released to me."

"You got it, you want her here or at your plane?"

"Let's make it to the plane, hey I talked with Queen Ana, from Latvia, and she told me that she has some seafood flown in for me, do you know where any of it is?"

"Well yes, but I didn't know it was exclusively for you, it's in the chef's room, for all to share?" said the Professor looking at Jack to realize it was wrong, to add, "I will correct this situation."

"No, don't worry about it, I just didn't know, when I get back, may I see what she has sent over?"

"Absolutely, ...Thanks" said the Professor.

Jack went to his room, and found his phone, he went to his refrigerator, to see a huge tin of caviar, he pulled it out, he saw a platter of cheeses and meats, he grabbed that too. Jack pulled out his phone to dial up Jim, to say, "Listen, I want a detail on both girls, coming out of the UN, and want Clarance recalled, ready in twenty minutes?"

Jack closed up his phone, to put it away, he felt refreshed, as he carried the food out of his room, a pathway was cleared, through the UN, to the hanger, he turned to see the girls were being escorted by the UN security force, to the waiting Casey and Paul, Jack closed the gap, to see the strike force waiting for him, Jack entered the plane, Jim was at the controls, up went the ramp, as he past the teams, he went to the cage, to see his rifle was gone, then sees Gia, he does a double look, then he hands her the food to say, "Can you fix me a hot tray of food, please."

Then he opens the door to his cabin, to see Mitzi and Tami at the desk, as he looks to his right, a stunner of a woman, as the flood of emotions are back in place, he stepped in, and in that instance, both Tami and Mitzi left his room, and closed the door shut. For her to say, "Mister Cash, My name is Natasha Rogers, I'm a big fan, is there any way I could do a story on you?"

"Sure, do you know why you're here?"

"Nope, your friend Mike escorted me here, besides who wouldn't want to meet the number one spy in the world, so can I ask, what is it like, I see that beautiful women surround you, And equally, lovely men, not to mention, those Black Ops boys, could get a woman hot."

Jack looked her over to say, "I have to tell you look amazing, so are you married?"

"Yeah, once, but it was really a cover up, I took a dead man's name to give it to my only son?"

"Why's that, where is your husband at?"

"Well technically I was never married, I met this wonderful guy in prison, and from that exchange, I got pregnant, and had a son, named after him?"

"Named after whom?"

"I guy I was in love with, his name was Jesse James, he was known as the outlaw in prison?"

"Really, where is at now?"

"That's just it, I can't find him, I've searched for twenty plus years and when I get close, it's a dead end."

"Well look no further, here I am."

She looks him over, and around to say,"No, you're not even like him, he was much taller, and really large, if you know what I mean?

"I do Marie-Elizabeth Duke", he said confidently, for her to stop in her tracks, to say, "How do you know my real name, it's been a twenty year secret."

"That's alright, I'm trying to find out my real name, I may have a living sister and a mother."

"Then I was way off, I had you only having a brother and living in Bonner Springs, Missouri.

"Wow, you mean like the real Jesse James?"

For Jack to say, "Yeah, but that wasn't even my real name, the guards called me that because the government called me a secret, even to you."

"What about us now?' as the two embraced. He felt her against him, as she held him to say, "Now I know it's you, and the two kissed, for her to say, "And ever and ever again?"

"Yes, will you be my wife?" asked Jack.

"Yes darling, I will, when can we get married?"

"After all this is over, as the two broke the embrace, for her to look him over, to say, "You have changed, now it all makes sense, so where do we go from here?"

"Well after the UN I'm flying over to Latvia, to get married to a Queen."

"Wait what?, I thought you said you and I would marry?"

"We will in due time, first, I need to secure relations with Latvia, for the US in order to maintain peace, and further keep Russia at bay."

"So this is for diplomatic reasons, I've heard of envoys marrying princesses of other countries for diplomatic reasons, alright I'll allow that one."

"Well to tell you the truth, three is sixteen, and after, the training one more."

"Wait, you have already sixteen wives?"

"Yes, and many more to come", said Jack.

"Wait, when will this all end?"

"Probably never, the US has told me I could have unlimited amount of wives."

"What does that prove, marriage is between one man and one woman?" said Natasha.

"Who said that?"

"Well it was what I learned, there was no one person say, it was the rule, why do you need more than one wife anyway?"

"Well it all started with my first girlfriend, she was a lesbian, and wanted other girls to join us, and then I went on a mission to Cuba where I met a super spy, he told me what was up, as a spy goes, the secret is have as many wives as you can, there loyalty will keep you alive, and so far he is right, you see its more about trusting, those around you and the love follows, as I was given his sister, Alba, as my first diplomatic wife, then, a princess from the Dominican Republic, named Alexandria, Alex for short, then as a token for what I did, I received from Havana the King's gift, his first daughter, Maria."

"I get the point, besides, I know a little of the spies, so your Carlos, Gomez's American agent, brother, I discovered that a while back, especially on the raid at Puerto Plata, your making quite a name for yourself."

Just then there was a bang on the door, Jack turned to open it to see Jim, for him to say, "Jack the UN has suggested something else, since the shooter Varfolomey, and his partner, is in the field grounds, all of the UN is on lock down, Tad Jones the brit, has taken up the fight, as well as Art Jackson, he too is set up and finally your son, Jesse has the Toussant, all three are going to position themselves around the shooter along with the rest of Black ops, and UN SAS, now comes the hard part, They want you to be a decoy."

"What, who's plan was that, yours Jim?"

"Well I did somewhat volunteer, once I told them, I could, keep you safe?"

"And how are you going to do that?"

"Simple, I can modify one of your wind breaker, to look like a jersey, as we speak, UN seamstress, as fabricating, teal, jerseys, with players numbers on it, and yours will have the number 15, also, UN officials have told, the players, to react once you get shot, go down, and the players will surround you, until a medical team will arrive, then you will be carted off."

Jack looked over at Natasha who looked back at him to hear her say, "You better get going, I guess it's time you catch a killer, I'll be here waiting for you, I guess." As Jim stepped out, and closed the door.

In room one, all the agents gathered, as it was evident Jack was not present, for the Professor to say, "We have had an incident here at the UN a breach, and the defective, Russian, KGB operator, Varfolomey Bartholomew is here, to assassinate, Jack Cash."

Tad raises his hand to say, "Is there anyway, I could help him?"

"In what capacity?"

"By a look out, I could set up, at the highest vantage point, and survey for the best shot?"

"It looks like you'll play next?"

"So what I don't care about this game, allow me to help out a fellow agent, and rid this world of terror."

The Professor thinks about it, to say,"Alright, I will allow it, under one condition?"

"Name it what?"

"That you have an UN advisor with you?"

"No problem, I just need my weapon?"

"The UN advisor will bring it to you, anyone else?"

"All raised their hand, eager to participate, as the Professor, assigned the roles.

As for the women, they were'nt told, as they were playing their first elimination games, Dana with number 1 ranked, Argentina won 4-2, over Turkey and Z'sofia. Next was Kellie, who searched high and low for Jack, too much avail, as she won, in a close match, 1-0, US, ranked 2, over Peleruth and Poland. Next was Freya, number 3 Mexico, falls, to number 10, Croatia, and Nina Ivan 4-3. Number 4 Spain, and Esmeralda, knocks off, Kendra and Russia, 3-2. Next up was Protima and Brazil, was 1-0, over Belarus, and Nina Toop, she really defended well, and was close, but a late surge, and a header, won the game. Next was France and Lea, she scored early, and kept Cami and South Africa from scoring and won. Number 9 Canada, took out number 7 Portugal, Darlene and Joana fought early and often, but Canada prevailed 2-1. The last game was abit of a blowout, as Honduras, Erica, took apart Chile, and Simone, 3-0. All the girls watched one others matches, not suspecting, an evil presence, was watching from the side lines, with Miss Erica Meyers, as her VIP pass, had unlimited access, to all areas, as she was guided by the UN, as special operations liaison to criminals, she choose the assignment, to be close to her lover as she was a double agent, as she walked freely, as she led the two of them up the stadium, for her to say, "Allow me to take you inside, confront him and you can kill him." She pleaded."

"No, it's a trap, The UN will shoot me on sight, show me to the high ground, all you have to do is make sure he is on the field."

"As I know as earlier as two hours ago, he is scheduled at his start time is 4:40, as they saw Egypt and South Africa take to the field, and the announcer said, "Round two games shall commence," the trio saw immediate scoring as South Africa wiped the field with Egypt it was 40-6, after the first half, while Varfolomey had one arm around Erica and the other on his gun case, as they all sat in the above seating all by themselves, much to the witness of the camera at the UN, a drumming in the second half, to finish, 80-20. 12:30, as play ended, and another two teams, went at it, as an older gentleman, Thomas, Jones, was moving slowly, trying to keep up as his Wales team, took apart Italy, as the young man Gordon Roderick, was blindsided multiple times, and on one occasion, knocked the ball forward, on a reset, the Wales team mounted a charge, then a breakaway, as the older Thomas followed, in the end, he received, a laid out, to deliver the ball for the try. It was successful, for five points, he set up and kick for extra, to make it 7-0, at half. As Varfolomey, heard Fyodor say,"Let's get something from concession stand?"

"You go, give me and Erica, some alone time to watch my favorite sport, to say, "You know, I won the cup, four years ago, with Russia, we beat the US, 56-10, they were weak then, as the second haft was more of the same, and Wales, won, 14-10. Just then Varfolomey, got up and began to cheer, as Russia took the field, his whistles, went on deft ears, as he saw his old friend Vadim, take the field, he smiled, as the opponents, came on as announced, Russia, will play, Turkey, Hendon, loved to hit, that was till he hit Vadim, then it was all over, as Vadim, punished him, with blindsides, as Vadim scored often and easy as Hendon was spent, as the first twenty minutes, was done, as the score was 14-0, all the while Varfolomey cheered, standing up, but also it became apparent to the women, as they noticed him, as some were questioning who he was, especially Lea, wondering if she could warn Jack. The next half everything was different, a line out, and Hendon took out Vadim's knee, and picked up the ball, and went for score, all the while Vadim, was seeking revenge, Hendon scored, and in the end, Turkey defeated Russia, 21-17. As they left, on came Greece and France, Jonathon was star struck by all the pretty women in the stands, cheering for them, as Andreas, took it to Jon, as the first half ended 40-8, it was pretty much the same the next half, as Greece won, 57-16. Next up was the young stud, or some say a ringer, as Tad Jones, look alike, took the field for England, as Benjamin Logan, was told, to stay away, and play your game, and he did, as he scored often for Columbia, to put up 14-10. Meanwhile, the real Tad, was readying himself, as he coordinated with the three other snipers, the field of fire, and their position, to hear,"Wait till he fires, then, each of you has one round, period. The second half, was more of the same, as England valiantly tried to come back but fell short, 41-32. Varfolomey sensed he needed to get into position, as the next teams came out, Australia and Norway. The three other snipers, they two were led up on the other side, with

Jesse on the far left to the north, Tad, in the middle, and Art on the south left, they all assumed a position, in a brief place, the closed box was between stands, and under some seating, as each laid with weapon in hand, waiting orders, as the game below was close. Inside the New Zealand locker room, sat all the players as the word came down, of what was to transpire, some had tears in their eyes, as Jack wasn't present, but they knew the sheer fact that if it's a head shot he will be killed, and knowing that fact was daunting to learn about, spy or no spy, he was their friend, all was quiet, in the other dressing room was Saudia Arabia, they too were told what was to occur, as Jamal, was somber, knowing he was mirroring Jack, as he was given a lightweight body armor to put on, as the UN advisors assured them, the only target was Jack Cash.

One raised his hand to say, "What if he goes on a killing spree?"

"He won't we have three of the finest snipers, honed in on his position."

"So take him out already?"

"He has one of our own, she is his hostage, we move in on him, and she dies?"

"Who is this woman you speak of?"

"Miss Erica Meyers, works for the Supreme Court of the United States, so you see our dilemma?"

They all shook their heads, acknowledging, as they got the notice, ten minutes to the field. In walks Jack, his teammates embraced him, in a long loving embrace, as they felt his jersey was of a little different than theirs, for the Pastor, to say,"Please hold hands, let us pray, dear father, we all go out in the face of danger, as we offer up this sacrificial lamb, to hopefully, he survives the shot, and hopes the staged execution will not be successful." The Pastor stop, to wipe his eyes, as others did, as he composed himself, to continue, "We know this is the spies work, but not knowing what and when it will happen, scares us all, so please look out for him and all the others on this field today, in loving regards, Amen.

The players, got up, and filed out, as the announcer, said, Australia beat Norway, 30-27, and our next game is New Zealand, who went to their box end and began their chant of the war cry, as Jack and the coach stood, beside him on the side lines, out from Varfolomey view, as he readied the weapon, and dialed in the scope, across from him three did the same. After the chant, Jack ran out onto the field, and shook hands with Jamal, and the game started, as a sense of security was among the players, as Varfolomey, was watching his prey. Jack was running all over the place, as Varfolomey, shot, no muzzle flash, as he silenced the barrel, the round was diverted into Jack's back, and to the magnet, Jack didn't feel a thing, as he just kept on going, as Varfolomey, said, "That should have been a head shot?"

As he adjusted his windage, while the others, were waiting a reaction to Jack falling, instead of the muzzle flash, which they could detect a heat signature. Tad saw what he was looking for, a single round off, and in that instance, spoke in his ear piece, "Upper deck, next to second window top right." aimed, and fired, the bullet, went into Varfolomey heart, as the bullet went in, but was held as the vest kept it from total piercing, but it did hurt, as Varfolomey, squeezed off another round, as he did, Art, saw his body move, and fired, his angle, he aimed for the pelvis, it hit, the hip, and instantly, sent Varfolomey, winching, but held on and shot one more time, as Jack stood, still he felt that one, and went down, in a heap, just as Jesse was the last to fire, the round came in and shattered Varfolomey right elbow, instantly making him a cripple. He was pulled out of there and helped along by Fyodor, as Erica helped disassemble the weapon. Varfolomey was finally successful, as he was bleeding, as Erica led them down the elevator, to an awaiting car, in the underground parking structure.

The players, broke apart, as medical teams, came to Jack's aid, as he turned and smiled, to say, "Guy's I'm alright."

"The UN advisor said, "Varfolomey has left the building with three confirmed hits to him."

They helped Jack get up, too much of the concerns of most of the women, as another player wiped off the three rounds, on Jack's back to say, "You were shot at three times."

"Oh, so I was, I only felt it once."

Jack continued with the game, as it was half, to a 14-12 game, the second half, was all New Zealand, as Jack won, 47-12. Jack walked off the field, with a entourage of people, namely Lea, who held his hand, to say, "Let's go celebrate, he let go of her hand to say, "You go, I need to speak with my crew, looking over to see the disappointed looking Francesca, for Jack to say, "Three shots for him, and look I was a defenseless and yet I still survived, oh, and I guess, you didn't get the memo, he was hit three times back."

She walked beside him, to his plane, as he went up the ramp, while she was being detained by Casey, still not understanding what was going on.

Jack went in, to his room, as others cleared out, took off his clothes and took a shower, cleaned up, went to his clothes drawer to pull out his protective clothes, he felt refreshed, and dressed in his clothes, he took a seat as Mitzi made her entrance, carrying a platter of food for Jack.

Natasha entered with her son Jesse, for her to say, for Natasha, to come close to him to say, "There is so much I need to tell you, I spent years trying to free you, you were wrongly imprisoned."

"I know, but this isn't why you're here, I asked Mike to find you so that I could protect you, as for us that was twenty years ago, our lives are different now, you're a journalist, and I'm well a spy of sorts, really a bounty hunter, so if you could leave the room, and send in Gia, please."

Natasha looked at him with a confusing stare, as she opened the door, she stepped out, with son in hand and Gia who was at the door, went in, and the door closed, as Kenny stood guard.

"I'll take it over here, thanks, how are you holding up, I know this isn't what you signed up for."

"Don't worry about that, I wanted to ask you something?"

"Go ahead, have a seat, what do you have?" said Jack eating the beef tips and mashed potatoes, chocolate milks in the carton, to hear, "I was thinking, if you would rather have Natasha trade places with me, this next week, I'm fine with that."

"Nah, it doesn't work like that, besides I'm looking forward to spending time with you, it's been a while, for your offer that is?"

"We could get reacquainted right now if you like."

She stood and was ready to undress, when Jack said, "No, not now, I need to go back in, and you're coming with me, I hope to have you all to myself are you ready to go in with me?"

"Yes, let's go." She said Enthusiastically.

"Well wait outside, and after I'm done assigning things to people, we will be off, so if you could send in Mitzi and Tami."

"Yes sir," she said with a smile.

"Oh one more thing, before them can you have Natasha come in?"

"Absolutely", said Gia.

Jack continues to eat, while waiting, Natasha appears, he has his phone out, he is sending out text messages, especially to ground support teams, thanking them for working with him over the whole Varfolomey incident. Natasha came in, as Kenny closed the door.

"Come closer, how do you like this, did you want to leave or what?"

"No, not at all, this is fun, I would like to get more involved."

"Good, I'm glad to hear that, after these next few missions, I'm sending you home, with me, I want you to be my wife."

"No that's not what I meant, I mean, working for you, in this capacity."

"How so, I thought everyone wanted to be a wife."

"Nah, I think I myself like being on your team, but that's it, is that alright?"

"I don't know, what are you writing a book?"

"Well I'm glad you asked, actually I am, and it's about you."

"Interesting, let me think about it, run along and ask Gia to come back in."

Natasha left, moments later Gia was at the door to say, "Sorry did I do something wrong?"

"No, but I have a question for you?"

"Sure, ask me anything?" she came to him, to stand beside him., she bit her lower lip.

"Why are you here with me now, is it to give me unlimited and lasting pleasure or be a spy?"

"Both why?"

"Who cares, I want a true answer, why are you here?"

"To learn as much as I can and go to spy academy?"

"Strip, let's see what you got" said Jack angrily.

She didn't hesitate, to unbutton her camouflage blouse, to pull it off, then her t-shirt, then bent over to undo her boots, she slipped out of them, to undo her pants, she wiggled out of them, she paused to decide what was next, she just popped her bra, to allow her perfectly breast out, then in one moment, slipped off her panties, to stand there in the nude, except for her brown socks.

"Turn around then grab your ankles."

Jack admired the view, he pushed the platter away, to rise up, he placed his hands on her butt and worked his way in, she didn't flinch, he felt her wetness, then said, "Turn around and rise up."

She was close to him, but stood at attention, to hear, "At ease soldier, good job, get dressed, you have passed."

"About that, if you will allow me to speak," Jack motions for her to continue, for her to say, "My issue is that I'm a civilian, all my life, and don't really know anything different, but I know at some point were going to need training, so just send me to it, no questions to ask and none to tell, and about this I would love to show you the same dedication and loyalty I've known you should have."

"Alright I understand, here is this platter, can you set me up another platter and the caviar?"

"Yes, absolutely, whatever you want."

Jack watched her get dressed, slowly and seductively, and then leave, as in walked Mitzi, and Tami. Jack sat back down to see them take a position on the other side of the bed, from Mitzi, and Tami, to say "Mitzi I need a status report on Brian's welfare, and I have a new mission for you, Mike, to look after Natasha, until I decide what to do with her, Mitzi agrees, to say, "I'll see to it that it is taken care of.", then leaves, to say "Tami, make sure Gia is going on to the first class at the academy."

Tami leaves to see Mitzi, to say, "What is your gut feeling on Francesca?"

"She is a looker, I'll give you that, he sure knows how to pick the young ones."

"She isn't what you're thinking" said Jack, standing at the doorway, to add, "Do you know if the tiger is tame?"

"Meaning to let out and roam, or just to pet it?" asked Mitzi.

"I don't know, have you let it out to run yet?"

"No, but if you're talking about the gift you received from Queen Ana, that has been gone with the President back before you went in."

"What's in the box over there?"

"Another gift from the Queen."

"What is it?" asked Jack, going over to look at it. There was holes for it to breathe, for Jack, to say, "I think it's another cat."

"Your joking" said Mitzi coming closer to him, to hear its breathing, for Jack,to say, "This box won't do, as he got up, pulled his utility knife out, sliced open the box, as Mitzi stood behind him, to look as Jack opened it up, then said, "Aw this is cute, and reaches in, and pulls out a baby Siberian tiger, it was a female, Jack showed Mitzi who said "No, No, No, get that away from me, as Jack sets it on the bed, to see it run around, for Jack, to say, "Ask Jim to come in here?"

Jack sat back down on the left side of the bed, and the baby tiger, came up, turned around once, then sat down, and placed its head on Jack's lap. Jack petted the tiger's rather large head, as it purred.

Jim came in, to do a double take, then walked carefully up, only to hear the cat growl, as its ears went back, Jack held it back or it would of charged, for Jim to say, "Another gift?"

"Yeah, can you and Jesse come up with a cage, to house her in it till I leave in a week?"

"What about the box" Jim said looking at the box, wondering what was inside of it, and now he knew, to say "Absolutely, once you go in, we will work on it, but for now, Jesse and I are inside working on the flight simulator...we will have it done, anything else?"

"Car ready?"

"Always, everything fixed, ready to go."

"Great and how is my two rifles?"

"Rebored, well-oiled and extremely cleaned, and the UN has classified it as a Russian relic, yet a priceless piece of art and the Russian's want it back, namely Varfolomey, he said he would spare your life in exchange for the rifle."

"Did he now, thanks for the info, give me a status into the UN, and send in Francesca."

"Yes, sir."

Moments later she appeared at the door, she stepped in, to see the true spy Jack looked imposing, the pearl handed smart gun he wore in a sidearm holster, his badge was exposed to see that he was indeed an International Bounty hunter, with one exception, he had the title of license to kill, trembling she came forward to see him and the tiger, who was being playful, to say, "Now what?"

"I don't know, I thought what would Varfolomey want to have happen to his girl, or are you just like all of his other recruits, he beds you once and you will die for his cause."

"It's not like that with me, he is my brother."

Jack laughs to say, "Doubtful, as Jack says, "Varfolomey is an only child, branded a traitor from the Ukraine, as you are, your accent gave it all away, so let's see your recruited by some organization, like the soviet secret police, no, no, it's now called the underground secret police."

"How do you know all of this" she said in confusion.

"It's simple when you're the best spy in the world you know all and see all, so tell me how your involved, and don't leave anything out, and by the way, don't you think you're a little over dressed?"

"Are you asking me to take off my clothes?"

"You seemed interested last night."

"That was then, this is now."

"You're not me, so let's have it."

"What do you want first the clothes or my confession?"

Outside his room, Mike and Mark, were pulled in on the task, which Jim laid out before them, on building the box, for Jim, to say, "You should see the young one he has in there now?"

"Enough, all of you, status report in the UN? Asked Mitzi.

"Two hour tops" said Jim, going back talking about the construction of the box.

Meanwhile inside the room, Jack watched as the last article of clothing came off of her, to say, "You keep yourself well groomed."

"Not for you, alright its true, I was recruited to get close to you, however you have people in more places more than we do, and Varfolomey and Fyodor have went back to Saint Petersburg, to await your challenge, if your man enough to do it?"

"Where does that leave you?" asked Jack admiring the view.

"All yours, till the day he kills you?"

"If you want, I guess you could be with your lover?"

"Your wrong about that, he isn't my lover, he really doesn't have one, I heard he was castrated, besides I've only been with one guy my whole entire life."

"Pity for you, who recruited you?"

"The CIA."

"Nice try, since 2002, the CIA is not allowed in the Ukraine, which means you're either a plant, or a double spy, which is it?"

"What do you mean by that?"

"It means this, you have a specialty, like you can speak a fluent language and to look at you, no one who ever suspect that, so that makes you a perfect candidate to be a double spy."

"How so, and why?" she asks honestly.

"Wait are you telling me, this had never occurred to you, oh my god, you really don't know, do you, they pay you a huge sum of money, to get close to me, even what sleep with me, in turn, they ask you everything about what you translated, however what you don't know is not what you translated, but rather the hidden message, and you don't know it but you gave them the answer themselves, good job, I don't need you any longer, get dressed, don't worry we won't do a thing to you except to release you to your countries consultant, so may go home to the town of Kiev?"

"How did you know?"

"The world spy network posts anyone and everyone associated to spies, and that's where I saw you, it was no coincidence you were sent to me, it was I that actually sent for you."

"How did you know?"

"Simple by the money, the trail always leads to someone, so good luck, and good bye."

"Wait" she said as she finished dressing, to say, "Alright I'll come clean, can I join you?"

"That's called a triple or no boundary agent, with that, it's tricky for you, instead of Varfolomey would be after you, so would the Ukraine who hired you in the first place, no, what you need is to go back home, lay low for some ten years, get married and have some kids, and look over your shoulder for the rest of your life, or do me a huge favor" said Jack, looking up at her, beginning to undress again, to say, "Alright I will sleep with you."

"No, it's not that, something more along the lines of loyalty."

"How can I do that when I know you can't trust me?"

"Precisely, I'll see just how naïve you really are, by going on a little mission for me, are you willing to play?"

"Sure what is it", looking at him, motioning for him to tell her to get dressed again.

Jack wasn't budging, he was admiring the view too much, to say,

"Commit this to memory, the person, you need to get her name is Rose-Marie Esland, living under that name in Nice France."

"And do what with her?"

"Bring her to the police station in Geneva."

"How long do I have?"

"Well you will be on the next flight out of UN."

"Alright I'll do it, can I get dressed now?"

"No."

"Then do something with me, big boy."

"That's not going to happen, I want you to call me as soon as you make contact with her."

"Alright, whatever you say."

"Now you can get dressed, and if you decide to run, I will find you and take you down, myself."

"No, don't worry about that, I'd rather prove to you my loyalty to you, rather than Varfolomey, that guy is a psycho."

"Go on, and if you do this then were cool, now go."

Jack watched her get dressed, yet it being slow, and teasing, to finally go, and Jack laid back, to continue stroking the cat's huge head, as he fell asleep.

Instantly Jim woke Jack up, by yelling at him, as he kept his distance from the cat guarding him. Jack lept up, and out of the room, down the ramp back into the UN.

Jack went through the doors, through a large room, that led to a courtyard where over a hundred of warriors, were in full combat mode, it was in slow motion, for him, seeing Tam-Lu, ordered her troops towards Jack, from boys to men, wield swords, with anger in their eyes, Jack pulled out his gun, hesitated, as he became overwhelmed, he lost his gun, as another unsnapped his watch, as he saw it being pulled off, the pin popped out, Jack was counting from Ten, as he was getting pummeled behind him, he could hear Tam-Lu, laughing, till a single missile came into the courtyard, with an explosion, taking out Tam-Lu, and those that were on the courtyard floor.

Jack stood as the dust settled, he picked up his gun, from a dead man's hand, to reload, he shot, and hit those around him, till the doors, were blown in, and men were carrying weapons, soon Jack was engulfed, as axes were swung into him, he was subdued, he used his phone, to launch the car's weapon system, he rolled over, with a dead guy on top of him. Explosions and shrapnel, was everywhere, as the dust settled, Jack peered out from under the dead guy, to see a far larger group of angry men yanked Jack up and was hoisted up, and thrown into the pit from the first explosion.

Men surrounded the pit, with automatic weapons, Jack moved, and they all fired weapons at him, his face felt was wet, Jack woke up, to see the large cat was licking his face, to an audience of Mitzi and Tami, who said, "That is surely cute, putty cat."

Jack pushed the cat away, to say, "Am I able to go back in yet?"

"Yes, about an hour ago, but I thought you needed the rest" said Mitzi.

Jack finally saw his son, Jesse as Jack got up to embrace him, to say, "I heard what you did, good job, thanks son."

"You're welcome dad".

Jack went out to the armory door. Casey said "I'll open the door for you."

Jack steps back to allow Casey to open the cage door. Jack walked into his armory while Casey stood at the door. Jack looked over the entrusted rifle, which sat on a professional stand. It was polished brass, with wood guards, it had a name plate that said "TOUSSANT 1" for Jack to say "I thought this was all gold, like the golden gun of its own kind."

"The report is next to it" said Casey respectfully.

Jack looked it over, to see the name of it, to the value it read "priceless", the stats were impressive from the Muzzle brake, to the 55" brass barrel, mahogany wood, to the deflector plates, for side and front shots being targeted at the shooter. Built in USB cable to a GPS and Rader, to the 20X scope. To the signature grip and trigger pull, especially designed for Jack Cash. 50,000 volts on the surface, several clips can go into the housing, 15, 30, 45, 60 and belt fed, as it was a gift from Henry, for the marriage of his two daughters.

Jack set the sheet down, looking a bit disappointed in that it wasn't gold anymore. Jim was at the door to say, "Jack the UN is waiting for you to go back in?"

Jack turned to the refrigerator, saw a soda, took it out and popped the top, and drank it down, Jack went past them, and out the ramp he went.

He saw Mitzi to say,"So what is up with Trixie, have you heard from her lately?"

"Last I heard was she was vacationing in the south of France, she said the mark is present, waiting till you were done at the UN.

"Fine, Fine," said Jack.

"One more thing before you go, Victoria Ecklon, texted me to tell you that she really wants to see you, and either or, kill Varfolomey, then, and only then will she rest peacefully, knowing she is truly safe." said Mitzi.

"Yes, let her know my first priority is going to Saint Petersburg and go after Varfolomey."

She exited, for Jack to say to himself, "What was I thinking, I gotta get my head back in the game, yes, Varfolomey is my next target, let's get through this next week, and graduate, he stood and paced thinking, "What, is going on with me, I'm sacrificing myself for what, a personal favor to a woman I don't even know, that's crazy, now what shall I do with Natasha, she seemed quite beautiful", Jack collected Gia by the hand, and took her inside.

Sometime later, a plane that carried US dignitaries, landed back at the UN, taxied, then went inside the hanger, the ramp lowered, to a parade of people, namely the highest ranking cabinet member was the Vice President, Linda Jackson, she entered Jack's plane, as everyone kept quiet, as Jim said, "Jack is inside the UN, but you can go inside."

She turned around and went into the UN, she was escorted to Jack's room, the door slid open, as Jack was finishing showing Gia around, to say, "Go into the bedroom, and close the door."

The door opened, to see Jack was back in that drab UN gear, she came in as the door closed on its own, to say, "That was lucky instincts to pull this whole thing off in the UN, quite frankly, I still think you should have done it yourself, how do you know he is confirmed dead?"

"He is dying, is all we know."

"Word from the UN, is that they are going to make you their number one spy, from your experience and extra-curricular activities, your first across the board, but that's not why I'm here, we recently discovered some shocking news, that affects you considerably, so here it goes, a couple days ago, Lisa and her team uncovered a message from Varfolomey, sent directly to Miss Meyers, she responded by giving the position of your spotter and the day and time of your projected arrival to Saint Petersburg."

Jack sat on the edge of the sofa, really couldn't believe this, to say, "Who authenticated this?"

"The Pentagon, encryption team, assigned to monitor this such event."

"Where is she at now?"

"On paid leave, were letting her go, where she must go, I'm sure we will find her and she will be dealt with, accordingly."

"Alright, anything else?" asked Jack.

"Well a security breach of this magnitude, has the President worried, so Lisa and her team are flying in, as we speak, I'll be here for the remained of the week, and as you know the

President is flying in on Friday, for the awards and special presentation, as for you, we as a collective group, we want you to stay here at the UN, relax, and finish out this week, then we will coordinate with the UN to see what your next assignment will be, as for your team, Trixie has been recalled, if you will allow I can send the 82nd airborne in to support Brian, and his position."

"No, let's wait, no, what am I saying, you're the Vice President, yes do what you think is right."

"No, Mister Cash, you don't work for me, nor the President, you're an entity in your own right, you're the expert, I'm merely a messenger, you know that there is a fleet of over thirty six ships at your disposal and over a thousand highly trained personal that will be here as you see fit, I'm mery just reminding you of what is available to you at all times."

"Yes, I don't know when I need them or like here at the UN, I am a bit over whelmed by their presence."

"Don't be, from this point forward, there will be no in subordination, the world is changing and the very most important person to us and the United States is you Mister Cash, so please use us in the future as you see fit" she said that as she was adjusting her bra.

Jack looked at her a bit funny, when she said that, to see her exited his room. For Jack to think, "Why would Erica become a traitor, he scanned his phone to see a E-mail from her, he opened it up, to read, the reason, she was involved in a game of counter terrorism, as only Lisa knows about it, she would have all the details and do not trust anyone, I'll be flying to Russia on Wednesday, let me know how I can reach you."

"No, No, No, you crazy bitch, why would you go see Varfolomey, who is this guy anyway, first it was the Premier's wife, now Erica, who is this guy ? "Maybe he has Francesca in his pocket as well." "Bizarro." Jack thought.

Jack left his room, to go back to room one, only to see it was empty.

Back on the plane, Tami waved, as she waved back at her, to see the Vice President was at the cage admiring the rifle, and for Jim to wait patiently. "Yes, lead the way, I want to see all the data and see what he has been up to," she said with a smile.

CH 14

Jack spends time with his friends

Sunday morning day 14, woke up was interesting, Jack was in the bed by himself, gone was Gia, and Debby, he rolled over and got up, he saw his swim shorts and slid them on, then went to his pool, and dove in, he began to do laps, un beknowst to him, he was being watched, shadows formed from the above skylight that showed there was a figure along the pool watching him, he stopped mid-way to see it was Linda Jackson, the Vice President. Who said, "Don't stop on my account, I'll wait."

"What do you need, I'll answer it now, said Jack getting out, and into the hot tub, to which he turned on the jets.

"If I had a swimsuit I'd join you."

"You can, then Jack spoke louder, "Call Debby, and have her bring the Vice President a swimsuit, I don't know her size?"

"Medium" she said, to add, "I guess you can have anything you want?"

Just as the door slid open, and Debby wheeled in a rack of swimwear, for the Vice president to choose from, she smiled at Jack and went to Debby.

Jack leaned back to allow the waves to cascade over his shoulders, to watch Linda choose from the many, she turned to face Jack with one in each hand to say, "Which one do you like?"

Jack stood up to see she held a small bright orange bikini, and a blue one piece, he pointed at the smaller one, which she placed the other one away, and went into the bathroom, and out of Jack's view, but Jack wasn't going to pass up this opportunity, he reached out, and up on his knees, to see that she left the door open, and was facing away, as she undressed slowly, he was on his hands and knees, watching the show, first was her blazer, then her shirt, which she neatly hung up, he ducked back then she popped her bra, she was fighting with the swim wear top, as she did she showed him her left breast, before she was able to control it, next was the skirt, she unzipped it, and squiggled out of it, only to step out of her heels, she pulled down her pantyhose, pausing several times to gain her balance and say something about a run, till they were off, as Jack waited, she slowly pulled down her white cotton briefs, but she turned and he was gone, he was ready to jump up and go look for her, when the toilet flushed, and he went back into the hot tub.

She appeared, wearing a bikini two sizes to small, he literally could see everything, especially down below, where it hasn't seen a razor for so long, she was busting out, on top, and down below, for her to say, "I guess this is model wear?"

"You look fine, come on in" said Jack smiling, as she stepped in, and down, and for Jack it meant he was right he saw everything, the nearly transparent suit covered nothing, only accentuated it, she kept messing with her breasts anyway, at one point one popped out, but she quickly put it back, for her to say, "This is way too hot for me, do you mind if I swim a bit?"

"Be my guest" he said, watching her adjust that tiny bottom, as she drove in. Jack saw she popped up her head, she stood, to turn, to show him that both breasts were free, and swaying as she shook out her hair, then she sat down.

Jack followed her in, and swam to the other side where she was at, he took a seat across from her, to see that she had covered up, to hear her say, "Do you know why I'm here?"

"No not really, for a swim?"

"Yes, no, well I wanted to tell you, they at the UN is allowing me full access around here, did you know they have the largest library in the world here, and the pool area, have you been to it yet, you would love it there are so many beautiful woman who lay out there?"

"There already spoken for, they are the girls of the other spies."

"Oh, anyway, I wanted to let you know, that I know about Erica, and what she is doing, it's like I'm left out of the loop" she said as she was still adjusting her top, to say "I don't know how they do it."

"Who does what?" asked Jack enjoying the show.

"This wear, this outfit?"

"What do you wear to swim in?"

"Usually nothing, I'm at home and we have an indoor pool."

"What about when guests come over?"

"Then I put on a one piece."

"You had one in your hand how come you didn't choose that?"

"It was a medium, and in a one piece I wear a large."

"Oh well, if its uncomfortable to wear just take it off, I won't mind" said Jack in a serious voice, not expecting for her to stand up and peel it off, and slid off the bottoms, a mark was left where it was once, and for Jack to see her in nothing was quite a turn on, as she could see it was well working, as she said, "Now it's your turn, you can take it off as well", only to hear "Miss Vice President Jackson, you have a guest waiting outside, shall I allow him entry or have him wait?" said the loud voice.

"I guess fun time is over" said Jack.

"No, it does'nt you wait here I'll be right back, oh by the way, do you have a robe I can wear?"

"Sure it's in the bathroom".

Jack watched her get up and out of the pool, she walked slowly, to the bathroom, moments later she wore a white robe, and to the door she went.

Jack saw the time, he himself got out of the pool, and to the bathroom, he was late.

Jack ran out onto the field, like an old pro, for match three. The stands were filling up. His name and that of Jonathan's of France, was posted as the featured match, he made it into the dressing room, Jack went to the side exclusively reserved for him, by the order of President Anderson. Two guards stood along an imaginary line, they only allowed Jack in and the rest of the team, kept quiet. Jack picked up his jersey, it read the number 13, instead of 15, he turns to show the coach, only for the coach to yell out "the Australians, are our rivals, let's put them down. they are a defensive team, that kick every possession, so I have moved you to inside centre, to play the ball, and allow Henry to back you up with his leg, for us it's a strategic move to get you the ball more, and more breakaways, you'll see what I mean after a few shots, don't worry you still can kick for penalty and for goal, everyone ready, let's go kick some boks" yelled the coach. Jack trotted on the field, only to see the Vice President in the Royal's box, next to a familiar face Queen Ana, whose appearance was unexpected.

The match started so unexpected, that it caught everyone by surprise, as Jack took the ball, broke the line, passed it back, and allowed others to follow him, and in the end, Jack scored on a breakaway. Half time came and the coach asked Jack if he wanted to take the rest of the game off, as the score was 34-12, of course he refused, and went on to lose to the Australians, 53-34. Jack chased Steven all over the field. he was ran out, but refreshed from all the running, and little hitting. As for his friend Jonathan, who was beat to a pulp, but managed to pull 18 more points as France lost to England, 38-30.

The match was over, the coach on the rampage, as was the team, Jack slipped out the back, showered and changed, with his pass in hand he went somewhere else, to get away from everyone, he got there, swiped his card, and was allowed entrance, it was the library, he was the only one in there, till Alfred showed his presence, to say, "What will it be today sir?"

"It seems every book I touched in the past, I've gotten in some trouble, so today I'm looking for Diplomacy and code of conduct."

"Both I can get for you if you want to wait, or have them sent to your room?"

"Nah, I'll wait" said Jack feeling a bit thirsty, to hear from Alfred, "Mister Cash, go inside that room, if you care for a drink, just ask, you must be a bit thirsty after a performance you just gave."

"You saw that?"

"Yep the whole UN was there, you know with this whole thing wrapping up in six days or so, each of us have come to know each and every one of spies, you know the winner will have his HQ here. To do with what he sees fit with, and with your lead, it will probably be yours" he had five books each in his hands to set on the table, to add, "What would be your first action if you were that spy" said Alfred.

Jack looked at him, then at the books before him, to say, "Well Alfred, I'd keep you aboard, and have you help a friend out, to qualify for college."

"Funny you say that, I'm actually doing that same thing right now, this man is truly a remarkable creature, his name is Ivan, and he is from Belarus."

"So you already met him?"

"Yes, indeed, Queen Ana has asked me personally to get him caught up to date, you know he is a great learner, but he holds you with the highest esteem."

"Thanks, that's nice to hear. You know I changed my mind, can you have the books sent to my room?"

"Yes Sir, was it something I said?"

"Nope, just want to relax."

Jack left the library, to realize it time not to hide, but to realize all that is his and much more.

Jack entered his Suite, it was quiet, he pulled out a flavored energy drink, and sat on the wrap around sofa, to hit a remote, that place a huge image on the screen, he drank and watched as investigative reporters uncovered a plot to assassinate someone, but was it real or fake, it had to be fake, why would someone put their lives in jeopardy for a story, then wait for the fallout, crazy, if it were true, someday, somewhere it may trigger the next world war." He thinks only to fall asleep.

Jack awoke, to have a pillow under his head, and a blanket laid over him, the television was off, and all was quiet, the clock read 3:35, what was it AM or PM, in those rooms it all looked the same, day or night, Jack got up and went to his phone, to see it was in the morning, thinking back he slept for over 15 hours, no way he though, then remembered the Queens visit, then Debby and Gia, so yeah, maybe that was accurate, he went into the bedroom, only to see both girls, he went over to Gia's side to lift the cover up to see she was in fact nude, then over to Debby's and did the same thing to see she too was nude, at the foot of the bed, he stripped down, then under the covers he crawled in between, them, deciding to face Gia's backside, he spooned her as Debby, spooned him.

The two girls were rustling around, to wake up Jack, to hear, "It's time to get up sleepy head" said Gia, to add, "Don't you have a match this morning?"

"Oh yeah, huh" said Jack, as he slid out, and went into the bathroom.

Debby finished dressing to hear from Gia, who said "I was expecting more sex, is he just that exhausted?"

"Nah, he is usually raring to go, but you have to remember, he is under a lot of stress, with all that he has to do, the main thing is that your here to support whatever his needs are, and be his eyes and ears beyond these walls."

"What do you mean?"

"Well take for example Francesca, had Trixie, who was before had done her job, she would have uncovered that she was trying to kill him, which Trixie failed to uncover."

"So what you're saying, is to get in with the other support team members and find out the scoop."

"That's pretty much it."

"I'm good at that, what about the other spy guys?"

"That's a tricky one, for me I realized, being with Jack, he is our protector, and none have yet to approach me, but you being younger and far more prettier, well, maybe, but remember, all they want is sex and to conquer you."

"Isn't that what all men want, anyway?"

"True, just be careful," said Debby.

"I will, and I won't forget that I'm Jack's eyes and ears" she said with a smile.

Gia left the room, out the door with her key card in hand, she knew it's been a whirlwind of a trip, with so many options, her mind was in the clouds, only to hear in a thick Russian accent, "So you're new?"

Gia looks down to see him, she stops to see he was leaning on the wall.

"Yeah, fairly new, I was told not to talk to strangers" said Gia coyly.

"So who do you belong to, no let me guess."

Gia looked at this beautiful man, sensing danger, but held back that information.

"Your with Louie? No, he is long gone,Ben???"

"No" said Gia, already annoyed with this man.

"Must be Tom."

"No" as she began to walk away, he was now becoming creepy, as he grabbed her arm, to hear, "Are you a member of the support staff?"

"Yeah, only for Jack Cash" she said smartly.

He released her arm, to apology, and to say, "He sure has a lot of women", but Gia was far ahead of him, to care, but at that moment she knew she had made the right choice, with Jack.

Jack adjusted his shirt in the mirror, then picked up his phone, to look over his e-mails, then the world news, and finally, his current ranking, in the UN, it said number one, and by a large margin, an iternery was on the table, brought in by Debby, it laid out the days event as a finals were next up, report to room one, at 0900 sharp. As Monday was here, day 15, after the finals, it will be onto the rifle and pistol ranges, tues was heavy equipment fire, and Intel at night, Wed, was Sniper training and counterterrorism, Thursday was all tests day, Friday was graduation, and assignments. Jack knew the hottest thing right now was Pirates off the coast of Somali, and in the Gulf of Aden. Sources sent to his phone is at Dante, is their HQ, and his name is King Sulemen.

Jack put his phone in the shirt pocket and went out.

The walk through the living area past the mess, he stopped to see, others that had trouble walking around, but allowed him access, rumors were abound, he was the top International Spy, and to give him that respect.

Jack saw that it was Lisa, and Ramon, near the entrance, for Jack to say, "They just let anyone in?"

"Only those with VIP credentials" said Lisa.

Jack smiled when he looked at her, to hear, "So you're happy to see me?"

"Maybe" said Jack.

"Ramon, leave us" she said, to add "I have some good news for you and some bad news, which do you want first?"

"How about the bad?"

"Alright."

"Then the good" he said looking around the stadium as it was filling up.

"Mark and Clarance want out?"

"Really, alright, did they say why?"

"From what my sources tell me, it's all about love."

"Will I get to speak with them before they go?"

"Of course, they may want out, but you know they are really just wanting time off."

"O Kay, I don't know what that really means but O Kay."

"It means once an agent always an agent till the day they die."

"So you're here, is that the good news or more of the bad?"

"Come on, we worked good together."

"Except for that, (meaning sex)."

"Who says we can't at least try it once, I know it's been a while for me, but I'll go if you want" said Lisa.

Jack looked at her weirdly to say, "Let me think about it."

"We have the rest of our lives to decide on that."

"So what's the good news?" asked Jack

"Well your down two members, I have brought the twenty plus girls to choose from, you know the ones I took from you."

"No big deal, I meet girls all the time, how about Casey, promote him."

"Sorry, he too wants to go back to Rangers."

"I thought he was a Marine?"

"Whatever, him, and his team, with the exceptions of the girls are all going, and I imagine the two girls want to go to your Academy, your first class, is in California in boot camp, shall I send Gia and Jill"

"Nah, keep them around, and about us, let me ponder it, any other bad news?"

"Natasha and Jesse are going to Washington, with Mike as an escort."

"Alright let me have Ivan?"

"Sorry he too is leaving, he wants to go to college, and he will fly out after he speaks with you."

"What's the good news if any?"

"Trixie is back."

"How is that good news someone wanted to kill her?"

"No, the story is that Debby and Jim are an item, and Trixie was threating to tell you."

"So what if they are, I already knew that, but I may choose her as a wife."

"You can, but then she would be out of the service, as you know, what you could do is to keep her and Jill and Gia as your assistants, and everything is good."

"I have Tami already."

"Nah, she is your secretary, she has handled all your inbound calls, but doesn't get in and do the physical stuff if you know what I mean" said Lisa coyly.

"Alright, let me talk with the girls and see if they want to stay, or what, I need to get going", Jack left Lisa behind, he trotted over the field to the locker room, to see the coach, who said, "Were moving you back to fullback."

"Why coach, we had so much success with me at inside centre."

"Wales, is a ground game team, Thomas Jones, is not too much of a runner, so I thought about moving you to number eight, at the back of the scrum."

"That's fine let's do that."

"Well, you're going to get beat up that's why?"

"What I'm no chopped liver," said Jack.

"No, not yet, but after the game you will be, there are big monsters in there, aiming to hurt you, and it's our job to protect you."

"Then I'll take the number eight then."

"Alright, then," said the coach to Jack, then announced Forwards come here, and set up the scrum."

Jack quickly dressed, to don the number 8 jersey.

"Now Jack here you are at the back of this scrum, guiding the scrum, usually the scrum half will get the ball, off to the side, for the fly half, but with you at number 8, he will hand it off to you for an inside plunge, or a drop kick, or a pass to yourself, as they may play up to defend the run."

Jack practiced getting the ball on the inside, and also following the pack, to say he was ready.

They trotted on the field, as the coach made the proper changes with the referee, as the match was to begin, he saw Thomas ready, playing inside Centre, his last position, and from the kickoff, it had become apparent, Wales had made a change in tactics, and New Zealand lost possession, and the wings were off to the races, easy catching Jack's team off guard, but it was the All-Blacks, and it meant a faster game than Wales, as Jack scored, and scored, and scored, it was a blow out by half time, as the score was 48-3, it seemed Jack was usefull in his current position. They left the field, as Jack asked for a change, as the coached apologized for his tactical error. With the number 13 back on, it was more of the same, Jack made all the penalty kicks as he could in the second half, but it was not needed as the results showed Thomas worn and defeated, allowed Jack the win, a first round win, 56-to 6. As all the others played first round elimination games, to include, Australia over US 56-30, Ben got hurt, as US valiantly tried, too little too late. Next up was Egypt over Cuba, the young Kyle took it to Carlos, as the score was, 42-26. Next up was England, mopping Israel up 34-0. Next up was Russia over Norway, 40-34. Favored South Africa, ended Columbia any chances early and often, as the final score was 55-14. In a close match, Saudia Arabia, over Greece, 18-10. Lastly it was Turkey over Japan, as Chu was out, and the score was 36-12.

Jack went over to sit into an ice cold whirlpool, it seemed like he was the only one, as he was given his space, till he left the room, then everyone else piled in.

Everyone stood at attention, as the President of New Zealand came in, Andrea Anderson, with a huge smile on her face, to congratulate the guys on a great effort, as she came to Jack to say, "Is there anything I can get for you?" she said in a seductive manner.

"No Miss Anderson" said Jack resting.

That was a cue for her to leave, an hour had past, and news of the semifinals were announced by messenger, as it was read,

Australia, number 1 versus, number 14, England.

Egypt, number 2 versus, number 8 Turkey.

Russia number 4 versus, Number 7 Saudia Arabia.

South Africa, number 5, versus Number 6 New Zealand.

Jack left the field, back in the classroom, to begin to take the necessary tests.

That afternoon, the men assembled after lunch, for the Confidence course, instructors all around to support the agents, as each of them took to the course with ease, even Jack felt this course was way too easy, thinking back at the spa in Virginia, was better.

All that attempted made it, it was fun as Monday was over, for Jack it was into his room, where the place was turned into a florist shop, the fragrance was intoxicating, he sees Gia, and Debby conversing, for Jack to say, "Debby, if you please, take the night off, I'd like to spend some alone time with Gia?"

Debby kissed Gia, and said, "Now you too don't have too much fun without me?"

"We won't as Gia smiles, to see her leave, as Jack motioned for her to sit, as she did, she looked at him, for him to say, "I have been wondering, how would you like to be my field agent partner?"

"Sure I'd love that, when can I begin?"

"Well here is the tricky part, I need you to go to the library, and ask for Alfred, he will then administer some tests for you, and get you caught up with the other agents, in the women's class, so by Friday you'll be able to enter a boot camp of sorts, what do you say?"

"Sure, when can I begin?"

"How about now?"

"Alright what about you and I together?"

"Well we could do this and that, but I thought you wanted to be a spy?"

"I do", she said sincerely.

"So get going he is waiting, and when you're through come back, I'll be waiting." She leaned over and gave him a kiss, to say, "Here is an opportunity to have me, and you want me to study, how do you do it?"

"It's simple, I respect you, and hope, you respect me, and do this so I can bring you out in the field, as for me, maybe tonight's a night of rest."

"Are you sure, say the word, I'll drop all my clothes in a second."

"Nah it's tempting, but I would really like for you to do this for me, and us."

"In that case, I'll go see this Alfred, and find out how I can best serve you."

Just then over the intercom, said, "Professor Benz, is here and is waiting."

"Allow him in", said Jack getting up, grasping Gia's hand and led her to the door, to see the Professor, she kissed him on the cheek, and left, for Jack to say, "The flight simulator done yet?"

"No, but I came to see you, to officially tell you, you are the top agent."

"Thank you I guess" said Jack.

"Yeah, about that Miss Holstein has asked me to see what you want for this position?"

"Like what I don't follow?"

"Well, simply, you oversee all the current spies in the field."

"What about Joe Simon he seemed better qualified than I?"

"Yes, this is true, he is, but he is shady, and not very honorable, and he isn't a favorite of Miss Hohlstein's either."

"Alright I get it, so what do you want to know?"

"First any special requirement?"

"Like what?"

"What do you need?"

"Nothing, I have everything."

"So then which spies do you want to keep?"

"Everyone!"

"Really how so?"

"There the best in the world so why not keep them at that level, weed out those that don't belong."

"Fair enough what of the Women?"

"All of them too."

"Really, all of them you say?" said the Professor. "Alright let me talk it over with the staff."

"In my opinion they are ready to go out, so let them graduate and move them along, already" said Jack.

"Don't you want anyone to stay here to help you?"

"Nah, I have someone for that role."

"Do you wanna see your office?"

"Oh about that, I prefer to have that out in my plane, oppose to sitting behind some desk, that way, I can fly place to place, and come in when a meeting is scheduled, now where are all those files so I may delegate whom to where, do you have a list of my available men and women?"

"Actually I wasn't prepared for this."

"Alright, when you are, bring them to me, I'm ready to go, anything else?"

"No I think that about wraps it up." The Professor left, and Jack went to bed.

Tuesday, day 16, it was the final four, and with any luck, it was Australia versus New Zealand, The place was packed, as Jack made his way onto the field, he looked over at the smaller players, as they kicked off, Jack was on the ball, and back, and it was like they had left off, he got the ball and scored, kicked the extra point, to make it 7-0. Jack waited to receive the ball, and it was same old by half time Steven was the stud, and with Australia, strong and powerful only way to score, walking around exhausted, Jack took it in and scored at will, by half time it was 43-43, it was a tie in the second half, there plenty of points available, as the game ended in a tie, 69-69. kicks for touch, line outs and a ground game, as Jack and the Full back just watched, till time ran out. The OT was played, and with one minute Steven pulled up for a 22 meter jump kick, and the game was officially over. Jack walked off the field spent, thinking, "Where can I get energy drinks?", then saw the President of New Zealand waving at him, for her, to say, "You did your best, sometimes the best doesn't always win."

"Aint that the truth, said Jack in passing only to think where can I find something with caffeine in it. Jack then thought about the mess and that delicious coffee, with a lemon, he went in, took a shower, changed, and went into the mess hall.

Others were coming back from watching the match, to congratulate him for a good game, Jack, and get in line at the mess hall.

Jack ordered, steak, potatoes, lobster and artichokes, coffee and lemon, and plenty of chocolate milk. He ate alone, as other went past him, the remaining spies had their own table, with their support members, his was not around, he thinks, "Maybe she has chosen to leave already".

He ate, then left. Outside he sees Lisa with Ramon, who comes to him to say, "Can we talk?" As the women all pass them to the field, as their semi finals were to be played, as it was announced, "Argentina and Dana Scott, plays Protima and Brazil, as Jack watched as it was a fierce game, back and forth still tied 0-0, at half time, Jack was served several drinks, and a hamburger and fries, the second half was a different game, as Dana took over, out pacing Protima, and scoring, and the game ended at 1-0. Next game that was called, US, and Kellie Ryan, against Spain and Esmeralda, US was a huge favorite and it showed early and often, as Kellie scored all three goals, and then in the second half, Esmeralda scored, and tied the game, to end in a tie, that's where it all began, three complete games later, it was still a tie, both exhausted as was the spectators, Jack was weary just watching it, as US Kellie made a break for it, and scored as no one defended her, to win, for Jack to motion to Lisa, follow me" said a weary Jack, making back to his Suite, the door slides open, they go in. Lisa asks Ramon to wait outside.

The door closes shut for Lisa to begin, as Jack lies on the sofa.

"Here is what I know?"

Jack looks up at her, for how long he isn't guessing, as he was tired and ready to sleep.

"Belarus has pledged at least 1000 troops, to occupy on along their border and so has Latvia, all 3600 plus from the north, and as we speak, Varfolomey and Fyodor with Erica is held up in the fortress, at your disposal is now 32 ships, part of them are in the Baltic sea, the rest are in the North Sea. The fighters are flying recon missions over Latvia into Russia, the Russian's have given us any support as we need it, especially to you."

Jack was sound asleep.

CH 15

Graduation with Honors- Special Mission

Next morning, Wednesday day 17, Debby and Gia woke up Jack together, He who slept on the couch, with a pillow and a blanket covering him. Jack held onto Debby's wrist, to say, "I need to ask you something?"

"I know what it is, Lisa asked me yesterday, and I told her, it's up to you?"

"What do you mean?"

"What I mean is do you want me to become a wife, or, no I want to say that."

"Say what" asked Jack finally waking up.

"Well I want you to decide if I could be your wife, before I make plans, elsewhere."

"So what you're saying, is that if I choose you to be a wife, you'll stay?"

"No, it's about the future, the deal from Lisa was, either I was in or out, being in, meant I go back to my job on the base, after the whole UN thing, if I'm out, then I go and get married to you and live with you under one roof, and with that there are problems with that."

"Like what, sounds good to me."

"My ability not to have children, and the fact that I'd like to retire from the service industry, so what are you thinking about?"

"It settles it, you'll be my wife" said Jack rather excited.

"Whoa, wait, I need you to say those words first?"

"What words, what are you talking about?"

"If you need to be reminded then it's over, and I'll be retiring then." she stormed out.

Jack was fully awake now, to see the stunning Gia dressed as he like her to be, tank top and super short shorts, for her, to say, "What she was meaning was for you to say you love her, as for us, I know it's a casual thing, heck we haven't even had sex once, I'm a bit disappointed, so I know I'm not getting a L word from you, and I choose to leave as well, to the academy, although being a mistress has its perks, but I'm really not cut out for that, so after graduation, for you I'm going to Camp Pendleton, with a new class, it's time to move on, and as for Jill, she has mentioned she would like to get to know you better, but would love to work in the President's cabinet, if you know what I mean, I hope I wasn't too forward."

"No, your fine, but what about working here at the UN." asked Jack.

"About that it was all a rouse, to save face the UN allowed the women in, but not to participate, after it's over?" said Gia.

"On whose authority?" asked Jack.

"What do you mean, on whose authority, The UN made that statement this morning according to Jill."

"That's non sense, according to my information, the women will all participate in the UN, if they don't believe you have them come see me, as for you, I might have an assignment for you?"

"Really you mean that?" she embraced him, for her to say, "I was actually, thinking of quitting on you, but now, what can I do for you?"

"Go find Debby and get her back."

"Will do, see you soon." She leaves and just like that Debby is there at the door, she came in, to say, "I so wronged you, and placed too much pressure on you, for that I am sorry, yes I will marry you."

"Yes, that will be fine, but I was thinking about what you said, and for that I'll allow you to serve out your twenty years as you so fit, upon that you'll receive a pension, but I was already going to do that for you anyway, after this is all over, I was going to sit down with you and determined what you want, then give it to you, but what I really wanted from you was to be my assistant here?" he waited for her to respond, for her to say, "Perhaps, that is interesting, and what would my duties entail, as she began to undress, as he led her to the bedroom, for her to say, "And what of our sexual encounters, what of them?"

"Oh they will still be there."

"Fine, and what of my duties?"

"Oh, typing, and filing, but instead of equipment, you'll be moving people."

"Fine, when can I start?" as the two kissed, as Jack said, How about now?" she looked at him to say, "So a big promotion, alright I will do it."

"Well then you better get going, they are waiting for you."

With that, she rolled out from under him to say, "So who do I go see?" as she was buttoning up her shirt.

"Go see Miss Hohlstein, tell her you're my liaison's officer here at the UN and you want the entire women's roster."

Jack watched her go, he got up, showered, changed, and out the door he went.

He was near late, as he fell into his number one chair, after eating breakfast, Professor Benz, and Professor Goins, waited till all sat down before beginning, "Behind me is your standings, with two more days to go, it's still anyone's race to win the number two spot, let's talk about some insensitive, first we have the official winner, which he gets, a free pass to the UN for the rest of his life, or live out his life in comfort, in addition to a stipend of 30 million dollars, a million a day, each of you will also get a cash prize for participating, in addition first choice at assignments around the world, as a UN International Super Spy, you'll have the entire backing of the World Court, and the operating UN, in addition to all the air or ground support you need, so let's open that book in front of you, today we are spending a bulk of the day at the ranges, for qualifying, the only one who is exempted here is Jack Cash, unless he wants to requalify, but currently he holds a rifle and pistol range records, Jack thought about it, and said to himself, "Why not, I'll go shoot", not thinking it was a huge mistake.

Jack opened up his book, to see the following "Jack Cash, by the highest order of the United Nations, has bestowed the honor of granting you the first number, 001, and your training is done. Please report to John- Philip French's office, to receive your first assignment.

Jack looked around, then closed up the book, he looked up, to see Professor Benz, motion him out. Jack got up, and never looked back, as he saw the UN's main office, inside a few men stood looking somber. Jack wore a smile, as John acknowledged, him, to say "Ah, here is our choice gentleman, let me introduce to you Jack Cash".

Jack shook everyone's hand, to say, "How can I help you gentleman?"

"Well Mister Cash, we are a group of businessmen, from the Eritrea, Zula, the port city is under siege, and our Prime Minister has been taken hostage by the Somalian pirates, his name is L'eouse Zein, will you be able to help us?"

"Absolutely he will" said John.

"Great when can he go?, were in a time crisis, and were prepared to pay the minimum fee."

"Right away, gentleman, if you will, allow me to brief Mister Cash on the details, he will be ready to fly out in an hour."

"Great thank you Mister French" said the wiser man, leading his colleagues out, to see the door close.

Jack sat against the desk, to hear, "This is right up your alley, the whole going into foreign countries and freeing those held captive, so are you ready to go?"

"You're asking me, like I have a choice?"

"Oh, you do, In two days were having the President of the largest country in the world will be here to see his number one spy, so I'd say you have till then to get this done."

"What about the championship game?"

"Oh don't worry, were saving that for Friday for all the dignitaries to watch, besides the women will keep them entertained as they play their championship game, while were waiting for your return, the star player and all that."

"What about the rest of my training?" asked Jack.

"I'd say you're done, you exceed everyone's expectation, and you're ready, actually I should have listened to you when you wanted to condense this to a week, we never realized how in demand you have been" said Mister French.

"What support do I get?" asked Jack.

"Same as before, Lisa Curtis is back in the fold, followed by the UN inspectors Gene and Roberta, and all that you have with the President's backing, and all his forces, all we ask is that you try to resolve it diplomatically, then if that fails or you feel it's necessary use your official license, here is your gold badge"

Jack took it to see it said "United Nations International Spy."

"With this badge, carries the official weight of all of the UN, and the world, in addition, that number indicates your ranking among other International spies, so when you're on scene, you're the go to guy, you're the general among men."

"Anything else I should know?"

"Just that the UN will officially announce this appointment so keep yourself from getting killed in the meantime."

"That's the first I've heard that from you," said Jack.

"Here is your folder, you know all the details."

"It's blank, the title" said Jack.

"That's because you need no title, its simply called, it's the Jack Cash's case now, what did you have in mind?, we will do whatever you want."

"I don't know, like number them."

"So this is Case number one," said Mister French.

"Exactly, do you have a pen?"

"Here keep mine" as he handed to him. Jack laid the document on the table to write "Case 1 (L'eouse Zein), to hear, "So from now on, you want the case, its number and the name of who you save?"

"Precisely, so may I have my team?"

"Absolutely, you're the boss now, all we are is the facilitators."

"Do I need to pack up the room I was in?"

"No, that is your forever, among a document that the world Court is finalizing, so go and have fun, oh and one more thing, from this day forward, you will be armed everywhere you go, including in here."

"What a relief, finally," said Jack as he opened the door to see the executives, to say, "Do you fella's need a ride back to your country?

"Nah, were fine, we have a private plane back into Asmera."

"I'll see you there" said Jack, renewed, thinking, "Do I have enough time to stop over and get a quick meal, Steak and eggs sound real good now." he thought. He made it to his room, he went in to see where his phone was, he dialed up Jim, to hear him say, "Yes?"

"Assemble the team."

"Were on standby and ready waiting on you boss."

Jack closed up his phone, looking around, thinking about Debby, and Gia, and more recently the Vice President, but left them all behind as he was on the move.

The doors were all open as he walked on out, into the hanger, he moved briskly towards the plane, the ramp was up, and the side door was down, at the door was Trixie, Jack stepped up and in, to a loud cheer, as he went right into his room.

The plane took off, as it taxied, then off it went, as it leveled off, over the intercom especially for Jack was spoken, "Three hour flight, all the air zones are clear" said Jim.

Jack washed up, and changed into his spy clothes and out of the UN's outfit. He hit a button on the wall, the intercom, requested the team's presence, to see his team was intact, starting from Mitzi, then Trixie, Mike, Mark and Clarance for Jack to say, "I thought you two wanted out?"

"After this mission if you allow" said Clarance.

"You can go anytime, but will you close the door" said Jack. As he waited, to continue "Each of you are binded to me in a form of a term, from this day forward, I want a year, two, three and so on, Mitzi will you draft up what they want, oh and one more thing, in addition, if anyone decides to stay with me till either my demise, or I retire, you too will be given the same entitlements, those who wish to leave, can go now, I want those who want to be with me regardless of who she is or him, either you work for me or you don't, and one more thing, Mitzi I want to enlarge the team to eight."

Mitzi looked around to say, "Were at seven now."

"Yeah, one more, elevate Debby as she is my liaison officer in the UN."

"That makes ten, is there any number you're looking for? She said sarcastically.

"Nope, maybe a personal assistant."

"You have one, her name is Tami."

"Nah, I want someone who can double as a translator."

"Will do boss, anything else?"

"Nah, you can all go and figure what you want to do, Trixie will you stay behind."

They left, only to see Jim at the door, to say "Jack may I have a word?"

Jack positioned himself in front of him, to hear, "Congratulations on your appointment, now can I see that badge and your wallet" Jack hands them to Jim, as he closes the door. Jim went to the cage, opened it up, and closed it to see Mitzi to hear "So Jim, Jack wants to know where you stand on his support?"

"All the way" he said as he worked, next to the rifle.

"How do you know what I was going to say?"

"You know I have an intercom."

"Oh, so I put you down for lifetime?"

"Absolutely, and you?"

"Right along with you" said Mitzi.

"What about the others?" asked Jim.

"Trixie is unsure, Mike is on board, well Mark is weighing his options and his love life, as for Clarance, he feels he has no choice but to re-up, for a year or so, you know he wants to elevate Debby, as he made her his liaison to the UN."

"Really, good for her, whatever he wants, it's been crazy around here, it's time we get back into the game, these three weeks have been a major pain."

"I hear you" said Jack, Jim opened the cage for him, as he stepped in, to admire the Toussant, as Jim hands Jack his wallet back to say, "I reinserted the activation, to the badge and magnetized the badge for bullet deflection, also I made up two new credit cards, one with the UN emblem, and the other is the US emblem, here is a bundle of local currency to allow you to do as you may with it, it equals ten thousand dollars, any other requests?"

"Anyone who doesn't want to be here, take back to the US, and extract Brian from Belarus."

Jim looked at Jack to say, "But, He is in deep cover?"

"I need some ground support in Eritrea, I believe there is a lighthouse in the port, I want him in place by tomorrow morning, with a support team, as we speak, Delta force is enroute to his location for extraction."

"Varfolomey will know something's up" said Jim, and what of the cat and mouse game, as honorable spies will do?"

"Oh I forgot, then send Clarance and I'll have Delta at the ready five mile mark, awaiting instructions.

"Precisely."

Jack exited, and left the two of them, on the opposite side of the cage, as Jim said "Till death or retirement do his part."

"Precisely" said Mitzi.

Jack was resting on his bed, as the door opened, to see it was Trixie, to sit up and say, "Hey what happen to the cat the Queen gave me?"

"It was swapped for me, and is being held in Washington, getting checked up."

Jack feasted over the meal, set in front of him. Jack said, "Thanks it's nice to see you again."

"As it is for me, so how was Gia?"

"Don't really know, nothing happened."

"That's too bad, anytime you want me, just let me know," she said with a smile.

"I will".

She left letting him think about her, while he ate.

Meanwhile back at the UN, Debby made her way over to the offices, by herself, unexpected, she arrived as men moved Quickly, to accommodate her, over to Miss Hohlstein, she was led in, Miss Hohlstein, motioned for her to sit, she took a chair, as Meredith ended the specialty call, to say, "So Miss Snyder, Jack tells me you are his new assistant, here at the UN, well welcome, I guess the first thing I can say, is you'll be working for me, as I get cases, I give them to you, I get a complaint, I give them to you, I get anything pertaining to the spies I give to you, so any questions?"

"Where can I find the list of all women spies, here and dismissed?"

"Why what does Jack have in mind?"

"To number them and send them out in the field."

"Really, I wasn't aware he was doing that?"

"To tell you the truth, neither did I, but you know Jack, he will find a way, to get the job done, and why not with the women, there all done, so let's get them out in the field."

"Wait a moment, who, what where and how?, who is going to coordinate them, first and foremost."

"That's easy, Jack, and second, they are all getting paid, so let's send them out and make some of our money back, can you show me the case files, and how does everyone get paid?"

"The case files are in the offices on the end, there are three of them, come let me show you around.", with that Miss Hohlstein gets up, and motions for Miss Snyder to follow, as they came to the hallway, they took a left, past other offices, through the glass out, Debby could see the lake, as they came to three offices, well furnished, for Miss Meredith to say, either one of these can be for you, but the end one is for Jack, all the case files, are here, along this bannister."

"Where are all the file cabinets?"

"Do you need some?"

"Yes, to file all the closed cases, and put some organization to all of this, look at the floor, files are everywhere, allow me to sort through them, and Jack will get the most urgent out of the way."

"Alright, that sounds fine, good luck." As Meredith exited quickly, to see Debby on the floor, picking up the files, thinking, "I could sure use some help here, and that of Gia."

The one hour mark was left as the climate in the cabin heated up. Meanwhile in the flight cabin, Mike was in constant talk with the two super hornets F-22, support aircraft mirroring the plane towards the hostile country, cleared to land, Commander, Bill Bilson guided the plane down towards the heavily guarded airport, as the plane landed, taxied, and came to a stop, as the ramp went down, as the hanger bay door was going down. The two special forces team rolled out, Mike was with them, taking a few with him to get cars.

Mark doing his job as a bodyguard, and helping Jim offload the car, the strike team, was missing Gia, who was at the UN. Jack stepped out of his room, to notice a whole new mood in the plane, he went out, to see the special ops group, with weapons ready. Jim held the door open for Jack as he slid behind the wheel, as he was already sweating, and wearing the jacket, even with this cooling system he was wearing. Jack fired up the car, turned on the cabin's cooling system, within a minute it was a cool 70 degrees, purified air, as the hanger door went up, the blazon sun, was instantly hot, as wave after wave hit the car, he pulled out his laptop, as his phone was in the dash, the car drove itself, in a stealth mode, going over hundred and half. His heads up display showed who his contact was and where she was going to be at.

Meanwhile, Bill, and Jim ordered all back on, and up went the ramp, and out went the plane, taxied, got the clearance to fly out, went to the empty runway, turned, and picked up speed, and they were off, going due north, towards Belarus.

The car slowed, then to a stop, outside a hotel. Jack pulled his phone out, then shut the car down, he stepped out, as a wave of heat surrounded him, as he stepped into the hotel. He saw a front desk clerk, as he passed by him, and into the elevator, up to the third floor, he stepped out, and down to room 314, he knocked on the door, the door opened, to see a familiar face, to say, "Weren't you at the UN?"

"Yep when we heard that the number one spy in the world was coming here, well I was sent down here, actually, I've been here about an hour or so ahead of you, maybe you should think about upgrading that relic of a plane for a Lear jet or for something newer."

"You're not my contact, her name was Maria-Rose, what happen to her?"

"I sent her home, you need a hard-nosed experience girl who could throw down with any guy, so what do you say?"

"Alright, so why don't you get dressed and we will go."

"Really, you don't like my outfit?"

"A see through sheer dress and obviously no panties."

She shows him he was right, to say, "I'm blending in."

"Then you'll need a veil to hide your face."

"That's Saudia Arabia."

"True, but also in this tightly ran community, at least wear a hat, and cover up" said Jack.

She came over to him, to tease him, she said "I thought we could get out our sexual frustrations before we go."

"Nah, I'm not interested, it's all about business, can you translate?"

"That's why I'm here" as she pulled off her see through dress, nude she walked around him. She dressed slowly, to catch his attention. Jack just looked around anxious to go, he patiently waited, till she finally dressed, in a provocatively sheer wrap around. Jack led them out of the room, down the stairs to work off the built up emotion, out the door, to the hot street. Jack got into the climately controlled interior, the car fired up, as she slid in, the car took off, he said "Sleep", instantly she went down. He allowed the car to drive itself, towards the prison. He pulled out his lap top, to see the current Intel, as it was streaming in, via the AWAX aircraft of the naval support that resided in the Indian Ocean, where he just got word, the plane was refueled in the air, and was on target.

The port was close, as the roads looked clear, the car traversed the twists and turns, down to the entrance of the Prison. He parked the car, she awoke to say, "Sorry I Must have been a bit tired."

"Depends on what you did this morning" said Jack facetiously.

"Just tired from the short flight, I guess."

"Is that what they call that nowadays," said Jack.

"No", she looked at him weirdly.

Jack got out to see the entrance empty, looking around, only to see her, who said "I sure thought there would be more people than this?"

"Where do you see anyone?" she said.

"Over there is a boy coming towards us, will you go talk with him, I'll go inside and see if L'eouse Zein is even here or has been taken" said Jack with his gun pulled, he went in. The dark damp prison, brought back memories, but only briefly, as dead bodies lined the empty hallways, as he followed them in, to a cell that was open, a single man held by two metal cuffs positioned on the wall, Jack lifted his head, using his phone he took a picture, checking to see he was still alive. He was indeed still breathing, it came back it was indeed, the Prime Minister, Jack holstered his weapon, and pulled a kit from his jacket a pick and key set, using the combination, he unlocked the first one, to see the man slump down, quickly he did the other, then Jack hoisted the Prime Minister up, and carried the man out.

Jack emerged to see a crowd had formed, mostly women and children, to the cheers upon seeing their leader, several men took their leader from Jack and all of them follow. Jack stops to see Z'sofia, to say, "What have you found out?"

"The boy said moment before we came, there was a huge ship here, and news of the silver shiny car was coming, that had a very bad man inside, was getting close, they fled, on their boat and disappeared around the cove."

"Really, a very bad man, doubtful, let's just see what they are up to" said Jack as he went to his car, slid in, pulled up his lap top, to see the last image, he locked in the coordinance, and said "O-1", instantly, a missile left the car, on a hot path, in a mere seconds it hit the hiding vessel, to a loud explosion, then as they all watched, from around the cove, into the port, came some men swimming, the current was helping them along, the Eritrea national guard, was waiting for them, rifles ready to fire, as Jack motioned for Z'sofia to settle down their arms. She was yelling down to them, as helicopters filled the sky, and were landing among them, Jack was thinking it was Lisa, but it wasn't it was, a big black guy stepped out yelling Diplomatic Immunity", instantly Jack recognized this guy, "Enzo Bonn's nemesis."

Jack had his weapon drawn, and held the three men at bay.

"Who are you, how dare you stand before me, for I am King Huffa, and declare this my country now."

Jack just looked at him, to say, "King Huffa your under arrest again, you others back away," said Jack hooking the giant up.

"Ha, Ha, Ha, by who's authority, your Prime Minister is dead, and what a lone man, with a shiny silver car is going to take me and all my men down, you and what army?"

It seemed like slow motion to them, but in that time, it was something of a bit of show of force, as what seemed like thousands parachuted from the sky, sea tanks from the red sea, and Marines stormed the beaches, as Seal teams, took down the swimming pirates.

Handcuffs were placed on all three men, as Lisa was instructing men where to go and what to do.

Jack heard "This isn't the last you heard from me" yelled the disposed King Huffa, as Jack pulls on his ear, to say, "Next time I'll castrate you myself, as his eyes got bigger, instantly remembering who he was, that he pissed his pants, like he had just expired..

Lisa saunters up to Jack to say, "Sorry I hope I wasn't troubling you."

"Nah, I had him in my sights, again, I'm calling the UN and getting to the bottom of who I arrest and then their released."

Lisa looked around to say, "Sure, you and a handful of the nation's guard, look we got the King pirate and you will get all the credit, I thought the mission went off well, they showed their force and we showed ours, besides we don't let anyone threaten our main guy now do we?" she said with a smile, adjusting his collar. She walked away, smiling.

Z'sofia, walked up to Jack to say, "Who is she?"

"Oh that is my boss, well once was?"

"So Jack now that were done here, how are you getting back to the UN?"

"Waiting for my ride?"

"That should be in five hours or more, come fly back with me, and we could have two hours of fun, she said, reaching for him, whom he said, "Need a ride to the airport."

"I was hoping you would ask" said Z'sofia.

"Get in, and then said, "Sleep."

CH 16

Varfolomey's disappointment

It was Thursday morning, day 18, The sun was shining brightly on the French Rivera, as the nude sunbathers lied on wooden made lounges, most of all looked the same, dark brown hair, with small breasts and dark red pouty lips, with a cigarette in one or the other hand. Francesca was on a mission, she fit in nicely as a young French girl, who was over dressed for the beach, wearing a Pokka dot bikini, her plan was set, she found Rose Marie, easily, her big nose stood out in the crowd, she was hiding in, Francesca, walked in the hot sand with her towel all rolled up, she saw a spot next to her, and knelt, then rolled out the towel, she sat down, long enough to see a man standing in her way of the sun, for her to say in her best French accent, "Mister move" loudly enough to see Rose Marie turn over to allow all to see her breast exposed, very white and clearly a tourist to all that saw. Unlike Francesca, who was topless, she stood to see her whole upper body was tanned, to say, "Go along, leave me alone", while the two saw Rose -Marie looking at him intently with a smile, he leaves.

Francesca, lies back, to enjoy the sun, while Rose-Marie turns to her side and looks over at Francesca to say, "Are you native here, do you speak English?"

Without looking at her, she had a straw hat over her head, to say "Somewhat why?"

Just then another boy stood at her feet, "Helena, where have you been, let's get together."

"Not now Jon, maybe later", in part French and part English.

The stallion walks off, to hear Rose-Marie gush over that one, only to hear, "You have a nice firm body?"

Francesca opened her eyes to see her man Henri, to say nothing she was speechless."

But Rose-Marie, kneels up to touch his firm stomach to say, "Oh you're a beautiful Frenchman, are you single?"

"Does it matter mademoiselle?"

"No I guess not" said Rose-Marie.

"Leave her alone Henri, get lost I'll call you later."

"Next time call me when you're in town, I'll set something nice up" he said walking away from her.

Rose-Marie had a smile on her face to say, "Are all those men yours?"

"Yeah, them and maybe a few more."

"How long do you plan on being here?"

"Oh maybe a day or two, depends."

"Depends on what" said Rose-Marie.

"Depends on who I meet and what they can do for me" said Francesca.

"I like that, are all men givers to you."

"They have to be, if they want my company."

"I wish, I could find a man like that, all I have is money to spend and no one to spend it on."

"Well you're in luck, you got me, how can I help you?"

"Well what about Jon, he was cute."

"Perhaps, but let's get you cleaned up, and see what we're working with?"

"What about these" she said playing with her breasts for her benefit.

"First off, any woman endowed, needs to hide these assets, look at those legs, tan them up and you'll be a huge hit, come on where are you staying at?"

"The grand hotel."

"So am I, let's go" said Francesca, rolling up her towel and lotion, she put back on her top, and waited for Rose-Marie, the two walked together, into the hotel, and up to her room, they went in, as Francesca looked around the room, to hear, "Do you mind if I take a shower?"

"No go ahead" she said as she heard the shower running, Francesca went snooping, only to hear, "What are you doing?"

Francesca turns around to see Rose Marie was nude, she said "Just making myself comfortable, besides, I was thinking, of taking a shower myself?"

"Well why don't you join me, I have plenty of room?"

Francesca followed Rose Marie into the bedroom, to see a huge black suitcase, a smaller one, and then walking past that to the bathroom that featured a double sided shower head system.

Francesca stripped, and followed Rose-Marie in. Each of them lathered the other up, as the water washed the sand away. Rose was laughing and giggling as each other touched one another.

Francesca was done with this it was time for action. She led Rose Marie to the bed, to begin an exploratory touch only to hear,

"What about Jon or Henri?" she pleads.

"Hush, this is our time."

"Alright I will allow you to play with me, only if you hook me up with one of them."

"You can have them both" she leaned her head back to say, "Oh boys come on in, she is ready for you", as she rolled off the bed, wrapped up in a towel, as Jon and Henri appeared with guns drawn, for Rose-Marie to hear, "By order of the French Police you are hereby under arrest for the embezzlement and theft of funds from the Klein family candy company" a frown appeared on her face as she said, "It was too good to be true, I should have known."

Back at the UN, Jack was resting in his room, while others were on the rifle range, a stack of newspapers on his table, he was reading them one at a time, his exemption was well received, the door slid open, in walked Debby, with a smile on her face, began talking, "It's all over the world, Lisa has been trying to get in touch with you, but I gather you're not answering her calls."

"It's not that, it's over there, just taking off some time."

"She wants to apologize for jumping in prematurely, are you hurt from that, is there anything I can do for you?" she said as she came up from behind him to massage his shoulders.

"Nah, I'm not hurt by that, it's between her and the UN."

"Why the UN and not you?" she asked. Honestly.

"Because I work for the UN now" said Jack with his eyes closed as Debby continued to work on his shoulders, she could sense his relaxed state, then her touched changed, it was more gentler, and with loving strokes, then she began to nibble on his ear, he looked over to see it was Sara. Instantly he turned and allowed her to set in his lap as the two were lipped locked, as Debby slipped out and went back to work.

That night was one to remember, and action filled, Sara rested on his chest, as he had the pillows propped up, for her to say, "Jack your letting me down, I'd thought you would have had multiple woman in your bed?"

"I've mellowed out, now."

"Now, you're making headlines all over the world."

"You heard about it in Alabama?"

"We have Secret Service and they know all and see all, Curtis tells me everything, you have been a very busy Spy lately, from some earth quake in Moscow Russia to the announcement of a royal engagement to the Queen of Latvia, so what is it like?"

"A bit like you, but older."

"Older and wiser" she adds..

"Nah it's just diplomatic."

"Come on Jack, I know you, so tell me what she really like?"

"You sound excited about this" said Jack.

"I am, she'll make sixteen, for a super spy, your way behind, how is she in the baby department?"

"She can't have any children."

"Oh I see now, all her other suitors weren't interested."

"How are you aware of all this?" asked Jack.

"Just what I read in the Tabloids', and bits of info here and there, do you know how rich she is?"

"No not really, that's not the reason why, were getting married."

"Well I know why you're getting married, and I told you I'm totally fine with that, besides that's why I'm here, she sent us all first class tickets, I am the first to arrive, then it will be Tia, Daphne and Isabella, as all the others will have to stay put, as Maria and Tessa, are looking over the families as the others aren't happy with it so they refused, so you just have me, for right now, how is the inside search for a wife?"

"Funny you asked, a girl, whom I rescued her sister wants to have me marry her, her name is Chloe Ryan?"

"That's nice, what is she like?"

"Similar to Daphne, but with stronger face features, but I'm trying."

"Well try harder, and find ones that like to share," said Sara.

"That's to be expected, princesses and Queen are all alike they don't want to share, but you're different, and that's why I love you, you're the first and will always be that."

"Your wrong Mister, I'm number two, Sam is first, and always will be."

"Fine", as he pulled her up towards him, as he held her and closed his eyes and went to sleep, the hours turned into the day, as they were not disturbed.

Friday morning, day 19, awoke them, as Jack was summoned into the training room, Sara dressed, to say "I heard there is a world class Spa here, I'll be at…"

"Go see Hendy, she will take care of you."

"Of course you know that, good luck honey on your tests, I know you'll do good."

Jack finished dressing in UN green garb, he slid his phone in, his chest pocket, as they departed at the same time.

Jack entered the room, to see his number one position, a stack of papers, as Professor Benz and his colleague said, "Come in, take a seat, as I was saying, before you is your tests as required by the UN, after you're done, turn the tests over, then exit the room, later today you will be notified of your standings and your cash prizes."

Jack pulled the first test from the pile, he saw his name printed on the top, he picked up his pen, he felt a draw on his writing hand, as he read the first question, his fingers stroked a box, as the page turned, he stopped, thinking what is going on?, it was as if the phone was answering the questions, as the triangular position, from the phone, to the watch, to his forefinger to the ball point pen, Jim gave him, the draw he could feel, but gave into to it, thinking "What the heck I'm a spy ain't I". Afterwards, the board showed the final standing to date, and by a two to one, margin, it was Jack Cash, as for him, he finished the final test, and was summounds by Professor Benz Jack put the pen in his wallet, in his chest pocket, under his trademark windbreaker was his gun and holster. And walked out with the Professor, down to a room, to see John –Phillip, who said, "Well done my boy, the Klein family candy company solved, except 200k was missing, now I know you make a million dollars a day, do you have it?, if so, I can deduct it from tomorrow's earnings, or what?"

"Well I do have an agent in the field, so I Imagine she maybe using it as a decoy, right now, but if you must take it out of my pay, wait, I thought I was awarded this job?"

"Well technically, yes you did, so what are you saying?"

"That I believe, I should have control over all my agents."

"You do, so your saying, let this all play out, and the rest of the money will all be recovered, and if not you'll pay for it?"

"Sure I don't care, so let me see, who I have to work with."

"Well about that, we at the council feel its unwise to send women into the field, as they may get hurt."

"Then why did you have them participate then?"

"Equality, and because you're a proponent for them."

"Your right I am, right now as we speak I have over twenty agents in the field."

"Don't say that very loudly, listen, go back to what you were doing, I'll take it to the council, and if it does get approved, I'll text them their names and current location, but in the meantime, take them to your academy, and after two years of training, then they shall be ready," said the Professor.

"Then let me have that list."

"Sorry that too is classified."

"What isn't classified?"

"Those files your assistant is working on."

"So of them, who is there to help me?"

"Well none, their all for you to solve, now run along, we have things to discuss, I say that in the kindest terms, but in private.

Jack left, and hit the mess hall, hungry, he ordered steak and eggs, sweet potatoes fries and chocolate milks, he sat down, in his booth to begin to eat, only to look up and see Z'sofia, slid in across from him, to say, "I was hoping we could still have our encounter" she said in her best English, speaking in Turkish.

"We had it" he said in between bites.

"No, no you're not getting away that easy, you're a super spy, and I need my time with you."

"Just tell everyone we did it, I'll go along with it."

"It doesn't work like that, I want to experience it."

"That was then, this is now, that does it for me, now move along."

"What that's it?"

"Mister Cash, asked you to leave" said a booming voice, as she looks over at the Giant, she quickly exited and past the massive man., who said, "I want to thank you for the tutoring and the entrance to college."

"You're welcome, I was doing what you wanted."

"Thanks' I'll never forget it" said Ivan the Giant, patting Jack on the shoulder, as he left.

A familiar voice said, "Do you mind if I take a seat" said the red head in apologetic mode, Lisa sits across from him, with a salad in hand, to say, "Let me begin by saying I hope I didn't intrude on your operation?"

"Nah, everything is fine" said Jack still eating.

"Can you tell me what's going on, it's me you know."

"Nothing, what do you want?"

"Well two things actually, first I need a home, and second is there any way we can work as a team?"

"How so, to your last request, as for a home you're here aren't you?"

"No, that's not what I mean, I'm literally looking for a place to set down the spy club, and Quantico, has said the area they earmarked is for you specifically, no ifs and butts about it, and as for us working together, well, it would be more of a partnership, then me always following you."

"No."

"Jack come on, you need me more than you think, the spy club is there for you, in every country and in the world."

"Even in Russia?"

"Well no, that's difficult, but were 10,000 strong and growing thanks to the whole coed network, and the hope that some may eventually work with or for you."

"Nah, I think spy club, is not that efficient, besides what purpose does it serve, knowing everyday people, can flip and have my back when asked or not, its that uncertainly, I'm having a problem with."

"True, true, but hear me out, what if, we put them under your roof, you say what, when and where they need to train, you know similar to the National Guard, and have a minimum and a maximum age."

"Hold on, you're going way overboard, there is no minimum, except eighteen, or a letter of consent, from their parents, nor maximum age allowance either there in or their out, how are you paying them now?"

"They aren't paid, they just want to serve our country."

"Well that's not right, you should install a pay system, and as a candidate achieves a certain level they advance upward, if they are ever activated on the spy level, then they get a lifetime exception."

"So you're considering the offer?"

"Perhaps."

She excitedly got up to reach over to kiss him, when he said, "Whoa, what are you doing, I said perhaps, go sit back down, let me think on this, you said you have 10,000 volunteers, how about this you send them off in groups of 250, till all your volunteers are trained, as I see fit?"

"You got it, what else?"

"I have complete access to everyone in training, and pull out if I see fit?"

"You got it, anything else?" said Lisa.

"Now lastly, why are you doing this?"

"Well I need to have a purpose to carry on your support, from what I started, and see it through."

"Fair enough, alright, I will let you stay in the barracks east of the airfield, that sit across the field, and I want you in the Academy offices, you know I do trust you, but if you ever cross me."

"I know you'll kill me, I've heard all before, but listen, I won't let you down, shall I run everything by you first?" asked Lisa.

"Of course, who do you think is paying for all of this?"

"You are, as she got up and went over to him, to kiss him on the cheek and whisper, "Maybe at some point I can really show you how grateful I am for this?"

Jack just watched her leave.

Jack finished lunch, to think about how nice it would be to have this same set up at his academy, but his main thought was about Lisa's proposal, and her motives, but he knew it would be better to keep her close, then far away, besides his mind was now on, he was on the move, back to his room, where he was going over the pallets, only to hear his phone ring, he answered it to hear "Jack Cash, Its Francesca, mission accomplished, money recovered, heading to Geneva."

"I heard you used your resources and got the UN inspectors involved, remember, I asked you to do it yourself?"

"But how was I to handle her myself?" asked Francesca honestly.

"That's what measures your value to me" said Jack.

"But I could still be valuable?"

"How, what can you offer me that I don't have?" said Jack.

"Varfolomey........ and Fyodor."

"Well make it happen, oh by the way when all the money was counted, it was short 200,000, do you know where that may be?"

A long pause for her, to say, "No, I just went into the room, and found the briefcase, that's as close as I came to the money, you asked me to bring in Rose-Marie."

"Your right I did, I hope you don't have the 200,000 anywhere in your person, or it connected to you at some point?"

"Well I don't, what's next boss?"

"Bring in Varfolomey."

"I could, but don't you want the glory for yourself?"

"Nah, I'm already full of glory, it's time we spread it around, you bring him in, and you'll be famous, and elevated to a full fledge spy or a traitor, once your with me, your with me, if you go back to him, then, you'll be sought out and killed."

"Hold on, my allegiance is to you only."

"Fine keep me in touch" Jack slides his phone shut, thinking about what was in play, to, make a call, it was Jim, as Jack said, "Abort, and pull them out."

"Will do."

Jack realized, his next mission is Varfolomey, once and for all. Case number two, Varfolomey, Fyodor, the Miss Meyers and now Francesca.

Jack saw the door slid open and in walked, Sara sees him, to say, "I was right, the spa is one of the best in the world".

"Sounds like you had fun, but I need you to do something for me?"

"Yes, what is it, as she was being coy with him, for Jack to say,"I need you to go see Queen Ana, and stick to her, when she flies out, you be with her, understand?"

"Yes I will, but now it's time you have fun" she said with a slyly smile, as she began to undress, to say, "Let's see is this the way Debbie does it," as she pulls off her tank top, to toss it off, with one hand and then dropped her bag. As Jack watched her, he put away his phone.

She undid her shorts, to allow them to slid down, next was her bra, she let it fall away, next was her creamy white panties, she pulled them down, stepped out of them, and jumped into Jack's arms.

Jack carried her to the bed, set her down, and fell onto her.

Back at the UN World HQ, "Frederick, this is a time of celebration, we have the bulk of the world at our fingertips, if all this plays out we will have all the world's spy's and finally get some control."

"I still believe we need to keep this all a secret, what happens if the public won't accept them, and then another issue is the control you have over Jack Cash, and the fact he wants the women to participate," said Frederick.

"Well he will lose on that one, besides, I thought it was going to be him, Vadim and Tad" said John-Philip.

"That's an understatement, he has all the firepower one hundred times any other agent, the question is will you ever really have control over him, because I really feel, he is hell bent on having women at his side, and all around him, what shall we do?"

"Nothing, I'll tell him no, and that solves it all, as for him, he will do as he is told, besides he is making a million dollars a day, now let's talk about all that's going on in the world today?"

"Besides North Korea, and the Pirates, Afghanistan, Pakistan, India, and the terrorist of D.C. which should we assign the world's number one, where?"

"That's the easy one, Washington, of course, he will be by his beloved spy academy, and also able to clean up DC."

"Is that the hot bed best suited for him?"

"It is, if we can get Washington behind us."

"Oh I see, your point, then it shall, prepare his new office."

"I will, and way ahead of you, that wing next to Miss Hohlstein, is about ready, for the top three, and what of the women, how many do we choose, or shall we allow Jack to do that?"

"Please keep that to yourself, which is a secret, but I believe I've made my decision."

"Yes boss."

Back in Belarus, Brian was laid out, as he watched the C-130 as it flew -by unscheduled.

Clarance was let out, as he soared to the ground, he landed near the valley close to Brian, he was on the ground, pulling in his chute, and then repacked it back, and secured it in the pack, then on the ground, he reaches Brian to say, "Were out, the mission is aborted, as Clarance assists Brian, with the hook-up, when he heard, "Don't bother, as the two saw the plane fly overhead, as Brian said, "There goes the plane."

"Yes but it will make another pass?"

"No, it's a one and done deal", said Brian.

"That sounds like that has happen before." commented Clarance, packing up the balloon.

"I'll reorganize the fields of fire."

"Wait your al-right with this?"

"Don't have much of a choice, now do we?" said Brian.

"You're not, but I am concerned about this?"

"Na, this is something you get used to, in SOG's it was the norm."

"Wait, you're with the SOG's."

"Yes, of course, every Super Spy, has several that surrounds them."

"So you're a SOG, only a handful had made it in that program" said Clarance.

"Yeah, it was tough, but it was the most rewarding experience I have ever been a part of."

"How does one become part of that exclusive group?"

"There isn't any, it's by invitational only, each year only a handful of the elitist, drawn from all the branches, from all the services, are pulled together, train till it's down to twelve, our mission is to capture, detain and extract a specific target, much like what is Jack's role as a diplomat, were actually the ones who do the dirty work, that is the part I really enjoy."

Clarance followed Brian into the bush, to a resting place to hear Brian continue, "Believe me, it's not one of recognition, it's all about the art of combat, that's why we're are either dead or end our career as an armorer's."

"Being dead, what do you mean?" asked Clarance.

"Means once in, you're always in, no if's ands and butts."

"You mean here?"

"Well yes or and no, I mean SOG's, before Jack came along, SOG's went into a country and used whatever means necessary to extract the threat. But more and more the outcry of the public, was the call for justice and thus Jack Cash was elevated to Super Spy status. Then he goes in, and is authorized to kill on sight, or be the face of the new diplomatic representative."

Clarance still looked puzzled, for Brian to say "Take Miss Curtis, for example, she is the head of the CIG group, her claim to fame was the whole thing about G I Jane, she petitioned the Supreme Court to become eligible to become an operator, after her training she became part of the SOG, now she is one of us, you know once a soldier, your always a soldier, our role within the SOG is now to support the Super Spy, as they need it."

"What do you mean by that?"

"Were in it for the rest of our lives, as Jack or Ben become worldly famous, it's our job, through the missions, in the hopes, to build his reputation. At some point, through his reputation, that once he shows up, it will be enough force, that he will strike fear in those that oppose him, will consider to disband or flee."

"I was considering, getting out."

"Why would you do that?"

"I felt it was time to do something else?"

"What could be that important other than helping the World's top spy?" said Brian, adjusting the sights on the sniper rifle.

"Well, I met a woman."

"Come on, a woman, their dime a dozen, you take as it goes, but in the end, I think it's a big mistake, once you're in, your always in."

"What are you saying, I really can't leave, for real?"

"Just like Jack, Jim and myself, are lifers, let's talk about the forces that surround us, did you know that there are groups of people out there just trying to kill our favorite spy, so it's our job, to protect, support, and give him our complete allegiance" Brian looked at the harden man, for a reaction, to continue, "Just think of how Jack feels, he has fifteen, I mean fourteen wives and a couple of children, and at the most he may get six weeks of alone time, but after that, duty calls."

Brian looked over at a man, who was caught in a stalemate of what he wanted to do, to see Clarance say, "What can I do to support you?"

"Good, so you decided to stay?"

"I'm taking it a day to day" said Clarance

"Carry the balloon pack, you'll be my spotter" and hands him, a set of ear plugs, and a set of infrared binoculars, to say, "Next climb the largest evergreen tree, go up about 100 feet, lie down, under the thick needle mat, look down, above the tree line, and at the suppose target."

Clarance looked at Brian, to say, "So you have eyes on our target?"

"Wow, so what you're saying, so if I do decide to leave..."

"Then you would be hunted down and divided up" said Brian seriously looking up at Clarance.

"But Jack allowed me to go, if I wanted to go."

"Did he really, or is that something you wanted to hear?" Brian used it as a mockery, to say, "Let's go do this, go ahead and find your position, then speak softly", said Brian, who took the rifle, up the hill, and onto the plateau, up to the position, he found, a small, borough of a ledge, as he laid down, he scooted up and assumed the position, above his vantage point, below was the check point, he pulled his phone, and hooked up the USB cable to the scope, as he dialed in each target, as each profile came up, on his screen, only to hear, "So why do you think they pulled the Rangers back?" asked Clarance.

"Hush", "We got company" said Brian, seeing a car come to the checkpoint, as Brian, adjusted his sights, to say, "Who is that?"

Francesca greets Varfolomey and Fyodor, they hugged and she kissed them both, she pulled a bag from the car, and hands to him, for him to say, "What's this?"

"A present, go ahead and open it up? "she saw that his right arm was in a sling, and he walked with a crutch. They walked back to the small cabin, as she helped Varfolomey who was messed up, it was pretty bad.

"Nah, I don't trust you, you're a little minx, what's inside?"

"Come on, when have I ever steered you wrong?"

"Well never, you're my sister, whom I can trust?"

"Then why would it be different now?" she said seductively, and while rubbing his lapels.

Varfolomey opens up the case, with his left hand, as she held it, to say, "What's this?"

"200,000 Euros, for your cause", she said innocently.

He closes the bag to say, "That's it, a mere two hundred thousand?"

"You said you always wanted money, so here it is?"

"No, what I said was I wanted Jack Cash dead, then take his millions and give it to me."

"Aren't you going to count it?"

"Nah, lock up that bitch, for all we know she might have defected herself."

Francesca looks over at Erica who came into the room, to say, "Varfolomey, at least accept her gift, you know all she was trying to do was help the cause."

"Her cause was to stop Jack Cash, by any means possible."

"Yes, but look at how many have tried, and failed, at least she is here intact and willing to help" says Erica, going over to the bag.

"Like you, you yourself had a chance to kill him" said the disgruntled Varfolomey.

"I did, but where do I do it, the Supreme Courts chambers, or how about the UN, not to mention all the eyes that are on him."

"What do you mean all those eyes?"

"I left him and America behind, for you" said Erica, she reached out and gave him a kiss.

"So you did, you take the cash, and spread it among all the troops."

Varfolomey turned his back, as Francesca, saw the open window, and escaped, she dove out head first.

As this time the bag, was opened, and out came an aerosol of gas, catching Erica in the face, the two guards, and Fyodor, who was trying to help Erica, Erica screamed till her last breath, as Fyodor, tried to close the bag, and clutched it, Varfolomey rushed to Erica's side, only to see she was gone, as was, his close friend Fyodor, Varfolomey was on the move, he waddled out of the room holding his mouth, he busted out of the door, to the waiting Francesca, as she inserted a knife into him, his hands went to his gut, and fell, he looked up at Francesca who was wearing a gas mask.

"Look what you have done bitch, you killed your lover Fyodor, and Erica, and now me, you betrayed us all."

Brian, looked through his scope, to say, 'It's going down, it's now or never, as he pulled off a shot at the man in and around Francesca, he had a clear shot at the intended target, he hesitated, then he and she were gone, out of sight.

Francesca was hoisted up by a big guard, as Varfolomey, received a shot in the neck, whereas he spun around, and went down, moment s later he had a helper and was helped to his feet, and along the side of the house. Francesca was kicking and screaming. Men were dropping like flies. Brian, kept the barrage of fire, and the hits kept coming, while he heard Clarance was on the move himself attempting to go rescue the girl, so said him.

Francesca, finally broke free, and ran past Varfolomey, who grabbed her wrist, and the two went down, he landed on top of her, as he yanked off the mask, to say, "Now you will die."

"No you first" she said as she picked up a rock and slammed it into his head, once, twice and the third time, as he allowed her, and she rolled and was on top of him now, bullets were flying past her, for her to say, "No Varfolomey, I got out when I got a better offer, it will be you that will suffer, as she hit him again, repeatly, as he took it in the head, to draw blood, for her, to say, "This is for all those that you killed, raped, and punished."

Instantly she was hoisted up off of him, by Clarance, as he shot Varfolomey, in the heart, in the same hole as Tad round went in, through the protective vest, his eyes fluttered, to finally close, for Clarance to say, "Let's get you out of here."

Brian provided cover fire for their escape, as he located interesting things to shoot at, like the fuel dump, ordinance shop, explosions were happening all over, as Clarance said, "We cleared the fence," as he spoke freely.

Brian was on his phone, asking for a an emergency pick up

It came back,"Authenicate this order?"

Brian, placed a call to Jack, who asked him, "I need a pick up code, we need to get out of here?"

Jack punched in,"Swan's are flying with one."

Brian sent that and he got back, "Will pickup in five mikes, set balloon, and be ready for pickup, he got the coordinates and the time to be ready, and he himself was on the move telling Clarance where to go and get the balloon ready.

Meanwhile back at the UN, in his suite, number one, on the men's floor, Jack just finished sending the pickup codes, to Brian, as he set his phone down, He and Sara were lovey dovey, in the pool, relaxing, when the call came over, Debby was pool side flirting with the pair, as Gia was the odd one out, Jack picked up his phone to see it say, "Varfolomey is confirmed killed, as is Fyodor and Erica.", Jack dialed up Lisa but changed his mind and switched it to a text, need a cleanup at the Varfolomey compound all clear to go in".

He sent it, only to think, what if it's still hot? oh well, with the leader down, the rest will follow."

Clarance had the balloon in the air, as both of the men wore a harness, and sandwiched Francesca in-between both of them, as a cargo plane made the run, it snatched them, and instantly they were lifted off, in the distance the Rangers were jumping, and parachuting down, a team of helicopters followed them, as the three were hoisted up, and to the receiving plane, to the bottom, and into the plane, as it veered off, towards the ocean, as the crew chief said, "Welcome Mister Cash, there is a room set up for you and your guests."

Brian walked past some fellow soldiers he knew, they looked up at him, and smiled, looking around it was just like their aircraft, inside, except, or maybe that was a car, under a canvas, they just passed, his cage, thought Brian.

"This way Mister Cash" said another, as the door was open, and the guy held out his arm, to help Francesca, up and inside, to hear, "Your meal will be ready shortly, we will be on the aircraft carrier in an hour."

The door shut, as Brian, looked at Clarance, and then at Francesca, who said, "Wait till they find out you're not Jack Cash."

Brian, was in an awkward position, he was ready for the door, when Clarance said, "No, go get cleaned up, you have been in the field too long, let me have your rifle, and you Miss take a seat on the sofa, over there."

"What about the bed?"

"Obviously it's not yours, nor I's, sit down. Clarance pulled out the portable chair, and set it in the floor, like he knew what he was doing, a tap on the door, he got up and turned the latch, to see a stunning girl, carrying the platter, whereas she said, "Where is Mister Cash?"

Clarance pointed to the shower, to say, "He is in there."

She stood there waiting, for Clarance, to say, "Just leave it on the counter" as Francesca came closer to them, for Clarance, to say, "Back off and take your seat."

"Sounds like you're his bodyguard, I guess I could leave it with you, if you all are hungry I have K-Rations available."

"That will be fine, we will take three, I mean two", she smiled and left.

"Hey let me have that platter", asked Francesca.

"I told you to sit down, and stay over there, this food is for Jack Cash exclusively."

"So why does he get it then?" she said pointing at Brian.

"Get what" said Brian. Refreshed from his light shower. He saw the platter, then said, "I hope there is another K-ration for me."

"Sorry bud, she is only bringing two, Brian looked over at the food that smelled so good, homemade, Brian looked around the room to see it was the same as theirs on the prop plane, except painted blue and white, for the Air Force. He also knew that most of everything was off limits, to him, her and his bodyguard.

The door opened, without warning, as one guard came in, with the server, this time, as Brian, went into the bathroom, to hear, "You can come out now, we know you're not Mister Cash, he is in the UN, our Admiral has informed us to keep you here in this room, till we land, we will however take that platter", as three K-Rations were set on the counter.

Clarance speaks up to say, "How did you know it wasn't Mister Cash?"

"That's easy, you gave no password, nor no tracker, or his gun?"

"Oh I see" said Clarance.

"Make yourselves comfortable, we will be landing shortly." said the guard sternly.

Back at the UN, Jack looked at his phone, while he held Sara in his arms, as she said, "That phone is a far cry from the phone I gave to you a while back?"

She pulled it to her to see a blank screen, to say, "Hey how come I can't see the screen?"

"Don't know, but leave it alone" said Jack, as he answered the incoming call, to see who it was, to say, "Yeah,allow them to stay, commend them if necessary, fly them to Riga, Latvia, said Jack pausing,...... for the wedding."

Jack slid the phone shut, to say, "One criminal down, ten million more to go".

Debby, was arranging the gifts from the constant deliveries, she slid the pool door closed, to see the flood of people, with gifts in hand, waiting at the door. As the UN advisor Christina, assisted Debby, as she took and carried them in.

Back on the plane, it was on approach, as the three braced for the aircraft carriers short runway, only to discover a soft long landing, the plane came to an instant stop, over the intercom, a voice said "Welcome to Germany, we will be in the hanger shortly."

"Germany, what's going on here?" said Brian.

"Maybe their refueling?" counters Clarance.

"Nah we can do that in the air, besides all I know is that Germany is the staging area for the Eastern Bloc countries."

The plane came to a hanger, then stopped, moments later the door opened, the sergeant stood at the door, to say, "Whose idea was it to launch the pick-up balloon?"

Brian looked at Clarance who looked back at him, to say, "I guess it was me" said Clarance.

"You come with me then."

Clarance was led out into the hanger, to see the massive size, and scope, there was all kinds of weapons, and everyone was dressed in blue, which he thought was quite odd, then he was whisked into an office complex, and led into a room, where the guard said, "Take a seat, she will be with you shortly, as the door closed.

Clarance looked around the room, to a desk, he took a seat, seeing that it was a integration room, moments later, the door opened and in walked Miss Lisa Curtis, with a file in hand, followed in by her apparent bodyguard, he stood by the door, as she spoke, "According to your file, it says your Irish, and so am I, My name is Miss Curtis, do you know who I am?"

"No, other than an associate of my boss."

"Your boss, you mean Jack Cash, last I heard, you wanted out, so it was approved."

"What are you talking about?" he said anxiously, looking at her.

"Let me put it this way, as she slides the picture of Gloria Thomas, towards him to add, "This woman has known ties to terrorist organizations, using her wealth and influence, to make things happen, and now, she is your girlfriend?"

"What, how do you know all of that?"

"If you hadn't realized yet, I will update you, were a spy organization, and from what I know were the best, anything and everything you say is recorded and sent to us, what you do, is recorded, we have a force of people watching your every move, let me address that first, Mister Cash, has his four team members in close, Jim and Brian work for me, and that leaves you the odd man out, you see Clarance, you were on a trial period, to see if we wanted to add you to the in close team, ... Or leave you out in the cold."

She prepares to get up as Clarance says, "Wait, I want to stay."

"Really from where I'm at, it seems like you meet a pretty rich girl and you want to bolt, how is that wanting to stay.?"

"Well I had a change of heart."

"A change of heart is the commitment, loyalty and trust that this will never happen again."

"It's there I promise."

"Really, for a tough guy like you, that must have been hard for you to say?"

"Nah, it was easy, I want to work for Jack Cash."

"Fine, I will allow your omission, under a couple of conditions."

"Yeah, whatever you want."

"First off you carry a phone that Jim gives you, you call in to me, to ask me something you don't know, like the balloon, pick up, as you may not be aware of, that is only reserved for Jack Cash himself to use, as an emergency escape, are you aware that it cost tax payers one million dollars for each pickup, next never get involved in anyone ever again, while in the company or performing a job or mission, either from myself or Jack himself, and lastly, leave any of the staff alone, regardless of any contact you may have with them, oh and one more thing, if you happen to see or come upon any of Jack's wives, treat them like the President's wife, you got that?"

"Yes" he said solemnly.

Lisa got up, and said, "Wait here and I will get you some place to stay, and Clarance thank you for your service and the completion of your last mission."

"You're welcome."

Lisa exited the room, to see a colleague who said, "Your pretty tough on him."

"Not really, we need to know who is loyal and who isn't, I think now we know we can trust Clarance" she said as she looked back, to add, "Get him on the plane, were going back to the UN."

Back at the UN, and in Suite one, Jack was dressed and looking over the boxes mounting in the living room, as Debby was working out a manifest, while Sara was still in the pool relaxing, the door slides open, for Jack to see it was Curtis, Sara's bodyguard, step in, to say, "They want, what I meant to say, "They would like you to come to the field, for the final game, between Australia and Egypt, and then on the soccer side the finals are about to start, if you like I can stay here with Sara."

"Whatever your orders are" said Jack setting down his phone on the counter" and walked out.

Curtis looked around at all the boxes, to say, "Do you peak inside any one of them, like this, is that candy?"

"Its poison?" said Debby.

"How so?"

"Think of this as the President's supply would you dig into it?"

"No, I guess not."

"Precisely, it doesn't matter what's in a box, or like his phone, get away from it" she said going over, she picked it up, and went into the bedroom, only to be followed by him, for her to say "Are you invited in here, this is Jack Cash's bedroom, if you don't mind wait in the living room, and don't touch a thing."

Debby, pulls out the top drawer, next to the white gun box, she sets his phone on a piece of velvet. She closed the drawer, she saw Sara in the shower, she closed the door, then went into the living room, to see Curtis, in a box, only to say, "Leave it alone, you're a moment away from me calling the advisors."

"Come on, isn't it fun snooping?"

"Not really, she said, as she closed up her phone, only to see the front door open and two burly UN men, grab Curtis and haul him out to, for him, to say, "What the hell is going on, do you know who I am, I'm a guest of Mister Cash, and guard Sara."

The door slides shut as Sara with a towel wrapped around her, says, "Was that Curtis?"

"That was Curtis, but he is gone now."

"What a relief, the guy is kind of creepy?"

"How so?" asked Debby.

"He always seems to know when I take a shower, and he pops in to see me."

Debby was horrified, as she says, "He sees you naked?"

"Pretty much so, I'd wish he would just back off, sometimes."

"Anything else" said Debby recording the conversation, with a smile on her face.

"Nah, do you know who is escorting me to the game?"

"Don't worry, it will be me" said Debby

CH 17

Scores are finally settled

Jack went down to the field, to see something just wasn't right, as on the board was a rematch between Australia and New Zealand, as Egypt was disqualified, for Kyle, failed a pop-up drug test. So Jack resigned himself to the locker room, to see the team dressed and ready to go, he finished dressing, in his all-black outfit, on the back was the number 12, outside centre, position, all was quiet as the Prime Minister of New Zealand, stepped in, she spoke to the team, then, came over to Jack, as her entourage, turned their backs to them, as she whispered in his ear, "This is a historic moment for our country, to be recognized by the UN, and yourself, whatever the outcome, Me, and our country is proud of you, we have sent a special gift to you, as Master Sergeant Snyder, will have it ready for your transport to your country."

"Thank you" said Jack.

"Additionally, please come to our country for a visit I'd love to show you around, personally."

"Perhaps, it may be a place I could visit in the near future."

"That would be great", she said enthusiastically.

"I'll call you personally, when that happens."

"Really", she said as she leaned in to kiss him on the cheek, it lingered, then off she went.

Jack ran out onto the field, with his other members, to a loud cheer and ovation. Jack waved to the crowd, they stood in the center, given time for the team to do their native pre-game chant of intimidation.

Jack looked up while participating to see a large contingence from United States, as well as all the participating countries in the UN. His eyes connected with his wife, Sara, then next to her was Queen Ana, who was waving down to him, next to her was her sister Queen Mary of Belarus, her husband King John.

After the ceremonies, for the final game, the teams lined up, for the kick off, Jack was back, as the ball was kicked in his direction, Jack caught it on the run, till he was instantly stopped, he lay back, as a semi-circle formed, as a skirmish broke out, punches were flying. Words were being spoken by the referee, as the New Zealanders were screaming at the tough Australian players. Jack was carried off the field, by the UN, much to the disgust of the New Zealander's not to mention the crowd, crying foul.

The match resumed, to a superior kicking game, lineouts, it took a heavy dose of smelling salts to reawaken Jack, who rolled off the table, staggered then fell flat on his face, he was dazed and confused, he was helped back up to his knees, given something to drink, he took a swig, only to spit it out to say, "What the hell was that?"

"Apple cider vinegar, water".

Jack took another swig, then downed it all down. He got up wavered a bit, got his bearings, waited, till the referee blew his whistle, to indicate a penalty kick was awarded to Steven.

Jack re-entered, the match. Steven's took a try at goal, he kicked it off the side of his foot, as a all-black's winger took it, on a break, Jack followed towards goal, as he threw it back to Jack, and Jack spiked it, just past goal line. He finished it off with an extra point. Jack heard the cheers, as he ran back to the 22 meter line, to receive the ball again, Jack, had the ball, he kick it, and Jack ran after it. He was close, but just like that, he was in line, and took the ball, and charged forward, instead of a huge collision, Jack was taken down softly, he let go of the ball, the ball was on the move, they played the ground game, trying to get Jack the ball, someone fumbled it forward, so the ball was turned over, and back the other way, Jack ran backwards, trying to catch up, and stay on side. The New Zealander's were reeling, as Australia was on the move towards goal, only to be forced out, at the five meter line. Line out, New Zealand wins it, and their off the other way, dummy half, to fly half, to winger, inside centre, and out to full back, Jack gets it on the inside, he was tackled down, Jack got up, and was back into the action. The game continued on, till the close of half time. Jack walked off the field, with the rest of his team. The UN soldiers were lined up to allow the players in, but kept everyone else at bay. Inside the locker room, stood the President Andrea Anderson of the New Zealand. She reached out to pull Jack's arm, he followed her into a room, to say, "We really need your help?"

"We, who, what are you talking about, you seem fine."

"No not me, my country?"

"It's out of my hands, contact the UN, I work for them now."

"That's not officially true, you actually have the weekend off."

"True, but I'm going be in a wedding this weekend."

"Well, it's not yours, so why don't you come to New Zealand."

Jack looked her over, to correct her, only to say, "Alright what do you have?"

"That's more like it, we just found out that Pirates from the East Timor region, are invading Melville Island, which bleeds over into the town of Darwin."

"Who was taken?"

"What do you mean?" she asked looking at him, in wonder.

"That's my specialty, is extraction, someone is taken, I will get them back, other than that, just send in the Marines, you have Marines don't you?"

She looked him over, to say, "But I thought you were a Super Spy that does it all?"

"That's where you were mistaken, my main function, is rescuing those under duress, and set them free, so if you don't have anyone dear to you that is held against their will, then call in your Marines to handle those pests" said Jack at the door.

"Wait" she said, as she got closer, "I really didn't know that there was specialty within the spy groups."

"There isn't, however, we generally do what we like to do, and for me, it's not storming Pirates on the open seas, just send in the Navy, wait, I'll actually do that for you, when I get to my phone I'll send a destroyer, a sub, and what five thousand Marines."

"Will you" she asked earnestly.

"Yeah, just let me finish out this game, and I'll take care of that problem," said Jack.

Jack left that room, and to his station to get a refreshment drink.

"You know you just crossed the line" said Professor Benz, as he stepped out from the shadows, to add, "Your making a huge mistake, asking the world's number one spy to assist your efforts."

"Well had you cooperated earlier, I wouldn't have to resort to this."

"Me, I don't have any authority?"

"Well that was some authority you gave to me last night?"

"That was chemistry" said Professor Benz.

"No it wasn't you used me" she yelled back at him, as the UN poured in, along with her bodyguards, and for Jack, to see the two in a compromising position. Jack left the room, shaking his head.

The crowd roared as Jack took to the field, he led his team to their location, Jack scanned the crowd to see the President of the United States; George White, Vice President; Linda Jackson, some of the members of the Supreme Court, the World Court, with Miss Meredith Hohlstein and then there was Sara, and next to her laughing was Queen Ana, down in a lower corner, was the remaining spies. They were lined up by order of ranking, Vadim, the blonde Adonis, then Tad Jones, his brother-in-law, Carlos Gomez, Ben Hiltz, then Thomas, Hendon,Jonathon, from France, Mustapha, Simon Jonas, Chu, and the others.

The rest of the Australian's players were set, they kicked off to Jack, who grabbed the ball and ran into the wall, bounced off and pitched it back, Jack fell away, and was on the move. He followed the play, only to get the ball, and he scored, and scored, and scored, till the game's horn sounded, it was over, they formed two lines and shook hands. Jack was called over to the newly formed stage, where he was awarded the game's MVP, the tourney's MVP award, and lastly the Teams cup. Jack turned to hand the cup to the New Zealander's team, then waved to the crowd as he walked off. Then the announcer came on to say,"Now it is the women's finals, Argentina, and Dana Scott, takes on the US and Kellie Ryan." They shook hands, as several of the male Professors shook their heads, and were leaving, as Jack and others watched, as the game got underway, Dana was strong, as she went down the middle, as Kellie tried to catch up with her, she then passed, and did a summersault, to get the ball back and wheel kick it in, to score, after that it was back and forth till half, they went off, as it was the awards presentation, first up was Jack, as the President of the US awarded Jack, the Freedom medal, and on the military side, the Congressional Medal of Honor, and lastly the Vice President, pinned on to his jersey the Navy cross, and a Navy SEAL's badge, to say, "For your gallantry in the field, we the President and I would give you the rank of Major General, as she hands him two five star emblems, as the two shook hands, he walked off, as others received their awards, to include all of the rest of the women, as some left, but it was second half, as some diginitaries left, Jack stayed, and went into the stands, to sit by his two Mates, to hear,Steven say,"Well mate we are out, not even a promotion as a field agent."

"There is still the Academy, if you want?" said Jack, patting the two of them on the back.

"We both would love to come" said Jonathon.

"It settles it, you will be in the first class," said Jack as the second part was more of the same, except the balls were going in, and now it was who had the ball last, on the big rugby field, whereas, before it was four fields, on this large pitch, but side to side, as they were tiring, as the game was tied, as Dana stumbled, and the US was working as a team, led Kellie all the way down, to set her up on a dummy pass, and she booted it in, the game was over. Every one flooded the field, as Jack went into the locker room, and showered, changed, and went right into the UN.

Jack entered the Suite, he looked around the room, to see the UN workers were packing up his things, by the direction of Debby. Debby went to retrieve Jack's phone, while he waited and Debby ushered them out. Jack went through his phone, looking over his vast contacts, and also the amount of money that was just placed in his account, 50 million, he pulled up his current list of charities, the first one on the list was the Helen White foundation, for breast cancer research, he clicked over a third to her foundation, waited, for the confirmation E-mail, with a personal thank you from Barbara White herself.

Jack closed up his phone, to see that Debby, laid a piece of paper down in front of him, and walked off. Jack scanned the contents to see his choices as the leader of the entire class, as to where his next assignment will be, thinking about the Academy, and his family to make his choice easy, Washington DC. He took the nearest pencil, and drew the line to that destination.

Debby smiled at him, as she took the paper away to say, "Everyone will be happy to have a break, from all this travel."

"Really" said Jack looking up at her. She left out the door.

The hours had passed, as Jack said his good byes to the whole staff of the UN, especially that of the spa, while Sara and the diginitaries were led out to their awaiting planes, an UN advisor, suggested to Sara,"Please come with me, your President would like a word with you."

The United Nations, held a press conference as they spoke of the new head of the UN spy department, Jack Cash from Germany. Jack took his place in the line of the newest crowned super-agent. The applause was deafening, as the UN delegates talk of a new race of fighters designed to put an end to all that is evil in the world. The following individuals were selected to be the face of the new UN.

Jack was listening and wasn't liking what he was hearing. It was getting way out of hand, especially with the crowds that were cheering. What seemed like the announcement for a sweeping change to corruption, only led to a new chant, that of the heads of these new agents, as the protest grew stronger, it was evident to post this live on world nation news, the secret was out, and now for Jack and the rest of the current agents, the noriety was over they were in real danger, as they were swept out and away from the stadium, each was given their assignment, with a piece of paper in hand. Just then commandos stormed the field, as they were shooting to kill, Jack was on the move with his two Mates trying to keep them safe, as he went past all others, into the UN, he was armed, and with his gun out, allowed them to go up the stairs, only to hear gunfire, as the targets was easy, to see, it was all the agents, Jack rolled out of the way from the bullet spray, waited, till the gunmen, came down the stairs, Jack tripped the closet one, as he went down the stairs, as Jack used his weapon, and fired at will to wound, shot after shot, each were still moving, he even aimed at each gunmen's head, to the point Jack was chasing the threat out of the UN and into the hanger, he was behind them, as some had a lead, and into the woods, as Jack stood at the door, wondering, how all of them made it. Jack watched their escape, and felt like he was useless, and pulled out his phone, to see the reports, seven agents feared dead, others un-accounted for, as for the top agent he appeared dead. Jack turned to see his team assembling, as he ordered them on board.

Jack stood on the ramp, as it went up, as the plane was moving, he stepped in, to see his car was under the cover, as the ramp came closed, the plane, left the hanger and never stopped, as it made its turn, picked up speed, and gently lifted off, around the aircraft, was a swarm of F-22 super hornets, escorting the newest Super spy away from the UN. Jack turned to address his support team, by saying, "From this point on, your all off for retraining, and for some a reassignment, let Mitzi know what you want to do, and she will make it happen."

"What about you boss" said Casey.

"Well for me, I have a small job to do, then, on the down low for six months."

Jack left them to ponder as he approached his two loyal seconds, to say "Mike and Mark, take a long holiday, till all this Spy thing blows over", then turned the handle and went into his room, to see Tami, at a chair and Francesca was sitting on the bed, he turned the knob shut, he faced them, to say, Tami, I need you to go back to the flight cabin."

She was still writing.

"I mean now, go on."

She left abruptly, for Jack to look over his phone, he patched his new coordinates, into the planes computer, as he received an encrypted message, to say,"Wait further instructions", he saw it and knew something was up, yet, he received the confirmed dead count, eight were all killed, Joel Robbe, Sean Calvin, Andrain Jonason, Roderick Gordon, Andreas Stauros, Kyle Devon, Stephen Moss and Benjamin Logan. As it said, all other agents are off and or either safe inside the UN. Jack closed up his phone, to begin to undress, not noticing the girl just watching over him, for her, to say, "Aren't you glad I took care of Varfolomey?" as she exited the bathroom.

"He escaped, so say my lookouts?"

"What, no, I took care of him and Clarance shot him in the heart."

"You did at that, by gassing him, which was clever, a real spy finishes the job."

"That's why I'm here, turn around Mister Cash, I want to see your face before I pull the trigger."

Jack turned to show her he was very vulnerable, but to his surprise, she stood wearing no clothes, offering up a pistol for his inspection, as she said with a smile, "This is Varfolomey's trick gun, I absconded with it, and now it is yours."

Jack takes it from, her and places on the dresser, then he pushes her head, as she falls back on the bed, and the two lip lock for some kissing, as his hands were all over her awaiting body, he spread her willing legs, mounted her and finished his business, he collapsed on her, while still inside of her, her real panting kept Jack hard, for another go around, till she got off, then he did the same, he held her, only to hear, "You were my third, guy that has ever had me."

"That's great, now what do you want?"

"What you promised me, a shot at spy school."

"Nah, I got a better idea, your gonna be my first agent."

"What's that, well then I think we have to go another round, think of it as a way for me to show my gratitude for what your about to allow me to do, and your welcome."

"You will be alright, your first mission, is to go to the US and more specifically to Washington DC and find a medical examiner, named Elizabeth Snyder, understand?"

"What is my mission with her?"

"Start cleaning up the place around her building, to name a few, first set up, blend in, and get established, see Jim before you go, get some bank, now off with you."

Jack laid back as Francesca got up and dressed quickly, only to cover the sleeping Jack and left.

The plane landed, as Jack was up and dressed, and ready for his new assignment, he was heavily armed, as he stepped out, to see first Mitzi who embraced him, then gave him a kiss on the cheek, to say her goodbyes, then it was Trixie turn, she wasn't as affectionate, but showed she really cared, lastly there was Jim, the two shook hands, for Jack to say "Take everyone home, or to their schools, then take six months of down time, then I'll see you in D.C in six month's or so."

Jack's phone rang it was the President of the United States calling, said Jack as he answered it, to say "Yes Sir, I know, but, yes, alright, if you would like, will talk then, as for me, well I'm doing someone a favor, then I'll see you later, out."

Jack slid the phone shut, he turned to see that the car was unveiled, "Get in if you still want to go" Jack said to Casey.

Jack waved to his crew, then slid in behind his car's wheel, the car started up, as he set his phone into the dash, he pulled up his lap top, that was on an arm of sorts, thinking, "It's something new, he thinks display, and a whole new format appears, on the windshield, only for his eyes only as Casey leaned back in the passenger's seat, he kept quiet, but Jack turned on a CD, of his choice, for Casey to listen too. Jack looked over his game plan, then manually backed up the car, down the ramp, onto the deserted, foggy, damp and wet overgrowing, landing field, the car was moving, the car displayed the map of the Island of Dago, off the coast of Estonia, and his target moved as the bleep showed him to do so, meant Brian and Clarance did their job, of planting a GPS on the target., and with all the Intel on him, all it will take is a single confertation, to end this problem, but as Jack was thinking, how about a full blown battle?"

The car slowed as it came to the fortress, the drawbridge was down, as he drove in, only to see people cheering a quick crowd recognition, indicated it was Belarusan, who were tipped off and beat him to the punch, and sure enough, there was King John, on his giant white stallion, smiling, Jack turned to Casey to say, "Now your free to go home, get out."

Jack also exited to see King John, to hear "Now my son, you have no excuses not to marry Queen Ana."

"Your right, and that's why I'm here."

"No worries my son, we will get you and your car back over to Riga, for the festivities, get in your car, and follow us," said the King, as Jack saw the Giant Ivan, with what appeared to be that of a head of Varfolomey, whom he was supposed to get, only to see the Giant with a huge smile and a wave to Jack. Jack saw Casey blend into the crowd, and disappear, as he slid back in, to type finished, on this file, turn the car around, and slowly follow the horse down to the dock, where a huge hovercraft awaited, as Jack and the horse led everyone on, all two hundred strong, Jack was up in the Royalty box, to see Casey wave off his old friend, as the boat turned, and quickly it was off. The ride was short, as they came to a rocky coast line, and around a corner, and into a slight tunnel, to a cove, where the hovercraft was home based. As it came to a halt. It was docked, and the ramp went down. Horses went off first, as Jack manned his car, got in and followed the horses, up and out of the cove, and off to the right, down into a valley, as the road disappeared into the earth, it leveled off, to a huge underground parking lot, a fence was open, as Jack drove through, then the gates were closed. A man in traditional outfit, directed Jack to the right, which the road opened up, his on board computer, was showing him going down, lights lit the highway, Jack let the car drive itself, while he looked on the heads up display for the map. He was trying to figure out the distance he was going to. The car slowed, a sign, on the left was the Palace receiving, on the right was the main entrance. Jack turned the wheel slightly to the right, and the car drove on, the car slowed coming towards a fortified guard stand, the gate went up and Jack was saluted. Another guard guided Jack to a parking spot. He parked the car, and put his lap top away, pulled his phone out, and placed it away. Jack got out and said, "Secure," Jack walked up the marble stairs, which glistened under all the lights. The door was open, for him, as he stepped in to see King John of Belarus. The door closed, a chain mail fence dropped down in front of it.

"Rest assured, my friend you will be safe in here."

Jack watched as the lights went out, bank by bank. King John led Jack his new son up a set of stairs, as the natural light came in, from the courtyard, a magnificent setting, trees of all types, maze of intricate manicured gardens, as workers toiled over them in the sun, ponds and pools, as water cascade over the falls, as Jack stopped to admire them.

"Come my son, we must get you ready for the Queens arrival."

Jack caught up with him, as they came to a set of double doors, as the King pushed on one, it opened as a guard, held it for him, Jack past by him, as the King led him down a corridor to a sign that said "King's Palace".

"Before we enter here my son, I will tell you that whatever you see in this area is yours to have, keep and take with you after the wedding."

A guard, pulled the door open, the King motioned for Jack to go inside.

Jack entered to a foyer, then he saw two doors, he choose the one on the right, as the other one seemed dark, he opened it up to see a room, a quick flashback to the first day at the UN, only to hear a voice say, "Mister Cash, please undress fully, set your weapon in the box provided for you, as for your wallet, place that on the counter, you will need no money here, when you're ready, tap on the door and a team leader will escort you to your next station."

Jack saw a replicate box, pulled out his gun, unloaded it and set it in to charge. He set his badge on the counter, he undressed completely, to see a closet, he opened it up, to see a single white robe, and a pair of slippers, after adjusting to the warmth and comfort of the robe, he knocked on the door.

The door opened, there stood in front of him, was a woman, dressed in white, her name tag said "Else", to hear "Come this way, Mister Cash."

He followed her as she led him down a path, of tropical trees, loaded with fruits, so close he could touch them. She turned to say, "The Queen has given us specific instructions, on what we need to do for you", she turned and continued to walk.

"Which is" asked Jack. Following her closely, but also looking around thinking, "If I need to rest and relax for six month's then this would the place to do it."

Women were all over, some wore grey shirts and others red, then others wore practically nothing.

The two stopped at a crossroads, for Else, to say, "Look around, do you see anything that you would like to do right now, or just lounge by the pool?"

"Well Else, I sure could fancy a mud bath, is that what those pools are?"

"Yes, matter of fact, those pools are red clay from France, and heated to 120 degrees, come with me, and let me introduce you to Gabrielle."

Off to his right were three girls dressed in blue, as the two went over to the pools, where a sharply dressed woman, was wearing see through grey shirt and shorts, smiled and had her arm and hand out, Jack shook her hand, as her name tag said who she was, only to hear "Mister Cash, I come to let you know if the Queen needs anything of you", she turns and leaves.

Jack looks over the pool, to say, "Do I just jump right on in?"

"No, silly, Mister, walk in over there, submerge and sit back and relax."

Jack did as he was told, walked over, slipped off the shoes, and dropped the robe, and stepped into the clay slurry, as it oozed in and around his body as he submerged, he found a seat, as Gabrielle, brought over a umbrella, and a pillow. Jack leaned his head back, into the pillow, and closed his eyes. Moments later a voice spoke "Mister, Mister Cash, would you like a refreshing beverage?"

Jack opened his eyes to see a half nude younger girl, with a tray.

"Sure, just set it down."

"Run along, leave the whole tray" said Gabrielle.

The girl set the tray down and scurried away.

"You didn't need to do that, I was admiring the view."

"I'm sorry, I didn't know, I thought she was a bother to you."

"No, on the contrary, it was nice to talk to someone, be it only briefly."

"Well you can talk with me?"

"Yes, but you're not topless" said Jack looking up at her.

"All you have to do is ask" she said as she pulled out her shirt and pulled it off.

"That's more like it, are you allow to get in?"

"Sure, whatever you ask of me?"

"Well in that case, take those off as well, then come in and sit next to me".

She didn't even hesitate, and unbuttoned her shorts, and let them fall away, showing him that she too was fully nude, for his viewing pleasure, she stepped in, as slowly made her way over to him.

She waited for him to speak, as Jack rested his head, and eyes, only to hear, "I'm waiting what do you want to talk with me about?"

"Come again, what do you mean" said Jack lifting his head up to see her.

"To talk, about what" she said in a demanding voice.

"Nothing, just wanted to allow you to enjoy this huge pool."

"Sorry it doesn't work like that" she said as she got up and began to walk out only to hear, "Wait, come to think of it, actually there was something."

Gabrielle was out, and then came back over, to say, "How can I help you now?"

"Well first off, don't be so sensitive, I don't know the rules around here, and second come back in your gonna bake out there."

"Your right about that", she said as she eased back into the mud, and back over to Jack, to say, "I guess Else, didn't tell you how all of this works?"

"No not really, only that whatever I ask for I get."

"Well that's true, except for one exception."

"Which is?" asked Jack.

"No sexual intercourse with the maidens."

"And who are the Maidens?" asked Jack eager to get his hands on her.

"All of us, were the Queens helpers, as you can plainly see from the color of the shirts most are wearing, the blue ones are Queens exclusive helpers, the Grey one are upper level helpers, we are the ones who have been here even before your arrival, and lastly there are those in red, they were chosen from a pool of 1000 volunteers, as the Queen had asked for, through an extensive personal and professional background check, they were excepted."

"This place is huge, what are some of the things I can do?"

"Well for starters, anything and everything, there are fifty acres here, do you want me to be your tour guide?"

"What's you angle here, do you get something in return?" said Jack looking at her, who was smiling back.

"Sure, lead me around."

"Servant out of the pool, assume your position" commanded the King.

King John watched her leave the pool hastily, as he slipped off his robe, and slipped in next to Jack, to begin the conversation. "Son, let's begin by talking about these servants, look around at all these girls, their servants as chosen by the Queen herself, as workers their here to provide us all the pleasures we so desire, so whatever you ask for, you shall get."

Jack leaned his head back and closed his eyes, to hear, "Furthermore, soon you will be their King, and then they will be yours to command."

"Maybe I don't want to command them?"

"Oh but you must, this is their job."

"That's just it, why even have them here, send them all away."

"No, no, no, that's not how it works here, here the monarch is recognized, and the Queen is the supreme ruler, yet it's a democracy, she still has the final say, unlike my reign, where I'm only a figurehead, believe me you're in for a treat, now let's talk about your compensation."

"What are you talking about" said Jack looking at him.

"Normally it would be a Prince who would be required to ante up a dowry, but in your case, she has put up the dowry for you." he paused waiting for Jack to respond, then continued, "Look around this is all yours, anything and everything a man could want, plus the women here, and there is a monetary factor, one billion dollars, in gold, smelted here in Latvia, in addition the people have also given you gifts as well" as the King raised his hand and one of the blue dressed maidens appeared to say "Yes, my King, how may I be of some assistance to you?"

"Explain to Jack here what the people of your country has donated to him in his honor."

"Well to start off with, there are at least 1000 of cows, we are setting up a milking station, and by the wedding, there will be fresh milk, cheeses and creams available, as for other animals, pigs, goats and American Bison, had just arrived, raised exclusively for the royal family, in addition, the palace in Belarus, has been transformed here on these grounds, with a an orchard of mature apple and nut trees, is there anything that Mister Cash would like?"

Jack looked up at her, to say, "Avocados, and pineapples."

"Will do" said Riona, to add, "Will there be anything else King John."

"No."

"How is it she gets away with mocking you" said Jack.

"How so son?"

"What about your highness or your majesty?"

"Oh, don't get me wrong, I feel some resentment in their voices, but I'm considered a guest as well, actually you have more power than I do, as I'm merely a guest, but don't allow them to impose their will on you."

"Oh you don't have to worry about that, I'm Jack Cash, Super Spy."

"Yeah, for here and right now, but out there, all the world's top spies are getting killed off, believe me your safer here, surrounding in this paradise, which has a force of 10,000 plus troops of her royal army, so this is pretty impregnable."

"Tell that to Hitler" said Jack.

"Alright maybe this place isn't as it could be, but the endless cave system, to the coast, and the royal navy is on ready response, so think of yourself as being safe."

Jack pondered that statement but knew otherwise, and when this fairy tale comes to an end, I'll be going hunting myself, especially if any of my friends have been hurt over this blunder."

"Jack what do you want to do now?"

"Oh, get out and hopefully eat some Avocados and fresh pineapples" said Jack getting out only to have Gabrielle there to say, "Well come with me, let's get you washed off."

Jack followed her, she used a hose to wash him off, then Jack, dried himself with a towel, then slipped into a pair of loose fitting trunks. She had waiting for him.

"The King had his own women, attending to him." said Gabrielle.

"So what do you have plans for me now?" asked Jack.

"First a massage from Romy, then an evening in the spa with Lotte." said Gabrielle.

Jack was led to a room, then led to a table, Gabrielle, said "Take good care of him" as she closed the door.

Jack was face down as Romy, was hard at work on his back.

Moments later, there was a bang on the door, the door flew open, a panicked, Gabrielle, yelled, "We need to get him out of here, the King is already in the safe room, come on help him up."

Shots rang out, Gabrielle, fell, Romy gasped, and she too went down, Jack was slow to move, but shots rang out and Jack rolled off the table, a mean look crossed his face.

Jack was moving his feet, as gunfire was over his head, a girl in red, pointed her gun at him, but wavered as he was coming at her full force, she took him and was driven back into the bedding plants, as Jack tackled her, then threw an elbow, he disarmed her, as her body went limp, shots rained down, he was moving, he was up and armed raised, he squeezed off rounds that found a home, those women who held guns against him, went down easily, and just like that the three remaining women were all Latvian, as Jack held the gun on them, as the massive doors went open and the royal guards came storming in.

Jack held his hands up, minus the guns, only to see the Queen, Queen Ana, stood dignified at the gate, she walked in, as everyone went silent, the three detained women, were all held down, as she approached, she spoke in her native tongue, and from the look on their faces meant sure death.

She smiled over at Jack, wearing but only his shorts, to say in English, "My soon to be husband, lower your hands you surely must be tired?"

Jack complies, to hear a soldier said some number, only for the Queen to say, "So even without your personal gun, you still put down fourteen, good thing we came in when we did or you'd be dead, now we can't have that."

Jack saw a new side to this woman, strong and defiant, and who was in charge, as she made a sign with her hand at her neck. Jack saw that sign before, in Belarus, all three were probably behind the attack.

The Queen came over to Jack, to say, "Sorry to disturb your rest time before the wedding, will you walk with me?"

She nudged him along.

He followed, to hear, "I'll be honest with you, there is a price on your head of one hundred million dollars, I can't guarantee your safety anymore, this once impregnable fortress, has been breached, so I can't offer you that safety."

Jack places his hand on her wrist, to stop her to say, "Don't worry about that, I'm here to protect you the Queen, from, all those out there, open up the gates, let them in."

"No, don't be silly, I feel we will be safe, as these three women, were only a last minute replacement, I've ask the guards for a complete lockdown, and to allow all my servants and maidens present."

"Then I'll be fine, let's get this wedding underway."

"Sorry we can't not until tomorrow, but tonight I will guarantee you will receive some pleasure before I see you", she looked over at the awaiting girls all dressed in white, a lineup of the volunteers for Jack's choosing, a mere fifty, to hear, "I know how you like your women, all shapes and sizes, if only King John were here, he'd be in heaven, so choose and she will be yours for the night."

Jack walked the line as the Queen watched, hoping to see a familiar face, there was none, these were all eastern Russian descent, and young, almost like Cuban, each girl had a name tag, the ones that smiled at him, he signaled them to move. All in all he chose four of the fifty, one blonde and three dark black haired women, all four girls had small chest and a petite bodies.

"Fine then take four, all see you tomorrow lover".

The Queen stepped out gracefully, to hear the doors slam shut. The girls led Jack through a new set of doors, it opened up to a room of white linens from top to bottom, to hear, "Welcome Mister Cash, to the white room, where all your desires will be fulfilled." spoke the blonde.

They all stood in, to see the door close and it was locked from the inside, Jack turned to see, they pulled off their tops and then wiggle out of their bottoms, they stood there in front of him, in bra and panties, they motioned for him to lie down, he laid face down, and went fast to sleep.

The President of the United States sat in his war room, with all of his advisors, time was running out as he stood up and announced "Each and every one of you has twelve hours to find, locate and allow me a chance to talk with our Super Spy, if not I'll turn it over to Miss Curtis, understood?", "get going."

The President really looked concern, only to hear the Vice President Jackson say, "We should have put him on Air force one, then onto an aircraft carrier."

"You might be right about that one, how do we lose our most valuable asset?"

"Well from all reports he is still alive, yet, either he is evading capture or just avoiding everyone, personally I think you should have Miss Curtis on this one, the two seem to get along, she knows him best."

"Perhaps, assemble his team, I want answers."

"Yes sir, will do."

"And send in Miss Curtis" said the President.

Lisa Curtis, was coy as she walked in, realizing her elevation, and newly found power, she was with a swagger, until she saw the President's demeanor, where she bit her lip and lower her eyes.

"Ah Miss Curtis, nice to see you, can you tell me where the world's number one spy is?"

"Well Mister President, the last report was Latvia."

"I don't give a damn about a report, I want someone on the ground, asking him to give me a call and say he is alright?"

"I could do that."

"Could you, how long will it take you to do that?"

"Within the hour."

"Really, you can do something the CIA can't do?'

"Well Mister President, I have a network well entrenched in that area, long before Jack went in, I know of the attack, it was controlled and our spy is fine."

"I'm glad you're assured, I want proof, with him talking to me, or you're out a job."

Lisa looked at him, to hear, "You're on the clock."

Lisa left the office to pull out her phone, and dialed up her contact.

Next in was his close team, the four stood next to each other, as the President of our United States, looked at each of them to say, "Your job is to protect Jack, what do you have to say?"

"Is he dead?" asked Mitzi.

"We don't know, I was under the impression, that you were all hired to support his every move."

"He sent us away" said Mark.

"Yes, I heard you but I was under the impression, you were his bodyguard, you're supposed to lay your life down for him, or shall I replace you?"

"No sir, I'll be on the next flight out", said Mark, being excused.

"And you, what he sees in you, you're a bit of a loose cannon, I don't know how many lives a person like you can have, but you're the handyman, a former spy, who will do anything anyone wants, I suppose I know your answer, you too get out of here", Mike left to leave the girls.

"I know about you two girls, you seem to be getting a bit soft, for you Trixie, you're on to boot camp, and for the most loyal, Miss Mitzi, no need for formal names, how have you been?"

"Fine sir."

"You know you can call me George."

"In Private or Public?"

"Private of course, now for you, we need to get you back in the game, join Miss Curtis, and I'll decide where we stand, you can go, and send in Jim."

Mitzi left to say, "He wants you next, then to Lisa, "Any word yet?"

"Nah, he is out like a light, she placed her hand over the receiver, to say, "I guess they rubbed him down with some sleep cream."

"Let me think, have them wash him down with apple cider vinegar, wait till he has an reaction and comes to?"

Lisa told them the first one, to wait for a response."

"Well we have to wait and see" said Mitzi to add "I hope will all don't lose our jobs, we should of listened to Jim." she said Quietly, to herself.

Jim made his way in, to hear, "Jim shut the door."

Jim did that to see the President, say, "Jim you know, you can do no wrong, yet you know better than leave an agent in the field alone."

Jim shakes his head, to say, "He isn't?"

"What do you mean?"

"He isn't, we have Sara."

"What do you mean, who is Sara?"

"It's his assistant."

"You mean she is there?"

"Yes sir, do you want to talk with them?"

"Do I, yes I do."

Jim dialed up Sara, to put it on speaker, go ahead ask her anything?"

"Sara, this is the President of the United States, can I speak to Jack?"

"Yes, wait one minute" said Sara, the car.

The President looked at Jim, to hear "Yes Mister President" said Jack's voice.

"Tell me how are you getting along?"

"Fine, just in paradise."

"Is everything alright, we heard about the attack."

"Everything's under control, actually, everything was staged, so that I may be lost for six weeks, so don't try to find me, I'll resurface after all this blows over, then I'll visit the UN myself, I need to go, take care G W, Out."

President looked at Jim, to say, "Listen I want you to devise me a transmitter that carries an explosive, so if this ever happens, we can touch a button and...."

"Blow off his head, isn't that a bit extreme?" asked Jim.

"Well he knows our secrets?"

"What secrets?, all he does is rescue those that have the secret, and what happens he survives, then he comes after all of us."

The President just looked at Jim, to say, "Well design something for the other group, dismissed."

A blonde in a bikini, was pulling on Jack's arm, as another was washing him down. Trying to revive him, as the steely-eyed, woman was in charge, barking out orders, in Russian.

"Get him up, we need to get him up now."

Jack was a bit drowsy, but able to see the four semi-dressed girls, except for the woman who was smartly dressed, to say, "Who are you?"

"Names Kate, we were sent in by Miss Curtis, she wants to speak with you?"

Wobbly, he walked towards her, to say, "Give me your phone", he takes it from her, to say, "What'sa want?"

He looked at the phone to exclaim, "Its dead, and tosses back at the blonde, who was frantically trying to regain the connection, as Jack, fell into the bed, and curled up and went to sleep.

CH 18

The wedding

Jack awoke as if he were in a dream, that had passed, the window was open, the birds were chirping, the sun, was let in, he slid off the bed, to look around to see he was alone, all he could think about was that tough looking blonde, where was she at?", he thinks, as he made his way over to the window, he pulled the blinds open, to see not a person present, yet the gardens below look magnificent., he looked up to see the glass dome was still intact, then there was a knock on the door, He said, "Come on in."

The door swung open, and two blondes entered, each smartly dressed, to say, "Breakfast is here for you, as one lifts the lid, to say, "Eggs, bacon, sausage, hash, corn grits and pancakes, just like you would find in the south."

Jack waves them on, to hear, "Would you like for us to stay?"

"Nah, I'll be fine, is there any chance that I could get butter and maple syrup." he said.

He waited till his request arrived, sat down and consumed a good portion of the food, then dressed, then waited to be summoned, for his room was locked, although his room was large and vast, he sensed something was getting close, as to the music he heard, from outside his walls, he paced the hallway, then into his game room, filled with everything he could play with, from pinball machines to billiards, along the wall, was a beverage and snack station, anything he could have, was available, then he saw the multitude of colored boxes of candy.

"Those ones from sweden, are the best" said King John, from the other side of the room.

Jack turned, around to see him, to say, "Not much into candy."

"It's all about the sugar, really", moving closer to add, "It would be insult to the Queen, if you had not tried at least one."

"Alright", Jack opens a bin, and uses a spoon, to hear, "Don't worry about that, these are all yours, all checked for any poisons, and such, actually everything you see here is yours, look around, these are only the small portions of gifts your about to receive, you're about to marry the Queen of Latvia, and right the wandering ship, these people need a strong viable leader, although you won't be King, you will, be able to live a safe and productive life here, as for that attack earlier, it will never happen again."

"How can you be so certain?" asked Jack grazing on some gummy fish, and things.

"From this point forward, only the experience is allowed in, those that have had extensive evaluations, and are on the most trusted status."

"And before?"

"Those were the result of volunteers, all of them are gone, all that remains are the four girls sent in to protect you, from what they call spy club."

"You mean last night?"

"Well about that, the Queen instructed, that you rest comfortably, and not to be disturbed, so your maidens slathered the sleep cream on your legs and arms, which will never happen again, in addition, all of your clothes and possessions, are in the other room, wait, before you get them on, Ana, wishes for you and her to take a boat ride."

"Alright, I feel like its safe, Jack said looking at his watch."

"Oh it is my friend, while you're in the dome, it is completely safe, you'll have others watching you."

"So how is all of this going to go down?"

"Well first, comes the ceremonies, then the presentation, then the dowry."

"What dowry?"

"For you it's nothing, your just like all of her other suitors, you're her tool, but in exchange for being that tool, you'll have privileges, beyond belief, first off, you will receive a stipend monthly for the rest of your life, and beyond."

"Beyond what?" asked Jack.

"Well that depends on how long you live, or out live her, the people may elect you to be their King, in the event that Ana goes before you, if its reversed, she may honor you, and may be buried here, it all depends on you, as I was saying, once the dowry is read, then the people of Latvia, may in turn pledge you some things, as I know of a goat farm on the outskirts of Riga, known for its sweet rich cheese, is essential, giving it up to you, as a gift, they will still run it, but all the profits will go to you and a bulk of the cheese, that's what we call, "Royal cheese."

"Then there is your proclamations, like what do you plan on doing, such as having a whole battle group, at your command, to use as you see fit, that in itself is huge, between you and me, you have more clout than any of her other suitors, then lastly the exchange of vows, then the 21 day period of conception."

"How does all that work?"

"Once you exchange the vows, your twenty one day period will start here, but with Ana's condition, think of it as a play session, as she has no possible way to get pregnant."

"Interesting" said Jack, continued sampling the candies.

"Come on over here my boy" said the King.

Jack held a plate of candies, to take a seat, to listen to the King talk,"Have you given any thought, to where you plan on living?"

"Here there and everywhere, I don't know, probably where my job takes me next."

"Where's that?"

"Probably Washington D.C., I imagine."

"Why do you say that?"

"Well its where my families will be, and where my home base is, now, as we speak a facility is being secretly built."

"Then what will Ana do?"

"She knew the arrangement before she wanted to do this, I have to admit, I married some Princess's, but never a Queen, it can't be that much different."

"Well actually it's not, unless, you yourself, have some royal blood lines, do you Jack, have royal bloodlines?"

"Doubtful, don't really remember, but what I do remember is a big field, that when I was a kid, I'd run forever it seemed, and that was the extent of that, say what do you think this is all going to happen?"

"Patient my boy, you're about to receive what only a few men have enjoyed, you're getting the girl and the kingdom all wrapped up in a nice package, you're gonna be a billionaire" said the King wisely.

"I'm already a millionaire, every person I arrest nets me a million, and then there is what your giving me."

"Yes, and much more."

"Besides, all the money goes to my wives, and all the rest I carry around with me."

"So if you like you can buy anything you want?"

"Sure, but I don't shop, I really just collect things along the way, like now, I'm collecting things, I don't know if I had ever, just went out and bought something, I take that back, several years ago, when Sara was working at the mall, I went shopping, but that was with someone else's money, maybe I will after this go back to Geneva and do some shopping, I wonder how the UN is doing."

"Read it for yourself" said a familiar voice.

Jack turned to see it was the Queen, who laid the paper down, to sit with them.

The big headlines were UN changes spy policy.

"Looks like I'm out of a job" said Jack.

"The world wasn't ready for the Super Spy yet I imagine" said King, getting up, to say "I'll leave you two love birds to talk."

Jack read the article as Queen, said "I don't want you to be angry with me, I did it so that you may have a restful day's sleep, instead of a night of sex."

"That's alright, I know your intentions were good, but we need to talk."

Jack looked over at the Queen who had her head down, for Jack to say "I don't know about this twenty one day brooding period, maybe one or two nights?"

"Wow, I was expecting something else" she said.

"I know, I was thinking of going home as well, I've had a few days to reconsider, so let's get this ceremony under way already?"

"Paitence, it will happen all day tomorrow, and then you can do whatever you like of me."

"How about now?"

"Sorry can't, I too have to prepare, besides I imagine the world wants to talk with you, so all of your personal effects are in you room, and I will see you tomorrow", she said as she got up to notice, then say, "So you're trying the candies, aren't they good, although a bit addictive, you know there from Switzerland."

Jack pushes the tray away, turns to see her leave, as four lovely girls appear, the most stunning of all appeared to say, "What would you like for lunch, Mister Cash."

He looked her up and down, to see that she was white American of descent to say, "Your American?"

"Yep, Californian born and raised."

"How did you end up over here working for the Queen?"

"I haven't, I'm with spy club, as the three others were here to protect you, in any means necessary, we were allowed in by a special envoy, so whatever you want I will prepare it for you, also we have been in contact with Lisa and she assures me that she and her team will be on the ground and here for the wedding tomorrow along with your team."

Jack looked up from viewing the phone to say, "What are your specialties?"

She shook her head to say, "I don't have any, it's whatever you want?"

Jack looked at her, to say, "Well in that case, steak and lobster, and could you make some artichokes, with butter and ketchup?"

"Certainly how would you like your steak cooked?"

"Medium" he said without looking at her, as she was gone.

Next to step up was the suppose leader, Kate the Russian, who spoke in very good English to say, "Is there anything else you would like for now?"

"Nah, I'm fine, does that mean you'll be staying in the room or will you be leaving too?"

"No, sorry, we will be here until Miss Curtis arrives", she said as she and the others left the room, seeing that Jack was bit annoyed. Jack went back through his phone, to see all of his calls, he deleted, most of his messages, and then sent out messages he was alright, and doing well, and that he was coming home soon.

Jack arranged his wives in order of standing and priority, and at the top was Sara, who after the attack, is with the President, and now is saying she too wants to go back to school to become a doctor, to be with her family, her constant messages are nice, and accepting, while the others are not as nice and are way too demanding, like Alba who wants to be a police officer, as for Maria, well she wants a lot more children, but knows she can't have anymore and on the other end of the spectrum, there is Alexandria, who wants none, and actually she is growing a bit restless, and wants to go back to her homelands. "Then there is the new batch, Isabella and Daphne runs the charter business, Maria Ingles, is pregnant, and Tessa has since joined her, the Shaw sisters, are doing wonderfully in their prestigious schools, Tia Riley-Cash, went back to school, as did the four others, Lindsay, Samantha, India and Melanie, and lastly there was Chloe, on to Quantico, to wait for Jack's arrival.

Jack began to ponder if he was making the right choice, if he wanted he could marry Dany the chef, she seemed nice, I guess I could be just like Ben, who has a girl for every occupation, to include the Supreme Court, what makes a good wife, one I could dominate, and control or one who is independent and doesn't need my support or a Queen that can support all of us, all I know after this I'll be done with women, and focus on my work."

Jack closes up his phone to see and smell the food coming in, which Abby placed down, to say, "Eat well and rest easy."

Jack waved his wrist across the food, to read his watch indicate it was clear, except a little higher sodium count."

A tub of melted butter, sat in a dish, waiting for the fresh, lightly cooked lobster, to sit and soak. Jack was hungry, as he tasted the chef's offering, not as good as Dany's but it was tasty, he thought and indulged in the rest of the food.

Meanwhile unbeknownst to him, aircraft, by aircraft, landed at Riga international airport, as American troops, exited in full combat gear, they occupied the whole eastern side of the airport, as planes sat on the tarmac facing the rest of the airport. Then a single smaller plane, made its approach, landed, and came to rest behind the wall of the massive jets, the landing ramp went down, and Lisa Curtis stood on the ramp, she turned to say, "Thanks for the ride Jim", then exited to an awaiting SUV, as it sped off.

Jim looked around to see the remaining support members, he didn't know either to kick them off of Jack's plane or simply let them do what they do best await orders, he turned to see Mitzi, who was obviously in charge, say "Mike and Mark, I need you both at the palace, get in close and hold your positions, that's all" as she used her hands to swoosh them away.

She turned, to say to Jim, "You were right, we should be here for him, till were all back stateside."

Jim looked at her to say, "It's not what I want it is what needs to be done, remember we work for him."

"Your right Jim, we need to listen to you more often."

"What is your plan with the support teams?"

"Well, Jill and Gia, are off to the Academy."

"What about all those girls?"

"What are you talking about, there are girls that come and go, all the time, and they are getting younger by the minute."

"You know, we were in Quantico, and there was at least twenty."

"Oh I know who you're talking about now, well, after Jack blew up the smuggling ring, they were dispatched to track down more, as to this date, we have captured over 6300 or so perps, the two stop talking to each other to see two strangers arrive, one carrying a huge box with carrying handles, for Mitzi to say, "Welcome back boys."

"Hi, "said Brian, passing them, to say, "Where's the car?"

Mitzi stood in front of Clarance, to say, "What's his problem?"

"Oh you know, there is someone more important than himself."

"So have you decided to get out or join us?"

"Yep, I'm on board till the old man retires" said Clarance.

"What changed your mind?" asked Mitzi.

"Well I had a long talk with this Admiral, and he was a huge fan of Jack Cash's, so much so that it impressed me, to the point, of considering, what my role is and what I should do?"

"Good, great to have you on the team officially, speaking of that, I need you to go with Jim, to the Palace, and link up with Casey, after the wedding concludes were taking Jack out."

"Really, why because he is a threat to national security?"

"No, never, I mean extract him out and on Transport plane, see all these jets around us, they are all decoy, we will all take off together, and us to a undisclosed place."

"Oh I gotcha, sorry".

An Suv, pulled up, on its side bore the letters U N the door opens, as Gene and Roberta slide out as Gene says, "Alright who needs a ride to the Palace?"

Jim, Mitzi, Roxy, Jared and Trixie, gets in, as Clarance takes his time looking over Gene, to say, "I don't know if it's safe to get into that vehicle, with you know the hit squads and assassinations out there."

"It's safe Mister Morey, get in" said Gene, taking the passenger seat.

The SUV took off, as Gene turned in his seat to say to Clarance, they might of gotten the jump on us, but seven of our super agents are safe, and well-guarded, waiting till number one is safe and regrouped."

"And as for Jack?"

"Well he is the last one left, and we have over 100,000 troops deployed, and his support team is here, on the ground."

Clarance was going to say something, but Mitzi, held her arm on his, motioning for him to be quiet. He did so, he wondered where Brian was at?

Gene gabbed on, only to Jim, who knew better than to speak, he sat in silence, to hear, "We are at the underground garage, is this your stop now Jim?"

Jim was looking at his handheld monitor, to see that they were close, to say "Right here will be fine."

Jim exited, with Clarance, as the SUV sped off.

They approached a guard shack, as Jim presented a Presidential order for the car, the guards confirmed it, and led Jim and Clarance, down a hallway, the guard punched in a code, the door opened, the lights went on, the two men, walked in, off to their right a huge door slide open, the room was made of red silk, to the red carpet, the car sat on, the immaculate looking car, pristine under the lights, the guards backed off, as Jim went through a sequence, to check for booby-traps and devices, and deactivate the defense measures, slowly the driver's side door opened for Jim, as he went to it, followed by Clarance, who said, "Can I drive old man?"

"No" said Jim, kneeling down, he accessed a hidden keypad, he punched in a series of three codes, then the car started, Jim slid out, as Clarance went around and waited at the passenger side door. Jim went to the driver's side door, to say, "Jack set the car in secure mode, I need to deactivate that then Jim hit the unlock button, and Clarance, slid in, to say, "Wow, this is space age stuff."

"Calm down, be quiet, said Jim nervously, as the laptop was in the up position, carefully he pushed it back down, Clarance was touching the sophisticated radio buttons, only to hear, Jim say, "Stop stop, touching the knobs, as Jim thought sleep, instantly Clarance was knocked out. Jim looked over at Clarance, to say, "It worked, I must keep my mind clear, as he said, "Close all doors, and manual placed it into reverse, he felt the car wanting control, but knew if it did it would go crazy, looking for Jack, so he drove it back, exited, on his beacon was Casey's position, and drove to him, out of the shadows, he stepped, to help Jim, with Clarance out of the car, while Jim drove off, Casey broke open some smelling salts to revive, Clarance who was a bit wobbly, he helped him, back into his hiding place, to see that he was waking up, Casey stood guard as other guards passed, and a bevy of beautiful women, but kept a secret where he was at, then a Blonde with long hair, was coming towards them to say, "I can see you there in the shadows, come out or I will call you in."

Casey stepped out, as Kate said, "I was just looking for you."

"Well you found me?"

"It wasn't hard, you and your partner are on all the security feeds for the Palace, every place has a camera on it, you might have as well been standing in the open, come with me, and bring your friend, Kate led them through a passageway, Casey carried his backpack, and Clarance brought up the rear, as Kate says,

"Miss Curtis informed me of what she wants to do, so I'll lead you to a room, that you can rest and relax, till the wedding is over, she led them down a passageway, that was well lit, on the walls were damp, as Kate says, "Were going under the pond, now."

They started upwards, to a courtyard, where hundreds of people were assembling cameras and video equipment, door slammed shut, they walked past the people, to a door, which, housed the UN, and CIA, and other agencies, to their spot, that said, Diplomatic contingence.

Clarance walked into a spacious quarters, with a huge window that looked out over the lake, and the pedestal, that had an arch over it, to say, "Looks like we get to watch the event."

"Were not alone" said Casey seeing Mark and Mike being escorted in.

"The teams all here" said Mike.

"Let's pull up a chair, as they looked over at Kate who says "Now you boys all stay here, and when it's over I'll bring Jack to you."

"Wait how are you able to travel so freely, and we cannot?" asked Mike.

"Because I'm a girl, and girls pose no threat, and besides I work for Miss Curtis."

She left them speechless, as she left the room, walked along a long hallway, she swiped her keycard, and was granted access, she was in the grooms, wing, over 100,000 square feet of living space, she was walking the marble walkway, passing countless living rooms, game room, swimming pool, there was everything in a room, under the sun, she entered the dining room, where Jack Cash sat, across from him was her boss Miss Curtis.

"It is of national importance, that you are air lifted out of here, and onto the plane back to the United States, and the security of Washington D.C."

"What about the honeymoon?"

"Well how about somewhere sunny and warm, like Hawaii?"

"I don't know, shouldn't that be left up to the bride?"

"Yes, but your much more important than her right now, allow me to call the President"said Lisa.

"Yeah, find out where he wants me to have it?"

"That's not what I'm going to ask him?"

As Lisa was on her satellite phone, making the call, Jack got up, to look over the newly received criteria paper, which Else, handed to him, to whisper, "We can get you in anytime for the fitting?"

"Whenever you're ready" said Jack, seeing her go, only to see Lisa get up and said, "I'm sorry."

She seemed a bit upset, as Jack said, "What did he say?"

In between sobs, she said "He said take as long as you like, and for us to back off, and wait at the airport."

"Wow that's a shocker, to think that you are ordering me around like that doesn't have some consequences of their own, well you better load up your boys and girls and get the hell out of here" said Jack smiling.

Just as Mitzi and Trixie step in, as Jack gave them both a nice reception, with a hug, and they gave him a kiss. They watched as Lisa and her team, left except Abby, who looked at Jack, but it was Mitzi who spoke up to say, "Sorry honey, you too won't be needed", so she left too.

While Mitzi and Trixie took charge, Jack went into the royal fittings, the alterations were done on the spot, as the magnificent suit, was assembled, by a team of tailors on the scene. Jack was ready, he slid in his badge, and wallet, he placed his signature weapon in its white box. As the door opened, to hear, "The time is ready."

Jack received a hug and kiss from his two faithful and loyal companions, they both had a tear for him, as he walked out into the hallway, that was actually, a large corridor, a white marbled walkway, as he walked he followed a young smartly dressed girl, who was motioning for those to move away, as they were in the courtyard, Jack took a left, to see ten guards each on both sides, dressed like him, at attention, he continued to the pedestal, where he went up to the top, as he looked over the lake to the right was a bank of windows that many faces and cameras were going off, then as he swept around to the officers, to the left side where, the red carpet showed the

Queen's side, plenty of dignitaries, and those from her royal cabinet, to include King John, and Mary of Belarus, and next to them was a box above the water was the orchestra, playing light sounding music, then everyone raised up, and the band got louder, then the Queen made her entrance with a nice white dress, and a long train, she wore a crown of her jewels, she walked proudly, as those in attendance clapped, then Jack noticed on the roof, large camera's, next to them a team of men with weapons, and scopes, the Queen's movement was slow and deliberate, till she turned left and up the pedestal she went, when all the music abruptly quit, from behind Jack, up from a boat, came a man dressed in all red, he made some noise climbing the stairs, but got to the top, as Jack watched him waver, then gain his footing, he stood behind them, a voice within earshot, he heard "Listen up, this is Elsa, I will translate, either all that the priest says or just what is directed at you, nod your head if it's all up and down, if it's just at you, side to side.

Side to side is all that Jack did, the priest spoke in somewhat good English, but the other is some Latin, the Queen held her face under a veil, but heard her say, "I Do", then it was Jack's turn, he waited then said "I Do, the Priest said some other things, then led Ana's hand to Jack's so that Jack could see the massive Ruby, on her finger, he pulled the Veil away, to see her beautiful face, he leaned in and gave her a kiss, on the lips, it ended quickly, as they took a bow, in front of the crowd that had gathered, then came the applause, in one motion, she pulled her train away, leaving a short dress and her bouquet, which she threw up in the air, and in that moment, Kate the Russian caught it. The Queen and Jack were down the stairs, to the waiting boat, each took a seat next to each other, as a boat guide led the boat out onto the lake, as everyone watched, she held his hand, as they went like into the sunset, but it was actually a huge screen of some sort, the boat circled the small lake, to the other side, and out of view, as behind them was a team waiting to help them off, and into what appeared to be a car on tracks, she sat in front, as Jack was helped into the back, a clear domed roof, came down and locked into place, then off it went, down, at first, then up into a circle, to a top peak, then straight down, it was a roller coast of a ride that took it around the palace, so that all could see, it was long and lasted five minutes, as it came to a stop, men undid the capsule, and others helped them up, they were led up the stairs, into a hanger, where a non-descript jet await, they went up the stairs, Jack kept looking around in hopes to see anyone friendly, he made it to an awaiting oversize chair, long enough, to hear the door shut closed, and the plane was moving, as was the two hundred plus aircraft that took off, and seconds later they were up in the air, as Jack turned in his chair to say, "Where are we going now?"

"Enough" said Ana, "You and I are on our honeymoon, all your people need to know, is that for the next two month's you will be with me," she stood, striping her dress away she announced "Off to Africa."

The End...